SAVANNAH

Also by the author

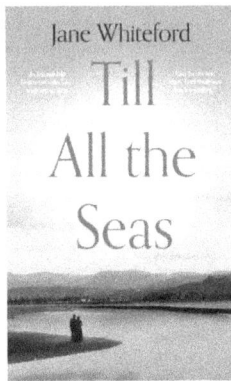

Shortlisted Lakeland Book of the Year 2023

www.janewhiteford.com

SAVANNAH

JANE WHITEFORD

The Book Guild Ltd

First published in Great Britain in 2024 by
The Book Guild Ltd
Unit E2 Airfield Business Park,
Harrison Road, Market Harborough,
Leicestershire. LE16 7UL
Tel: 0116 2792299
www.bookguild.co.uk
Email: info@bookguild.co.uk
Twitter: @bookguild

Typeset in 11pt Adobe Jenson Pro

Printed and bound by CPI Group (UK) Ltd, Croydon, CR0 4YY

ISBN 978 1916668 690

British Library Cataloguing in Publication Data.
A catalogue record for this book is available from the British Library.

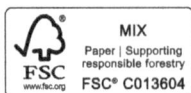

MIX
Paper | Supporting
responsible forestry
FSC
www.fsc.org
FSC® C013604

For Rose

ONE

Northwest England, 1870

He hammered frantically on the door and waited impatiently. As he raised his fist to pound again, he was relieved to hear the bolt slide back. A gust of rain-sodden wind propelled him over the threshold as the maid struggled to hold open the door against the unrelenting storm. He was soaked; his hat and coat dripped into puddles on the marble floor of the hall. Behind him, a second figure, carrying a small leather bag, his cheeks stung red with the cold and wind, loomed out of the dim light of the lamps under the *porte-cochère*. The stable master, who had waited to attend to the horses, plunged out into the stormy night and the maid heaved the door shut behind him.

"Is there any change?" asked Will, shaking out his coat and hat before dropping them on a chair nearby.

"I cannot say, sir," Sarah replied. "Thank goodness you found the doctor at home."

He waited for the doctor who, with the maid's help, was divesting himself of his drenched hat and coat, then hurried up the stairs to his parents' bedroom, the doctor on his heels, and tapped on the door.

"Father, it's Will. Dr Greenwood is here."

He heard his father's footsteps cross the floor, then the door opened. William, white-faced and haggard, heaved a sigh. "Thank

God. Thank God, you're here, Richard. She's in such pain. Please do something." He stepped aside to admit the doctor.

"Can I help, Father?" Will asked.

"No, thank you, Will. You've done well to fetch Richard so quickly. I'll hear what he has to say, and I'll come down to you shortly."

His father guarded the door so he could not see into the room. Then his mother howled a scream that seemed to come from the depths of hell itself. He looked in terror at his father.

"Wait for me in the study. I need to get back to her. I'll come down soon, I promise." William squeezed his son's arm and gave a wan smile of reassurance before gently closing the door.

It was a foul night. The wind rattled the rain-lashed windows and boomed in the chimney. The clock on the mantelpiece showed half past eight. Will bent down to throw some more logs on the fire, then poured himself a measure of brandy from the decanter on the side table, which he knocked back in one gulp, gasping as the sharp warmth hit the back of his throat. The terrible howl coming from his mother had alarmed him. He had no idea that something as natural as giving birth could be so horrible and shocking. He had watched a horse foal, a cow calve, a sheep lamb, and they just grunted and heaved the newborn into existence without, it would seem, such agony. What was happening with his mother he did not understand, other than the baby was coming early and was a cause for concern.

It had started so quickly and without warning. They were in his mother's sitting room after dinner, and everyone was in good spirits. It was his mother's favourite room in the house and, with the lamps lit, the fire blazing, the candles on the mantelpiece glinting in the mirror above, and the curtains drawn against the moaning wind, it was cosy and warm. He had arrived from Stillingford, a village near Liverpool, the day before, after spending a few days with his aunt – his father's sister – and cousins on his journey home from Oxford for the Christmas holidays. His mother, approaching the eighth month of her pregnancy, was looking well although she had complained of backache earlier. She was sitting, legs stretched out, on the sofa working on her embroidery. He could see her as he chatted with his father. She was smiling to herself, pretending to be busy and casting the occasional glance in the direction of her 'two favourite boys', as she called them. Her husband, tall and handsome, strong and trim, the lines at the corners of his mouth and his dark brown eyes and the flecks of grey in his dark brown hair betraying his age of forty years, was generous, honest, thoughtful and good humoured. Her clever son, mature for his age and often serious, but always kind and considerate – who had fussed over her, plumped up the cushions and moved the side table so she could reach her drink – was so like his father in looks, apart from the dark blue Hamilton eyes. Her eyes. Then she cried out.

"Marianna, my darling, what is it?" said William, leaping from his chair and rushing to her.

She had dropped her embroidery hoop to the floor and was clutching her stomach. "Oh, no!" she wailed as she felt the wetness between her legs and tried to rise. "The baby is coming. It is too soon."

Scooping Marianna into his arms, William carried her upstairs.

"I will go for the doctor," Will called out to him. "And I'll stop by the lodge and get Mrs Dummigan to come."

"Yes, yes. Good lad. Be as quick as you can."

Will had changed into his nightclothes. He poured himself another drink and sat in one of the leather wing chairs by the fire, pulling his dressing gown tighter to keep out the draughts that seemed to come from every corner of the room. The study had once been his grandfather's. It was wood-panelled; the windows to the front and French doors to the side offered views across the lawns to the wood in the valley. There was a well-used but comfortable sofa with sagging cushions against one wall and, on either side, two tall, glass-fronted bookcases, always locked as they contained several rare editions. A wide, mahogany desk positioned near a window, with captain's chairs either side, was shared by his parents as they attended to their business affairs. A thick book lay on his father's side of the desk for recording the names and breeding lines of his horses; on his mother's side was a pile of ledgers containing the household accounts, estate accounts and rent records for the tenants. There was a photograph in a silver frame next to the walnut stationery box at the end of the desk of his mother and father with Aunt Lizzie, a baby – his cousin Meg – in her arms, and her husband George, who had died years ago in America. His parents looked so young, but were solemn faced, as though they knew of the heartache that lay ahead of them. Will closed his eyes for a moment and willed his mother to be well.

She was so dear to him. For his whole life he had been the centre of her world and he shared everything with her; she knew everything there was to know about him: his successes and failures, his dreams and insecurities. But since his father came into his life the year before, he had been consumed by a carefully hidden, resentful jealousy. And soon, this very night possibly, there was to be another intruder to demand a share of his mother's love.

He got up to stretch his legs and wandered over to one of the bookcases. His grandfather, Henry Hamilton, was a kind, gentle, wise man. Will, his short legs dangling over the edge of the seat, often sat with him as the old man smoked his pipe and chatted to him. He was allowed to choose a book, one of these special books that were kept here: big books that weighed heavily on his knees and needed both his small hands to turn the thick pages; beautifully illustrated books about birds and animals; strange people wearing unusual costumes; maps of the world showing countries with unfamiliar names and maps of the stars which his grandfather would patiently explain to him. This was one room untouched by his mother's whirlwind of redecoration when she had moved permanently with William to Longridge Hall. She had loved her father and wanted the room to be as he had left it.

It was nearly half past nine. Will sank down in the chair and drained the glass of brandy. He wondered what was happening upstairs. He put his head in his hands and willed his mother to be well. The door opened and he shot up from the chair.

"How is she, Father?"

"In pain, Will. A lot of pain. The doctor's given her something, a touch of chloroform, but he's cautious as he must think of the baby and getting it delivered as soon as possible."

"Will Mama be all right? The screams. They were…" He shuddered.

William saw the fear in his son's eyes and said, "Yes, she will be all right. She's in good hands."

But he said it to reassure himself as much as Will.

"How can you bear to be in the room and watch her suffer so much?"

"Prospective fathers are normally banished but I cannot let your mother endure this without me by her side. I'll go back to her now. I just came to see how you were. You're ready for bed, I see. I don't know how long it'll take. Perhaps," he said, eyeing the empty glass on the table, "you should go up and try to sleep. I'll come and wake you if there's news." He turned at the door. "And thank you, Will. You did well to bring the doctor so quickly."

"I could not sit and do nothing, Papa."

William went to him and hugged him. He was touched that his son who had never called him Papa before had done so at this difficult time.

At two o'clock in the morning, Marianna delivered a baby girl. The labour may have been relatively short, but it was bloody and excruciatingly painful. She was weak from loss of blood and exhausted by the effort. The child was small and silent. The doctor had worked on her for several minutes, as Ada Dummigan, the housekeeper and cook, stood anxiously by his side, before she drew breath and uttered a feeble whimper.

With the baby safely swaddled in her mother's arms, the doctor washed and dried his hands, rolled down his shirtsleeves and began to pack away his instruments.

"Richard, will you stay the night?" asked William. "You're more than welcome as it's dreadful out there."

"Thank you, William, but in half an hour I can be in my own bed and Ellen will be waiting up, no doubt, until she has heard all is well here."

"In that case, would you mind giving Ada a ride home? She's been soaked once this night."

"Certainly," replied Richard.

William turned to Ada, who was busy clearing away the detritus of the birth, and asked her to send Sarah to the stables to summon Andrew with the doctor's gig.

"Give her our news, and that I don't expect her or Andrew to be up first thing in the morning. The same for you, Ada. It's been a long night. Leave a note for Polly to see to breakfast."

"Thank you, sir. Dr Greenwood." Ada beamed. "Ain't it wonderful to 'ave a new life in the 'ouse? Such a bonny, little thing too. I'll get rid of these," she said, nodding at the bowl in her hands and the sheets over her arms, "and fetch my coat."

William waited for Richard to take one last look at his patients before accompanying him downstairs to the hall where Ada was waiting. He helped Richard on with his coat and then disappeared, returning a few minutes later with three glasses of brandy on a tray.

"Thank you, both of you. Here's a little something to warm you before you venture out and to toast the arrival of our daughter."

"Your very good health. To Marianna. To Miss Hamilton-Read," said Richard, raising his glass.

"To the family," said Ada. "Good 'ealth to all."

They clinked glasses and downed the liquor.

"I shall return at nine tomorrow." Richard laughed as he saw the time on the grandfather clock in the corner of the hallway and corrected himself. "I shall return mid-morning to check on mother and baby. With plenty of rest for a week, I do not foresee any problems for Marianna. I believe you have arranged a nurse for her lying-in? Perhaps you could notify her to come at once. The child is small; we must keep an eye on her. Send for me if you are at all worried."

After they had gone, William took the stairs two at a time and went to knock on Will's bedroom door, but there was no reply, so he left the boy to sleep and hurried to his own bedroom. Marianna was propped up on pillows. She was pale, her face blanched by the pain and hours of labour as though the pink-cheeked child swaddled in her arms had sucked the blood from her as she travelled to the light. She was, because of her childhood experiences, a strong, single-minded, sometimes stubborn woman, but now she looked fragile, her eyes ringed with dark shadows, her hair lank with sweat from her exertions. She looked up at him and smiled. His heart lurched with love for her. He climbed onto the bed and put his arm round her shoulders. She rested her head on his chest.

"She is a bonny, little thing," she said. "But what a struggle. I'm exhausted, William."

"It's over," he said. "She's here at last. Sooner than expected, but safe and well." He kissed the top of Marianna's head. "I love you so much, Marianna. Thank God you are well too."

"I had a difficult time when Will was born. She looks like him, the same shock of dark hair as Will had."

"She is beautiful. Will you listen to that wind! She was desperate to be born and couldn't wait to come to us. Even on such a night as this. And now she sleeps through it all."

The windows rattled under a shower of hailstones and the curtains moved slightly as a heavy gust of wind thumped the front of the house and screamed round the chimneys, causing the coals in the fireplace to sputter and glow. They waited a moment for the noise to subside. William shivered. "Will did well to ride out in this weather."

"I hope it is not an omen."

"Of what?"

"A stormy life ahead for this little one."

"Marianna, no dark thoughts at this happy time. We will both be here to watch over her." He took his daughter's tiny hand in his and said, "Have you decided on a name for her?"

Marianna shook her head.

"I'd no idea until I saw her and then it came to me. I'd like to call her Savannah."

"Savannah," repeated Marianna. "I like it. Pretty, but unusual. How did you think of it?"

"I heard it in America. It's the name of a town in Georgia. I always liked the sound of it, although I've never been there."

"Savannah Hamilton-Read," said Marianna, kissing her daughter, "welcome to Longridge Hall."

TWO

Six months ago, they had arranged for the carriage to meet them at Melchester Station rather than Newbridge, which was closer to Longridge, as they both wanted to see the bay again. The carriage was halted by the side of the road just beyond the village of Keer Bank. They walked to the rocky outcrop, the same place William had stood nearly twenty years before on his way home to the hamlet of Netherton on the Loop Hall estate on the other side of the bay, full of excitement and trepidation at the thought of seeing his wife again after his enforced exile.

The tide was out, and the air smelt of salt and wet earth. The sun glinted on the silver ribbons of water and pools left by the ebbing tide. In the distance, on the far shore, under the looming limestone crag, they could see the terrace of cottages at Netherton where they, a young, newly married couple, had lived so happily. It was a view that had impressed and inspired them when they first crossed the sands from the hiring fair at Melchester all those years ago and held a special place in their hearts. Birds swooped, mosaics of black and white – oystercatchers, lapwings, terns – rising and falling in choreographed movements; the breeze rustled the grasses; the sunlight glinted on the windows of far-off buildings; a train clattered over the viaduct.

That was the day Marianna had told William she was expecting a child. He was overjoyed at the thought of celebrating their second chance of happiness with a new life. Since the death of Marianna's second husband Bennet Foster, and their own remarriage, they had visited Longridge several times. The house and estate had been left to Marianna by her father, Henry Hamilton. As he wanted his grandson, Will Read, to inherit eventually and carry on the family line, the surnames were combined. Now she and William were reunited, there were plans afoot to redecorate the house and extend and improve the stables to fulfil a long-held dream of William's to breed horses. It was agreed between them that she would run the estate – which included three farms and private and commercial property in Newbridge – and manage the household: the estate was hers. She knew, though, that she could rely on William's support, advice and business expertise. William was wealthy in his own right thanks to his profitable investments, as well as the import and export business in Liverpool overseen by his manager, Frederick Hartley. The horse breeding at Longridge would be his domain. They had also agreed to set up a charity, as William had done in Stillingford, where he had lived with his widowed sister, Lizzie, to provide bursaries for local children to continue their education after elementary school. It was a cause close to William's heart, inspired by his late brother-in-law, George Hindle, who decried the lack of opportunities for children from poor families to advance themselves through learning.

Longridge Hall, an attractive, well-proportioned house built, in the Georgian style, in the local pink-red sandstone to replace the Jacobean farmhouse destroyed by fire in the eighteenth century, stood on high ground in front of one of the Westmorland Fells from which the house took its name. A long driveway left the private estate road at the lodge house to arrive at the front door with its *porte-cochère* to protect visitors from the changeable weather. Across the sweeping lawns, the bellcote of the family chapel could be glimpsed between the trees in the valley below. The rooms in the house were spacious. On the ground floor, the full-length windows added to the lightness and airiness of the rooms, which included a drawing room, Marianna's sitting room with a door that led out to the walled rose garden, a dining room, a morning room, a study, a billiard room and a library laid out around a wide hall, the walls of which were adorned with the portraits of past Hamiltons. The grand, central staircase divided on the first floor under the stained-glass window depicting St George slaying the dragon and led to the ten bedrooms split between each wing of the house, with more bedrooms in the attics where the servants slept. A door under the main staircase led down to the kitchen, butler's pantry, wine cellar, game larder and other service rooms and the back stairs to the attics.

A few weeks after their arrival to live permanently at Longridge, Marianna began to feel unwell. This particular morning, she was sitting, thinking, on a chair in the hallway. The ground floor was a hubbub of frenzied painting and decorating as workmen bustled past with ladders, buckets, dust sheets and brushes to the various ground-floor rooms; all part of her plan to eradicate as much as she could of her mother's imprint on the fabric of the house. There were gaps on the walls, glaring black outlines left after her mother, Carolina, had removed paintings following Henry Hamilton's death, including the only portrait of him, to take with her when she returned to Portugal, the country of her birth. Marianna was contemplating the idea of her and William having their portraits painted for when she rehung the pictures. She was also thinking of commissioning a small portrait of her father, copied from a photograph, to hang beside all the other Hamiltons – some handsome, some plain, others severe and disapproving – descended from the Scotsman who came south after the union of the Scottish and English crowns with a hoard of gold plate and a pair of solid silver candelabra for reasons never recorded.

Despite all the windows and doors being open, the smell of paint and turpentine was everywhere, and she felt queasy. She was thankful all the upstairs rooms had been decorated before they had moved in. She was uneasy too, as she often experienced a sharp twinge in her stomach, and she wondered if she was doing too much: organising, ordering paints and fabrics and supervising. She did feel tired. Perhaps it was the summer heat. She was staring into space and looking troubled as William came down the stairs.

"What is it? You remind me of the young girl I knew who often disappeared into sombre thoughts."

She jumped slightly at his voice, looked up and smiled weakly. "Will you walk with me, William, as I feel in need of some fresh air? The chaos is getting on my nerves."

She led the way across the hall, stepping carefully over the sheets laid to protect the marble floor, through the open front door. She took his arm and said, "It is not just the noise and busyness. Do you mind if we walk to the chapel? It's the anniversary of my father's death and I should like to spend a few moments there."

"I didn't know," he said. "Of course."

They walked in silence along the road that led away from the house and through the wood, down to the small family chapel. It was a simple, stone building, built sometime in the late seventeenth century by one of Marianna's more devout ancestors, with a bellcote at one gable end over the porch and a stone cross at the other. The bell had been taken down many years ago and left to gather dust on the floor in a corner of the chapel. The chapel had never been used for its purpose by any of the more recent Hamiltons, who were not known for their adherence to any religion – apart from Marianna's mother, a devout Catholic – except at times of birth, marriage and death.

William and Marianna passed under the arch of two yew trees guarding the gate set in the stone wall which surrounded the burial ground, where the yellow lichen-smeared headstones of generations of Hamiltons poked through the long, uncut grasses. Marianna gazed at her father's headstone next to the path. *Henry Baillie Hamilton. Aged sixty-four years. Beloved husband and father.* His epitaph simple but true. She stood, head bowed, for a few moments, and William waited for her a few paces away, to allow her the quiet of her private thoughts. He had never met her father, but he knew how much she had cared for him. He had been her ally and a source of comfort when she returned to her family after so many years lost to them, a buffer between her and her harsh, disapproving, difficult-to-please mother. He had taught her all he knew about managing the estate.

Marianna turned to William and hesitated, debating whether she should tell him what troubled her. It was a fleeting hesitation. "I need to speak to you, William. Let us sit a moment."

There was a wooden bench near the porch and in the cool shade of the building.

"What is it, darling?"

He did not care to see her beautiful face and stunning blue eyes clouded with worry.

She rubbed her stomach.

"Is it the baby? Is something wrong?"

"I don't know. But I am concerned. It was at this time in my pregnancy when we were newly married that I lost our first baby when we lived in Mossbrook—"

"You're worried you may miscarry?" he interrupted. "But you had Will, and everything was all right then?"

"I lost a second baby, William."

He looked at her quizzically, unsure he had heard her correctly.

"At the same stage in my pregnancy, I lost Cuthbert Robson's child."

Marianna, unable to look at him, was staring at the ground in front of her, where ridges of moss grew between the slate slabs of the path. Muffled bleats of distant sheep blended with the twitterings of sparrows in the bushes and the cooing of pigeons in the wood. William was breathing hard, but he said nothing. She remembered very well her lover, the handsome widower whose wife had killed herself.

William knew of her affair with the steward of the Loop Hall estate, where they had lived some twenty years before until their cruel separation; she had told him not long after they had been reunited the previous year, but he knew nothing of her pregnancy and subsequent miscarriage. He could not think what to say; this man, Robson, whom he had thought when he saw them together after his long journey back to her following his exile, was Will's father; this man whom he had thought had married her; this man who had caused him to flee in despair and live without her for nineteen years... Marianna was speaking. She had not lifted her gaze from the path.

"I could not tell you as I felt it was enough that I confessed to my affair with him. I did not tell him either. I didn't know I was pregnant when I left Netherton. I miscarried here at Longridge. No one knew."

William sighed. He said nothing. What was he to say? He loved her. This was ancient history.

"I was ill, very ill, when I heard you were still alive, knowing my mother knew and kept it from me, and that I had just missed being with you again. Then discovering you had gone to America, and I would never see you again, I was in *Hell*, William. It may have been something to do with my illness that I lost the baby weeks after that. I don't know. Yet, I am concerned there is something in me that means I may not carry this child to full term. I have been feeling a little unwell lately."

"You've been doing too much. You should've waited perhaps before embarking on this redecoration project."

"Have you been listening to me?" asked Marianna, turning to him. "Have you nothing to say about me keeping something from you?"

William took her hand and said gently, "We all do things we are sometimes ashamed of, Marianna. We get to a point in our lives when we look back with regret on things we did in the past. I know I do. You had an affair with Robson. It is not impossible to believe that a child would result. I'm sorry you suffered when you lost it. But it's all in the past."

"It is not just that, William," Marianna said, lowering her eyes. "The affair was my doing. I went to Cuthbert Robson. I made myself available to him. That is not the behaviour of a decent woman, surely?"

"Marianna, you've told me this. It happened years ago. Why are you talking of it now? Why does it bother you now?"

"Because I have thoughts that happiness is such a fleeting thing. We were so happy all those years ago and it was snatched from us when you disappeared, and everyone thought you had drowned in the bay. These last few months with you have been the happiest I can remember for a long time, and I feel it will all be snatched away.

Again. I feel if I confess to you, in some way, by confessing, I am making amends for what I have done wrong. God will forgive me and grant me a stay of execution—"

"For goodness' sake! Marianna! Look at me!" exclaimed William, taking her by the shoulders and turning her to face him. "Execution? That's a bit strong."

Her face was twisted in pain. "I felt so guilty, William, because I knew in my heart of hearts you were not dead. I loved you so much I knew I would have felt something if you were dead. I sensed you were not on the coach that perished in the bay. I clung on to that hope for a long time because I knew you would not have abandoned me. The months passed. Will was born and still you did not return." Marianna began to sob, and he pulled her to him, but she resisted. "No, I need to look at you. I need to see in your eyes that you forgive me." She could barely control the tears. "I began to feel something lacking in my life – a physical need, a very strong physical need. I was aware that Cuthbert Robson had a liking for me. I will confess I found him attractive. I went to him and offered myself to him to satisfy my needs. He loved me and asked me to marry him, not once, but many times. I could feel your presence sometimes, your spirit, and I knew I should wait for you to come back. I was betraying you. I felt so guilty." The sobs welled up from the depths of her. "I was on the point of accepting his proposal when my mother came for me."

William moved again to take her in his arms to comfort her, to reassure her, but she raised her hand to stop him. She took a moment to calm herself and searched for her handkerchief to wipe her eyes.

"Then when I was married to Bennet… The men I lay with. I did not love them. Some were *married*, William. I am shameless. Selfish. Putting my own needs first. I had a young child, for goodness' sake."

"But I know this. You've told me of the circumstances of your marriage: that you were deceived, that your husband did not lie with women, and he told you to seek comfort elsewhere. Why should I judge you? I've behaved in this way too to satisfy a need. You cannot change the past, Marianna. Let it go, I beg you, or you'll make yourself ill again."

Marianna was twisting the handkerchief in her fingers and sobbing convulsively. Again, William reached to comfort her, but she moved away. She needed to unburden herself further.

"I am being punished, William. I did not want our baby when we were newly married. I was too young. I wanted to have a life, just the two of us, for a while. I got what I wanted. We lost the baby. So, God took you away from me because He saw me for what I was."

"This is nonsense, Marianna. There is no God with a master plan. It is we who make what we can of our own lives."

She did not seem to have heard him. "Now, I have found you and I am so happy, so loved and full of love, God moves to punish me again for my past behaviour by taking this child."

Marianna's wild ramblings and sense of persecution alarmed William. He knew she found comfort in prayer, but her belief that God was punishing her, her belief in the cruel judgement of her by God, was not founded in a deep faith, more a superstitious need, instilled in her by Agatha Mislet when she was a child at Coldbarrow, the isolated farm where they had both been taken against their will. Agatha Mislet used the hellfire and brimstone of the Bible as a means of control over the children who lived there and which, for Marianna, had now mutated into an insurance policy for when she was called to account on the Day of Judgement. For him, it was all illogical nonsense.

"Is there something wrong with the baby? I shall send for the doctor."

"I am having some of the symptoms I have had before. But more than that, I am filled with an overwhelming dread."

"You will not lose this child, Marianna," William said gently. "Please, my darling, these sombre thoughts that trouble you, you must speak to me... share them with me." He had witnessed these black moods years ago when she thought she had been abandoned by her family and did not know her true identity. But this was the first since their reunion. "You must rest more. You're doing too much. We have years ahead of us to make all the changes we wish to make." He shuffled along the bench to take her in his arms and hugged her close. "Do you remember the time when we ran away from

Coldbarrow and slept out on the fells?" He could feel her nodding. "Do you remember you were so cross with me when we climbed down into the valley to look for water as we were so thirsty and there was none? You sat down and refused to move, and I left you to fume. That was the first time I was aware of your stubbornness. Sometimes, Marianna, it's a good thing to be stubborn and hold on to what you believe in, but not this... this holding on to dark thoughts that make you so sad. Remember, when all seems hopeless, have hope. Promise me that when you feel sad again, you will come to me." He felt her nod again. "I love you. I love you. Remember that I love you. Remember what we promised all those years ago, that we would love each other 'till all the seas gang dry.'"

Surely, if she could draw strength from his deep love for her, she would find peace. She was an assured, capable woman, evident in her managerial and organisational skills in running the estate and household; all overlaid with her gentle femininity, natural charm and empathy, which was returned by the affection and devotion shown to her by the servants, even after the few months they had been at Longridge.

She sat up, took his hand and tried to smile. "I love you so much, William. You are so good to me. What would I do without you? My beautiful man." She clung to him and sobbed out her tears, her pain, her sadness, and he rocked her gently. They held each other for a long time without speaking. It did not matter what dark secrets she told him. He loved her.

Dr Haddon had attended the Hamilton family for many years and arrived in the late afternoon. He was old, white haired and overweight, and puffed his way up the stairs to their bedroom. He put down his bag on a side table and came to the bedside to peer at Marianna over his half-moon spectacles. She grimaced as he wheezed his stale, beery breath in her face. He felt her pulse, pulled down the skin under one of her eyes and patted her hand.

"A little nervous episode, my dear. Nothing to worry about." He picked up his bag to leave. "I seem to recall, some years ago, you had something similar. Are you eating well? Sleeping well?"

Marianna nodded.

William was unimpressed by his cursory examination and asked, "Should we not be concerned because she's with child and her age? Marianna is usually so well."

Dr Haddon sighed in condescending exasperation. "Our dear Queen gave birth to nine children, the last at the age of thirty-eight."

His remark was flippant, dismissive; he did not appear to register William's concerns for his wife's health. Marianna was thirty-seven, she had suffered two miscarriages, and it was nineteen years since she gave birth to their son. William was unimpressed, considered the doctor old-fashioned and his competence questionable. He thought he should be put out to grass like a retired horse, but he held his tongue despite his frustration. He accompanied him to his carriage waiting at the front door.

As they shook hands, Dr Haddon said, "I shall be retiring soon." His words were music to William's ears. "I have sold the practice to my assistant, Dr Richard Greenwood, who will be taking over at the end of the month."

William seized on the opportunity afforded by this news. "In that case, Dr Haddon, would you be so kind to ask Dr Greenwood to call on Marianna as soon as possible so we can make his acquaintance and determine if we wish to be under his care?"

Richard Greenwood arrived the following morning. He had been at the practice in Newbridge for two years. He was thirty years old, a Yorkshireman, descended from a long line of doctors, of medium height with light brown hair and green eyes, a friendly demeanour, personable, calm and reassuring and, to William's relief, was modern in his ideas. Marianna was equally impressed.

He spent some time with her privately, letting her talk to him and listening patiently. Then he examined her. She had not told William about the blood-spotting on her underwear.

"It is a minor concern," Dr Greenwood reassured her, "and sometimes happens at this stage of a pregnancy. However, to be careful, I advise bed rest for a few weeks. Get up at least twice a day to go for a leisurely walk and get some fresh air, but rest as much as you can, and" – he wagged his finger at her – "no lifting of anything heavier than a teacup. You will have to issue orders for the work you are having done from the comfort of your bed." He smiled at her. "You are a little anaemic, so I'll suggest some additions to your diet. I shall call again in a few days and then every week to keep an eye on you. If you have any concerns, you must send for me immediately."

Marianna was dozing on their bed after luncheon as the heat exhausted her. On the side table was a thick, leather-bound book, her memoir, begun in the days after her mother brought her back to Longridge. She had told William that she wanted him to read it as she had recorded in it her thoughts and emotions, beginning with her time at Coldbarrow, and she wanted him to share every part of her; they would have no secrets.

William kissed her gently on the lips. He would join her for tea later. He whistled tunelessly as he made his way down the road in the warm sunshine, relieved that Dr Greenwood had set Marianna's mind at rest, which eased his own concerns about her. He passed the walled kitchen garden and walked through the stand of trees to the stables. His workmen were hard at work; he nodded to the foreman. He was very satisfied with the work that had been completed so far to fulfil the ideas and plans he had put to his architect.

The original stables had been built in the early eighteenth century around the old pele tower that, centuries before, had protected the original inhabitants of Longridge from marauding Bordermen. William had remodelled the layout: the pele tower would house their carriages with a tack room behind and storage on the upper floors. To one side he had rebuilt stables for the carriage horses and prospective stallions and, to the other, stables for the mares and their foals; and storerooms that could be converted to stables if his breeding project proved to be a success. All the doors looked out onto the yard to provide some interest for the horses. New, more modern accommodation had been built to one side of the yard to replace the old, run-down dwellings, with a large cottage for his stable master and two smaller cottages for staff, should the need arise. Opposite, the old barn had already been renovated. In a nod to the elegance and grandeur of the stables on the Loop Hall estate, which he could not afford to match, a weathervane had been added to the pele tower above the clock.

"Any problems, Mr Stott?"

"Nay, sir," the foreman replied, removing his cap and mopping his brow. "Although this heat is summat else. Work's progressin' well. We should have th' main cottage ready by th' end of this week."

"Good. My stable master and his family are anxious to move out of their lodgings." William smiled and wandered off to find Andrew to see how the carriage horses were faring in their temporary home in the barn alongside the carriages and Andrew's furniture. He was pleased with the appointment of Andrew Kerr as stable master. He had impressed him with his knowledge and experience and was as excited as he was to be at the birth of a new venture. He was a well-built, dark-haired Scotsman, twenty-nine years old, with an open, honest face and a quiet, self-assured manner round the horses. He was married to Catriona, a shy, homely woman, pregnant with their second child, who was very much looking forward to moving into their new, comfortable and well-appointed home.

William had waited years for the opportunity to fulfil his dream of breeding horses and it would soon come to pass. Trains had superseded coaches, but ladies would still ride out in their carriages and gentlemen would still like to ride for sport and pleasure. Now, all he needed was a virile stallion and some brood mares.

"Do you think we shall be happy in this house?" asked Marianna.

William had just entered her sitting room to join her for tea after riding out with Andrew to exercise the horses, and they and the horses had returned soaked in sweat, so he was feeling refreshed and invigorated after a bath and change of clothes. Her question, asked without raising her head to look at him, stopped him in his tracks and lowered his spirits. The optimism he had felt earlier had dissolved with her words. She was sitting in a chair by the closed door that led into the rose garden. Arthur Dummigan, the gardener, had been explaining how and why to prune the roses, and the manure he had placed on the flower beds in spring still smelt ripe because of the heat and made her feel nauseous, so she had come back into the house.

"What do you mean? Come and sit beside me and tell me what you mean."

Marianna rose to join him on the window seat overlooking the lawns at the front of the house. "I have never really lived here," she explained. "I was so young when I was taken and then, when I came back, I could not settle because of my mother. I felt on edge all the time. The only time I felt relaxed was when I came here on holiday with Will after I inherited Longridge. It *is* a beautiful house, William, and I do not wish to sound ungrateful as we have so much but…" She paused as she saw the shadow of unease in his eyes. She knew he was concerned that she could sink into one of her dark moods. "Do not fret, William. I'm not unhappy in that way. I just wonder… You uprooted yourself from Stillingford for my sake. Do you feel settled here?"

"I do because you are with me, we've a child on the way and so much to look forward to."

"It's just that I feel obliged to live here as I am really only the guardian of the estate until Will takes over. I feel obliged to carry out my father's wishes – he was so thrilled to have a grandson to inherit one day – and I wonder, if that was not the case, where I should like to live."

"Your father left the estate to you first, Marianna. He wanted to make amends for the difficulties you endured, and you *were* his eldest child. He must have recognised your capabilities to entrust it to you. The fact you have a son with his name to pass it on to is a bonus. This is a special place. Generations of Hamiltons have nurtured it, and we must do the same and instil the value of their legacy in our children."

"Are you happy to live here then, William? If you are happy and it feels like home to you, then I shall be happy."

"I am happy. There's so much to enjoy here and you always wanted to live surrounded by countryside such as this."

Marianna kissed his cheek and got up. "Then we shall say no

more about it. You have put my mind at rest. Would you care for some tea?"

"Yes. Thank you," he replied.

She went to ring the bell beside the fireplace. The conversation had planted the germ of an idea in his head.

THREE

Five months into her pregnancy, Marianna was blooming. She was keen to start the next phase of decorating, but William was firm with her. To keep her mind occupied, she busied herself with the baby's layette; she was a skilled needlewoman, taught by Agatha Mislet, the woman who had dominated her childhood at Coldbarrow. William took her for rides in the carriage, and they went by train from Newbridge to go shopping in Melchester or Penistone. He encouraged her to invite to tea local women, recommended by Dr Greenwood's wife, Ellen, and her warm hospitality led to new friendships, as a result of which they were both invited to social gatherings in the area. In return, an invitation to attend a dinner party at Longridge, often in the company of local dignitaries, was much sought after. William did not think he had seen Marianna so happy. The brooding, dark thoughts seemed to have gone. She glowed, her dark blue eyes shone, her hair was sleek, her figure had filled out, and he desired her as much as ever but had been afraid to love her since the alarm about her miscarrying the baby.

One afternoon, Marianna was resting on their bed after taking a bath. William had been to the stables to check on the mares he had purchased at the auction in Melchester and brought her a cup of tea from the kitchen. As he turned to leave, she reached for his hand. She was wearing a light silk dressing gown and, as she moved, he glimpsed the curve of her rounded breast as the robe opened slightly.

"Stay, William."

He lay down on the bed beside her and gazed at her. He longed for her, but he was unsure of the intention behind her request. She seemed to read his thoughts, began to stroke his face, moved her hand to unbutton his shirt to caress his chest. She wore the smile he knew so well. Then she sat up to undress him, all the while caressing and stroking and kissing him.

"I want you, William. Make love with me. It has been a while."

She sat astride him, and he was overwhelmed by his love for her, intoxicated by the smell of her, entranced by her beauty: the heart-shaped face, the dimples which appeared as she smiled at him, her deep, deep blue eyes, her richly coloured hair cascading round her shoulders. Her lips parted; her eyes were dark with longing; her belly round and swelling; her breasts round and full. He wanted her.

"Are you sure. I don't—"

She put her finger to his lips, leant forward, her hair falling over his face, and whispered, "You cannot hurt me or the baby."

They had been quiet for a while; happy, contented. He sat comfortably, sinking into a pile of pillows; the sheet covered them. She was lying between his legs, her head resting on his chest; he could feel the bump of the unborn child, the weight of it, on his thigh.

"The mares have settled in well," he said. "I wanted to talk to you about acquiring a stallion."

"William!" Marianna burst out laughing and pushed herself up to look at him. "Your own prowess has made you think of stallions!"

He laughed with her. "Am I so conceited? To be serious, we need to think about the breeding to start paying for all the expense."

"I shall come with you the next time you go down to the stables," she said, nestling into him.

"Yes, and you can think of names for the mares. Andrew says he is tired of calling them Number One and Number Two." William was silent for a moment as he knew that what he was going to say next might prove difficult for her. "I need a stallion of quality. He'll be expensive if he is to sire the horses I want."

"Where would you acquire such an animal?"

"I was thinking of writing to Charles d'Anson at Loop Hall."

Marianna rolled away from him and sat up awkwardly as she shuffled into a comfortable position. A look of disquiet passed over her face.

"Why there? You got the mares from the auction in Melchester."

"Because I know of his reputation. I know how they do things there: the standards he has, the bloodline."

"That was twenty years ago," she said darkly.

"I spoke to breeders and buyers at the auction. His reputation is sound. He is still highly regarded."

"What if someone should recognise you?"

"Does it matter?"

"If you are determined to do it, then I shall not object. What else can I say, William?"

But he knew she was unsettled.

That evening, Richard Greenwood came to dinner. His wife had taken their young son Jack to visit his grandparents in Yorkshire. Richard and Ellen had become valued friends and they often spent time together. Richard shared William's love of horses and they went out riding as often as Richard could spare the time. Although not as skilled, Ellen shared Marianna's love of needlework and was eager to learn and improve.

Marianna retired early to bed and William invited Richard to join him in the study for a nightcap. It was a warm late evening. One of the French doors was open. Both men removed their jackets, loosened their collars and settled comfortably into the chairs either side of the fireplace. After some general chit chat, Richard said, "May I ask, William, if it is not too private a matter? There is quite a gap between your son and this baby."

William swirled his brandy, watching the colours change in the glow of the lamplight. He liked Richard very much. Although he was younger than he was by ten years, they had common interests and ideas; they shared the same morals and values. There was a long silence.

"Of course, it is private. Forgive me. I do not wish to pry."

"No, it's not that, Richard. You're a doctor. You cannot betray a confidence."

"You do not need to tell me anything that you wish to keep private."

"To be honest, I wouldn't know where to begin."

William got up and, taking his drink with him, went to stand by the open door to give himself time to think and whether he could trust this man with his and Marianna's secrets. He sipped his drink. The ticking clock on the mantelpiece filled the silence. The western sky was blurred pink, yellow and mauve as the light faded. He breathed in the air heavy with the scent of a climbing rose. Bats flitted across the lawns. A moth was fluttering against the glass, and he closed the door. He took another sip of his brandy. He decided to give Richard the benefit of the doubt.

"You'll have heard the rumours about Marianna's past," he said, returning to his chair, "when she was kidnapped as a child, only three years old, by her nursemaid? It was a scandal at the time and I'm sure it's still a fascinating source of gossip for some."

Richard nodded. Dr Haddon had told him. The nursemaid had been infatuated with a manipulative scoundrel who wanted to ransom the child, but she lost her nerve, and he took the child anyway. Nobody knew what had become of her until years later; at least, they knew only what her family had chosen to tell.

William, nursing his brandy, sipping it occasionally, was ready to tell their story. "I was taken from my family too, a poor, working family in Mossbrook, a mill town in Lancashire. You'll have noticed that I've not completely lost my accent." He smiled. "We ended up in the same place, Coldbarrow, a farm in the middle of nowhere, to work on the farm and in the mill. It was owned by a man called Heaning Mislet and his sister, Agatha, who bought and sold children." Richard groaned. "And renamed them. We were Jacob and Mary. And yet," he smiled wryly, "it was there that my love for horses began."

They had grown up together, fallen in love, and then ran away to find William's family as Marianna could remember nothing about hers. They found his married sister, but his father was dead – his mother had died two years before he was taken – and his brothers had gone. William worked in a cotton mill. He and Marianna married and, months later, she suffered a miscarriage.

William sighed. "We could not settle. The dirt, the cramped streets and houses, the filthy air. We both craved the countryside as it was what we had grown up with. So, we decided to leave and went to the hiring fair in Melchester. We found work on the Loop Hall estate, not far from here, owned by the d'Anson family."

Richard nodded. "I know of it."

"I was a groom and Marianna worked as a seamstress for Mrs d'Anson. We were very happy. Very happy. Then everything changed."

Richard saw the grimace of pain before William emptied his glass. He lowered his voice as though he did not trust the walls not to betray his secret. "Please, I must ask you never to divulge what I am about to say. I've a dread, rational or irrational, I do not know, that my past may come back to turn our lives upside down again."

Richard could not imagine what he meant but reassured him that his words would not leave the room.

William went on to describe how, on returning from a job delivering a horse to its new owner and, whilst waiting in Melchester for the coach to take him home across the sands of the bay, he had been caught up, unintentionally, in a political meeting organised by the Chartists, that had descended into what the authorities later described as a riot. He had seen with his own eyes that the disturbance was deliberately started by provocateurs. He was wrongfully arrested, convicted and transported to Australia.

Richard gasped. "Transported! Good Lord! How did this happen if you were innocent?"

William rubbed his chin and shook his head sadly before saying, "They weren't interested in my innocence, Richard. They wanted scapegoats. There were witnesses attesting to my conduct. All lies." A flash of anger in his eyes as he struggled to control his emotions. What these people had done to him. "My faith in justice died that day as I knew they had been bribed to speak against me. I was guilty in the eyes of authority, and they were not going to listen to my pleas. I was bitter for many years that the truth could be so distorted to satisfy their own ends."

He went on to relate how the prisoners were marched all the way to London, and then on to Portsmouth to board the barely seaworthy convict ship, wrecked in a storm in the Atlantic some ten days into the voyage. Everyone drowned; but he, who could not swim, had somehow survived, washed up on the beach of an island, along with the ship's doctor who died not long after. He fell into silence. He occasionally had nightmares about his ordeal: the waters closing over him as he resigned himself to his fate and sank, his lungs crushed, until some instinct drove him to the surface. He shuddered, seeing again the bodies of men, women and children scattered on the sand amidst the debris. Richard was watching him, his brow creased with concern.

William briefly described the long months of hardship as he made his way from the island, where he had been cared for until he recovered, to Spain, and then home on foot, hundreds of miles, as he had been robbed of the money given to him and he was terrified of the sea, unaware that Marianna was pregnant and had given birth to their son. He explained that when he had not returned home that fateful day, he was presumed drowned in the bay as the coach he was supposed to be on, delayed by the trouble in Melchester, was late and missed the guides who took travellers across the bay in safety; it was caught out by the tide and quicksands, and everyone perished. He spoke of his return, many months later, to Netherton, the hamlet where they lived, when he was given reason to believe that Marianna, thinking he was dead, had remarried. He was heartbroken, knowing he could not reveal himself to her, and set off on his travels again. He ended up on the road near Longridge Hall and came upon a carriage accident involving Carolina Hamilton who, grateful for his actions in coming to her aid, had given him a temporary job whilst the coachman recovered from his injury. It was from the coachman he learnt about the Hamiltons and the taken child, whose name was Marianna.

"I told Carolina Hamilton where she was. Until then, I did not know her true name. Of course, I could not stay at Longridge."

The clock on the mantelpiece struck ten. William paused, and on the last chime looked at Richard, who nodded that he understood.

"You thought she had remarried. You were alive. A difficult and delicate situation."

"Yes. I was in agony about what to do," William said ruefully. "I left Longridge for Mossbrook to discover my sister had emigrated with her family to America. I followed."

Richard heard how he had found employment and began his search for Lizzie. After several years, by which time he had started his own successful import and export business, he found her living in poverty in Philadelphia as her husband, George, had died.

"I brought her and her children to live with me in New York. Lizzie never settled so we returned to England. If only I'd known that Marianna had waited for me…" William closed his eyes and sighed. "It pains me so much to think of what I have missed because of a misunderstanding." He paused to gulp back a sob and to collect himself. "Marianna did remarry when Will was seven years old. A wealthy lawyer in Manchester." William raised his eyebrows as he shot Richard a look. "It was more than seven years…"

"I understand completely what you are implying." Richard shuffled uncomfortably in his chair at the thought that the crime of bigamy may have been committed a second time. "This happened years ago," he added, trying to think of some reassuring words as he processed all the information he was hearing. It just went on and on. So many things happening to one couple.

William laughed, a short, bitter laugh. "Marianna told me that her mother did not approve of me. The wrong class." He laughed again. "She still disapproves of me even though I am a wealthy man. I think she is ashamed, too, as she did not tell Marianna that I was alive and had been here at Longridge…" William waved his hand. "No matter. Not long ago, last year in fact, I met Will by chance. Then Marianna's husband died."

William avoided mentioning the sham marriage of convenience arranged to provide the veneer of respectability for the homosexual Bennet Foster, who had agreed to a divorce but, before the petition was started, died in Italy from cholera at the home he shared with his lover.

"And here we are." William exhaled noisily, unsure whether with relief that he had reached the end of the story, or with misgivings that he had told it at all. He looked at Richard for a reaction. "It's a ridiculous history, isn't it? So ridiculous it doesn't sound believable."

Richard could think of nothing to say for a moment; the story was extraordinary. His friend had suffered greatly. Marianna too. He shook his head in bewilderment and puffed out his cheeks. He realised that he had not touched his drink for some time and finished it before shaking his head again. "Your secrets are safe with me." He replaced his glass on the side table.

William was staring at his clasped hands.

"I am having difficulty taking in all you have told me. And you found each other again. That is remarkable. What a stroke of luck! You deserve to be happy, both of you."

"She is the only woman I have truly loved," said William softly, still staring at his hands, keen now to steer the conversation away from their difficult, complicated past. "I've never been happier." He thought back to their lovemaking that afternoon: how beautiful she was, how she had pleased him, thinking of his needs before hers. "I adore her. If anything happened to her…" William's voice faltered. He looked at Richard. "She is doing well, isn't she?"

"Yes, very well. I am pleased with her."

William rose from his chair to refill their glasses.

"And I am pleased she has you to take care of her."

The response from Loop Hall to William's letter arrived a week later. They were breakfasting in the morning room. It was a gloomy day; rain streamed down the windows and the lamps were lit. William scanned through the letter thanking him for his interest and extending an invitation to visit. He put down the letter and looked across the table to Marianna, who was buttering a piece of toast.

"I've been invited to Loop Hall next week to look at some prospective horses. Would you like to accompany me?"

The knife clattered onto the plate and Marianna looked at him in horror.

"It's all right," he reassured her. "He's not there. At least, I assume he's not there, as the letter is signed by James Bell. Steward."

Marianna dabbed her mouth with her napkin. "Whether he was there or not, I would not go. The baby... The travelling... No, I do not think so."

"I thought you might like to revisit the place."

"Next time, perhaps. If there is a next time." She picked up the newspaper and began to peruse the front page of advertisements as if they were of extreme interest to her. Cuthbert Robson, who became her lover after William's presumed death, whose marriage proposal she had rejected when she returned to her family, whose child she had miscarried, was no longer the steward of Loop Hall. She wondered what had become of him and his daughter, Eleanor, who had so resented her as a rival for her father's affection, and as a replacement for her own mother who had killed herself years before Marianna knew them. Marianna felt her cheeks flush as she remembered him, the handsome, kind widower: how she had loved him, the physical love they had shared, the pleasure they got from each other and, if her mother had not come to claim her, whose wife she would now be.

William had talked of fate and how it was impossible to fight against it. Regrets cannot change anything, he told her. She had no regrets regarding the relationship with Cuthbert Robson. She was a passionate woman who needed sexual contact. He had satisfied that need. She raised her eyes from the newspaper to look at her husband. He was perusing some other letters. Tears pricked her eyes, and she looked down again quickly. Thank God fate had intervened and she had not married Robson. Now, she had her beloved William back again and life was wonderful. They adored each other. They had something, a bond, forged in their difficult childhood, which had been tested, broken and remoulded. She was determined, despite her frequent descents into sombre thoughts, to relish every moment they had together.

William took the train to Kirkby by Sands in the county of Lancashire. As the train crossed the viaduct at Belside, he craned forward to take in the panorama of the bay and to look for the teeming flocks of birds that came to feed on the rich sands, a sight which had always enthralled him. He had crossed the sands many times on the coach, the journey dependent on the tide and the skills of the guides who shepherded the travellers through the gullies and the rivers, away from the treacherous quicksands. He supposed the work of the guides was limited now that the trains could pass safely across the bay; perhaps their services used by those too poor to afford the train ticket. How convenient it was to be able to cross safely and more frequently. How strange to ride above the water.

The hamlet of Belside he had ridden through so often on his way to deliver Charles d'Anson's horses to customers had grown with the coming of the railway. A few shops lined a small promenade which led to the station and rows of houses clung to the hillside. Gulls bobbed on the water. Some boys were hanging over the railings on the promenade, their lines cast into the sea to catch fish. In the distance, on the opposite shore, he could see the spire of Kirkby Church and, further still, the limestone crag towering over the cottages at Netherton where he and Marianna had lived. As the train chugged slowly over the viaduct, the wheels clattering on the rails, he looked east to the hills near Melchester and west to the fells of the Loop Hall estate that surrounded this vast expanse of water stretching to the horizon, silver-grey in the pale sunshine. Kirkby Station had been built near the old coaching inn on the outskirts of the town. Mr d'Anson's steward, James Bell, was waiting to collect him. He felt strange as they trotted along in the gig pulled by a Fell pony, trying to concentrate on the steward's conversation whilst, at the same time, taking in the sights which stirred so many memories. Despite the passing years nothing had changed. As they rode past the cottages at Netherton, there was a lump in his throat and he had to avert his gaze – the row of neat, stone cottages, the woodwork painted in the forget-me-not blue of the estate colour, was unchanged. He wondered who lived in their old house. The tide was ebbing, and he watched the gathering flocks of oystercatchers, curlews and terns, crying, swooping and swirling, impatient for the rich sands to be exposed.

They turned off the main road near Middleton Church to follow the road that led to the hall, the road he had walked along on his way to and from work. They passed into the dark woods echoing with birdsong, and he could identify most of the calls he heard. They came out into the sunlight, turned again down the road that led to the stables and passed through the arch under the clock tower into the yard. He remembered that the arch, under the building across the yard with the weathervane he had copied, led to the paddocks. Nothing had changed here either, the standards maintained as he remembered: tubs of pale pink pelargoniums stood at regular intervals round the perimeter of the spotless yard; the paintwork was fresh; the windows gleamed. He could hear the chatter of the lads in the tack room; they had been banished there as was the custom when Mr d'Anson was showing his horses.

Jumping down from the gig, William removed his hat and approached the unmistakable figure of Charles d'Anson. He was greyer, fatter than he remembered, but Mr d'Anson had never spoken to him, probably never registered his presence, in all the time he had worked for him.

"Good morning, Mr Hamilton-Read. Did you have a pleasant journey?"

Charles d'Anson never sold horses to customers he had not met personally. He bred horses to make money, but he cared for them enough to ensure they went to good homes.

"Good morning, Mr d'Anson. I did. Thank you. Thank you for sending your steward to meet me."

"Not at all. Mr Malkin" – he turned to the young man standing next to him – "Jupiter first."

With a curt nod, Jonny Malkin retreated to the stables. He had not recognised William. William would not have recognised him either if he had not heard the name, as he had changed so much from the skinny, bashful boy he remembered. He was the son of his former boss, the stable master and head coachman, Ambrose Malkin, from whom William had learnt so much about horses, and had obviously, as William had always presumed when he had worked there, succeeded his father in the job.

When Jonny returned, leading Jupiter by the head collar rope, Mr d'Anson invited William to inspect the handsome, black stallion with a white blaze down his muzzle. William studied his conformation, ran his hands along his back and hindquarters and down his legs, and checked his teeth and feet. Jonny walked him up and down the yard and then trotted him as the steward described his pedigree. William had recognised the traits of the stud stallion, Sultan, who had sired many of the horses he had ridden out to customers. Jupiter was tied to a rail in the yard, then Jonny fetched the second horse, Marquis, who had been bred from a different bloodline. He was a bay and very handsome too. William examined him and watched as Jonny trotted him up and down. William asked if the stallions were proven studs, how many mares they had covered, whether any of their offspring were still at the stables and if he could see them. Mr d'Anson said Mr Bell would show him and then, as he had satisfied himself as to the suitability of this prospective customer and he had business elsewhere, he excused himself and they shook hands.

"If you are interested, Mr Hamilton-Read, then speak to Mr Bell. He will arrange everything."

William asked the steward if he could lead each horse himself. It was the second horse he was drawn to. The first followed him reluctantly, tugged at the leading rein and there was a spark in his eye – a spark of defiance. However, the second followed him quietly, stopped when he stopped and nuzzled him when he patted his neck. William trusted his instincts. This was the horse he wanted. This horse, with the gentler eyes, trusted him.

The deal had been done and arrangements made for payment and delivery. William shook hands with the steward who said, "I have arranged for one of the lads to take you back to the station, Mr Hamilton-Read."

William thanked him and went to wait next to the gig. He patted the pony's neck then turned as he heard the lad approaching.

"I'm to take thee to th' station, Mr Ham…" The lad's words died on his lips and his mouth gaped in shock. "William? As I live and breathe…"

Joseph Ainsworth, his old friend – his closest friend in those days – and colleague, who had hardly changed at all over the years, cropped ginger hair and freckled face, the hint of a paunch perhaps, stood, his eyes wide in disbelief, wondering if he had committed a faux-pas and made a fool of himself.

William shook his head and said, "Not here, Joseph."

They climbed into the gig and Joseph slapped the pony's rump with the reins. William waited until they were out of sight of the stables and asked Joseph to halt the gig in the woods.

"I knew a Mr Hamilton-Read were comin' today but I nivver thowt it'd be thee. Th' name?"

"It's me, Joseph. How are you?"

"But thou died," said Joseph, still unable to comprehend why his old friend was sitting next to him. "Drowned in th' bay."

"As you can see, I'm alive and well."

"Very well, from th' look of thee. A gentleman. What on earth happened to thee?"

"I had an accident," said William. "I lost my memory." It was simpler to lie. It was the answer to be given which had been agreed between him and Marianna to avoid awkward questions being asked.

"But we thowt thou were dead. Mary. Poor lass. She had a babby." Joseph looked anxiously at William as if imparting news he was ignorant of. "She had a lad. She left. What a strange story that were; tekken from her family as a bairn."

"I know all about it, Joseph. And my son, Will. We found each other, hence the name. We've combined our names."

"She came from wealthy kin," said Joseph, looking at William's expensive clothes, implying he had done well from the marriage.

"I made my own fortune in America, Joseph, before I found her again. I'm not a kept man." He laughed, to spare Joseph any embarrassment.

"Wher'st thou livin' now?"

"Near Newbridge. Perhaps, you'll deliver my horse to me?"

34

"It's all different now, William. They go by train now. Progress."

"So I understand. Mr Bell told me someone will accompany the horse to ensure its comfort and safety. Do you still enjoy the work here?"

"Aye, that much hasn't changed. Jonny Malkin learnt well from his faither who's retired to Kirkby."

"Is he as harsh and strict?"

"Strict, aye, but friendly wi' me. He grew up wi' me, remember. I'm th' senior groom now. All th' other lads thou knew have moved on. As did Cuthbert Robson. Th' steward?"

Joseph had turned as red as his hair when he realised that he should not have mentioned him, unsure whether William knew of the relationship between him and Mary that had caused quite a stir on the estate at the time.

"Where did he go?" asked William, as if asking about an old acquaintance.

"I divn't know. He left years ago."

"And Martha?"

"Aye, we're very happy. Will thou stop at th' cottage an' see her? She'll need to see thee wi' her own eyes. She'll nivver believe me otherwise."

William considered Joseph's request, noted the eager anticipation on the smiling face, then nodded.

After dinner, William and Marianna settled together on one of the sofas in her sitting room. It was the first room Marianna had insisted on redecorating; not because her mother's taste was offensive to her but because she did not care for her mother, and to leave the room unchanged would be a constant reminder and a source of irritation to her. The decoration was plainer: the busy-patterned wallpaper removed, and the walls painted in a muted, dusky pink, a colour she considered more in keeping with the age of the house. The furniture had been reupholstered, and there were some ornaments and pictures. She did not subscribe to the fashion for cluttering rooms with *objets*. She snuggled up to William, who was nursing a glass of brandy, relaxed in the warmth and smell of him, the strength and steadfastness of him, the comfort of him.

"Tell me about the rest of your day."

At dinner, William had described his journey and what he had seen of Loop Hall. He told her about Jonny Malkin, the steward and, of course, his new horse. Now they were alone, with no one to overhear their conversation, he told her about Joseph, who had recognised him immediately, and how he had explained what had happened to him in the manner they had agreed. He had called on Martha on the way back to the station. When Joseph asked him, he had debated whether this was wise, but he would have offended Joseph by refusing, and he reckoned the news of his miraculous reappearance would spread whether he called on her or not. They lived in their old cottage which seemed very small to him after all these years. Martha and Joseph had three children, all employed on the estate. She was still the same, warm and friendly, a little plumper and asked to be remembered to her.

Marianna smiled. "She was a good friend to me."

"If the breeding goes well, darling, and Marquis proves his worth, I'll not need to go back to Loop Hall. I can buy another stallion elsewhere if I need to. It was interesting and satisfied my curiosity and, of course, I was entranced by the beauty of the place, but as I left, I felt a great sadness and a great sense of relief as though I'd buried a very sick relative. I'm pleased I went, but it's time to put the past behind me." He sipped his drink. "Do you remember how I longed to find my family when we were at Coldbarrow and what a disappointment it was when we returned to Mossbrook? My dream did not match reality. I felt I had to go back to Loop Hall to put something to rest. Now I have and I'm satisfied. However, you must ride on the train over the viaduct. It felt strange to cross the bay in that way rather than by coach. We shall take a trip round the coast to Castleton one day."

William stroked her hair and Marianna shut her eyes, comforted by his touch. After a few minutes, he said, "Are you not going to ask about him?"

He felt her flinch. "He is gone then?" she asked quietly.

"Yes, he's gone, but Joseph didn't know where to."

FOUR

William cradled Savannah, now ten days old, in his arms as he walked round the drawing room, talking to her about the furniture, the pictures on the wall, the view from the window. Marianna was resting on a sofa, feet up, a cup of tea in her hand, smiling contentedly at them. It was the first day after her 'nine-day confinement', but Richard Greenwood believed that a change of scenery, a little exercise and fresh air were of more benefit to a newly delivered mother than being imprisoned in her bedroom, so she had been up and about for a few hours each day.

"I could look at her all day," William said. "And she looks at me. She's frowning now with concentration."

"That may be wind, William," Marianna teased. "I don't think babies are able to focus their eyes at this age. You are probably a blur."

"I'm telling you, darling, she's listening to what I'm saying." He kissed tenderly his daughter's cheek. "She's looking at me with intense curiosity. She's fixing my features in her memory and attaching them to my voice."

"As you wish," she said benevolently.

"Yes," he cooed at the baby. "This is your papa speaking to you. You're as sweet as a little mouse. We're going to be the best of friends."

The child let out a squawk.

"Are you sure about that, William?" Marianna said and laughed. She reached to put down her tea on a side table. "I think she needs a feed." She unfastened the bodice of her dress and stretched out her arms to take the baby and put her to her breast. William sat down opposite, put his feet up on a footstool and sighed. His wife, head bent towards the baby, stroked her cheek as she suckled. Despite her frailty and the shadows under her eyes, she was so beautiful, serenely beautiful.

"I missed this with Will," he said.

"The disturbed nights? The crying? And the contrariness? She's fallen asleep!"

"That's the price we pay. No, I meant the joy of meeting your child for the first time. The instant she was put into my arms, I was overwhelmed. A big man like me overwhelmed by a tiny mite. I felt a surge of love for her. And Will is smitten." He jumped to his feet suddenly as he remembered something. "I promised Will we'd go for a ride. You don't mind?" He kissed mother and baby. "Shall I ring for the nurse?"

It was a crisp, sunny day with enough light left to go for a good ride round the estate before darkness descended.

"I'm so relieved Mama is well," said Will as they walked down to the stables.

"Yes, she's still a little weak and tired," said William, "but Richard says another week or two of rest and then she should start to feel more like herself. And what do you think of your new sister?"

"I cannot say what I think. She is so small and delicate. I am not used to babies, and she seems a little uninteresting." Will did not feel that was the right thing to say to a proud father. "But her name is unusual and pretty."

William stopped, put his hand on Will's arm and gazed at his son. He was as tall as he was, of slighter build and, apart from the Hamilton eyes, was almost his mirror image. He was a handsome, young man. He hoped his son had his own caring nature.

"You'll grow to love her, Will. You promise me you'll love her and take care of her?" He saw the puzzled look in Will's eyes. "And you promise you'll look after your mother?"

"Papa?"

"I don't mean anything untoward in my questions. Only, there's nearly twenty years between you and the baby, that should anything happen to me, you'll be the adult to look after her, to help your mother to look after her."

"Of course, I shall look after them. This conversation, Papa, has a morbid tone to it, when it should, in the present circumstances, be more optimistic and hopeful."

"Indeed." William laughed and patted Will's shoulder. "I suppose it's a sign of impending old age to worry about such things. Come. Let's admire Marquis and then saddle up and go for that ride."

The first snow of winter covered the tops of the fells. The air was sharp with frost, the horses' breath hung in clouds as they rode along the road that would take them to a lonning through the woods, the trees stark and bare of leaves, and down to the Beulah, the river which flowed on to Newbridge. The circular route would bring them back to the fields of Fell Foot Farm where they could gallop across the stubbled, unploughed ground. They were both accomplished riders and there was a glint of competitiveness in their eyes as they nodded to each other before spurring their mounts and riding headlong for the wide, toppled trunk of an old oak tree at the side of the field. They slowed their horses as they approached the gate which would bring them back to the lane to the house, their faces red-glowing, eyes laughing; it did not matter who had won the race, it was another shared experience that brought them closer.

Their relationship was still new. William did not meet his son until he was a young man, eighteen years old, brought up by Marianna and, from the age of seven, another man, Bennet Foster; his character and personality already formed, whether by nature or nurture, William did not know. He was clever, which he surmised he could have inherited from either of his parents. He was well-mannered, thoughtful and quietly determined, and William hoped he was happy. Their relationship was friendly and respectful, but

William was aware he preferred to confide in his mother; there was still, even after a year of being acquainted with each other, a hesitancy, a reluctance to show his true feelings to his father. Yet, William was patient and, whenever his son was at home, took the time to be with him, on their own, to talk to him in the hope the barriers would come down. There had been a glimmer of that on the night Savannah was born when Will had first called him Papa. And continued to do so.

Andrew Kerr, the stable master, took their horses after they had untacked them, and they walked back to the house.

"I'll have to find a lad to help Andrew," said William. "He's a lot to do with the horses we have."

They came to the front of the house; the light was beginning to fade, and Sarah could be glimpsed through the windows, passing from room to room to light the lamps and close the curtains.

"Do you think you'll go directly into law practice when you've finished at Oxford?"

"That is the idea, yes."

"I was wondering whether you'd like to travel first before putting your nose to the grindstone?"

"I had not thought of it."

"If you wanted to, I could help. You could go to America. I can arrange that for you. Maybe see how a New York or Boston law firm operates?"

"It's a tempting idea, Papa."

"You'll still be young when you qualify. You'll have the rest of your life to be a lawyer. It'd be interesting and educational to travel and see a bit of the world." William stopped under the *porte-cochère* as they reached the steps up to the front door. "I'm very proud to have you for a son, William Peter Hamilton-Read. I cannot take credit for the way you've turned out; that is down to your mother and Bennet Foster. But there's something of me in you. Your mother notices it and has told me so."

He placed his hands on Will's shoulders and stared into the young man's eyes. Will blinked, a little embarrassed by the show of affection.

"We've not known each other long," William went on. "But I want you to know I love you. I want you to know you can talk to me about anything. You can come to me for anything at any time."

He pulled his son into his arms and hugged him. Will did not resist.

"Now," said William, standing back and grinning at him, "it's Christmas soon. We must go out tomorrow and find a tree for the hall or your mother will not be pleased. We must take care of her, Will. You and me. She is the most precious creature. To both of us."

"Indeed, she is." Will smiled at his father. He had been touched by his genuinely warm words. He hesitated, unsure if he wanted to break this intimate moment or use it as a bridge to a deeper understanding of this man his mother loved so much. He decided on the latter.

"Papa, may I speak with you again? Perhaps later, after dinner? Just the two of us?"

"Of course." William eyed the darkening sky, heavy with yellow-tinged clouds. "I think we may have snow in the night." He took Will's arm. "Shall we go and see your mother and the baby?"

His father had poured him a small brandy and they sat in the comfortable, leather armchairs either side of the fire in the study. William remembered how Will had helped himself to a drink on the night Savannah was born.

"I recall," he said, "the advice of an old man I knew once. Never rely on drink to solve your problems. It is wise to heed him. My experience has shown that drink makes your problems worse and adversely affects the people round you. But a small measure, now and again, will do no harm."

"You have had experience of those whose lives have been ruined by drink?"

"My father for one, after my mother died. He used it to drown his sorrows and neglected his family. The owner of Coldbarrow, Heaning Mislet, was violent when drunk and became a wretched human being. Now, what did you want to talk to me about?"

Will stared into the fire, watching the golden flames flickering, their light reflecting on the brass grate. He raised his eyes to his father, who was waiting for him to speak.

"You have already told me about your life until the time you left for America. I wanted to know how you made such a success of your business as you started with nothing."

William laughed. "You think I made my fortune by nefarious means?"

Will was horrified. "No, sir! I meant—"

"I tease you, Will," his father interrupted. "Perhaps you don't approve of me profiting from the war in America?"

"I cannot say, Papa. Is it for me to judge? If I was to be pragmatic, I would say if not you, then it would have been someone else."

"I did not sell guns. My conscience would not allow me to do that. I sold woollen goods from England such as blankets and cloth to make uniforms, and anything else that was needed."

"I suppose your blankets kept some soldier warm at night."

William ignored his sarcasm and shrugged his shoulders.

"Many people here starved because of that war," said Will bitterly, "when the supplies of cotton dried up."

"Many did not," said William, "thanks to people like your mother and Bennet Foster and…"

"You, Papa?"

William nodded slightly, sipped his brandy, then nestled his drink in his hands.

"And now there is a war in Europe," he said. "Here we are in December 1870, and the people of Paris are starving as the Prussians lay siege to the city." They contemplated the horrors of this until William said, "To go back to your original question: I started out, when I first arrived in New York, working for a Scotsman who sold woollen cloth, but I soon became concerned about his business practices as he owed money everywhere, so I left to work for a trading company in New York, where I was promoted because I was prepared to work hard. I rose very swiftly to the board. I was paid well and made investments in the railways amongst other things. I then decided to work for myself. I worked long hours as I had no family to distract me. Well, not until I found Aunt Lizzie and her children. I think you know they had fallen on hard times in Philadelphia after George died?" William reflected for a moment. "I might've been a different man with a different life if I'd not been kidnapped as a child. I would've followed my father into the cotton mills with no chance of bettering myself. Long hours in the mill to stave off hunger and poverty. With the advantage of hindsight, I bless the day I was taken. I would never have met your mother either. I am who I am. By birth? By accident? What does it matter? The instinct that drove me to survive as I drowned in the Atlantic when the convict ship sank needed to be honoured. My life was saved. My life needed to be celebrated. My life was worth something. That drove me to succeed. I've been successful through luck and hard work. I've never made a drama out of what was done to me but got on with my life and stubbornly pursued my goals. I was never ruthless, and I've done what I thought was right and I don't believe I've caused harm to anyone. I was never ruthless," he repeated.

William sipped his drink and rolled the liquid round his mouth to savour it. He thought Will might say something, but he was silent. He had enjoyed a more privileged upbringing. His father's world, its hardships and deprivations and struggles, was alien to him.

"When I was taken as a child, seven years old, snatched from the street, taken to live with strangers, I detached myself from my fellows. I set myself apart. It was my way of coping. I had one very good friend, Peter, the boy whose name you have, who made my life bearable. He ran away one night but was caught. He was killed by the drunkard, Mislet, and I missed him very much. I learnt to watch, Will. I watched how people behaved. I listened to what they said and watched as they contradicted themselves. I learnt how to mask my own feelings. I learnt how to read people, their mannerisms, the things they did not say as much as the things they did, which came in useful later in my business dealings. I learnt how to behave by watching others and refined myself, rubbed away the coarseness in my behaviour and speech, and became more skilled in etiquette. I moulded myself into a gentleman in the same way your grandmother transformed your mother into a lady." William paused to take another sip of his drink before going on. "She used to talk like me, you know, until her mother insisted on elocution lessons." He smiled. "At Coldbarrow, your mother helped make my life bearable again after Peter died. She gave me something to live for. I had to be less selfish to care for her. She was my best friend and shared my life for a number of years. I've loved her since I was fourteen years old. That day in Liverpool when fate brought you, a complete stranger, into the hotel to sit at my table must count as one of the best days of my life. You brought her back to me." William leant across to squeeze his son's hand. "You brought her back to me."

Will smiled shyly at his father. "I am glad your story has had a happy ending, Papa."

They subsided into silence. For Will, overwhelmed by the power of his father's story, it was an opportunity to absorb and reflect on the strength of his father's character: living on his wits, his determination to better himself despite the hardships and injustices he had suffered, and yet, shining through it all was his humanity and kindness. His father was a remarkable man. In comparison, Will felt puny and inadequate, still a callow boy, and wondered if he would ever measure up to him, ever become a man to compare. His mother had suffered too; something he had learnt the previous year when she had revealed her past to him, but which he could never have imagined as she had never allowed him to witness any trace of her unhappiness and sorrows.

The clock on the mantelpiece struck the hour and they sat waiting for it to finish its chime. Both had finished their drinks; neither felt the need to replenish them, neither wanted to move, each content in the other's company, each aware that every conversation between them, when they spoke honestly with each other, cemented the bond between them.

A log crumbling in a shower of sparks roused William to toss another on the grate. "So," he said, settling in the chair, "you've chosen the right path to follow in life? With your studies, for example?"

"You asked me earlier."

"I did. But would you, at some time, consider doing something other than law?"

"You mean would I consider working in your business?"

William grinned at his acuity and said, "Or running the estate here."

"There is time yet for that. You and Mama manage it well enough. Is there something troubling you, Papa? This is the second time today you have mentioned what may happen in the future."

"No, I just like to think about things. I know from bitter experience how things can change in an instant. I'm acting out of self-interest, planning ahead. One day you'll have to come back and take over. It would be reassuring for your mother to know that's what you wanted." He paused as he saw Will's uneasiness in being pinned down to making a commitment he did not feel ready to make. "You are young yet. No need to make decisions now."

Will wanted to change the subject altogether. He had not entertained any thoughts about his future beyond enjoying his time at university, the freedom to behave as he wished, learn things about the world, about himself, about women, more women, as many women as possible, away from the scrutiny of his parents, unencumbered by thoughts of responsibility and duty.

"I'm glad you decided to leave this room as my grandfather had it. It holds special memories for me and the time I spent in his company."

"Yes, your mother didn't want to change it and I don't mind at all. Your grandfather had many interests if his collection of books is anything to go by." William stood up as he sensed Will's discomfort. "Enough talk. Let's have a game of billiards and you can let your father beat you this time."

The next morning, they woke to a covering of snow, the crystals glinting in the morning sunlight. The lawns like freshly laundered tablecloths, pockmarked here and there with the tracks of nocturnal animals and the newly wakened blackbirds probing in the snow in search of food.

Breakfast was interrupted by an urgent message from Andrew Kerr for William to come to the stables. Will went with him.

Andrew was muffled up against the cold, stamping his feet on the cobbles, and, beside him, the most pitiful creature either had ever seen. The mare – it was hard to tell which breed – was emaciated; her mane long and dirty; her tail trailing on the ground; her ribs protruding through wet, matted patches of coat, where the snow had melted, that surrounded the scabby, bare patches on her skin. She trembled, showing the whites of her eyes: with hunger or fear, it was hard to tell. Her breath steamed in the cold air as did a stinking puddle of urine. Andrew said her feet were inflamed and she struggled to walk.

"She was found by the milkman on his rounds, tied to a gate at the end o' the estate road and he brought her here. That she's been neglected is plain to see. I reckon she's been badly treated too as she's sae frightened if you raise your voice."

"And heavily in foal," said William.

They tied the pony's legs to stop her kicking out and, between them, they carried and heaved the bewildered animal into one of the stables, where she eyed them warily.

"We should leave her to settle, poor, wee lass," said Andrew. "I'll put out some hay and water for her and keep an eye on her. You give your permission, sir, for her to stay until she's foaled? I dinnae think it'll be long."

"Of course, Andrew. Where else will she go?"

"She's a bit moth-eaten," said Will. "How can anyone be so cruel?"

Andrew was right. The mare foaled early the next morning, but was weak and exhausted, and did not survive beyond two days. Her foal was small and sickly, and it was thought he would not survive either, but Andrew cared for him, sleeping next to him in the stable, encouraging him to feed with the milk he had coaxed from the teats of his dying mother. They were all watching as the foal struggled to his feet and took his first, wobbly, hesitant steps. It was Will who named him Moth.

FIVE

Not long before Savannah was born, a comment made by Marianna had planted an idea in William's head that, as he was a man who liked to plan ahead, made him think of the time when they would be ready to hand over the estate to Will. The idea flitted into his mind now and again and it had taken years to come to fruition. Recently, he had heard about a farm, a few miles to the west of Longridge, which was soon to be put up for sale and, at Christmas, when Will came home from Liverpool where he was now employed as a solicitor, he took him to see it. They had ridden over the fells to have a look without telling Marianna, as William wanted Will's opinion, and whether he thought Marianna would approve of his plan. Will was as captivated by the place as his father and encouraged him to buy it. William negotiated a reasonable price before it was offered on the open market. Until the purchase and legal matters were completed and the family solicitor, Mr Birch, sworn to secrecy, William found it difficult to contain his excitement until Mr Birch handed him the keys.

The very next day, a crisp, sunny February day, William suggested a ride out in the gig to Marianna and eight-year-old Savannah was left in the care of Sarah. They drove into the next valley and, as they approached the entrance to the farm, William halted the carriage and insisted on tying a large handkerchief round Marianna's eyes, much to her annoyance, as he would not explain the need for it.

"What are you doing, William? Why the cloak and dagger?"

"Ssh!" he ordered. "Just humour me."

Marianna continued to protest about the blindfold as they travelled up the long drive between a wood and fields bounded by drystone walls towards the house, situated on a slight elevation in the middle of the valley. William pulled on the reins to stop the gig.

"Welcome to Hapenny How," he said, removing the handkerchief.

"Why have we come to look at an empty house?" asked Marianna, somewhat confused as her eyes adjusted to the daylight. "The Palmers left months ago."

"It's ours."

"What? We have a house already. What on earth are you talking about?"

"Our house. A house we've bought together and where we'll live when we retire."

"A house we have bought *together*?" she said slowly. "That is news to me."

William was disappointed. Marianna had not reacted in the way he had hoped. He thought that she would be as charmed by the place as he had been, but she seemed annoyed. She had not been consulted.

"It's meant to be a surprise. You said once that you didn't feel as though Longridge was home to you. I've thought about what you said for many years. I wanted to do something for you," he said sadly.

"Oh! William, darling, I am sorry," she said, clutching his arm. "It is such a shock that you go out and buy a house without telling me."

He looked at her hopefully. She was smiling.

"I have always thought it a beautiful house. I visited once with my parents when it was owned by the… I can't remember the name. Before the Palmers, who were not at all sociable. Can we go inside if it's unoccupied?"

William reached into his coat pocket and jangled the keys in front of her. He jumped down from the gig and went round to help her down and straighten her skirts. Slipping her arm round his waist to hug him, Marianna said again, "It is beautiful."

Hapenny How was a white-rendered, Gothic-style Georgian house with chimneys at the gable ends, triple-bay windows on the ground floor and first floor on one side, a long, arched window above the front door with its pedimented portico, and arched windows to the right of the door. The farm was surrounded by fells. A stream tumbled down one of the fells and meandered through the meadows. The farm buildings, a collection of stone barns and outhouses built many years later, stood beyond a wide, open yard behind the house which was shielded from them by the judicious planting of trees.

William opened the front door and stepped aside to let Marianna cross the threshold. She gasped; not because of the whiff of mustiness that prevailed, but because the window above the door and the small windows to each side flooded the parquet-floored hallway and central staircase with light. They moved into the sitting room, which was spacious with a large marble fireplace, a high, plasterwork ceiling and cornices. There was a dining room of similar proportions and decoration on the other side of the hallway, and a morning room and a small library. All the windows had wooden shutters that William opened and closed as they passed, their footsteps echoing, through the rooms now bare of furniture. A door near the stairs led to the back of the house where the kitchen, pantry, scullery, laundry room and boot room were located. Upstairs, the master bedroom matched the proportions of the sitting room below and there were five further bedrooms, with rooms in the attic accessed by the back stairs off the kitchen. The views from the front of the house stretched southwards down the valley where the stream twinkled in the sunshine.

"The Palmers must have been sorry to leave," said Marianna, as they stood in the bay window of the master bedroom admiring the view. "Financial problems."

"There's gas but there's scope for further improvements," said William. "We've the time to do as we wish and introduce modern conveniences. It's well situated, Marianna, and we're not too far from Langwater."

Marianna was having second thoughts. "But can we… can you afford it? We have so many commitments and the Palmers couldn't make it pay. I know it is your money, but we usually discuss…" She sighed. "I'm quite cross with you, William."

"Rest assured, I have thought hard about this," said William, trying to conceal how cross he was with her for not seeming to appreciate what he was doing for her or giving him credit for his years of experience in business. "I have made discreet enquiries. Palmer had gambling debts, nothing to do with the viability of the farm. If we cannot find a tenant farmer to take it on, we can let the house and rent the land to our neighbours."

"Remind me how many acres it is."

"Two thousand or thereabouts."

"Two thousand acres to farm when we are old and decrepit?" She raised her eyebrows.

"It's mostly fells for sheep, as you know. When we want to move in, we can sell off the land we don't need. There's many a landowner round here looking to increase their holdings." He laughed. "We could sell the land to Will."

"Hmm." She smiled at him. "Yes, you have thought about it, haven't you?" He sensed a softening of her position. "The house is charming, and the situation is peaceful. We could be very happy here…" She paused, then said with the twitch of a smile, "I suppose."

He kissed her cheek. "I'm so relieved. Will knew you'd love it."

"Will? Will was in on the secret?"

He nodded. "I shall tell you something else, Marianna. When I read the deeds, I discovered that it once belonged to your great-grandfather, James Baillie Hamilton. What do you think about that?"

"I never knew!"

"Should I tell you he built the house for his mistress, Georgina Forster? He rented it to her for a halfpenny a year; hence the name."

"Is that so?" She frowned at the mention of the paltry amount as she gazed once more at the view from the window. "I still need to be convinced this was a wise move financially, William."

It was Easter Sunday. The servants had a day's holiday, and it was decided the family would go to the bay, an hour's drive away, for a picnic and to watch the many birds that gathered there, as both Will and his father were keen bird watchers. A picnic by the bay was a special treat and sometimes the Greenwoods would accompany them, but not today, as it was the last day of Will's holiday – he came home frequently to see them – and the trip would be family only. Will had gone to the stables with William to harness the horses to the carriage and Savannah, who had helped her mother prepare the picnic, waited with her in the hall for their transport with the rugs and hamper, the binoculars and, for the first time, Henry Hamilton's old telescope that William had found at the back of a cupboard in the attic.

William had been told of a particular spot they had not visited before where bar-tailed godwits, winter visitors to the bay, could be seen. It was a fine but cool day with few clouds in the sky, and the sun shone on the pale sheets of water left by the ebbing tide that exposed the vast, slate-grey sands of the bay. The horses were unhitched from the carriage and tethered. Will filled a bucket of water for them from a stream nearby and, when they had drunk their fill, he watched as Savannah, talking softly to each horse, expertly attached their nosebags. She was a beautiful child, tall for her age, with long, dark hair tied back with a ribbon that was frequently lost, and the dark blue, almond-shaped Hamilton eyes. Marianna had spread the rugs on the grass behind a sand dune and settled down to work on her embroidery whilst the others went to sit on the ridge overlooking the sands, taking turns to look through the binoculars or telescope at the flocks of birds wheeling above the bay or feeding in the mud, each vying to be the first to spot the godwits.

Savannah was having difficulty focusing the telescope, which was also clumsy and heavy for her to hold steadily. She had scanned the railway viaduct and saw, in the distance, something white and blurred that was moving about but could not work out what it was. Her father had a look.

"That's Netherton on the far shore," he said, adjusting the focus. "Someone's hung out their washing. That'll displease some on this particular day." The breeze that ruffled the water trapped in the gullies flapped the sheets on the washing lines at Netherton. "Look." William handed back the telescope and held the end up for her. "See the row of cottages? Mama and I used to live there many years ago."

This was news to Savannah, who thought they had always lived at Longridge and never imagined her parents had a life before she was born.

"Tiny!" she exclaimed.

Marianna called to them that the picnic was ready, and they went to join her. As the food was passed round and lemonade poured or ale dispensed, Savannah asked them why they had lived in such a small house. William knew and instantly regretted the moment he had mentioned it because her natural curiosity would be piqued. Marianna exchanged a concerned look with him, as there were parts of their history that they had agreed would upset their daughter and they should wait until she was older before telling her.

Will had intercepted the look and said, "Tell her. She has as much right as anyone to know."

Savannah looked expectantly from her mother to her father. William took a deep breath and began to tell the story of how they had both ended up at Coldbarrow, trying to explain the taking of them in a dispassionate way so as not to frighten her, but Savannah was horrified and had put down her plate and nestled in her mother's lap. William hastily reassured her that they were not badly treated and, if he had not gone there, he would never have met her mother. He kept the story brief, concentrating on the good times, especially how happy they were living in the tiny cottage on the other side of the bay.

William swallowed hard before continuing, "One day, Mouse, I had an accident and I got lost." He gave Marianna and Will a look to tell them he was sparing Savannah the truth. He could not tell her that he was thought to have drowned in the bay as it was such a special place for them, and he did not want to spoil her memories. "Because I was lost and did not come home for a long time, many people thought I was dead."

Savannah gasped, her eyes wide with horror, trying to understand what he was saying and reached forward to grab her father's hand. Marianna sighed as this was not the picnic she was hoping for: a few hours together, happy and relaxed, before Will left the next day. She cuddled her daughter.

"It is not as it sounds, darling." She glared at William.

"No, indeed," said William. "For as you can see with your own eyes, I'm here and full of life. A kind man, Mr Foster, looked after Mama and Will for me until I managed to come home again. It was a while, Savannah. Now we're back together again. And we all lived happily ever after, didn't we?" He reached forward to stroke her face. "I'm still hungry, and you and Mama have made such a delicious picnic it'd be rude not to eat it all up, wouldn't it?"

When it was time to leave, Savannah helped Will to pack up the picnic things. William and Marianna had wandered off to a grassy knoll. William had both arms round Marianna's waist and held her close as she rested her head on his chest. Savannah looked at them wistfully with tears in her eyes.

"What is it?" asked Will, taking the folded rug from her and placing it in the carriage.

"I'm scared, Will."

"What about?"

"Bad people who take children from their mamas and papas."

"Come here," he said, wrapping his arms round his adored little sister. "You are safe. Mama and Papa will never let anything bad happen to you and neither will I. I promised Papa when you were born that I would look after you." He kissed her cheek and held her at arm's length. "You are safe. You believe me?"

She nodded. "But what if someone comes to take them away again?"

"It was a long time ago and nobody is going to come and take them away. I promise." He held up his fists in a boxing pose and said, "Papa will fight them off."

"It is so sad what happened to them," said Savannah, trying to smile at him.

"Yes, it was. But look at them now," said Will as they watched

53

their parents. He was no longer the callow boy who resented having to share his mother with his father and Savannah. His jealousy in the year up to his sister's birth had withered in the warmth of belonging to a family that loved and cared deeply for each other. "They were so happy, then a bad thing happened to them and now they are happy again. They love each other so much. You can see how much, Savannah. And they love us too."

"Do you have someone to love, Will? Like Papa loves Mama?"

He grinned at her and tapped her nose playfully. "Can you keep a secret?"

Savannah's eyes widened in anticipation and a smile appeared. "You have?"

"I have met someone. That is our secret though. Promise you won't tell as it is still early days?"

She nodded and crossed her heart.

"Now, would you like to sit next to Papa for the ride home?"

"Please."

Will lifted her in his arms, kissed both cheeks and spun her round. She squealed. Then he placed her in the driving seat and tucked a blanket round her.

The following afternoon after Will had left, and as the weather was still fine and dry, they decided to climb Longridge Fell. As she was forbidden from coming alone, it was a treat for Savannah to climb up to view the never-ending, wild spaces that stretched for miles north to another country, and Devil's Seat, an imposing, limestone crag that loomed above the moorland, with a fifty-foot drop to the rocks below. They took a picnic, prepared by Ada, and a rug to sit on. They walked together along the path past the walled garden, then through the stand of larch and Scots pines that took them to a short cut, a set of steps set into the drystone wall which bordered the field at the bottom of the hill. William helped Marianna over the wall as Savannah scampered ahead, scattering the sheep which grazed there, stopping occasionally to pick up stones she spied that were placed in the basket over her arm to fulfil a family ritual.

The summer after she was born, William had carried Savannah in a basket to the summit to show her their kingdom and Will had gathered some stones lying about on the ground and had laid them out in a circle, and each time the fell was climbed stones were collected to add to the construction which, after several years, resembled a small cairn.

It was a strenuous climb following the well-worn sheep track to the top where, after catching their breath as they waited for Marianna to arrive, the stones were ceremoniously placed in position on top of the cairn and the view admired. In the distance stretched the wide expanse of the bay surrounded by fells and hills. Sometimes the tide was in, and the light would change depending on the colour of the sky. At other times, when the tide was out, the sands would be light or dark, shadowed by the clouds and striped by rivulets of water. The fells would change too, depending on the season, from the washed-out browns and greys of winter before the snow came to the rich purple of the blooming heather in late summer.

As Marianna set out the picnic in a sheltered hollow, Savannah sat down next to her father on the ridge of the fell and slipped her hand into his.

"Why do people like views, Papa?"

"Do you not, Mouse?"

"I like this view because I can see for miles, and I feel as if I am on top of the world."

"It's the same for me. It also makes you feel quite small because you realise how big the world is and how we'll never have the time to see it all and know all there is to know about it."

"And lonely too, Papa."

"What do you mean?" William asked, giving her hand a friendly squeeze.

"If I was here by myself, the big spaces round me would make me feel lonely. If I couldn't see our home, I would think the world was empty and I would be a little frightened."

"Sometimes, my sweet, little Mouse, it's a pleasant experience to be on one's own to think and clear your mind."

"What do you think about, Papa, when you are on your own?" Savannah was intrigued.

"All kinds of things. But mostly how happy I am and how much I love my family."

Savannah released her father's hand and climbed onto his lap to hug him.

"As we all love you, darling Papa. You are the best papa in the world."

He kissed her cheek. Savannah turned her gaze to the landscape laid out before them. After their last climb up the fell, William had shown her the maps rolled up in leather tubes that were kept in the study, which her great-grandfather Augustus Baillie Hamilton had commissioned from a surveyor and cartographer, Theophilus Emmett, so that they could satisfy their curiosity about how high they had climbed. Longridge Fell was 595 feet. Devil's Crag was 640 feet. Calf Fell was 721 feet. "How did Mr Emmett work it out, Papa?" she had asked.

"He had paid attention in his arithmetic lessons," her father replied, winking at her, and she knew that he did not know the answer either. It was not until years later she discovered that her father had had no formal education. But at that moment they shared something as he knew how much she hated arithmetic. How she loved her papa.

"Is this all ours, Papa?"

"Quite a lot of what you can see from here is ours. As far as the road by the school in Newbridge to the south, and then behind us, as far as the road that crosses the moors into Yorkshire. Five thousand acres in all."

"And it will all be Will's one day?"

"Yes."

"What will I have, Papa?"

"Well…" William pondered this difficult question for a moment. "What would you like to have?"

"A place to keep horses, dogs, lions, tigers and elephants."

"A zoo, perhaps? Behind the stables? That will not be a difficult task. I'll see what I can do. And you will be the zookeeper and I'll have to find you a smart uniform and a peaked cap. And a big net in case the lions escape."

"You are funny, Papa."

"Are you hungry yet?" called Marianna.

As they ate their picnic, William and Savannah competed to identify any birds they saw or heard. Then, William stretched out on his back, his head resting on his clasped hands, and closed his eyes, and Marianna took up her book. Savannah decided to amuse herself by exploring the other side of the hill where winter rains had washed away the topsoil and exposed the rocks and stones underneath. She took the basket to collect her finds. When she had half-filled it and it was still light enough to carry back, she clambered up the slope and stopped at the top. Her parents did not realise she was there, and she stood silently watching them. Her mother was lying on her back, her fingers entwined in her father's hair, and he was almost lying on top of her, propped on one elbow, stroking her face and running his hands down to her breasts and caressing them, and then they were kissing. Not a peck on the cheek. She had seen those. She had experienced those. She dropped to her stomach so she could just see them through the heather covering the slope of the hill.

She was spying on her parents, but they knew that she was about, so she did not think it was something she should not see. This kissing. This was long, passionate; they seemed to be eating each other. Then they stopped. Her father rolled onto his back and took her mother's hand and kissed each of her fingers in turn. Her mother sat up, turned to him and said something and kissed him, and they were off again. She knew her parents loved each other; she heard them say it. They told her how much they loved her and Will and each other, Will had said as much yesterday. But this was different. This was a special kind of love and kissing was their way of showing each other that love. She hoped she would love and be loved as much when she was grown up. A long way off. She was only eight years old. But she did not know what to do and how long she would have to wait before they stopped, and she was feeling left out. She decided to take action.

"Ouch!" She poked her head above the heather. They were sitting up. "It's nothing," she said brightly. "I just tripped. I have some more stones for the cairn."

Now she had their attention and was the centre of their world again.

SIX

William hoisted Savannah onto his back. She squealed with delight and tightened her grip round his neck.

"Come on, Mouse, or we shall be late for tea with Mama. My goodness! You're heavy." He pretended to stagger, and she squealed again. "And don't forget to compliment her on the paintings."

The portraits of him and Marianna, which she had commissioned the year before, had been hung either side of the stained-glass window on the landing that very morning.

"Why do you call me Mouse, Papa? I have never asked before."

"It's ironic."

"Why are you 'ronic, Papa?"

"Ironic. All one word. Because you are as far from being mouse-like as one could imagine, and I'm going to have to put you down before my legs give way."

They had been out riding to keep out of the way as Marianna was chairing a meeting in the library of the charity committee she and Ellen Greenwood had set up. William knew when Moth was born that he would keep him for his new daughter. From a pitiful, gangling scrap, he had grown stronger each day and, although small, he was a handsome little fellow, somewhere between a Shetland and a Fell pony. William had put Savannah on him before she could walk, and she had taken to riding immediately. She was fearless. At first, they had walked out; him on his mare, Sorrel, her on Moth led by Thomas Longmire, the stable lad, but, before long, she was impatient to discard the leading rein and take charge. Just now she had cantered along the track at the side of the field and cleared the trunk of a fallen birch tree without batting an eye.

William adored her and she adored him. Her mother sometimes despaired at her antics: sliding down the banisters, climbing trees, walking along the top of stone walls, cartwheeling across the hall floor. Antics which often resulted in bumps and scrapes and torn clothes. She was high-spirited, funny and headstrong, and did not settle to her lessons with the governess who, apologising for her failure to teach their daughter, resigned in despair. She would rescue injured animals and birds and make homes for them in one of the outhouses until they recovered. She had friends in the Greenwood and Kerr children who never turned down an invitation to play with her, in the house, in the grounds, making dens in the woods, playing with the yard cats, taking turns to ride Moth in the paddock, and it was Savannah who could be heard above the others, directing what they should play.

"So, what do you think about starting school in Newbridge on Monday?" asked William, taking her hand.

"I shall tell you what I think when I've tried it, Papa."

"That is a sensible and honest answer."

"And if I come home and say I do not think much of it at all, Papa, what will you do?"

"Send you to your room and feed you nothing but bread and water until you agree to return."

Savannah giggled. "In that case, darling Papa, I will come home on Monday and say I think very well of it."

"And that, my sweet, little Mouse, is the right answer."

They both laughed and she kissed his hand.

Marianna looked up in surprise as the door to her sitting room was flung open and Savannah rushed towards her to give her a hug.

"Your picture is a picture, Mama." She sniggered at her witticism. "And I've learnt a new word. Ironic. I do not need to go to school after all. Papa can teach me at home."

Marianna hemmed. "A good try, Savannah. You will go to school on Monday. You will make new friends and Dr Greenwood's children will be there to look after you."

Savannah pouted and threw herself on a chair.

"And what does ironic mean?" asked her mother, as William came into the room, flipped up his coat tails and sat next to her on the sofa.

Savannah shrugged.

"More reason for you to go to school." Marianna smiled at William and handed him a cup of tea. "Did you see Ada on your way in? Did she mention whether the food parcels for delivery to Newbridge were ready?"

"No, we didn't see her."

"Would you like some cake, Savannah?" asked her mother.

Savannah shrugged again.

"Perhaps they will teach you manners at this school. You are sadly lacking in that regard."

"Sit up properly and have some cake," ordered her father. "It'd help if you placed the napkin on your lap."

She shook out the napkin over her skirts and sulkily accepted the plate he offered her. "It *would*, Papa, not it'd…" She clamped her mouth shut when she saw his stern look.

"How did your meeting go?" William asked Marianna as he helped himself to another sandwich.

"Very well. Ellen had a private word with Dora Cavendish, who has agreed to support our idea for a charity ball and even suggested she approach the mayor to put his name to it."

"A lot of work for you. I'll help you if I can."

She nodded at him and said, "I shall hold you to that," before picking up some letters lying on the table next to her.

"I have had a letter from Aunt Lizzie to say they are all coming to stay; one from Mr Hartley who is not because his wife is expecting another child and one from Will—"

"Is Will coming?" interrupted Savannah, her mouth full of cake, showering her lap with crumbs. "Oh, I am so glad."

Marianna rolled her eyes at William but said nothing about her daughter's eating habits. "Yes, and he wishes to bring some friends so we shall have a houseful and I must make arrangements to employ the extra staff needed to help Ada and take care of us all."

Every year, William and Marianna invited his sister Lizzie, her children and their spouses and children to stay for a week in June.

"Will we all sleep in the attic again, Mama?"

To free up the bedrooms for the adults, the older children slept on mattresses on the floor of the old nursery next to the room shared by the maids, Sarah and Polly. For Savannah it was an adventure, especially when the Greenwood and Kerr children were allowed to stay the night. Marianna handed William the letter from Will. He scanned it quickly and looked across at her; her eyebrows were arched in anticipation of his reaction to the contents.

"So!" he said. "Will wishes to bring a young lady to meet us with her friend as chaperone. Has he ever mentioned Miss Harriet Miller to you before?"

"Not to me. How interesting! How intriguing! He says nothing of her or her family. All we know is her name and that of her friend. What do you make of it?"

"I know all about her," said Savannah importantly.

"Pardon?" said her mother.

"Will told me at Easter he had a friend and swore me to secrecy."

"Is that so?" said Marianna, not quite believing her.

"She must be important for him to drag her all the way up to these northern wastes to meet his parents," said William. "I hope we impress her. Better get Savannah to start polishing the silver!"

Savannah groaned and then saw her father was smiling and realised he did not mean it. If it had been her mother's suggestion, she would not have been so certain.

"Mr Crompton is coming to look at one of the geldings, Jericho, later this afternoon. Would you like to come to the stables with me, Savannah?"

"Yes please, Papa." She beamed at her father. "Will he fetch a good price?"

"I hope so. Although Mr Crompton is known for being a little stingy." He grinned at her. "But don't tell him I said that."

"Well," said Marianna, "if you have finished your tea, Savannah, you may go and fetch me your reading book. I shall listen to you for ten minutes or so and test you on your times tables before I go out."

Savannah jumped to her feet and skipped out of the room, banging the door behind her. Her mother winced and held up a fourth letter. "Another from Alessandro Paluzzi." He was Bennet Foster's lover for a number of years before Bennet died.

"He is well?"

"Yes, he misses Bennet even after all this time, but he has found love again with…" Marianna searched the text of the letter. "A bookseller called Sebastian Nardini. He repeats his invitation to visit him in Italy."

"Well, perhaps next year. We'll need to plan to ensure everything runs smoothly with my business and the estate if we're to be absent for some time."

Marianna held up another letter that William saw was black edged. "My mother," she said flatly. "She is dead."

"Oh! I am sorry, Marianna," said William, putting down his teacup.

She flicked the letter dismissively and said, "It's from my sister. Verity was staying with her in Portugal. Without her own family it would seem. Mother had a heart attack. The funeral was a month ago. Only now do I hear the news."

William edged towards her and took her hand.

"I feel nothing, William."

"Even so, your sister could've written sooner, sent a telegram, and given you the option of attending the funeral."

"I am relieved she did not. I would not have gone. All that way for a woman who did not like me. My conscience has not been troubled by the dilemma of making a choice."

Marianna had endured a strained relationship with her mother, a proud, controlling woman, who had been mortified, on being reunited with her missing daughter, to discover she had married a common groom and borne his son. She had concealed from Marianna the identity of the person – William – who had told her where to find her daughter on the Loop Hall estate and, by the time Marianna had drawn the information out of her that confirmed William was still alive and knew about their baby, it was too late, and William had left Longridge and gone to America. Marianna had never forgiven her mother for her deception and blamed her for her breakdown. Mother and daughter had clashed over the years as Carolina Hamilton tried to mould her daughter into the young lady befitting her status and was glad to see her eventually married to the wealthy Bennet Foster. Marianna had no relationship at all with her younger sister, Verity, who had resented her return and subsequent claim to the Hamilton estate which she thought would have been all hers. Her sister had been spiteful and unwelcoming and taunted her about her lack of education and manners. She had married an aristocrat for his title, and he had married her for her money. It was not a happy marriage. Following the sudden death of Henry Hamilton, Marianna arrived for his funeral to find her mother and sister helping themselves to the family treasures which belonged legally to her and, offended that they had not asked her first as she would have surrendered them willingly, had banned them from ever setting foot in the house again.

"Well, she is gone," said Marianna. "I have often wondered if I had not been taken as a child, how different in temperament and outlook I might have been. How much I might have resembled her. What a hateful, snobbish woman I might have been." Marianna laughed. "Can you imagine her horror at the thought of Savannah attending the local school and mixing with the local children?"

"We agreed we could not bear to send her away to school and we decided she needed the company of children her own age. And one thing we do not suffer from, Marianna, is snobbery. But it's sad your mother never met her granddaughter. She couldn't stand the thought of seeing me again after what she did. It was her loss."

"Let us speak no more about it. Rather, we must plan for the arrival of our guests and speculate about Miss Harriet Miller. Where *has* Savannah got to?"

"Oof!" exclaimed Savannah, dropping the basket of freshly picked vegetables onto the kitchen floor. "I told Arthur I would manage but it was heavier than I thought."

"Oh, goodness me!" exclaimed Ada. "Look at the state of you. What'll your mother say?"

"It's my riding habit, Ada. She is used to seeing it dirty." Savannah wiped her hand across her cheek and left a muddy smear.

"Into the scullery with you," said Ada. "Polly'll get you cleaned up."

Polly picked up the basket and Savannah followed her to the scullery and allowed herself to be subjected to a vigorous scrubbing of her face and hands at the sink.

She was crossing the hall when she had heard the voices from the kitchen coming through the open door at the top of the stairs, and she had immediately forgotten what her mother had asked and went down.

The kitchen was a happy room. The copper pans gleamed on their hooks. The open shelves of the dresser were filled with old recipe books, Ada's own well-thumbed notebooks, grimed with butter and spots and stains of meals past, and interesting gadgets which Ada sometimes let her use, like the apple corer, and they would take turns to see who could peel the longest skin from the Bramleys. One wall was covered with built-in cupboards which reached the ceiling and were off-limits to her as they contained glassware and dishes. A long, wooden table with chairs either side took up the middle of the room and, once, Polly had let her and Jack Greenwood, sworn to secrecy, take turns to ride up to the dining room in the dumb waiter. There were two gas cookers and ovens – the gas installed in Henry Hamilton's time – and there was always a smell of something tasty and delicious to tempt the appetite. In winter, when the fire was lit, it was cosy to sit on the Windsor chairs by the fireside. Polly, the kitchen maid, as short and plump as her cousin Sarah, the housemaid, was tall and slim were always laughing and sharing a joke. Ada's husband Arthur, the gardener and handyman, his assistant Ezra and the two ladies from Newbridge, who helped with the chores, would pop in sometimes for a cup of tea. Savannah listened and learnt. Arthur had been a gardener before he joined the army and had seen elephants in India, but never a tiger. Ada was a Londoner, an orphan, who always wanted to be a nurse but had been put into service as a scullery maid and worked her way up to the position of housekeeper in a big house before she came to Longridge. Savannah liked to be there with them, not only because it was a happy place, but because they made a fuss of her, and sometimes, despite the attention from her parents, she was lonely. Arthur had finished his tea and Savannah had offered to go with him and Ezra to the kitchen garden and bring back the vegetables for dinner.

Ada was a small, solidly built, motherly woman with bright, twinkling eyes and a ready smile. She was in her late forties and had been married for fifteen years to Arthur, who was in fifties. She loved children but had none of her own and liked nothing better than when the Greenwood and Kerr children piled into the kitchen with Savannah and any other waifs and strays that she had picked up to sit round the table, drawn like bees to the honeypot by the enticing smells of her baking.

Savannah came back into the kitchen and stood beside Ada, who was slicing lard into a bowl of flour. Her sleeves were rolled up past her elbows and the string of her apron had disappeared in the rolls of flesh somewhere in the region where her waist should be.

"What are you doing, Ada?"

"Makin' pastry for the pie for dinner."

"May I help?"

"If you like, but you'll need to put on a pinny first, my pet."

Ada retrieved a clean apron from a drawer in the cupboard, pulled it over Savannah's head and tied the strings. Savannah knelt on a stool beside her as she began to work on the pastry.

"Now your turn. Mix the flour an' fat with your fingers, nice an' gentle. We don't want your papa crackin' 'is teeth."

Savannah chuckled. Polly came and sat at the table with the washed vegetables.

"Arthur says Ezra's making eyes at Sarah," said Savannah.

"Does 'e indeed!" exclaimed Ada.

"Does that mean they'll get married? If you make eyes at someone? Can you scratch my nose, Ada? I've got an itch."

Ada obliged.

"Why divn't you ask her when she comes down?" asked Polly, winking at Ada as she made a start on the peeling.

"Is anyone making eyes at you, Polly?"

"That'd be tellin', Miss." Polly chortled and wrinkled her freckled nose.

That *would*, Savannah was on the brink of saying and then remembered her father's severe look. It was rude to correct the way someone spoke, unless it was Mama correcting her.

"Arthur must have made eyes at you, Ada."

"'E most certainly did not!" snorted Ada. She was visiting her cousin in hospital with a bag of oranges tucked under her arm. Arthur was coming out of the front door after visiting a friend who was recovering from surgery. He laughed as she tripped, and the oranges spilled and rolled down the steps. "A gentleman would 'elp a lady in distress," she had said, glaring at him.

"Arthur says it was his fine moustache and whiskers that did the trick!" said Polly.

Yes, thought Ada. He was a handsome fellow, and behind the gruffness she found a kind and gentle man.

"What do you mean, Polly? Did the trick?" asked Savannah. "Was Arthur a magician?"

"'Ave you finished the peeling, missy?" asked Ada to stem the flow of this conversation which might be innocently repeated upstairs.

"So, why did you come all the way from London to Longridge?" asked Savannah.

"Arthur 'ad just left the army an' wanted to come 'ome an' 'e got taken on by the man who employed 'im before 'e joined the army. I was the 'ousekeeper." She had no strong ties in London. They settled down to their new life, were comfortable with each other; each knowing this might be their last chance to find companionship for their old age. Love came slowly. "We came 'ere when Mr Telford died. Very kind, old gentleman, 'e was."

Marianna, wondering where Savannah had disappeared to, appeared at the foot of the stairs. Savannah, the pinny reaching to the floor, was elbow deep in flour and concentrating hard. Ada saw the mistress and was about to say something, but Marianna shook her head and smiled. She nodded at the boxes on the floor by the back door and Ada nodded in turn to confirm they were ready for distribution. Then Marianna went back upstairs.

"That'll do nicely," Ada said to Savannah. "Now go an' wash your 'ands. Would you like some cordial?"

Savannah gulped the contents of the glass in one long swallow. Wiping her mouth on her sleeve, she said, "Will you teach me to cook, Ada? I should think it would be a more useful skill than learning times tables."

"You need to know your arithmetic to cook, my pet. You need to weigh things an' add, subtract an' multiply. So put your mind to learnin' your tables. We can ask your mother if you like. I'd be more than 'appy to teach you." Ada put down her teacup, reached for Savannah and said, "Come 'ere, my little pumpkin."

Savannah settled into her ample lap. Ada put her arms round her waist and cuddled her.

"I remember the night you was born."

"I know. You have told me before. But you can tell me again," she said kindly.

Polly smiled at her. Polly had heard the story too. Many times. Savannah enjoyed hearing how Will had been so brave to go out in the storm to fetch the doctor; how the wind had tossed Ada onto the grass verge as she made her way up the drive from the lodge to come and help her mother; how small she was when she was born. "I think that's why your papa called you Mouse. You was tiny an' quiet. Not like now!" How Ada helped Jack's papa; how worried they were until she took her first breath. Ada would tell her the rain fell in torrents and the wind howled, uprooting trees, tumbling chimneys and blowing slates off roofs and sheep flying through the air to land miles away.

"How did they get home again?"

"They're 'efted, ain't they?"

The more times she heard it and the older she got, the less inclined Savannah was to believe Ada's tale about the storm, but she knew how much Ada enjoyed telling her and she was very fond of Ada, who was always kind to her.

Sarah came down the stairs with the tea tray. "Miss Savannah, your mother says you're to fetch your readin' book and go to her in her sittin' room."

"Oh no! I completely forgot," said Savannah, jumping up from Ada's lap. Polly caught her eye and jerked her head. "Sarah! Are you getting married to Ezra?"

Sarah blushed crimson. "Really, Miss! What a question!"

Savannah scampered up the stairs. "Sarah loves Ezra," she sang. "Sarah loves Ezra."

* * *

William threw back the curtains.

"There's not a cloud in the sky, Marianna. Aren't we lucky?" He was in a contented mood. He had made love with his wife, bathed and dressed, the weather continued to favour the house party and today, the day of the picnic, was no exception. "I'll have a quick breakfast, and then go and make sure the tables and chairs have been set up."

"In the shade, William. Lizzie, for one, does not enjoy the heat."

"I sometimes think how lucky we are," said William, sitting on the bed beside her. "From the hard beds at Coldbarrow to the feather mattresses here. From a slop of oatmeal for breakfast to a sumptuous picnic. From chapped hands and chilblains to fine clothes. And now, a picnic with our dearest friends and family."

Marianna sat up and settled against the pillows. "I shall lie here a while longer and try to think of something that will arouse the interest of you-know-who."

William patted her hand. He recognised that she was upset that, despite all the planning and arrangements, it was not always possible to satisfy everyone; although good manners should dictate that a guest did not advertise their dissatisfaction so openly.

"We have done our best, darling. I know Newbridge does not have the grand shops of Liverpool, but it has other charms."

"Melchester was a disappointment too. Lizzie told me. Even with the attractions of the priory and castle."

"Don't fret, Marianna. We shall have a wonderful day today."
He grinned at her. "Despite you-know-who."

At noon, the guests assembled in the hall, boaters and bonnets on heads, parasols over arms, excited, talkative children counted and inspected. Lizzie was there with her daughters: Meg, married to James Cunningham, a schoolmaster, and their children James and Mary; Beth, her husband Robert Winter, a clerk, and their daughter Millicent; her son George, a doctor, married to Alice Barclay, the daughter of his professor at Medical School, and their sons, Georgie and baby Harry. Will was accompanied by Harriet Miller and Esme Lambert, a friend of Alice's. Richard Greenwood was accompanied by his wife Ellen, and their children, Jack and the non-identical twins, Madeleine and Isabel, and his new assistant, Doctor Martin Ashbourne.

The cart carrying the hampers of food and drink had set off thirty minutes before. The gaggle of chattering children preceded the adults down the road to the newly mown hay meadow by the River Beulah, with its view of the chapel. Long trestle tables had been shoved together in the shade of a copse of trees, covered with crisp, white tablecloths and surrounded by a motley collection of chairs and benches. The servants had laid out the crockery, glassware, cutlery and plates of cold meats and salads, sandwiches, tarts, jellies and cakes under Ada's supervision. Bottles of wine, jars of ale, lemonade and water had been placed in a makeshift chiller, a circle of stones piled up in the river shallows.

There was no standing on ceremony: the guests sat where they liked, and the servants were to join them, as well as the tenant farmers, farm workers and their families who were already gathered in the field. It was William's and Marianna's way of thanking the people who worked for them, although every year the same thing happened: the servants congregated at one end and the children took possession of the middle tables. William, as host, and helped by Will, Andrew, Thomas, Arthur and Ezra, served drinks to the guests. Then William made a short speech welcoming them all, especially their new guests, the Misses Lambert and Miller and

Dr Ashbourne, and thanking the servants for all their hard work in preparing the picnic. William touched briefly on the current problems in farming and looked forward to better times, and then a toast was made to the health of them all.

Marianna had strategically positioned herself opposite Will and Miss Miller so she could keep an eye on them and note, not for the first time that week, how they were with each other. Harriet Miller was tall and slender. Her features individually were fine: piercing blue eyes, full lips, round chin, straight nose, but the arrangement of them on her long face was discordant – the eyes too close together, the gap between her nose and mouth too wide – and Marianna failed to see why her son was attracted to her. She had had one conversation alone with her and realised how serious-minded she was, quick-witted with a sharp, cruel tongue which Marianna had overheard directed to Miss Lambert, mocking something Lizzie had said and her 'common' accent. Her friend, sitting on the other side of Will, was slim, fair-haired, grey-eyed. Not beautiful, but pleasingly pretty, helped by her ready smile and her engaging personality. She kept glancing at Will and blushing if he said something to her. She radiated warmth and made more of an effort than her friend to be sociable: they were as different as light and shade.

When the meal was over, the house servants cleared away the dishes, loaded the baskets into the cart and disappeared back to the house. The others were then free to sit in the shade and chat or spread out on the rugs and old carpets laid on the grass or stroll along the riverbank for an hour or so, before the house servants returned with more cakes and refreshments in time for the obligatory cricket match. Umpired by William, it was a game with few rules, with mixed teams of anyone, young and old, male and female, who wanted to join in. Meanwhile, the children removed their shoes and stockings to paddle in the river, jump across the stepping stones, skim stones and collect branches and stones to make dams. Misses Miller and Lambert had wandered off along the riverbank, arm in arm, sharing a parasol, and William saw an opportunity to get Will on his own. They collected a couple of chairs and glasses of ale and went to sit apart from the others.

"I wanted a moment with you to get something off my chest and I've not had the chance this week to speak to you alone."

"This sounds serious, Papa." Will, like his father, had removed his jacket, loosened his collar and rolled up his shirtsleeves.

"Well, maybe. I'm disappointed Fred Hartley wasn't able to come, as I wanted to discuss the future of the business with him away from the distractions of Liverpool. I wanted to involve you in those discussions and get your opinion. Sound you out." William swallowed a welcome glug of chilled ale.

"Glad to help if I can."

Will and his father had grown even closer over the years and enjoyed a warm, easy, often teasing relationship. His father often sought his advice on legal matters.

"You seem settled with Longthorne and Halliwell. Your prospects are good? You may advance there?" It was William who had heard of the opening at the firm from his own solicitor in Liverpool and suggested Will put himself forward.

"They seem satisfied with me. I have brought in some new clients for them."

"You took up my offer to spend some time with Fred and see how the business worked here and in America after Oxford. Is it something that might appeal to you?"

William told his father that he was glad to have had the opportunity to see how the business operated but repeated what he had told him at the time that he did not have the skills, the financial skills, to ensure the continued success of the business as he was not suited to haggling and dealing and lacked the confidence required.

"I understand. I think you're following the drift of this conversation and I think we're of the same opinion – that you don't wish to take over from me. I've been mulling over what I want to do as I have mentioned to you before, but I just wanted to take this opportunity to make certain of your position – which hasn't changed."

"I'm sorry, Papa. We have many interests. But not that one."

"No need to be sorry. I'd never insist on you doing something that you have no interest in. But the estate and our farm at Stillingford are more attractive propositions?"

"I would say so, although times are hard as you mentioned in your speech, but I should like to practise law for a while longer."

"It's a shame you leave so soon, as your mother and I have been discussing that very topic and how to adapt for the future to protect the integrity of the estate. But that'll have to wait for another time. Perhaps your next visit. You take Misses Miller and Lambert home tomorrow. I hope they've enjoyed their stay and, of course, they're welcome to come again. I shall interrogate your mother later to find out what the situation is there." William laughed and patted Will's shoulder as he looked away in embarrassment. "Now, let's rejoin our guests."

Will went off to join George, Richard Greenwood and the new doctor, who would no doubt be discussing something medical. William mopped his brow with his handkerchief and looked round for Marianna, who was walking with Ellen Greenwood amongst the guests and stopping to talk to them. They were very dear friends, a friendship forged by the closeness of their children and a shared love of needlework. They often visited each other's houses to sit and sew and chat. Ellen was a kind, calm, level-headed woman, and very suited to being a doctor's wife, as she often had to deal with her husband's distracted, anxious patients. She was petite and pretty with a friendly manner. Everyone who met her liked her instantly. William decided to leave them to it and stood watching the children. There were fifteen or more playing in the shallow river. There was an excited babble of chatter, laughter and splashing. *The cricket teams will not be short of players*, he thought.

Lizzie was sitting in the shade of the oldest tree in the field, a proud oak with a stout, gnarled trunk whose limbs spread low, almost touching the ground. There was no breeze, and she was fanning herself furiously. She had just given baby Harry back to his mother. William collected a glass of lemonade and went to join her.

"I may walk back to the house, William, if you don't mind. I do so wish ladies' fashions would accommodate the heat."

"I can send Thomas for the pony and trap." He handed her the lemonade.

"That'd do nicely. I told Alice I'd take Harry back for his nap."

William returned five minutes later, sat beside her and asked if she had enjoyed the luncheon.

"As always, William. A feast. Mrs Dummigan's such a treasure. And such a good company of people." Lizzie took a long sip of lemonade. "All the family together, and I do like Dr Greenwood and his wife. The new doctor's shy."

"Will leaves tomorrow to take his guests home."

"Marianna told me. They're leavin' earlier than she thought. Do you know the reason?"

"No. She'll tell me, I've no doubt, as well as report back on her further impressions of Harriet Miller."

Lizzie pulled a face and he laughed.

"Go on, Lizzie. You've always been quick to assess someone's character and you're usually accurate."

"I don't like her, William. But that's all I shall say as it's really none of my concern. Her friend, Miss Lambert, is much more natural and friendly, and I don't say that from any biased viewpoint, seein' as she's Alice's friend. Still, you don't think Will's serious about Miss Miller?"

"To be honest, Lizzie, I don't know anything about his thoughts or feelings regarding her. I hope he's confided in his mother."

"I suppose at his age he's thinkin' of settlin' down, but to rush into it and choose the wrong person is a mistake."

"Indeed. Your children are all happy and settled, which must be a comfort to you."

"Yes, I'm fortunate, and it's kind of you to let Beth and her family live with me. Robert's a good, kind soul but will never set the world alight. They would've struggled to afford their own home on his salary."

"They're company for you, Lizzie. You'd rattle around that house on your own."

Lizzie reached over to squeeze his hand and said warmly, "I bless the day you found us in that hovel in Philadelphia with barely a morsel of food between us. I still have nightmares about what would've befallen us after my beloved George died if you had not."

He patted her hand affectionately. The day he found her, he was shocked: thin and worn out, her hair prematurely grey from the stress of her difficult circumstances, when the hope of a better life working in the mills in America, built on false promises by those peddling the dream, luring the millworkers of northern England, had turned to ashes, and then George had died from the stress at the thought that he had let them all down by uprooting them from England. Now, she was matronly but still the same Lizzie: devout, honest, loyal, loving and a doting grandmother. They had lived together with her children at his house, Meadowside, in Stillingford, near Liverpool, for several years before Marianna came back into his life. She had looked after him and his house. He would do anything for his sister.

Lizzie sipped her lemonade and fanned her face. There was a shriek followed by peals of laughter.

"Savannah's a handful, William," said Lizzie, identifying the source of the shriek. "She's more in common with the boys."

"High-spirited, I think you mean, Lizzie. She behaves as she does because it's in her nature to do so. She does not do it wilfully to test us. She knows where to draw the line and one look from her mother warns her not to cross it. She's a joy. I adore her."

Savannah came running across the grass; she was soaking wet, her clothes clinging to her body, her hair plastered to her flushed cheeks. "I fell in, Papa. We were building a dam and I slipped and went in up to here." She pointed to her neck. "Mama is cross with me and says you must take me home to change."

William knew this was Marianna's way of letting him know it was partly his fault their daughter was so unladylike and got into so many scrapes. He said as gravely as he could, "I think we should leave you to freeze to an icicle and teach you a lesson. What do you think, Aunt Lizzie?"

"I think you may be right. Go and tell your mother I'll take you, Savannah."

Savannah looked at them both, her brow creased in bewilderment. "How would I freeze to an icicle in this heat? Sometimes you say the most ridiculous things, Papa. Don't you agree, Aunt Lizzie?" She ran off before her bemused aunt could reply.

"That one's goin' to be trouble, William. Mark my words."

They could hear Savannah shouting to the other children she would be back soon once she had changed and not to start the cricket match without her.

"The Greenwood boy's devoted to her, isn't he?" remarked Lizzie. "She bosses him about. I think he'd do anythin' for her."

"They're very good friends. In the holidays they're inseparable, thick as thieves. His sisters follow, and the Kerr children, all in thrall to Savannah. Jack's a sweet boy. Clever too. He helps her with her arithmetic, and she helps him by bringing him out of his shell. His mother says he has a lot more confidence, thanks to Savannah."

Lizzie got up to gather her belongings as she saw Savannah coming towards them, followed by Thomas with the pony and trap.

"What'll happen when they're older? They can't stay at the school in Newbridge."

"I believe Jack will go to his father's old school in Yorkshire. As for Savannah, I don't know. We haven't discussed it. I can't bear the thought of her going away from home. She is only eight. There's time yet."

Will left after breakfast the following day with Misses Lambert and Miller to catch the train from Newbridge. His parents had sat up late in bed the previous evening discussing their son and his new friend, and William asked why Miss Miller wanted to leave.

"I don't know, but Will was embarrassed. I have to say, William, I do not care much for Miss Miller. She hasn't made much of an effort to get to know us or involve herself in anything despite my attempts to make her feel welcome, make sure she was comfortable, introducing her to everyone, even suggesting a round of cards in desperation – you know I hate playing – showing her the library, telling her about the family history. To try to persuade her to stay longer, I even suggested a riding lesson with Andrew as something novel for her to try but she turned quite pale and the look of revulsion…" Marianna sighed. "She is pleasant looking and intelligent, I grant you, and comes from a good family, quite wealthy, I believe, but she is haughty and there is something shallow and a little nasty about her. Do you know? When she saw we had invited the staff to share the picnic, I overheard her say sarcastically to Miss Lambert, 'How very egalitarian!' I don't think we are grand enough for her."

"Lizzie isn't impressed either. She prefers her friend."

"As do I. Will did not pay much attention to Miss Lambert at the picnic other than to be polite, but she could not keep her eyes off him. I think she may have feelings for him, but he does not notice."

"Did Will confide in you at all? Does he have any serious intentions regarding this young woman?"

"No, he's said nothing, which is unusual, and which makes me think he is having doubts, so does not need to reveal his thoughts to me. I hope so. I hope he saw how she behaved and has the sense to see her for what she is. They are not suited, William. She will be too demanding and critical. If this liaison continues, I may have to say something."

"Tread carefully, Marianna. He's a grown man now. We'll have to trust him to make the right decision. I'm disappointed we didn't manage to speak to him about our plans for the estate. I like to involve him, as what we do now may affect his future inheritance."

"Then *he* will have to trust us, William. Farming is changing because of what is happening in the world, with the market flooded with cheap grain from America and the recent bad harvests here. We must act or there will be no estate for him to inherit."

"Next week will be stressful, I fear, when we see the bank manager."

"He will not refuse us the loan. Our plans have been so carefully worked out and costed."

"If we agree to Thomas Crossley's idea to build a much larger hen house, a hen barn, in fact, he will insist we put up his rent. The same with the Binghams' wish to build a new byre for their dairy herd. As for the idea of using the moorland for deer stalking or shooting, which we know nothing about, he may fall off his chair laughing, as it'll take time to stock the land with birds and we'll need to find a gamekeeper. He may think us fools."

"Nothing ventured, nothing gained, William. At least we have found a good tenant for Hapenny How, and we could release some capital if we sold some of the commercial property we own in Newbridge."

"Let's change the subject, darling. Sometimes I come out in a cold sweat thinking about it!"

SEVEN

It was the last day of the summer term. William waited on the road outside the schoolhouse, holding the reins of Sorrel and Moth, who stamped his foot impatiently. When the weather was fine, William would sometimes turn up to surprise Savannah with the horses and they would ride home together. The bell rang to announce the end of lessons, the door opened, and Mr Harrison, the headmaster, allowed the children, already lined up, to leave in an orderly fashion. William could see Savannah peering through the throng of faces, grinning at him, itching to escape the strict discipline of the classroom and her teacher, Miss Barnet. As soon as she crossed the threshold she broke into a run, her dark plait flying behind her, shouting her farewells to her friends. She had many friends. William and Marianna believed this was because of their daughter's cheerful, warm and friendly disposition and not, owing to the family's status and wealth, because other parents encouraged their children to seek out her friendship for their own purposes.

"Papa! Papa!" Savannah stretched up on tiptoes to peck his cheek before he hoisted her onto Moth's back. "It's the holidays at last!"

The school was situated on the outskirts of Newbridge, and they were soon on a bridlepath which led across the field to the woods and up the hill to Longridge.

"Can we go through the woods and then into Mary's Lots, Papa?" Savannah liked to canter.

"If you wish." William stretched to open the gate into the wood and let Savannah pass through. "Walk, Savannah. We don't want Moth to trip over tree roots."

"I had to read out my composition, 'A Good Deed', to the class as Miss Barnet said it was very good. Billy Davis got the best marks for arithmetic this term, and for spelling. He is very clever, Papa." Mr Harrison had already mentioned the station porter's son to him as a candidate for a bursary to continue his education at the Grammar School in Newbridge. "And Ben Kerr had to stand in the corner again for talking too much. It was Jack's last day too. He got a Bible as a leaving present."

"What else did you learn today?"

Savannah turned in her saddle. "Did you know Sir Walter Raleigh brought potatoes back from America? For which I am very grateful. I do like potatoes."

William smiled. They walked on in silence through the dappled shade of the wood as far as the gate into Mary's Lots, a flat, open area of grazing land. After letting Savannah pass, William leant along Sorrel's neck and pulled the gate shut. Without waiting for him, Savannah excitedly kicked Moth into a canter and was heading for the copse of trees where the fallen tree lay, which she had often begged her father to allow her to jump, but he always refused. It was a solid, wide trunk of oak and far beyond the capabilities of Moth, who was too small to clear it. He yelled at her. "No, Savannah. Stop! Stop!" But she was too far ahead to hear him or chose to ignore him. He could see Moth was now galloping flat out. Savannah was shrieking with excitement and stirring the pony to go faster. He kicked Sorrel and set off in pursuit, cursing his daughter's reckless impetuosity, praying she would lose courage and change her mind. He knew she would not. And then, everything seemed to slow down. He heard Sorrel's hooves thudding on the hard ground. He felt the breeze on his face. He tried to shout again for her to stop but his mouth was dry with fear. He saw her legs move out sideways to kick Moth on as she positioned herself in readiness for the jump.

He saw Moth rise to her command, his head and neck stretched out. He saw the front hooves clip the tree trunk. He saw the pony pitch forward and come to a juddering halt, stranded across the bole. He saw his darling daughter fly over Moth's head and, in a flurry of skirts and petticoats, disappear from sight. He heard the thud as she hit the ground. He heard the anguished cry escape from his throat, "Savannah," as he arrived seconds later and threw himself from his horse and staggered across the grass to find her crumpled, limbs lying awkwardly, face down, immobile.

"Savannah! Savannah!" he screamed.

Moth, wide-eyed, reared his head in fright at the sound of him and began to struggle to free himself, snorting wildly in distress. William fell to his knees and rolled her gently over. Her face was white, ghost-like, her eyes closed, her mouth open. He could see no blood.

"Savannah, darling. Mouse. Can you hear me?" His face was wet with tears. He leant close to her face, praying he would feel her breath on his cheek. She was alive. He sobbed with relief. He felt gently along her arms and legs, but nothing seemed to be broken. Sorrel nudged him in the back and whinnied as if to hurry him in his actions. Moth had disentangled himself and stood trembling beside the tree trunk. William got up and quickly looped the reins round the stump of a branch so he could not move off. He scooped Savannah into his arms and, asking Sorrel to stand quietly, placed his foot in the stirrup and heaved himself into the saddle.

As he approached the stable yard William yelled for Andrew, who came racing out of Marquis's stable at the desperate sound of his voice, followed closely by Thomas. They saw the deathly pallor of the unconscious child clutched in his arms and Andrew reached up to take her as William dismounted.

"My God! What's happened to the wee lass?" asked Andrew as he handed Savannah gently back to her father.

"She's had a bad fall. Go for Dr Greenwood, Andrew. Take Sorrel and be as quick as you can. Thomas, fetch Moth. He's tied to the fallen oak in Mary's Lots. Check him over. He may be injured. He's in shock. Be gentle with him."

Panting heavily, his mind racing with all kinds of dreadful thoughts, William ran with Savannah up the road to the back of the house, kicking open the door into the kitchen, ignoring the startled faces of Ada and the maids as they sat drinking their tea, and up the stairs to Savannah's bedroom.

"Marianna! Marianna!" he cried as he passed through the hall and took the stairs two at a time.

Marianna appeared at the door of the drawing room and saw the stricken child in his arms and, hoisting up her skirts, raced up the stairs after him, crying out, "What happened, William. Why is she so pale?"

William placed the limp child on her bed. She had not opened her eyes or uttered a sound.

"She fell from Moth. I don't think anything's broken. Andrew's gone for Richard. She's hit her head and I can't wake her." He unbuttoned her boots which had left a smear of mud on the counterpane.

"But what can we do?" asked Marianna, her voice rising in panic, her fingers twisting together, as she stared down at her seemingly lifeless child. "Why is she not moving? Savannah, darling. It's Mama. Wake up, darling."

There was a knock on the door. It was Ada, who had come unbidden with a tray and two bowls: one of warm water and the other chilled, and some cloths.

"Oh, thank you, Ada," said William, grateful for her thoughtfulness.

"Can I do anythin' else, sir?" she asked, her eyes filling with tears at the sight of Savannah, pale and motionless on her bed.

"Would you please ask Sarah to wait by the front door as I've sent for the doctor."

Marianna sat on the bed beside Savannah and pushed her hair from her face and gasped. A lurid lump the size of a duck's egg had appeared on her left temple. She took the child's hand and squeezed gently but there was no response. Marianna wrung out a cloth soaked in the warm water and began to wipe the smeared dirt from Savannah's face and then placed a cold cloth on her forehead.

"It may help with the swelling," she said as she did not know what else she could do.

William was standing by the window looking down the driveway for the doctor. "He's here," he said, rushing from the room – it was Dr Ashbourne who had come – to tell him what had happened. He did not yet want to incur the wrath of his wife by having to explain the circumstances of the accident in her presence.

"You gave us quite a fright, young lady," said William, tucking the blankets round Savannah.

"My head hurts, Papa, quite badly, and if I move it, I feel dizzy and a bit sick."

"Dr Ashbourne says you're to stay in bed for a few more days. You have concussion. Did you understand what he was saying to you? You shook your brain up when you banged your head. Do you remember what happened?"

"I remember you came to school for me, and we rode home. We were talking about potatoes."

"You fell off Moth. You tried to jump the log I've told you repeatedly not to jump, so I'm cross with you, Mouse, because you disobeyed me and hurt yourself. You hurt Moth too and you frightened him. He's too small for such a jump."

"Don't scold, Papa. I'm poorly. It will not do to scold a poorly child."

"You may be poorly, young lady, but you need to know how much you've frightened Mama. And me. You must learn to do as you are told, Savannah. You're nine years old—"

"Nine and a half, Papa."

"Even more reason to know better. We tell you not to do things precisely to stop you doing something foolish and coming to harm."

Savannah looked suitably chastened.

"Where is Mama?"

"She's resting. She watched over you last night and she's tired."

"I'll tell her I'm sorry." Savannah's bottom lip began to quiver. "I'll say sorry to Moth too."

"Make sure you do."

"I am sorry, Papa. Truly I am."

William went to see if Marianna was awake. She was curled up on their bed, fast asleep. He stood, watching her, her mouth slightly open, her chest rising and falling gently, the recent worry on her face eased by the release of sleep. He kicked off his shoes, crawled onto the bed and lay next to her. She had been badly shaken by the accident. When he came to relieve her vigil in the early hours of the morning, she whispered to him, "See! Happiness is a fleeting thing. God has punished me again."

He ran his fingers slowly along the line of her eyebrow, down towards her cheek and across her mouth and kissed her gently. Her lips twitched and she opened her eyes and blinked groggily. His face was inches from hers and smiling; she smiled back.

"She's sleeping," he said.

"Good. She will suffer no ill effects?"

"Dr Ashbourne says not. He was very sweet with her. He left about half an hour ago. I didn't want to wake you. And if the conversation I've just had with her is any indication, she's well on the way to recovery, so no more dark thoughts. Promise?" He kissed her fingers and held her hand.

"Promise. Please, William, you must try and discourage her from this recklessness, this disobedience. She has no idea of the consequences of her actions."

"I've told her, and she has promised me she'll apologise for upsetting you. I should be stricter with her, punish her more." He shuddered at the thought. "As you did last week when she trailed muddy footprints across the hall floor. Her face was a picture when you handed her the mop and bucket."

"She needs to learn to appreciate the work the servants do for us. Mrs Matthews had just cleaned it. I love her dearly but sometimes she is so aggravating and wilful. She needs reining in. She must learn to be more ladylike."

"I'll speak to her again when she's feeling better, and I understand your concerns. I will forbid her to go riding for two weeks and she'll miss the Greenwood's party to show her the consequences of disobeying me. She gave me such a fright, Marianna."

Marianna pushed away the lock of hair that always flopped over his brow.

"I do not recall Will being so troublesome and worrying and stubborn."

William rolled onto his back and put his hands behind his head. "She gets the latter trait from you, darling. We must hope that Savannah grows up to be more restrained. There's time…" He sighed. "Perhaps I've been too lenient."

He had missed so much of Will's growing up it felt churlish to begrudge him the attention he bestowed on his daughter, so Marianna said, "I am not saying you are too indulgent, William. Well, perhaps a little. I think it is in her nature to be high-spirited. She has many endearing qualities. She is an intelligent child, thoughtful and caring. How many creatures have we found in her bedroom over the years?" Marianna laughed. "How did she smuggle the lamb up? Do you remember?"

"I do. It was almost as big as she was and most upset at being taken away from its mother."

"Yes, she is good-natured and kind. I do not despair totally."

Marianna snuggled up to William and he put his arm round her.

"I've been thinking," he said. "What about a holiday? In a couple of weeks, perhaps, when the doctor's happy with her recovery. We could do with a change of scenery. There have been some difficult times these past few years and we'll be busy in the months ahead as we put our plans for the estate into action at last."

"Yes, it would be pleasant to go away for a few days. Have you somewhere in mind?"

"Westport. The sea air will be beneficial. I used to go there with Lizzie and the children when they were small. There's a fine hotel there, the promenade, the pier, the beach, plenty of entertainments. And we could call on Lizzie on the way home. See Will." He paused, then added, sighing, "I need to speak to Fred Hartley too."

William decided Savannah needed a new pony, something a bit bigger than Moth, who seemed to have lost his nerve since the accident. Within a fortnight, he had acquired a Welsh Mountain Pony, sweet faced and dark eyed, and, although she had been broken in, he needed to put her through her paces to ensure she would be a calm and steady ride for Savannah. Marianna had resisted the idea at first, as it would be further to fall if Savannah had another accident, as surely she would. Savannah was beside herself with excitement once she had been reassured that they would keep Moth as a pet.

Marianna, Savannah and Thomas the lad, watched as William led the haltered pony into the paddock. He stood for several minutes talking to her, letting her smell him and stroking her neck, before running his hands along her back and down her legs. He walked away from her and turned slightly to see the ears prick, then waited for her to follow him, which she did. He talked to her, patted her neck, repeated the same process and walked away again. He saw the lowering of her head, the act of submission, as she began to follow him. He saw in her eyes that she was not afraid of him and trusted him. He spent another ten minutes repeating the process and then waved to Savannah to join him. Thomas opened the gate for her, and she walked quietly towards her father.

"Let her smell you and talk to her gently, and then do as I did. Stroke her neck. Now run your hand along her back and keep talking to her. Everything done slowly. Every word spoken calmly. Patience and trust, Savannah."

When they walked away, the pony followed.

Marianna rested her arms on the gate and watched them: father and daughter together, sharing this bond, their love of horses. As she watched, she knew this was one of the many things she loved about William. It had been the same at Coldbarrow where they had grown up together. He was always gentle and patient with the younger children and animals. Now, gentle and patient with Savannah. They came back towards her, Savannah leading the pony. She heard William say that tomorrow they would put the tack on her, and Savannah could ride her round the paddock.

"I think your punishment expired today," he said. "Perhaps we shall ride her out before we go on holiday."

"Oh, yes please, Papa."

"Now go with Thomas, give her brush and make sure she has some hay and fresh water. Talk to her so she gets used to your voice."

"What will you call her?" asked Marianna.

At that moment, a ladybird landed on the back of her hand and folded its wings.

"Ladybird!" said William and Savannah in unison.

* * *

It was the penultimate day of their holiday at the seaside resort of Westport and the first day that promised a long spell of dry weather to allow them a walk along the mile-long promenade. Most days the weather had been changeable but there were plenty of amusements to keep them entertained. They had been to the circus, to the zoo, to the theatre, and snatched walks along the pier and on the beach between the rain showers. The hotel had a games room and William and Savannah played billiards and he taught her the rudiments of chess.

Savannah had been promised an ice cream if she walked nicely with her parents all the way to the park where a brass band would be playing. She acquiesced. Her behaviour had been impeccable throughout the week, as though she had at last accepted that she must think before acting. Although not yet ten years old, she was astute enough to realise how much she had frightened her parents and she loved them too much to cause them such pain. She sat quietly, licking her ice cream, fascinated by the peaked caps, the gold braid and buttons on the musicians' bright red jackets, listening to the stirring music, her feet tapping along with the beat, and held her mother's hand as they returned to the hotel along the promenade an hour later.

As they passed one of the set of steps that led down to the beach, a small black and white terrier raced past and bolted along the promenade, followed by the desperate cries of an elderly lady, who came puffing breathlessly up the steps, waving a collar at the end of a lead.

"Badger! Badger! Come here, you rascal."

Savannah shook off her mother's hand and set off in pursuit of the errant Badger.

"Don't worry, ma'am. I'll catch him," she cried over her shoulder.

"Savannah!" shouted William and Marianna in unified exasperation and hurried after her.

Some thirty yards ahead of them, Savannah had come to a halt, as had Badger, by a wicker bath chair in which sat an old woman, dressed in black, attended by a younger woman. Savannah crouched down and picked up the dog and seemed to be engaged in conversation with the old lady. As they neared her, Marianna grabbed William's arm, pulled him to a stop and exclaimed, "Good heavens!"

William turned sharply and saw Marianna's pale, tight face and said, "What is it?"

"It's Agatha Mislet."

"What?"

"It is Agatha Mislet. No doubt at all. She's talking to Savannah."

They set off again, slowly, towards their daughter. Then William said, "Wait here. I'll fetch her."

Marianna was anxious. Now they were so much closer, she knew she was right. It was indeed Agatha Mislet; the woman who, with her brother Heaning, owned Coldbarrow Farm. The brother who bought and sold children to work for them in the mill and on the farm; his sister who had taught her to sew and had, over time, come to regard her as a daughter, and from whom she and William had run away to find William's family. She felt a pang of guilt as it was the inebriated Heaning Mislet's riding accident that had provided the distraction to enable their escape. They had learnt later that he had died as a result of that accident. Marianna accepted a long time ago that what the Mislets did was wrong and illegal despite Agatha Mislet's kindness towards her. Agatha Mislet was a ghost from the past she never thought she would see again. Nor wanted to see again.

Savannah had turned round at the sound of her father's voice and came towards him, the dog in her arms licking her face enthusiastically.

"Take the dog back to his owner and wait with Mama."

He was relieved she had not embarrassed him and obeyed him instantly. The elderly dog owner had caught up with them and was chatting volubly to Marianna about how grateful she was, asking Savannah's name and inviting them all to take tea with her the following afternoon, until Marianna was able to usher her away.

"Why is Papa taking so long to talk to that old lady?" asked Savannah crossly.

William stood for a moment, eyeing Agatha Mislet. Unmistakably her. The woman who had bound his wounds after her brother thrashed him with his riding crop – he still bore the scar – thinking he had helped his friend Peter to run away. Peter who had died because of her brother. The long face was lined, the jowls sagged, the deep crease between the eyes which gave her face a permanent frown was more pronounced, the hair white, a rug wrapped round her despite the warm sunshine. Peter had called her 'th'owd crow'. She was always dressed in black in those days too. She stared back at him, wondering why he lingered and whether he knew her and intended to speak. Her brow creased further. There was something about him. She looked past him towards the little girl standing next to the strikingly beautiful, well-dressed woman. She had noticed the child's deep, deep blue, almond-shaped eyes as she explained about the runaway dog. Something about the eyes stirred a memory – but what was it? Her own eyes narrowed as her mouth twitched. And still he stood, silent, defying her to recognise him and say something.

"Jacob?" The young woman who stood beside her – *her nurse*, William wondered – gasped, and repeated, "Jacob?"

He saw the flicker in Agatha Mislet's eyes as she put the name to the face from the past. He turned his gaze on the young woman who had spoken. She was in her early thirties, small, fine-featured, dressed plainly in a brown, cotton skirt and jacket.

"Leah?" he said before he could stop himself.

"Aye." She broke into a smile. "Was that your daughter? So pretty. And the lady yonder? Please tell me it's Mary. Please say it is so?"

"It is," he said. He had no grievance with Leah, one of the Coldbarrow children Mary – as Marianna was known then – had taken under her wing.

"Will you not ask her to come and speak wi' us?"

William shook his head. "You go to her. I've something to say to your mistress."

"May I go?" Leah leant towards Agatha, who waved her hand in consent.

William waited until she was out of earshot before saying, "You're unwell?"

"Old age. I cannot walk far but I like to take the air. You look well, Jacob."

"My name's not Jacob, as you well know. It was a name you foisted on me, but I never forgot my real name or who I was." He turned slightly towards Marianna, who was now engaged in animated conversation with Leah as an impatient Savannah twirled her skirts beside her. "And she's not Mary. She found her family again."

"So, all is well with you both. No harm done."

"No harm done? What a strangely deluded woman you are. She was kidnapped. Did you know that? I was snatched too. Both of us taken from loving families. You should be in prison for what you've done, or that brother of yours should be. But he escaped justice, didn't he?"

"You sound bitter despite your obvious change in circumstances," she sneered, looking him up and down. "You will not make me feel guilty for anything I have done. I made the lives of all the children in my care so much better than the lives they came—"

"I had a decent life, as did she," interrupted William. "We were stolen. Made to work long hours. Then you would've sold us, like the others, until your brother made a mess of things with his gambling and debts."

"You waste your breath with your vitriol. I cannot see, looking at you now, that I have been the cause of any harm to you, either of you. Leave me. Send Leah back to me. You deserted me despite everything I did for you."

William clenched his fists at her lack of compassion, her blinkered acceptance of what her brother did, her lack of understanding about taking children from families who wanted them and loved them and the damage it caused. He could feel the anger rising as he thought of the times he had cried himself to sleep at the loss of his family who did not know what had happened to him. He pictured Peter's body lying on the cobbles in the yard where Mislet had thrown him after whipping him, as an example to the other children not to run away, his eyes glazed, blood oozing from his head. He remembered the day when he hid in the stable and heard the conversation between Mislet and one of the men to whom he was in debt.

"Your brother was going to sell her as a whore to pay for his debts," he spat out.

"I would never have allowed that; she meant too much to me. And your conscience is clear, is it? You did nothing to help him that day; the day you ran away, the pair of you, and did nothing. He was badly injured, fatally injured. You said you were going to help him, as I recall." She lowered her eyes to hide the darkness of her guilt. She had smothered her brother with a pillow to bring his pain to an end – she knew his brain was damaged – and she knew, may God forgive her, it was to rid herself of him.

"And your God may punish me for not going to his aid," said William. "But I feel no guilt after what he did to Peter and to me. And the others? Their graves were found. Did you know that?"

"Those children died of sickness. Peter died accidentally. My brother meant him no harm."

He could see she thought her conscience was clear, she was not troubled, she had made peace with that God of hers.

"You have no shame?" he asked to provoke some reaction.

"Me? None at all. Nothing that happened in those days was as a result of anything that I did."

Agatha Mislet rearranged the rug over her knees and turned her head away from him. He knew he was not going to gain anything by prolonging the conversation. She would not apologise, she would not acknowledge her part in what had happened, even if she had been only an onlooker to her brother's actions.

"I made you, Jacob. The man you are today." Her eyes glinted as she turned back to look at him.

Her self-delusion caused him to snort in derision. He began to wonder why he had stayed to speak to her in the first place. Perhaps he was seeking some kind of compensation for what had happened to him, Marianna, Peter and the others with an apology from her and recognition of what her brother had done. The look of defiant, self-satisfaction on that wrinkled face was too much. He reached into his coat pocket and threw a handful of coins – silver and copper – into her lap.

"The money I stole from you to enable our escape. My conscience is now clear. Is yours?"

He turned on his heel and strode back to his family. What could be more precious?

Savannah, hunched and swaddled in her pale, lilac coat, like a puffed-up squab, her brow furrowed, her lips pursed, stared hard, first at her mother, then her father, willing them to notice her. They were on the train to Liverpool, from where they would take a cab to her father's old house at Stillingford to visit Aunt Lizzie. Marianna was talking to William about the meeting on the promenade.

"Leah seemed happy, didn't she, William?"

"I told you last night you didn't need to worry about her. You said she is married, and they both work for her."

"A boarding house, though. Does she strike you as someone to welcome strangers into her home?"

"I doubt she mixes with them. Leah and her husband will do all the work."

"And she has changed her name. Mrs Woodhouse. Leah said she lets people assume she is a widow."

"Let's forget about them. I do not care to remember Agatha Mislet."

William settled back in his seat to gaze out of the window at the passing scenery.

"What is it, Savannah?" asked her mother, taking in the scrunched-up face. "You look as if you have swallowed a wasp."

"I am thinking hard, Mama."

"About?"

"About how to ask you both if I may have a badger."

William jerked his head and looked askance at Marianna, his eyebrows raised in disbelief.

"A badger?"

"The dog yesterday," explained Marianna. "He was called Badger."

William stifled a laugh, relieved that his daughter was not entertaining the thought of having an actual badger. "Why do you want a dog?"

"Because he was very sweet and friendly and licked my face to show me how much he liked me." The words tumbled out. "And I am *very* much in need of a dear friend," she said pleadingly.

William laughed. "You have many friends of the human variety, Savannah."

She was not to be deterred in her quest. "Yes, but I need a friend at home." She pouted and turned her mournful eyes on her father. "I am so very lonely."

William and Marianna laughed together at her acting.

"A dog is a responsibility," said William, "and I'm not sure you're responsible enough to care for a dog."

He heard Marianna exhale in relief beside him as he resisted his daughter's wiles, and then breathe in sharply as she heard him say, "Mama and I will think about it." This would be another victory for her daughter, who could twist her father round her little finger. Their conversation after Savannah's accident regarding 'reining her in' seemed to have been forgotten. Savannah turned on her most winning smile.

"As you wish, dearest, kindest Mama and Papa. You will not see a more beautifully behaved, dutiful, responsible child in your life."

"Geoffrey!" exclaimed Marianna, taking his outstretched hand.

He bent over to kiss the back of her hand.

"Aunt. All yours?" he asked, stepping back and looking towards the open front door where the children had gathered.

Marianna laughed. "No. My daughter and her friends." She turned to Sarah, who was hovering in the background, in her hand the silver salver on which she had borne Geoffrey Wallington's gold-embossed visiting card to the sitting room and, ignoring Savannah's questioning look, asked the maid to take the children down to the kitchen for tea.

The Greenwoods had come to visit for the afternoon to hear all about their holiday. William and Richard had gone out riding. She and Ellen had been working on their embroidery in her sitting room when they noticed the children, who had been playing with the young Kerrs on the lawns at the front of the house, had gone quiet, before the crunch of wheels on the gravel of the drive alerted them to the arrival of a visitor. The children's curiosity, or rather Savannah's curiosity had drawn her to the house to find out who the stranger in the taxicab was.

Marianna sat opposite her nephew in the drawing room. He had refused her offer of refreshment as he did not have much time and the cab was waiting to take him back to the station.

"I need to be on time and not miss my connection to Liverpool," he explained, glancing with curiosity round the large, light-filled, tastefully decorated and well-furnished room which he barely remembered as he had only visited Longridge for short holidays as a boy.

"Well!" said Marianna. "It is lovely to see you. How you have grown!"

"Not so surprising, Aunt." He raised an eyebrow at her. "It has been more than twenty years since we last saw each other."

Geoffrey, an only child, was of medium height, stocky, with his father's build and his mother's fair complexion, and there was no mistaking the Hamilton eyes, his best feature, as his nose was hooked and his lips thin, giving him a sharp, predatory look.

"How are your parents?" Marianna asked out of politeness. She had little interest, if she was honest, for she barely knew his father and there was no love lost between her and her sister Verity. The letter informing her of their mother's death was the first communication between them since she had banned them both from Longridge.

"My *parents?*" said Geoffrey sarcastically. "Well, whether they have been parents to me is a moot point. My father is an alcoholic womaniser and my mother leads her own extravagant life in London with her lovers, as far away from my father as possible."

"Oh!" Marianna was shocked. It was obvious to everyone at the time that Verity, encouraged by their mother, married Lord Herbert Wallington for his title, political connections and entrée to the higher echelons of society, and he married her for her money, as his father had mismanaged his inheritance. It was not, even from the early years, a happy marriage. He was a weak man who allowed his wife to bully him because she held the purse strings. Marianna had also seen her at work, dripping poison about her husband and his shortcomings into the ears of others, including her young son.

"I shall soon be rid of them, for tomorrow I sail from Liverpool in search of a new life in America. Your mother left me a generous bequest, so I beat a hasty retreat before either of my parents gets their hands on it." He laughed an embarrassed laugh. He hardly knew this woman and here he was talking so openly. "My mother is draining the coffers with her expensive tastes and my father has drunk his way to ill health and lost all interest in his affairs and maintaining the house and estate. There will be nothing left for me to inherit when the time comes." He smiled ruefully. "However, I have not come all the way from Derbyshire to bore you with my travails." He reached into his jacket pocket to retrieve a small package and letter and passed them to her.

Marianna glanced up to see William and Richard passing the window. She eyed the envelope and recognised her mother's handwriting. She did not know how she was supposed to feel about this woman now she was dead. She never thought about her: dead for three months but dead to her daughter for years.

"I am here at my mother's request to give you those," said Geoffrey.

"What are they?"

"I have been told of the rift between you, your mother and sister. However, when my grandmother died in Portugal, my mother found a letter with them instructing they should be given to you. As I was on my way to Liverpool, I was asked to make a detour to put them directly into your hands." Geoffrey stood up. "I have completed that task so I must really be on my way."

The door to the drawing room opened and William came into the room.

"I heard we have a visitor. I've arranged for tea to be served in your sitting room, darling."

Marianna rose from the sofa.

"This is our nephew, William. Verity's son. Geoffrey Wallington."

William strode across the room to shake the hand of the nephew he had never met. He had never met his parents either. "Pleased to meet you. I am Marianna's husband. William Hamilton-Read. Will you join us for tea?"

"Pleased to make your acquaintance, sir, brief as it shall be."

"Sadly, Geoffrey has a train to catch, William, and cannot stay," explained Marianna.

Geoffrey took her hand and kissed it. "My apologies for having to rush off."

"It was good of you to come. May I wish you a bon voyage. And Geoffrey…" She thought of his relationship with his parents and wondered how much he had suffered. Enough, evidently, to want to cross an ocean to get away from them. "If you wish to keep in touch, please do."

"Thank you, Aunt. It was good to see you again after all this time." He smiled and bowed his head.

Marianna sank down on the sofa as William escorted their visitor to the front door. She put down the letter and turned the small package over in her hands until curiosity got the better of her and she ripped off the string and paper to find a small, red velvet box. Inside was a miniature in a gold frame studded with diamonds and sapphires, beautifully painted, of a young man in dark clothes with a gentle smile and eyes as blue as could be. She gasped. It was her father, Henry. She was less keen to open the letter but was intrigued as to why her mother thought she should have the portrait. She had not bequeathed her anything in her will and there were no bequests to her other grandchildren, Will and Savannah.

Dearest Marianna,

When you read this, I shall be dead.

Blunt as always, thought Marianna.

The miniature is very special to me as it was given to me by your father on the occasion of our betrothal. I give it to you as a token of love from a mother to her daughter, as I know how much you loved him.

Every day I have regretted our disagreements and the subsequent rupture in our relationship. We are so alike, much as I know it will displease you to accept this. We are both strong women – strong-willed and stubborn. However, I will not apologise for my behaviour. I acted only in your interests when you came back to us. I wanted the best for you, but you could not see this or accept it. You must acknowledge, though, that I have made you the lady you are now.

I hope, now you are older, wiser, and a mother, you appreciate how much I was affected by your loss when you were taken as a small child. What it was like not to know what had become of you for all those years. It was torture. An agony. I would not inflict it on my worst enemy.

For you to throw back in my face all my endeavours to improve you to make up for the lost years was very painful for me. Your ingratitude was heartbreaking. However, I forgive you. I cannot go to my Lord and Saviour without making amends, which is why I write to you after all these years and ask you to understand and find in your heart some love for your mother. I pray for you, querida. I pray for your soul. I pray to God to forgive you the pain you have caused me—

"Pah!"

In disgust, Marianna tore the letter into shreds and tossed them into the fireplace, put the miniature inside her bodice and went to join the others for tea.

Despite Marianna's misgivings, William had acquired a puppy from a litter on a neighbour's farm that he had left in the care of Andrew and his family to house train, as the stable master had more experience of dogs than either of them; and all the Kerrs were under strict instructions not to breathe a word. The day after the stranger's visit, Savannah wondered why her mother was coming with them to the stables, as she rarely rode out with them. Marianna was a nervous rider as she did not learn until William encouraged her after Savannah was born and became more nervous when she saw the manner in which her daughter rode. Savannah's interest was piqued when her father went instead to knock on the Kerr's door.

"He's in the kitchen," said Andrew, opening the door to them and letting them pass.

Catriona, smiling shyly, rose from her chair beside the range and curtsied. The puppy was dozing in a box at her feet. He was small; a rough-coated terrier, black and white and brown, with a black patch over one eye and a docked tail. The Kerr children were kneeling beside him and got up quickly to move aside as Savannah rushed towards him.

"Quietly, Savannah," said William. "You mustn't frighten him."

Scooping the puppy into her arms, Savannah buried her face in his fur. "Is he for me? He is adorable," she said, sighing, her eyes brimming with tears. "And he is almost like Badger. I shall call him Badger too." She rushed to her father, the bewildered puppy still in her embrace, and reached up to kiss him and then her mother, breathless with excitement, and squealed, "Thank you! Thank you!" Then she turned to the Kerr children and exclaimed, "Andy! Ben! Joanna! You knew about this!"

They beamed at her. Ben, who was in the same class at school, chuckled. "Your pa swore us to secrecy."

William smiled. "You must thank the Kerrs for looking after him."

"Thank you all," said Savannah. "Have you ever seen such a happy child? Is Badger to come home now, Papa?"

"Yes. Andrew says he's fully house-trained, but he still needs more training so that'll be your job. You must take the responsibility for teaching him to sit, come and walk nicely on a lead."

"Yes, I will. I think I am the happiest girl in the world." She kissed the puppy's head. "Come, Badger, it's time for your first lesson."

William waited behind as Savannah left with her mother and Badger. He winked at Andrew and handed the Kerr children their reward: a florin each, for their wonderful powers of self-control in not divulging the secret.

To Marianna's great surprise, Savannah took her canine responsibilities seriously, rising early to take Badger outside for his morning toilet, feeding him in the kitchen, and taking him for short walks across the lawn until he grew stronger. She taught him to sit and take a treat nicely from her fingers, rewarding him with praise and kisses. The dog was devoted to her and, although her parents had insisted that he sleep in the kitchen, it was not long before he found his way up to her bedroom, where he slept in his basket by her bed on a cushion specially made for him by Marianna and embroidered with his name.

William had never owned a dog and was secretly flattered by the dog's attention. When Savannah was at school, Badger would come to the study where he was working and lie across his feet under the desk and trot behind him when he went down to the stables. Badger liked to chase the yard cats. In the afternoon, to hedge his bets and keep in with all the members of the family, Badger would join Marianna in her sitting room, and if she was not busy with her sewing, nudge his way onto her lap and into her affections. Everyone was charmed by the new addition to the household.

For the last year, on a Wednesday afternoon, Jack Greenwood had come home with them after school to help Savannah with her arithmetic, the one subject she struggled with. She was bright and imaginative, according to Miss Barnet, her teacher. She wrote the most wonderful stories in her beautiful, copperplate handwriting, and her reading and spelling were far above average, but she seemed to lack the patience to concentrate and memorise her times tables, which was hampering her ability to do multiplication and long division. Jack came willingly; it was not a chore for him to spend as much time as possible in her company, preferably alone, when she gave him her undivided attention.

They would sit together in the study as Jack patiently recited her tables with her and explained the confusing process of where to put her numbers when she was doing her working out. When Savannah had enough of schoolwork, they would look at her late grandfather's books, play billiards or chess or walk Badger in the grounds until it was time to take tea with her parents. It was Savannah who decided what games they would play although Jack was two years older than her. She would boss him about and he was so in thrall to her, he would obey her every command. He adored her; she was funny, lively and popular. He had none of those traits; he was clever and bookish and was happy to follow her and bask in the glow of her personality. He was a handsome boy, fair-haired and green-eyed like his father, kind and considerate, but shy and quiet. Nevertheless, as his mother had commented on many times to William and Marianna, the change in him since their friendship had grown was remarkable.

"Well," said William as they sat down to a high tea in the dining room, "are you seeing any improvement, Jack?"

Jack had walked from Newbridge to spend the afternoon with Savannah. Marianna had asked him to practise the times tables with her for ten minutes each time he visited as she was determined Savannah would know them all before the end of the holidays. Jack was an obliging teacher; Savannah was a reluctant pupil. It was the summer holidays after all.

"Yes, sir. It is just the seven times table that seems to be proving more difficult."

"Very well, we shall practise it, Savannah, so you shall know it by the start of the new term."

"Do you know, Papa and Mama, that the nine times table is most peculiar?"

"How so?" asked Marianna.

Savannah smirked knowingly at Jack before asking her mother, "What is nine times two?"

"Eighteen."

"Nine times three?"

"Twenty-seven."

"And nine times four?"

"Where is this going, Savannah? I know my nine times table. And please do not feed Badger titbits under the table. It is not good for him and will make him fat."

"Add the numbers together, Mama," said Savannah triumphantly, wiping her sticky fingers on her dress. "What do you notice?"

"Oh, very good. Does that help you to remember it?"

"Jack told me. Even Miss Barnet has not pointed that out. Jack is a mathematical genius."

"Ssh!" William laughed. "He'll ask for payment for his services."

Jack blushed. "I would not, sir. It pleases me to come and help Savannah."

William gave Marianna a knowing look.

"You'll be off to a new school soon. Are you looking forward to it?"

"Yes, sir," said Jack hesitantly.

Marianna saw his discomfort and offered him a plate of cakes to change the subject.

"I shall ask Mrs Dummigan to put some cakes in a box for Madeleine and Isabel. We don't want them to miss out. Are they looking forward to Saturday?"

"Yes, Mrs Hamilton-Read. They are looking forward to it. We all are."

The Greenwood children were coming to spend the night, as their parents were going to the theatre in Manchester.

"Savannah's papa should be home by then. He is going to Liverpool tomorrow."

EIGHT

William turned the horse's head for home. The August sky had darkened considerably; slate-black clouds threatened in the west and the blackness made the leaves and grass seem greener. The air was oppressive after two days of summer heat. A weather front – a wall of pressured clouds – loomed. It reminded him of the storms in Spain when he had walked home all those years ago after the convict ship was wrecked in the Atlantic when, suddenly, everything would go quiet, birds seemed to drop out of the sky and the leaves rustled vigorously in the warm wind before the black sky split open. He could sense the mare's unease and kicked her to a canter but pulled her up sharply as she began to limp. She had cast a shoe somewhere. He had offered to ride out the mare for his neighbour, David Thompson, who was thinking of buying her and wanted William's expert opinion. David had often loaned him a horse when he lived at Meadowside, and he had not minded doing him this favour.

They had walked, trotted and cantered along the bridleways as he put the mare through her paces and she was a comfortable ride, calm and steady. He had been to Liverpool that morning and signed the papers which, after a couple of years of frustration and unforeseen difficulties, had finally terminated his involvement in his company. He had sold out to a consortium of businessmen which included Frederick Hartley, backed by his father-in-law, and he was more than happy with the price he had achieved. It was a relief too; he would not need to return to Liverpool as often as he did now – twice a month – which meant days away from Marianna. He missed her. He had been without her for nineteen years, now every minute with her was precious.

As a boy growing up at Coldbarrow, despite his imprisonment there – for what else could it be called – he had never lost hope. He hoped he would leave one day, with her, and he had fed that hope with his own endeavours, saving, or stealing rather, the money he made from selling at the weekly market in the nearby town the extra eggs and the rabbits he took from the snares to fund his escape. Later, his success as a businessman in America, achieved through his own doggedness and determination, which filled the void after he lost her, made him content. He had everything he needed to be comfortable; his lovely home, Meadowside; he looked after Lizzie and her children; he knew other women. He was content with what he had achieved despite the loss of Marianna.

He had, too, a contented pride in himself, in the way he lived his life, the way he conducted himself. He was satisfied with his lot and had tried not to dwell on mourning the loss of her, although he never held out any hope of finding a woman to match her. Marianna. Just thinking of her brought a smile to his face. He had always loved her, and he had often thought about her over the years they were apart and could still not quite believe, even after all this time, that they had found each other again. He never loved another woman as he had loved her. He did not know, until she came back to him, what it was that he lacked in his life. Happiness. He had known it when they were young, but then it had seemed a normal part of life, something achieved by two people who loved each other unconditionally. Now he was older, he understood the depth of their love for each other; love tested by daily life, love tested by tragedy, and he understood love in all its ways. She was his lover and closest friend. She made him complete as a man. He was a happy man. He could not wait to get back to Longridge.

The mare still limped. He slid from the saddle and picked up her rear offside leg and indeed the shoe was gone. He muttered an expletive as lightning flickered in the west. Then drops of rain spattered the ground and there was a distant rumble of thunder. They were still three miles from home. The ground was soft, so he remounted and clicked his tongue. He would trot her to the road and then dismount. He pulled his hat low over his forehead and pulled his coat lapels round his throat. He was not dressed for a storm which, as the minutes passed, came closer and the rain began to fall in sheets, soaking him to the skin, and he began to feel very cold.

He arrived home an hour later having given the horse to David's stable lad to take care of. Lizzie, who had been out all morning at a meeting of the Stillingford Ladies' Charity Circle, met him in the hallway and took one look at him.

"Joan." She called for the maid. "I'll tell Joan to fill a bath and you get out of those soaked clothes immediately. You'll catch your death."

William came down to the sitting room half an hour later, warmed and dry, where Lizzie had a hot toddy waiting for him. The sky outside the windows was still black. The thunder rolled in the distance as it made its way eastwards. The lamps were lit to dispel the gloom and the fire blazed in the grate.

"Thank you, Lizzie," he said, as she offered him the glass. "Apart from the soaking, I enjoyed the ride until she threw a shoe. David will be pleased with her. She's a good horse. How was your meeting? Did you resolve your disagreement with Miss Scarborough?"

"Yes. Clarissa conceded finally that the stained-glass window in the church would be more suited to the position I suggested, and the vicar agreed with me."

William smiled. His sister could be quite determined when she set her heart on something.

"She admitted she should've been more gracious as you'd made such a generous donation to the commissionin' of it. And your business in Liverpool?"

"It went well. All over with, thank goodness. I had luncheon with Will. He managed to escape from the office for an hour."

"He doesn't see Miss Miller anymore, I believe. Alice told me."

"No, much to Marianna's relief. She did not think them suited at all. But he is seeing Miss Lambert. Did Alice tell you that?"

"No. Does she know or is it a secret?"

"Best not say anything in case it is. We met her family after our holiday in Westport, so it must be serious. Owt to eat, lass? I'm clemmed."

She smiled at his choice of words: echoes from their impoverished past in the mill town. She got up to go and arrange something for him and, in passing, kissed the top of his head.

"We've come a long way since Mossbrook, haven't we, William?"

William woke in the night, sweating and feverish; his throat was raw and it was painful to swallow. He tossed and turned, unable to get back to sleep. He was glad when the light filtered through the curtains and he could get up, but he felt weak and unsteady on his feet. He wondered if it was the result of his soaking the day before. He washed and dressed slowly. He was due to go home today, and he was determined to do so. He glanced in the mirror and saw his cheeks were flushed. Lizzie would make a fuss and insist he stay, but he wanted to get home to Marianna and Savannah. He made his way downstairs, deposited his bag by the front door and went to the morning room. He poured himself some coffee and tried to drink it. His cab would arrive at nine to take him to the station. Lizzie was up and he could hear her speaking to the housekeeper in the sitting room as they discussed the menus for the following week. The empty plates on the table told him Robert had already left for work. Beth appeared in the doorway, holding her daughter, Millicent, by the hand.

"Good morning, Uncle William."

"Good morning to you both," he replied as cheerfully as he could muster.

"Are you unwell?" Beth enquired, noting the pinkness of his face.

He detected the concern in her voice and was relieved to see the cab approaching along the drive so he could deflect her question.

"Time to go. Will you give your Uncle William a kiss, Milly?" Millicent ducked behind her mother's skirts.

"Never mind," said William, laughing. "Take care, Beth. Regards to Robert." He went out into the hall. "My cab's here, Lizzie. I'll see you soon."

He did not want to wait for her, picked up his bag and hurried outside. She would see the state he was in and delay him by telling him all the reasons why he should wait a few days until he was feeling better. She appeared on the steps as he settled back into his seat and waved to him. He did not remember much of the train journey home as he slept a while, vaguely remembered changing trains, and dozed off again. The carriage was waiting for him at Newbridge. Andrew, alarmed by his appearance, asked him if he was unwell as he took his bag.

"A chill, Andrew. Just get me home as quick as you can. I need my bed."

The carriage came to a halt at the front door and Andrew helped him down, otherwise he feared he might have fallen. He was extremely hot; his cheeks burning, beads of sweat dripping down his face, and his head throbbed. Savannah rushed out to meet him and threw herself into his arms; he almost fell over. Badger was yapping excitedly, and the sharp, piercing sounds made him wince. He had forgotten the Greenwood children had come to stay and they stood on the steps next to Marianna, who took one look at him.

"Savannah, children, go inside. Savannah, tell Badger to stop making that racket."

She shooed them inside and she and Andrew took William by the arms and guided him through the front door.

"He's no' well, ma'am," said Andrew, placing William's bag on the hall floor. "Will I help you with him to his bed?"

After Andrew left William sitting on the edge of the bed, Marianna began to undress him. His shirt was soaked with sweat, and he shivered. She pulled aside the blankets and he collapsed backwards. She lifted his legs, tried to make him comfortable and covered him, saying, "I shall be back in a minute."

William groaned and shut his eyes and drifted off into a fitful sleep. He did not hear her return or feel her wipe his face with a cooling cloth, moisten his lips, or see the concern etched on her face.

The Greenwoods arrived mid-afternoon the next day to collect their children. After politely enquiring about the trip and hearing how much they had enjoyed themselves, Marianna took Richard to one side and asked him to look at William, explaining he had got soaked two days before and was now feverish. William was huddled under the blankets, bright eyed, flushed and shivering. Richard placed a hand on his forehead and took his pulse.

"I do not think you are unwell as a result of the soaking, William, although it has not helped. I am certain you have picked up an infection from somewhere. Stay in bed. Plenty of fluids. A little light food," he ordered. "If there is no improvement by tomorrow, send for me, Marianna. Now we will take our children and leave you in peace."

Richard Greenwood was sent for the next day. William was worse. Savannah was told she could not visit her father as he was too poorly, and Marianna knew the slightest sound set his nerves on edge. He had started to cough, an irritating cough that caused him pain in his throat and chest. Richard took his temperature, felt the swollen glands in his neck, examined the inflamed throat, listened to his chest, diagnosed tonsillitis and bronchitis and recommended soothing honey drinks and further bed rest. He asked Marianna if she wanted him to arrange for a nurse, but she said she wished to care for him herself.

The new school term began. Marianna breakfasted with Savannah and then, when she had left for school, sat with William, quietly doing her embroidery, letting him sleep, sleep broken by fits of coughing that racked his body and, when he was awake, talking to him softly and stroking his hand, offering sips of water, trying to coax him to take the broths and jellies Ada made for him, bathing him, lying next to him to grab some moments of sleep whilst he slept. When she left the room, Badger was there, lying outside the door, whining softly.

"Marianna," he said as she finished washing him one morning, "you know how much I love you, don't you?"

"And as much as you love me, I love you more," she said, leaning forward to kiss him.

"I'm frightened, my darling." He grabbed her hand and gripped it tightly.

"Please, William. I am here to care for you. You will get better. You must get better."

"I remember Daniel. The doctor who died after the shipwreck. He drowned in the fluid in his lungs. I see the same symptoms in me. I'm struggling at times to breathe, Marianna."

"No, William. It is bronchitis," said Marianna, alarmed by his words as though he was not going to fight to get better because he thought it pointless.

"Promise me. Promise me that you'll be brave and carry out the plans for the estate. We've done so much already, Marianna, and it will work."

"But you will get better, William, and we shall do it together."

His head fell back onto the pillow, and he whispered, "Be brave, Marianna. Do it for me, darling."

Richard came every day, and, on Friday evening, there was a knock on the bedroom door and Richard came in. "Sarah said to come straight up."

He saw the distress on Marianna's face. He examined William, who was propped up on pillows as he found it more comfortable, and, despite his reassuring smile at the patient, Marianna saw the shadow of concern cross his face as he listened to William's chest, but he did not say anything, and she feared to ask what he thought. She accompanied him down the stairs.

"Why don't I take Savannah home with me for a day or so and you can look after William without worrying about her. Ellen asked me to invite her."

"That is kind of you, Richard. I appreciate it. She's wandering around like a lost soul when she comes home from school. She misses William's company. Do you mind waiting while I pack some things for her?"

Savannah took her mother's hand as they went into the bedroom. Her father seemed to have shrunk in size. He was almost disappearing into the mountain of pillows that supported his frail body. His drawn face was mottled with fever. She clutched her mother's hand more tightly, a little frightened at the sight of him.

"He is sleeping, Mama."

"It's all right. Go to him and tell him your news."

Savannah let go of her mother's hand and crept towards the bed and whispered, "Papa?"

William's eyes flickered and opened, and a wan smile appeared on his pale lips as she bent to hug him gently.

"I am going to stay with Jack, and Mrs Greenwood said Badger can stay too."

"That's kind of her," croaked William. "You'll be a good girl?"

"Of course, Papa. Will I see you when I get back?"

"Indeed, you will. Now give me a kiss, my little Mouse, and give Badger a pat from me."

She kissed his hot, flushed cheek and, unsure what to do, turned to her mother, who beckoned to her.

"Dr Greenwood is waiting, Savannah."

On the landing, Savannah threw herself into her mother's arms. "Is Papa going to die, Mama?"

"No! No! But he is very poorly. We must pray for him to get better as soon as possible so we can have him as he was before. Our darling William."

The following morning, Marianna was looking at some correspondence in the study. William had become very agitated and asked her to check all the papers regarding the sale of the business had arrived from his solicitor in Liverpool. There was a knock on the door.

"Come in."

It was Sarah. "Ma'am, the dog is here."

Marianna was confused and raised her eyebrows. "Dog?"

"Miss Savannah's dog, Badger, ma'am."

At that moment, she heard his shrill yap and hurried past Sarah to the hall. Badger was lying by the front door, lifted his head at the sound of her footsteps and ran towards her, jumping up at her and barking, short, demanding barks, and then running to the door.

"He were scratchin' and barkin' outside the door, ma'am. I heard him as I were passin' and let him in," said Sarah.

"He has run away from the Greenwoods," said Marianna as she bent down to pick him up in the hope of quietening his barks, which she was sure could be heard upstairs and would disturb William. But he wriggled so much she had to put him down. He ran to the door, pawing at it and whining and then turning to her to bark, a short, sharp, insistent bark. Marianna was perplexed.

She did not understand his behaviour. He was trying to tell her something. She opened the door and Badger raced away down the road and stopped to see her hesitating on the steps, so he barked and ran towards her before turning again to run off, stopping to see if she was coming and barking to urge her on. Marianna lifted her skirts and began to run as he bounded away down the road. He stopped now and again to check if she was still behind him. He was making for the chapel. He did not wait for her to catch him up and open the gate into the burial ground but scrabbled under a gap in the stone wall and disappeared in the long grasses surrounding the gravestones. She heard his yelp coming from the direction of the porch.

Marianna found Savannah on her knees in the porch, hunched over, her face in her hands, rocking backwards and forwards. Badger was lying, panting, beside her.

"Savannah," she said softly as she struggled to regain her breath.

Savannah looked up in surprise at her mother's voice; her face was wet with tears. She got up and rushed to her outstretched arms, crying, "I came to pray for Papa. But I could not open the door and now, because I have not asked God to save him, he is going to die."

"No, my darling child. Why would you think such a thing?" She hugged Savannah close.

"I heard Dr and Mrs Greenwood talking," she sobbed. "I heard Dr Greenwood say Papa was very ill. You said we must pray to God, so I came."

"Did you tell them you were coming here?" Marianna asked, although she already knew the answer. The Greenwoods would not have let her come alone. They would be wondering where on earth she had got to.

"I couldn't open the door, Mama."

"It is very stiff and heavy. Would you like to go in and say a prayer for Papa?"

Marianna turned the heavy iron ring which opened the door and gave it a shove. It creaked on its hinges and scraped over the stone flags. The interior smelt musty, unventilated and damp.

Cobwebs draped from the rafters and grimy windows and dead flies littered the window ledges. The bell her grandfather had taken down for some reason lay shrouded in dust on the floor behind the door. She had not been in the chapel since her father died. His coffin had lain there overnight before being taken to Newbridge church, as her mother had insisted on a Christian service and a funeral cortège processing through the streets of Newbridge; whether that was in accordance with Henry Hamilton's wishes, no one knew. He had been brought back for the interment next to his ancestors. The building was as simple inside as out, unadorned, apart from a few pews and the stained-glass window above a stone altar. The gold chalice, candlesticks, paten and cross were locked up in the safe in the study.

Marianna and Savannah knelt together in the front pew and bowed their heads, silently putting into words their hopes and fears: Savannah's hopes her darling papa would get better; Marianna's fears he would not. This God she sought in times of trouble who found, each time she was so happy, a way to punish her. And this was the worst punishment.

As they came back up the road to the front of the house, Marianna saw Richard's gig and the door opened. Richard came hurrying towards them. Badger bounded forward to greet him. "Thank God," he said. "I came as soon as we were aware she was missing."

"I am sorry, Richard, that she has caused you to worry. She was at the chapel. That little dog," she said, nodding towards Badger, "came to tell me."

William deteriorated further over the next few days and Marianna's anxiety threatened to overwhelm her. She sent a telegram to Will, urging him to come home immediately. She needed him. William's temperature fluctuated alarmingly, he was short of breath, his lips tinged with blue, the pain in his chest was sharper and more painful and he was coughing up phlegm. He struggled to eat, and the weight seemed to be dropping from him. Richard came again. As he examined him, noting the racing pulse and tachycardia, William sat up suddenly and coughed out a thick yellow-green phlegm, and Marianna saw the concerned look of alarm on the doctor's face. There was blood in his sputum.

Richard took her to one side to show her.

"I am sorry, Marianna, but this is serious. It is pneumonia and I fear the worst."

"Is there nothing you can do?" she whispered, unable to conceal her anguish.

"No, I fear not. We do not have the drugs to cure this infection spreading through his lungs which weakens him daily. Some would try bloodletting, but I do not subscribe to it. He is weak enough and I fear it would be a waste of time." He took a moment to compose himself. "I must warn you to prepare yourself. William is dying, Marianna. I am so sorry."

It was no use; with patients he was able to disconnect his feelings and remain professional, but William was his friend. He could not keep the emotion from his voice as he gulped and blinked away the tears. "There is nothing I can do. As a doctor, I feel so helpless and useless. As a friend, I feel despair. Perhaps Savannah should come and say goodbye."

Savannah picked up Badger, who had waited for her outside the bedroom door, and buried her face in his fur. He twisted his head to lick away the warm, salty tears that flowed unchecked. She saw her papa was very ill; he barely acknowledged her, and she held his hand for a long time, unwilling to leave him until Marianna guided her away. She thought she understood what her mama was telling her, but it did not seem possible. Tomorrow he would be better, they would go out riding, tell each other stories and laugh, she would climb onto his lap for a cuddle, and he would tickle her, and she would smell his cologne and feel the roughness of his cheek when he kissed her.

Surely, it would be so? Badger wriggled in her arms, so she put him down. The grandfather clock in the hallway below chimed.

"Time for tea, Badger."

The little dog pricked his ears, wagged his tail and led the way downstairs to the kitchen. Ada was stirring a pot of something on the cooker. She had already chopped up some meat for Badger and his bowl was on the table. Savannah put it down on the floor for him and he sat, watching her carefully for the signal that told him he could eat. She waved her hand at him, and he leapt forward to tuck in. Savannah stumbled backwards, her chest heaving with sobs and felt Ada's arms go round her. She was led to the chair by the hearth and lifted onto Ada's lap.

"Come, come, little pumpkin. Come, come."

Marianna undressed and climbed into bed beside William and kissed him gently, and then snuggled as close as she could and lay her arm across his chest. She thought he was sleeping.

"I love you so much," he whispered and reached for her hand. "These last years with you I have been so happy. I know why I have lived my life. For you…" His eyelids fluttered and he soon drifted away to sleep. His breath rattled in his chest, and he grunted as he tried to snatch a gasp of air. His once healthy, vigorous body was now thin and wasted. He had vomited twice that day and looked up at her as she held the bowl to his lips. His face was grey and gaunt. His beautiful, dark, gentle eyes were dulled and filled with fear. He sank back onto the pillows, exhausted by the effort and reached for her hand and pulled her with what strength he had towards him and whispered, "I love you. Till all the seas." She had turned away, his words of farewell, seven arrows, each stabbing, unforgiving arrow piercing her heart, her being. She turned back to him. He was watching her and raised his hand feebly to touch her face. A tear rolled down his cheek. She could not bear it. She could not bear it. But she smiled at him.

"I love you too. More than I can say."

"Kiss me," he wheezed. "And then lie with me. I want to feel you next to me."

The moon lit up the room. The curtains had been left undrawn and the shaft of pale moonlight stretched across the floor. Something had woken her. She heard the haunting cry of an owl in the wood drifting across the lawn. She lay for a moment; her arm was stiff, and she moved it tentatively from William's chest. And then she knew. He was dead. He was gone. Too soon. Too soon. His breathing, difficult and laboured, was no more. His silence had woken her. She began to cry, soft tears. Tears of relief he suffered no more. Tears of gratitude that she had known this man at all. Tears of love for him and everything he meant to her. Tears for the son and daughter he had given her. Tears of love. Tears for all the love, freely given and received. That was his legacy: his undying love for her must live on in their children.

"My beautiful man," she whispered, as she leant over to kiss him. "My beautiful, beautiful man."

NINE

The day she buried him the wind blew the spitting rain into their faces. His coffin was borne on a wagon dressed in flowers to the burial ground, where his grave had been deeply dug to leave room for her when her time came. Will, Richard Greenwood, nephew George and Andrew had lowered him into the ground. Will and Richard had said a few words, eulogies from a son and a friend about what he had meant to them all, and she tried to read Rosetti's poem *Remember*, but could not finish it, and Ellen had taken the paper from her hands to read it for her. The simple service passed in a blur, voices murmuring, hands squeezing hers, Savannah sobbing and clinging to her so tightly she could barely walk, the scent of flowers heavy in the sodden air, throwing a clod of muddy earth onto his coffin as her knees buckled under her and kind arms reached out to take her as the rain began to fall in sheets.

"Papa! Papa! Papa!"

The wailing pierced the stillness of the night and dragged Marianna from a fitful sleep. She pulled on her robe and rushed from her room. A door opened.

"Go back to bed, Will. I'll see to it." She glanced across the landing, relieved to see no one else appeared to have been disturbed.

Savannah, a silhouette in the darkness, was standing on her bed, the blankets tossed aside, her fists clenched at her sides, sobbing uncontrollably. Badger sat at her feet, looking up at her, quivering at the pain in her cries.

"Darling," whispered Marianna, unsure if her daughter was awake or in the middle of a night terror. Approaching the bed cautiously, saying again in a soft voice, "Darling, it's Mama," she reached up and pulled her daughter gently down to sit beside her on the bed and folded her in her arms. "Hush, hush, my darling."

"Where's Papa? I want my papa."

"I know, sweetheart. I want him too. But it cannot be. Do you understand, Savannah? Papa is not here anymore."

"I want my papa. I want my papa."

Marianna wept, the tears falling silently as her child shook in her arms. She did not know how long they sat, nor how long it took for Savannah to grow quiet. But that night she took Savannah to share her bed and held her daughter until sleep finally came, and Badger watched over them from the foot of the bed.

There were nights when Savannah slept in her mother's bed. There were nights when, encouraged by Marianna to sleep in her own bed, she woke screaming for her father. There were nights when Marianna woke to find Savannah had crept into her bed and brought Badger with her. There were days when she refused to go to school. It was Ben Kerr who came up to the house and asked to talk to her and said he would look after her. There were days when she refused to eat. It was Ada who took her down to the kitchen and they would make something together and Savannah would be tempted to eat their efforts. Jack came with his father and tried to engage her in games of chess, but she could not concentrate. The first time Marianna heard her daughter laugh again was down to Badger.

Richard had called during his rounds to check on Marianna, who was not sleeping well. He had left pictures drawn by Maddy and Izzy and a bag of carrots and apples for the ponies from Jack, which were left on a chair in the hall. His children were confined to the house as Izzy was unwell with a temperature and sore throat that he thought might be contagious. Marianna was in the study with Ada, their first meeting since William's death to discuss household business, and she had left Savannah in her sitting room with a piece of tapestry to begin work on a sampler. But Savannah soon lost interest trying to form regular cross-stitches and sank back against the cushions, the sewing discarded, and shut her eyes.

"Mama! Mama!"

The cry brought Marianna and Ada hurrying across the hall to find Savannah standing on the sofa. When she saw the two women framed in the doorway, their faces betraying their alarm, she burst out laughing and pointed.

"Look what he's done! Just look what he's done!"

They ventured into the room to see. Badger, tired of being ignored by his mistress, had been on a scavenging mission. Displayed in a neat line on the rug in front of the sofa were his lead, a ball of wool that Ada recognised, a ribbon, a glove that Marianna recognised, a rag doll, a mop head, two apples and a carrot incised with teeth marks. The little dog sat proudly on his haunches, tail thumping, eyes gleaming with mischief.

In the afternoon, Badger, followed by Marianna walking hand in hand with Savannah, who was clutching the bag of apples and carrots, led the way down to the stables. The first visit. The first painful visit. To see the horses without William.

TEN

Savannah waved furiously at the departing train. Marianna took her hand.

"Will can't see you, Savannah. There is too much smoke."

He caught his breath. The beautiful woman, dressed in black, next to the child also dressed in black, stood on the opposite platform, revealed to him as the last carriage moved away. She coughed and flapped at the smoke swirling round her and the child and glanced momentarily across at him. Then, they were gone, lost in the swirling mist. He wasted no time and set off to the stairs on his side of the track, pushing past passengers who had just disembarked from the northbound train, and rushed to the bridge which crossed the tracks to the station exit. She was walking briskly, the child by her side, hand in hand, making for the street which led down to the centre of Melchester. He hastened his pace to cut her off at the top of the street, and then stopped. What was he doing? He was not even sure it was her. But then she was coming towards him, saying something to the girl. It was her. No doubt at all. Even after thirty years he knew it was her. Beautiful. Elegant… Dressed in black. Why? Perhaps he should not intrude. He turned away slightly and saw from the corner of his eye that she had seen him and stopped. He raised his hat and smiled. The spark of recognition crossed her face. Tall and distinguished. The handsome face, now creased with deep lines round the mouth; the grey eyes that crinkled when he smiled; the hair, long to the collar, fair and now tinged with white.

"Mr Robson," she said, nodding her head in greeting. "It is you? I am not mistaken?"

"Indeed, it is, Miss Hamilton." He was flattered that she had not forgotten him.

"Miss Hamilton?" said Savannah, intrigued. "I am Miss—"

Marianna cut her off. "My daughter, Savannah."

"How do you do," said Cuthbert Robson, offering Savannah his hand, which she shook and then stared hard at her mother, waiting for an explanation. *She is so like her mother*, he thought. *A real beauty.*

"Mr Robson is an old friend. If you will excuse us, Mr Robson, but I promised to take Savannah shopping and for tea before we caught our train home."

"Home?" he asked.

"Longridge Hall."

"Of course."

"I believe you no longer live on the Loop Hall estate."

He wondered how she knew. She saw his confusion.

"My late husband went to buy a stallion there."

That would explain the mourning dress. "I am sorry for your loss."

She nodded at his condolences. "Where do you live now, Mr Robson, if I may ask?"

"Denton, a small village not far from town. I have my own farm now, Moss End. I was just seeing Eleanor onto the train. You remember my daughter?"

"I do."

"She is a teacher at the school she went to in Castleton."

"Well, we shall not detain you further, Mr Robson. Savannah is impatient to buy a present for her dog."

Marianna held out her hand. Robson took it and bent to kiss it, his eyes raised to her, and held it for a moment longer than he should, staring deeply into her eyes, her sad, shadow-rimmed eyes, looking for something. What exactly? This woman he had loved so passionately and wanted to marry. This beautiful woman, still beautiful despite her loss, who had haunted him for years. She smiled kindly at him. Then she turned, took her daughter's hand and walked away.

Savannah had had enough. She and Jack had taken tea with her mother and afterwards he had insisted she spend more time trying to understand decimal points and why it was important to put them in the right place. He had explained it several times and it was still as dull and uninteresting as it was fifteen minutes ago. She admired his patience, but she was itching to get outside. She told him she had something to show him.

They slipped out of the study door and crossed the lawns, making for the gate into the woods. Ezra was mowing the grass and stopped to wave to them. The path down the hillside was steep and, about halfway down, Savannah pushed her way through the nettles and brambles to a small clearing, and Jack followed.

"Badger found it," she explained. "He stopped the other day and started sniffing like this." She held her nose in the air to imitate the dog's excitement before he disappeared into the undergrowth and she, naturally, with complete disregard for her dress which snagged on the brambles, followed him. "It's a badger's sett. See! Badger found a badger." She chuckled.

A pile of freshly dug earth was scooped onto the mound in front of a hole under the roots of an ancient beech tree.

"We won't see them," she explained. "Thomas told me they only come out at night, and I have to ask Mama if he can take me out one night to watch for them. Perhaps you could come too."

"I'd like that."

They sat down on a tussock of grass. The sunlight drifted down in glimmering shafts through the thinning canopy, a light breeze rustled the leaves already on the turn, pigeons cooed above their heads. Two small beings, hidden in a glade, rained on by sunbeams. Just the two of them. The older one in thrall to the younger one – the puppet master – ignorant still of all the feminine wiles, yet fully aware of the hold she had over him. The two of them, innocent, so close, the best of friends.

Jack said, "I go away soon. Next week."

He had missed the start of term at his new school as he and his sisters had contracted chicken pox.

"I know," said Savannah, "and I shall be so very sad. You are my best friend in the world… after Badger," she added.

"Your ribbon is loose," he said, tying it for her. "You're always losing ribbons. Will you write to me, Savannah?"

"Of course. You must write to me too and tell me what your school is like and what you get up to. I cannot imagine what you will do all day. There are only so many times tables and spelling lists a child can bear."

"There will be sports, like cricket and rugby, to learn, and there will be outings. So I've been told."

"Are you scared, Jack? I would be scared to leave Mama and Badger."

"I am. But don't breathe a word. I have to be brave about it and not upset Mama. I am scared because I'm so happy at home, and I worry I will not like it very much. And as I'm late going, everyone will have made friends already."

"Then you must come home. I cannot bear to think you will be sad."

"You must write to me and cheer me up. I shall miss you, Savannah." He grabbed her hand and made her jump. His eyes were sad.

"Are you making eyes at me, Jack?" she asked.

"Pardon?"

"Boys make eyes at girls when they love them."

Plucking up the courage to declare himself, Jack blurted out, "I do love you, Savannah. Do you love me?"

"You know I do, second best after Badger." She corrected herself. "Third best, I forgot Mama." She paused. She had been trying so hard for the last week to be brave. Her darling papa. Did he count? She blinked hard to drive away the tears. Of course he did. "Actually, seventh best. I forgot Will, Moth and Ladybird."

"Stop teasing, Savannah. I mean proper love. Not the love between friends, but like the love between grown-ups, between men and women." Leaning towards her, he kissed her gingerly on the lips. "Will you marry me? I want to look after you now your papa—"

"Marry you?" she interrupted, wiping her mouth on her sleeve. "I am not yet ten years old. Do I want to get married at ten years old? I think not."

"Will you promise to wait for me then, until I have finished school and you are older? Will you swear to me that when I ask you, you will say yes?"

"Savannah! Jack!" It was her mother, her voice carrying across the lawns to the wood.

"It's time for you to go home, Jack."

"You didn't answer me," he said, taking her hands; his were damp with sweat.

"Yes, I will marry you."

She jumped up, giggling, and kissed him on the mouth, then bounded up the path and raced across the grass to the front of the house, where Thomas was waiting with the gig to take Jack home.

"Mama! Jack and I are getting married," she panted, hands on knees as she gathered her breath. "I have kissed him, and I have accepted his proposal and—"

Jack arrived, breathing hard, to hear what she was saying and turned crimson, and in a state of extreme embarrassment, clambered as fast as he could into the gig. Marianna handed him his jacket and he mumbled his thanks, unable to meet her gaze, praying for the seat to swallow him up and for Thomas to get a move on.

"I was saying, Mama, we shall be married when Jack finishes school. Isn't that so, Jack?"

* * *

Marianna was in the study, sifting through papers and putting them into piles. The agent who collected the rents from the tenants in Newbridge and supervised repairs had called and left her with receipts, ledgers and lists of work needing to be done. Savannah was sitting to one side of the desk, Badger stretched out at her feet, doodling on the piece of paper in front of her. She was writing to Jack and illustrating her description of the new, young master who had arrived to teach them at the beginning of the school year and, in Savannah's opinion, spent too much time on arithmetic. He was exceedingly tall and thin with a face covered in pimples, which Savannah was gleefully colouring in green under his shock of ginger hair. He was terrified of the children and Savannah ran rings round him, much to the amusement of her classmates, but that had incurred an angry interview with Mr Harrison in front of her mother and an ultimatum to mend her ways. Now, she was seeking her revenge by drawing attention to Mr Ollerton's many disagreeable features. They both looked up as Will entered the room.

"I didn't know you had been out so early this morning, Mama," said Will, bending down to rub Badger's stomach.

Marianna looked at him quizzically.

"To the chapel. There are fresh flowers, daffodils, on Papa's grave."

Marianna went every week to place posies of flowers or cuttings of foliage on William's grave. Savannah would not go, even eighteen months after her darling papa's death, as it upset her too much. She could still feel the heat of his skin as she kissed him farewell and the thought of him lying cold in the ground, mouldering and being eaten by worms, as one thoughtful schoolfriend had told her, terrified her.

"They are not mine," said Marianna, looking puzzled. "I am not aware anyone else leaves flowers."

"Oh," said Will, straightening up. He peered over Savannah's shoulder. "Who on earth is that grotesque creature?"

"My teacher. And I hate him."

"Savannah!" exclaimed her mother. "You do not hate him. Hate is too strong a word to be used in such a cavalier fashion."

"Do you want to come for a quick ride out with me before luncheon, Savannah?" asked her brother.

She looked hopefully at her mother, who nodded.

Will had been home for a few days' holiday and was going back to Liverpool later that day, as he had an important social event to attend the following evening. He had been very upset he did not arrive home in time to see his father before he died. He had told his mother that although Bennet Foster had played a part in his upbringing, and they had enjoyed a close relationship, he knew there was something stronger with his father. They had, during the past eleven years, despite his initial wariness, found a connection. "I loved him, Mama," he had sobbed as he collapsed in her arms. "I loved him and never told him."

"He knew, Will," she had reassured him.

He was a wonderful support to his mother in the days following William's death and took on the responsibility of dealing with the bureaucracy, organising the funeral and contacting Lizzie, and William's former colleagues in Liverpool. Marianna had felt so detached from everything. Richard had given her a draught of something to calm her. It was just like the days when William had gone missing at Netherton which had also passed in a haze; she could not sleep or eat, and her head throbbed with the lack of food and sleep, and she felt constantly nauseous. Lizzie was inconsolable but she had nothing left to give her. What she had her daughter needed. Will came and sat with her, saying little, just holding her and letting her be and she was grateful. He understood. There had been a painful disagreement with Lizzie about the lack of a religious service, but William was not religious, and she had to do what she knew he would have wanted. Although she did not have the unshakeable faith of many, she had more faith than William, and nursed a belief in the resurrection of the soul and hoped they would be reunited one day.

The day after the funeral, Mr Birch, the family solicitor, came to read out William's will. As she listened to the wording of it, Marianna was convinced that William knew he was going to die before his time and she struggled to keep her composure. He had left Lane End Farm in Stillingford to Will to do with as he wished and had instructed Will to sell the land he owned near Manchester and Liverpool and the money to be put into trust for Savannah until she reached the age of twenty-one. Lizzie was to live at Meadowside until her death, with the same income he already provided for her, and then the house was to be sold and the proceeds divided between his nephew, George, and nieces, Meg and Beth. Everything else he owned, including Hapenny How, he left to Marianna. Before Mr Birch departed, he handed her a letter from William which she did not have the courage or peace of mind to read, and it was stored safely within the pages of her memoir.

There had been a difficult conversation with Will about how she was to manage the estate without William's support, especially with shouldering the responsibility for the innovations William had proposed, and she sensed Will's reluctance to give up his life in Liverpool so soon. He told her she was more than capable and reassured her that, at some time in the future, he would come home to take over as his grandfather had wished. Although she knew if she pressed him he would acquiesce, she could not begrudge him his desire to enjoy what he had for a few more years.

Marianna, outwardly confident and assured, had been filled with self-doubts since William died, and struggled to come to terms with losing him. At Coldbarrow, he had proved himself hardworking and reliable and the Mislets came to depend on him. To her, as a young girl, he seemed so sure of himself, mature, confident and determined to leave to find his family, that he made her feel safe as well as loved, and she ran away with him because she trusted him implicitly to care for her. And he had. When plagued with dark thoughts, he comforted her. Who would do that now? Who could she ask for advice knowing that it was in her interests? Who could she trust? Who could she confide in? And Savannah. Who was there to share the raising of their daughter? And there was gossip. Ellen had overheard some in their social circle criticising her behaviour as unseemly in a woman in deep mourning. She knew who the main culprit would be – Dora Cavendish, wife of the accountant in Newbridge who had taken offence when Marianna had taken her business to Melchester to be attended to by the firm who managed her father's affairs. Mrs Cavendish and her cronies did not approve of her running the estate when William was alive: it was not a woman's place to be involved in men's work. But what did they expect her to do now?

She had an estate to oversee. People depended on her for their livelihood. She could not shut herself away. Sometimes, she felt lost and empty and often she did hide herself away as her grief overwhelmed her. William was irreplaceable. William was her lover, her confidant and her best friend.

For the first time in her life, she felt uneasy when she went to bed; so much so, she had taken to rising in the dark hours, wakened by an imaginary creak of the floorboards, probably the shriek of a fox; or the sound of heavy breathing, probably the soughing of the trees in the wind, and went downstairs to check the doors were locked, berating herself for being silly. Sometimes she wished that she had been more forceful with Will and insisted he came home to Longridge. But she did not bully her children as her mother had done. She despaired at her own weakness and feebleness of character. Now, as she waited for her children to return from their ride, Marianna was relieved she had at last reached one decision: a decision regarding the horses and she would talk to Will after luncheon. The letter was in her hand.

Will settled beside his mother on the sofa in her sitting room: he had grown into a fine young man and, although he had inherited William's looks and some aspects of his character, she knew Bennet Foster had played his part in helping to raise a mature and kind man. She had always been close to her son, and she had always been honest with him and, now William was gone, she would have to turn to him for his advice and counsel. Marianna handed him the letter and he read it quickly and passed it back to her.

"Who is he?"

Indeed, who is he? she thought. The handsome widower whose wife suffered low spirits after the death of a child, constantly feared the loss of her second and killed herself. The handsome widower she had relied on to satisfy her longing for physical love after William's disappearance. The handsome widower who had appeared at Melchester Station like a ghost from the past.

"He knew you when you were a baby. He was the steward at Loop Hall. I wrote to him for advice as I wish to sell the horses, and he knows a lot about horses. I know nothing of breeding, and it is an expensive business."

"What about Andrew?"

"Mr Robson is making enquiries about finding him another position. It is the least I can do as he has been a loyal servant. Your father thought very highly of him. I will not speak to Andrew until I have some certain news. I do not want to worry him."

"And Thomas?"

"I will keep him on. I still need a carriage and Savannah will want to keep her ponies. If there is a horse you wish to keep for riding out when you are here, then we shall do so. Thomas wants to get married and has already asked if he could move into one of the cottages. I have agreed."

"Robson asks when he can visit."

"Yes, he wants to meet Andrew and get some more information about the horses and their pedigree. Questions I cannot answer."

"I think it is a sensible decision, Mama. You have enough to care for with the house, the farms and the tenants."

"Thank you, Will. The fact you agree with my sentiments has confirmed I am making the right decision. I cannot carry on what your father started with the horses. It saddens me to think I am letting him down as it was a cherished dream of his, but I do not have the expertise. And thank you for everything you have done. You have been a great help to me." She squeezed his hand. "Will you keep Lane End Farm, do you think?"

"No, Mama. I do not have the time to devote to it and farming is difficult these days. I think it will be more prudent to sell it." He paused. "And, if I may tell you a secret?"

Marianna smiled at him. She knew what he was going to say. "Miss Lambert?"

"Yes, I have asked her if she would marry me before I speak to her father. If I had some ready capital I'm sure it would sweeten my request. I was going to tell you when I had his permission. I know you like her."

"I do. She is a charming girl and from a good family. You will need to make sure she understands what she is letting herself in for in the future if you come back to Longridge. I don't think she has experience of living in the country. You must ask her to come with you next time you visit us."

ELEVEN

The room was stuffy with the smell of tobacco and perfume and the crush of so many people; the air filled with the buzz of conversations, laughter and the clinking of glasses; the music of the string quartet in the hallway disjointed and muffled by the hubbub of noise. Will weaved between the huddles of guests to join Harry, who was on his own and looking lost. They knew few people in the room and were there to represent Longthorne and Halliwell at this soirée, a charity fundraiser organised by Mrs Vernon Shepard, whose husband owned a shipping company, at their very grand house on the outskirts of Liverpool. As he pushed his way through the throng, he stood on the hem of a dress whose owner turned round in surprise and he stifled a gasp.

Time stood still for a moment, everything frozen, movement and sound, and it was just the two of them. She was stunning; fair hair and big, brown eyes framed by thick lashes, her figure voluptuous in the tight-fitting bodice of her pale blue silk dress. She swung the skirt away from him and set the world in motion again. She smiled, baring her perfect white teeth in a most disarming smile and held out her hand, saying, "That's one way to get my attention, Mr..."

He recognised the accent – American – but not from where in that vast country, despite spending some time in Boston after leaving university. Her voice was sing-song, girlish, and she was laughing at him, waving her hand for him to shake. He took it and kissed it as she squeezed his fingers. The look in her eyes was telling him something. What? She was as attracted to him as he was to her? He could hope it was so.

"Leonora Brown, Mr?"

"Will Hamilton—"

He did not finish as a husky voice sounded behind him.

"There you are, Leonora."

"Mother."

A tall, fair-haired woman with a lined face, dressed in a shimmering, low-cut, grey silk gown, which exposed the age-puckered skin of her neck and chest, rings glinting on her gloved hands, appeared at Leonora's side.

"I am looking for your uncle. I need to speak to him."

"Good evening, Mother," said Leonora, leaning towards her to kiss her cheek. "May I introduce Mr Hamilton."

She barely glanced at Will but glided past. "Ah! I see him, Leonora. Good evening, young man."

"Please forgive my mother. I shall put her rudeness down to weariness. She has been away for a few days and has been rather tired. I did not expect her to attend this. Now, you will notice, Will, that my glass is empty."

"What brings you here?" asked Will, handing her a glass of champagne he plucked from a passing waiter's tray.

"Here? Or to England?"

"Both."

"My uncle is an old friend of Vernon's. They were at the University of Oxford years ago. We are visiting England on holiday before going to France and Italy. This is our last evening in Liverpool as we go to Oxford tomorrow, as my uncle wishes to travel down memory lane."

Will was disappointed.

"You have the most beautiful eyes. The first thing I noticed about you," said Leonora and, in the next breath, asked, "Why are you here at this frightfully dull party?"

Will was non-plussed by the compliment and ignored it. "I

work for a law firm, Longthorne and Halliwell. They act for the Shepards, and my colleague and I have been sent, under orders I may add, to put in an appearance, as Mr Longthorne cannot attend and Mr Halliwell has been dead for years."

She laughed a tinkling laugh. "What do you say we creep away? There's a garden through this door."

Leonora led the way along the path between the box hedges of the parterre garden and across the lawns to a summerhouse beside a small lake, some distance from the house where the lamps were being turned on.

"Oh my!" said Leonora, sitting on a bench. "It is quite chilly out here."

"Here," said Will, removing his jacket and placing it round her shoulders before sitting next to her.

"Thank you, kind sir. I am so glad you are clean-shaven. I do not find men with beards and moustaches in the least attractive, despite the fashion for them."

Will was confused by her leading comments and whether he was supposed to read something in them. What could be more leading than her inviting him out into the garden?

Leonora finished her drink and placed the glass on the floor, opened her reticule and took out a gold cigarette case and asked him to light one for her. He had to confess he did not smoke and would not have the first idea. He had never seen a woman smoke before. She laughed, lit one herself and let him take a drag. He shook his head and spluttered, "How do you stand that?"

She laughed again, the tinkling laugh, then said, "I also prefer tall men and you are reasonably tall. Do you live in the city?"

Will got the impression she was teasing him and chose to ignore her flattery. "Yes, I share lodgings with Harry." He nodded back to the house. "My colleague."

She took his glass and placed it next to hers on the floor. She tossed the half-smoked cigarette away.

"Kiss me, Will."

"Pardon?" From flattering words, she had moved on rather swiftly to unexpected demands.

"Come on," she drawled. "We both want the same thing. I saw it in your eyes the moment we met. Let's not beat about the bush. Kiss me. I want you to kiss me."

He was glad she could not see his flustered face in the fading light. He had never encountered such a forward, plain-speaking woman in his life. He put his arm round her waist and pulled her in close and kissed her. He tasted the tobacco on her lips. She opened her mouth to him and forced her tongue into his. He kissed her, more passionately than he had ever kissed a woman before. He felt her hand go to his crotch to feel him and he stopped, sitting back in shock and embarrassment as she knew he was aroused.

"What are you doing?"

She laughed and got up, hitching the skirts of her dress, to sit astride him, and kissed him again and then, she pressed his face into her bosom as she moved on him and he had to push her away to spare himself the inevitable, the worst embarrassment.

"You will come to Oxford," she said, sliding off him, completely unabashed by what had taken place.

"What? When?"

"We shall be there for a week. We are staying at the Randolph. I like you. You interest me. I shall not know anyone in Oxford. I shall be *so* bored. And I can show you some fun. Come to me as soon as you can."

"I know Oxford," Will said, as though he was agreeing to her command. "I studied there."

"Excellent. You know it well enough to find some secret places. You will come as I have bid you."

He thought it a ridiculous idea, as Oxford was nearly two hundred miles away, and he wondered if she had had too much to drink and was teasing him again, but she tapped the side of her nose and began to issue instructions as she plotted their rendezvous.

"Shall we go back in?" she asked, handing him his jacket. "I'm shivering still. You didn't warm me up as I had hoped, and I am sure we will have been missed."

He followed her back to the house, not quite understanding what had passed between them and what he had let himself in for.

The next morning, Will, who had hardly slept the previous night as he debated the idea of going to work or taking up Leonora Brown's blatant offer, lied to James Longthorne and said his mother was unwell and he needed a few days' leave. James Longthorne was not at all pleased and commented he had just returned from visiting his mother but relented as he had no cause to doubt him.

Will settled into his seat on the train. He struggled to recognise himself in this rash behaviour which was totally out of character. His friends, who were not connected with the legal profession, regarded him as conservative in his ways, but he had his reputation, and his firm's, to consider. Although he went drinking and chasing women with them, he never overstepped the mark. He never drank too much, and he was the one they relied on to see them home safely when they had overindulged. He never saw the point of gambling away his jealously guarded income, as he had plans for it. He never visited the brothels in the city with them. He preferred to satisfy his urges with a better class of woman, and he never had any problems finding a willing lover as he knew he was handsome and attractive. His employers considered him a safe pair of hands; he was steady and thorough and methodical in his work and charming with clients. His mother! He shut his eyes and tried to put her out of his mind. He knew what she would think. He felt uncomfortable about lying to Mr Longthorne, a man he respected, and by the time the train arrived at the next station, he had given himself a good talking-to and rose from his seat to catch the return train to Liverpool.

But the image of Leonora Brown, the effect she had had on him that he could not quite fathom, the fact she had taken control and ordered him to come to her – how could he resist? She intrigued him. She excited him. He had never before met a woman like her. Someone for him to taste and enjoy before settling down to marriage. He sat down to resume his journey and, by the time he reached Oxford, he was not regretting his decision at all. He knew why he had made it and why he was meeting Leonora. He booked himself into a boarding house near the railway station and went immediately to the Randolph, where he left a note for her at the reception desk to say he had arrived and to meet him at three o'clock at the tearoom in the street round the corner.

Leonora was on time and floated into the room, dressed in a low-cut, green silk dress with a tight-fitting bodice that pushed up her full breasts into half-moons. Modest she was not, and the hum of conversations ceased, and eyes swivelled to watch her as she walked slowly towards his table, swinging her hips from side to side, well aware of the effect she was having. Will kissed her hand and held out her seat for her, struggling to think of something to say, as he was filled with an uncontrollable urge to ravish her there and then. He ordered tea and they made small talk until the waitress returned, each knowing what the other wanted as they exchanged lingering glances. She rubbed her foot up and down his leg under the table and he tried, as a gentleman, to avert his gaze from her magnificent décolletage which swelled enticingly with her every considered breath.

Leonora took a couple of sips of tea before saying what he had been summoning up the courage to say himself. "Enough of this. Where are we going?"

She was astonishing. *Is this how American women behaved?* Will asked himself. *So forward? So direct? Or just American women on holiday in a foreign land? Thank God she has taken the initiative*, he thought. He was struggling with the etiquette of the situation, how to broach the subject of what was so obvious to them both. He was captivated by her, but more than that, he was very, very attracted to her and wanted her desperately.

"I know," Leonora said, as innocently as she could, as she had already mapped out her planned seduction. "My room is thirty-four. Give me fifteen minutes then go directly into the hotel, straight up the stairs to the third floor and look as if you know where you are going so as not to arouse suspicion. My mother is visiting colleges or chapels or something incredibly dull with my aunt and uncle and won't be back until dinner."

Will tapped on the door. No one had batted an eyelid as he passed into the lobby and strode up the stairs. Leonora called to him to enter. She was completely naked. Her fair hair flowed loose around her shoulders. Her hands were clasped behind her, and she had turned sideways, one foot in front of the other to strike a pose. *A practised pose*, he thought, *to show off her incredible figure*. Her breasts were large, round and firm, as were her buttocks, her waist narrow, her hips curvaceous. She held out her arms to him and, kicking the door shut with his heel, he went to her, already roused by the sight of her and what she offered him. She put a finger to his lips and began to undress him and he struggled to control himself as she touched and kissed every part of him and, when he was as naked as she was, she led him to the bed and pushed him backwards before mounting him.

Will did not know where the time went or how many times she loved him. He had already suspected that Leonora Brown was no virgin. She was very skilled and very much the dominant partner and he was her willing pupil. He had never known such pleasure. When he was a student, he had taken serving wenches from the local alehouses into the back alleys of Oxford, and paid them a half-crown for their time, and they were glad to give him his pleasure and escape. He had courted and lain with women who let him do what he needed to do. A perfunctory business. Leonora did things to him he had not known were possible. She asked him to do things to her he did not know gave women so much pleasure.

When Leonora had satisfied herself, she got up to wash her intimate parts in the bathroom and left the door open, and Will watched her. She was as he imagined a courtesan to be at the court of kings. She was completely unembarrassed and sure of her charms; so much so, he could not resist her and went to her and pulled her back to the bed. His unquenchable desire and stamina seemed to impress her and, when he had finished, she said, as he lay panting and sweating on top of her, "You must come to dinner this evening with my mother."

Will was aghast, raised his head and stared at her. "How do I explain my presence in Oxford?"

"You'll think of something." She laughed. "If you do, I shall reward you by entertaining you again. You are such a handsome fellow I am surprised you still have so much to learn, and I shall enjoy teaching you."

Will sat opposite Helena Brown in the hotel's dining room. Leonora's aunt and uncle were dining elsewhere with an old friend. Will knew his reason for being in Oxford – on business on behalf of his law firm – was a feeble one. Mrs Brown's eyes absorbed his every feature as she stared unremittingly at him, and he wished she would not. She could not be described as beautiful; her features were sharp, and her skin was loose and wrinkled, her eyes pale and hooded and her figure solid and rounded and maintained by her corsets. Will imagined Leonora had inherited her womanly figure from her mother but her looks must be from her father. Perhaps he was being unkind and Mrs Brown may once have been beautiful, her looks faded with age and sorrows in her life. Despite this, she had a presence that implied she did not suffer fools gladly.

"How long will you be in England, Mrs Brown?" asked Will, after she had described her afternoon visiting her brother's old college, and he had told her of his time in Oxford.

"For as long as my brother decides. We are his guests."

"Where are you from?"

"Leonora has not had the time to tell you? How busy you must have been."

Will's ears were burning. He reached for his drink to cover his discomfort. What were these two women? Her mother knew what she was doing?

"We are from New Jersey, Will," Leonora said, replacing her cutlery on her plate. "My late father was a congressman. My uncle has brought us to Europe as a treat. My mother is lonely at home, and I tire of keeping her entertained."

"Thank you, Leonora, for your brutal honesty, as always. So, Mr Hamilton, where do you come from?"

"Actually, Mrs Brown, it's Hamilton-Read. My family has an estate in the North, some miles north of Melchester, if you have heard of it?"

Helena Brown's jaw tightened as she clenched her fists in her lap.

"My mother runs the estate."

"Not your father?" Leonora asked. "I am intrigued."

"My father died more than a year ago."

"I am so sorry," said Leonora. "We both are, aren't we, Mother? We know what it is to lose a loved one."

Helena grimaced. She did not know how she managed to get through the rest of dinner. She found herself staring even more intently at the young man opposite, noting his good looks, his mannerisms, and she contributed rarely to the conversation. She was relieved when, finally, the meal came to an end and Will rose to bid them a good evening and offered to pay the bill.

"That is kind of you," said Helena with forced politeness, "but my brother will take care of it."

"Shall we have luncheon together tomorrow, Will?" She saw her daughter wink at Will as she proffered her hand.

"We certainly shall," he replied, bending to kiss it.

"Let me walk with you," said Helena as they went into the hotel lobby and all heads turned to watch Leonora sashay her way up the stairs to her room. "In fact," said Helena, opening the door to the reading room which she was pleased to find empty, "come in here." She went to sit in one of the alcoves next to a desk covered with crumpled editions of the day's newspapers and nodded to him to sit down. "I shall get to the point, Mr Hamilton-Read. You will leave Oxford first thing tomorrow and you will never set eyes on my daughter again."

"Is that for you to decide, Mrs Brown? Leonora seems to be a woman who knows her own mind."

"Oh, she knows her own mind, of course. She does as she pleases. I have no control over her at all. You don't think you are the first to be seduced by her?"

"I do not regard that as any of your business."

"But it is my business, young man, if you are fucking my daughter."

Will gasped in shock. He had never heard a lady use such language. He did not think refined ladies, certainly the ladies he was accustomed to, knew such language. The common girls in the alleyways did; they told him he was a good fuck to get another shilling out of him. Esme Lambert did not. Sweet, gentle Esme, who had let him fondle her breasts, lifted her skirts for him and lay quietly, trembling, and winced as he entered her. She would never use such a word. Esme, the woman with whom he had an understanding that they would marry. He felt a pang of guilt as he thought of her. But Helena Brown's crudeness had appalled him and, a little ashamed of his betrayal of Esme, he answered in kind.

"She was a good fuck. A very good fuck."

Helena smirked. "Spoken like a man. Another score on the tally sheet. Go back to where you came from and forget her."

Will did not care for Mrs Brown's tone nor being told what to do. "She has promised me a fuck tomorrow." He could not help himself.

Mrs Brown leant forward aggressively. "You will leave her alone," she hissed, the skin round her mouth puckering into creases, her hooded, pale eyes narrowing into venomous slits. "You are fucking your sister."

Will jerked back in his seat and looked at her. The wizened face full of thunder, the fists clenched in her lap. Then he laughed. Scornfully at first. Then incredulously. This was ridiculous.

"That is pathetic," he scoffed. "To warn me off by saying such a thing is beyond belief." But something in her dark, threatening eyes told him she was not lying. He felt the blood drain from his face as his skin turned a washed-out shade of grey and his head began to swim. What on earth was she saying? "Bitch!" he spat at her. "Lying bitch!" He had lost control: the foul, uncouth language.

"William Read. Businessman. Importer and exporter with an office in New York. Recently deceased. Buried in the family plot on the Longridge estate near Newbridge. I went to lay flowers on his grave the day before yesterday on behalf of the daughter he never knew about."

Will clamped his hands on his knees as his legs were now out of control and shaking violently. In his mind, he saw the bunch of fresh daffodils on his father's grave. She had been to the private family burial ground. Unobserved. Gained access on one of the paths from the main road, no doubt. She had trespassed. What had she said? His father had another daughter? He had slept with his sister? He felt sick; he could feel the recently digested meal churning in his guts and rising in his throat and he swallowed hard.

"A very handsome young man, your father. Younger than me but I like younger men. So much more entertaining. More stamina too." She cackled. "I met him in the foyer of a theatre in New York." She closed her eyes momentarily, remembering. "Twenty-six years ago. I was not interested in the play as I had other things on my mind. The seduction of your father. There he was: so handsome, smiling, a beautiful smile to melt a woman's heart, absolutely charming, with some friends from his business. I was on holiday alone. I often travelled alone. On the hunt, Mr Hamilton-Read. My husband, the congressman, too busy in Washington to pay his wife much attention. We had an affair. Extremely passionate, as I recall. Day after day for the month I was in New York." Will cringed. "I went back to my husband, unknowingly pregnant with the child he could not give me. Your father was not informed, and it did not matter as I knew I would not see him again. Your father was one of many lovers, but he was the one who gave me the gift of my daughter. When I knew that we were coming to Liverpool it was too good a chance to pass up. A chance to see him again. Curiosity? I don't know what I hoped to achieve. I made enquiries at his office to find out he had sold the business, but they told me where he lived and that he had died. I am sorry you have lost your father."

Will had heard enough. To hear this vulgar woman talking about his father disgusted him. To think his father had made love to this crude woman repulsed him. He stood up and took a moment to collect himself as his mind was whirring, the blood pounding in his ears, and he did not feel completely in control of his legs and thought he might collapse. He was not sure either he could contain himself and resist the urge to wipe the gloating look from Mrs Brown's ugly face. He had slept with his sister. His half-sister. Did the half make it better? Half as bad? He did not know at the time who she was. He could not be responsible, could he? She had seduced him. She had thrown herself at him. Why had he allowed himself to be manipulated by her? Why was he so weak? Like mother, like daughter. Leonora and her mother deserved each other. No, he was not the first she had tempted – perhaps the first on this extended tour of Europe and the bedrooms of its menfolk – and he would not be the last. He had to get away from this vile woman. If only he could get his legs to work. He breathed in deeply to calm himself. Mrs Brown was watching him with a barely concealed sneer on her face. He summoned up as much dignity as he could muster.

"I apologise for my inappropriate language, Mrs Brown. A gentleman should not speak to a lady in such a manner. However, I doubt whether you and your daughter could claim to be ladies. Good evening, Mrs Brown."

TWELVE

The clock began to strike the eleventh hour. Marianna paused at the entrance to the stable yard dominated by the centuries-old pele tower. It was an attractive, well-designed and well-kept space: a credit to her darling William. She could see Thomas, through the trees, heading for the paddock with a wheelbarrow and fork to clear away the horse muck. Some of the horses stood, faces peering inquisitively over the top of their doors, snorting, ears twitching, hooves stamping, watching her as she remembered William and the love and hard work that he had put in to realise his dream. A deep, shuddering sigh shook her, and she fought back the tears she could not shed at that moment.

She knocked on the door of the Kerrs' cottage and Catriona answered.

"Come away in, ma'am."

She led the way to the kitchen at the back of the cottage, where Andrew began to rise from his seat at the table. Marianna motioned to him to remain seated and sat down in the chair next to him. A kettle hissed on the cooker.

"Would you like a cup o' tea, ma'am?" asked Catriona.

"No, thank you. Please, Catriona, sit down. I wish to speak to both of you."

Catriona lifted the kettle from the flame, turned off the gas and glanced anxiously at her husband. Since the master's death, they had had many conversations as to what would happen, and the mistress's request the day before for a meeting, not with Andrew on his own up at the house, but together on their territory, and the words that came next, confirmed what they both had feared.

"I have made a decision regarding the stud horses. I have decided to sell them."

"But, ma'am," said Catriona. "What—"

Andrew held up his hand. "Let the mistress speak, Catriona."

"It's all right, Andrew. Your wife is concerned regarding what this will mean."

Marianna told Andrew how valued he was and how highly William regarded him. She explained that Cuthbert Robson, an old friend, someone more experienced than she was in equine matters, would be coming the following week to look over the horses and arrange their sale. Andrew fixed his eyes on his clasped hands resting on the table and nodded occasionally. Catriona, eyes glistening, stared at something beyond Marianna's head. They were good, honest, dignified people which made her task more difficult.

She told them that she had asked Mr Robson to enquire about a position for Andrew which he would discuss with him and which he was under no obligation to accept and, of course, Andrew could seek employment elsewhere if he wished. She reassured the Kerrs that they would continue to live in their cottage and Andrew would continue to receive his wage until their future was settled.

"I will not turn you out," said Marianna, "and you know that, as that is not the way we do things at Longridge."

Catriona rustled on her chair. "I love this house." She lifted her apron to her face and stifled a sob. Marianna, seeing her distress, said quickly, "As I have said, your time with us has been much appreciated and I am grateful to you for your service and loyalty. I will of course provide excellent testimonials."

Andrew nodded. "Thank you, ma'am." He got up and went to stand behind Catriona, placing his hands on her shoulders to reassure her. "It's good o' you to come and speak to us and let us know what's to happen. What about Thomas? He's to be married soon."

"He will stay on," replied Marianna. "We shall keep the carriage horses, the ponies, and, perhaps, a couple of horses for Master Will. You think Thomas will prove satisfactory? I should seek your advice before I speak to him?"

"Well." Andrew laughed. "I've taught him all he kens so it would reflect badly on me if I spoke ill o' him."

Marianna smiled. "He will manage then?"

"Indeed, ma'am. May I say, ma'am, it was a privilege to work for Mr Hamilton-Read. For you both. The master is much missed. A fine man indeed. And we've loved living here."

Catriona looked up at her husband and smiled at his gracious words. Marianna rose and shook their hands and, flouting the usual social constraints, hugged Catriona and kissed her cheek.

* * *

Cuthbert Robson settled into his seat on the train from Melchester and placed his hat on his knees. The carriage was full, and he was glad of the window seat and the view, as he disliked cramped spaces. The trees beside the railway track were in full leaf and daisies and dandelions grew in scattered clumps on the embankments. The sun appeared intermittently from behind the breaking clouds. As they passed through Keer Bank and he saw the sands and mudflats exposed by the retreating tide, he wondered what had happened to the guides he had known, who shepherded the many travellers, including him, across the bay and were no longer needed thanks to the railway. He thought of her husband, of course, who died so tragically, drowned because the coachman, who was late, had missed the guides, and ignorant of the route and not knowing where the quicksands were, had risked the lives of his passengers and could not outrun the speeding waters of the incoming tide. Her letter was in his coat pocket. It had arrived out of the blue and had unsettled him for a few days before he plucked up the courage to answer it. Since their chance encounter at Melchester Station more than a year ago, he could not get her out of his mind. She had changed little since the last time he saw her when she came to his house to tell him she was leaving to rejoin her family at Longridge. She had promised to return to him, if she failed to settle, and marry him. Whether she had failed or not he never knew, but her letter then, so brief and formal, dashed all hopes of them being together.

He had noticed the fine lines round her mouth and a hint of grey in her hair, but her eyes – the first thing he had noticed about her when he saw her at the hiring fair in Melchester all those years ago – were stunning. How he had loved her. Indeed, how they had loved each other, passionately. He had never loved a woman as much as he loved her. Yet he always knew he was second best to the dead husband. And now it would seem she was a widow again. She had remembered from their brief encounter outside Melchester Station the name of his farm and the village which surprised him, and he wondered if he should make something of it. Her letter, like the one rejecting him, was again brief and formal and straight to the point. She looked to him as a knowledgeable friend to help her as she lacked expertise in what had been her late husband's enterprise. She also asked him to find a position for her stable master, Andrew Kerr. That was it. Nothing personal apart from a correspondent's usual enquiry after the recipient's health. He had responded in the same vein: he would be delighted to help her and offered some alternative dates for a visit. Then there was her signature at the end – Marianna Hamilton-Read. What on earth did that mean?

Andrew Kerr met him at Newbridge Station. It gave him an opportunity to sound out his knowledge and experience and discover something about the set-up at Longridge.

"Where are you from originally, Mr Kerr? I detect a Scottish accent."

"The Borders, sir."

"Then I think we must be sworn enemies." Robson laughed. "I am originally from Northumberland."

Andrew laughed too. "Well, it was a long time ago since our ancestors, the Reivers, fought each other. I think we can forgive each other after all these years."

"Tell me about the horses."

"We have one stallion, a magnificent animal," said Andrew. "Purchased from Loop Hall. A proven stud with a wonderful temperament, gentle and calm. We have four brood mares, one in foal, and two colts. There are other horses that Mrs Hamilton-Read wishes to keep."

Robson saw his opportunity at the mention of her name. "Her husband died, I believe?"

"Aye, and very sadly missed. He kent what he was about with regard to the horses. He told me it had long been a passion o' his to breed his own. We have done well ower the years selling everything we bred, and the two colts are ready to go."

"Your mistress's name – I thought it was the Hamiltons who owned Longridge."

"She joined the Hamilton name to her man's when they remarried."

Robson was confused. She was already a Read, Mary Read, when he knew her first. Her husband, Read? He was dead. Remarried? How was this possible? He was very confused. Shocked.

"They had children?"

"Aye, a son, Will, and a much younger daughter, Miss Savannah."

So, William Read, he mused, *you did not drown as she long suspected; she never gave up hope you were still alive. She had found the great love of her life and lost him again.* Robson was glad to lapse into silence as he mulled over his thoughts. They left the main Newbridge to Penistone road for the private estate road which passed through the wood that skirted the south side of the estate, the trees vaulting over them and casting the road into shade, until Andrew turned off at the lodge house. Robson cast his eyes from side to side as they trotted along the tree-lined drive, where a thrush high in the canopy sang enthusiastically and the buds were bursting on the rhododendrons, past the fields of grazing sheep framed by the pale fells. It was a picturesque spot and so unlike the flat, open landscape surrounding his own home. The drive opened out into a gravelled semi-circle and Andrew brought the gig to a halt under the *porte-cochère*. Robson thanked him and jumped down.

"Mrs Hamilton-Read said she'll bring you to the stables, sir."
Andrew touched his hat and moved off. Robson took a deep breath;
he was aware his heart was beating faster than usual, and his palms
were sweaty. He wiped his hands down the front of his coat as the
maid opened the door.

"I'm to show you to the mistress's sittin' room, sir," she said as she
took his hat and coat and placed them on a chair by the door. Sarah
led him across the wide hallway where the central staircase divided
beneath a stained-glass window, depicting a figure he thought might
be St George, framed by two portraits – he recognised both subjects
– to the western end of the house. The maid knocked and opened
the door, stepping aside to let him pass.

Marianna was standing beside the fireplace with her hands
clasped in front of her. She was in half mourning and was wearing
a pale lilac, moiré dress with her hair pulled back in a thick,
plaited chignon. Robson checked his step and tugged nervously to
straighten his waistcoat. His heart was beating faster still, and his
tongue clung to the roof of his mouth. Since he had agreed to visit
her, he had often wondered what his first words would be, but now
his mind was jumbled, the words were stuck in his throat and he felt
like a lumbering, tongue-tied schoolboy.

"Mr Robson." She came towards him to shake his hand. "How
kind of you to come. Please sit." She gestured towards one of the
sofas. "Would you care for some refreshment?"

He sank gratefully into the cushions before his knees betrayed
him. He noticed she wore no jewellery apart from the two rings on
her left hand.

"No, thank you."

"Did you have a pleasant journey?"

"No. Thank you. Yes. Indeed, yes." The words tumbled out in a
confused mess.

"Luncheon is at one," said Marianna, sitting down opposite
him and folding her hands in her lap. "I have been presumptuous in
expecting you to eat before seeing the horses."

"Not at all," he said. "It is kind of you." More time in her company.
More time to find out what had happened to her and to him – the

dead man who had clouded their relationship as she refused to give him up and devote herself exclusively to him. *My God*, he thought, *how beautiful she is*. He glanced round the room to give himself time to compose himself. A feminine, tasteful room, full of light and not crammed with furniture: everything there was for a purpose and—

"So different now with the railway," she was saying, interrupting his thoughts. "No need for a guide over the sands. Have you travelled over the viaduct?"

"Yes." He did not know how to speak with her, what to say to ease the conversation. Years before, they were master and servant, although he had never condescended to her, and they had never been awkward with each other. Now she was a lady. A fine lady. The common accent gone. Poised. Elegant. "Have you?" he asked lamely.

"Yes, we went to Castleton, round the coast. It was beautiful; the sea to one side and the majestic fells to the other. I wonder what the d'Ansons made of having the railway crossing their land?"

"A lot of money."

She tossed back her head and laughed. "Of course!"

They had broken the ice. He felt the tension ease in his chest; at last, he could think of something to say. "Eleanor is in Castleton."

"You mentioned it when we met last. She likes teaching?"

"Yes, very much. For her it is a vocation. She is headmistress now."

"How proud you must be."

"And your son, Will?"

She smiled at him. He had been kind to her baby son.

"He is a lawyer in Liverpool and is recently married. He and his wife are on honeymoon in Scotland and will call in next week on their way home."

"How time flies! He was a baby when I saw him last. So, you live here alone?" he asked and instantly regretted it. "I'm sorry. What I meant to ask was if you manage the estate yourself since…" His voice trailed away.

"Of course. My late father instructed me."

There was an uncomfortable silence as he wanted to ask her about her husband and she, knowing what he wanted, did not want to tell him. Her memories of William were too precious and raw and, many years ago, she had betrayed him with this man sitting opposite. But one thing her mother, a stickler for manners, had taught her was not to embarrass guests, so she said, "I am so pleased you agreed to sell my horses for me. I have absolutely no knowledge of breeding or pedigree and fear it is an expensive business, which alarms me greatly."

"Mr Kerr has explained on the way here."

"You told me you had found a position for him."

"I will put it to him this afternoon. I have, on your recommendation, put forward a good case for him with a Mr Graham of Thorneythwaite Hall, near Kirkby Martin, whom I know from my time at Loop Hall and who has extended an invitation to interview him. Though it will not be a position as stable master."

"Thank you, Mr Robson. It is a weight off my mind, as he has been a valuable servant. I have told him he is under no obligation to accept, and I believe he and his wife have been thinking of moving back to Scotland to be near their families."

There was a knock on the door and Sarah entered to announce luncheon was ready.

After they had eaten, the conversation confined to generalities – the weather, Longridge, what a fine spot it was, the opening of the Natural History Museum, trips they had made to the capital – Marianna accompanied him to the stables and left him with Andrew, telling him to meet her in her sitting room and report back what his considered opinion might be before he left.

Robson returned an hour later.

"I am most impressed," he said. "There will be no problems selling the horses. I will contact prospective buyers who may wish to come and look at them first, whereas others will take me at my word. Failing that, there is always the auction in Melchester, and I would be quite happy to act on your behalf. One of the mares has taken my fancy and I would not mind buying her."

"That is good news. Will it be a long process?"

"Not at all. I'll make a start as soon as I get home. Of course, one thing."

"Yes?"

"We did not discuss my fee and expenses."

"I trust you, Bertie." He caught his breath. The first time she had addressed him informally and she had done it instinctively. "Sell the horses and deduct your costs. You have spared me a lot of heartache."

He could not take his eyes off her. He wanted to go to her, even just sit next to her, feel her breath on his skin, smell her. He was struggling with his emotions. There was so much he wanted her to tell him, so much he wanted to understand. Understand if there was still a chance.

"And Andrew?" She was speaking, eyebrows raised. She had been waiting for an answer to the question he had not heard as he was so lost in his thoughts.

"Oh! He is grateful for your efforts, and I shall meet him at Melchester Station next week to take him to Thorneythwaite."

"That is kind of you. Well, Mr Robson, we must conclude business for today. Andrew will take you back to the station."

His heart sank. Now she was businesslike and formal again. He rose to shake her hand and held it as he gazed into her eyes.

"Marianna…"

She understood his look and was offended by his familiarity. Had he forgotten her situation? She wrenched her hand from his grasp. Her eyes blazed. "Andrew will be waiting."

The following week, Will and Esme called in at Longridge on their way home from their two-week honeymoon in Scotland. They were to stay for a few days. Marianna could sense there was distance between them, not the closeness to be expected in a recently married couple, and she noticed they hardly spoke to each other or barely looked at each other. Marianna was worried that Will might have regretted the marriage. Although he had courted Esme for many months, the wedding, a civil ceremony, had been arranged very quickly after a short engagement, causing Marianna to wonder if there was a child on the way and Will had done 'the right thing'.

Will had taken Savannah out riding and Esme wandered aimlessly through the rooms downstairs, stopping to look at a painting or pick up an object from a table or stare out of the window. Marianna had noted her restlessness and went in search of her. She was sitting in the library, an unopened book next to her, staring into space, absent-mindedly stroking Badger who had wormed his way onto her lap.

"What troubles you, Esme? Are you unwell?"

Esme looked uncomfortable and her hand went to her throat to fiddle with the pearl necklace Will had given her as a wedding present.

"No, I am well, thank you."

"Are you sure? Is it something I can help you with?" Marianna sat down beside her.

Esme shook her head and looked away. Marianna shooed Badger from her lap.

"I can see something is not right between you and Will. You can tell me to mind my own business, or you can talk to me. We are friends, are we not?"

And then it all spilled out – all the things she could not imagine speaking about to anyone else, including her own mother – as though Marianna's kind words had unplugged a dam of pent-up emotion, worry and despair.

"There is something wrong. There is something wrong with me. I fear he does not love me. I fear he thinks he has made a mistake in marrying me."

"Why do you say such things?"

"He cannot bring himself to love me." She began to fiddle with her necklace again. Marianna took her hand and squeezed it warmly. Esme blushed and lowered her voice to a whisper. "He comes to me, but he cannot complete the…" She swallowed hard. "The act. I fear I must be repulsive to him." She clutched Marianna's hand in desperation. "How will I have a child? A child I long for. How can I please him? I love him so much. What must I do to make him love me?"

"Oh, my darling girl!" exclaimed Marianna, embracing her. "Of course he loves you. How can he not?" She sat back and examined the downturned mouth, the flushed cheeks and eyes full of sadness. "You are beautiful, Esme, sweet and kind. May I ask you something?" Esme nodded. "You did not know other men intimately before Will?"

"Mother-in-law, please." Esme's face reddened further. "What must you think of me to ask such a question?"

Marianna got up and took Esme's hand.

"Come. Come with me. We shall go somewhere more private. To my room."

"Ladybird is looking well," said Will as he and Savannah set off down the drive.

They had waved at the library window, but Esme and their mother were deep in conversation and did not see them.

"I love her. She is very comfortable, and I feel a bit more grown up as she is a good four hands taller than Moth."

"The little fellow seems to be enjoying his retirement."

"You are glad we kept him, Will?"

"Of course! I remember when he was born. Such a scrap of a thing. I think you should be riding aside now, Savannah. You *are* growing up. I shall speak to Mama about a new saddle befitting a young lady."

Will urged Juno into a trot and they were soon out of the front gates and onto the road that led to the fields below Calf Fell, where they could canter safely as there were no fallen trees to tempt Savannah to jump.

They pulled up their horses. Savannah's face glowed. She puffed out her cheeks. "That was good."

They turned the horses' heads to walk home, dropped the reins, and the horses ambled easily, rocking their riders from side to side. Savannah enjoyed riding out with Will when he came home, as she had him to herself and he talked to her like a grown up and would tell her about his childhood at Longridge before he moved to Manchester when their mother married Bennet Foster. He had told her he found his grandmother distant, and he thought she did not like him. It was not until much later when he knew about William that he understood her hostility, that she could not accept him as the son of a common groom, and he could not forgive her for her snobbery. His grandfather, though, he loved, and Henry Hamilton treated him kindly and with great affection. He did not, unlike Ada, talk about the night of the storm, the night she was born. He had answered her the first time she asked with a wave of the hand. "It was nothing, Savannah."

"Do you miss Papa?" asked Savannah.

"I do. He was a good man."

"I miss him terribly. I do not think there will be a day when I don't miss him. Mama still cries, you know, Will. She does not know I hear her sometimes."

"Then you must be kind to her and not give her cause to worry."

Savannah knew he meant that she must behave at school. He was always telling her that she must be good and not upset Mama, who had enough to worry about.

Will sighed. "I am jealous of you, Savannah."

"Why?"

"Because I didn't have my childhood with him. I knew him only as a grown man."

Savannah thought for a moment and then said, "If we put the pieces of my memories to the pieces of yours, together we will make a big jigsaw, a picture of Papa. And we will remember him together."

Will looked across at her, her cheeks pink with exercise, her eyes fresh and sparkling, and smiled. She sat well on the pony, her hands resting lightly on the reins, an accomplished rider. She was wearing her favourite riding habit of royal blue twill that set off her eyes. Wisps of hair had escaped the matching ribbon that somehow was still in place. He smiled again at this miniature version of his beloved Mama. A sweet, endearing child he loved very much. Sometimes, she said the most extraordinary things and she had an empathy he thought a child of her age incapable of. But he did not, in truth, know many children to compare her to.

"Indeed," he said. "A picture of a good, kind man we loved very much and who loved our mother beyond words." He sighed again. "I hope to find such a love."

Savannah was puzzled and did not understand him as he had a new wife and, surely, you did not marry someone you did not love, but she did not think it her place to ask. They rode home in silence.

When they returned to the house, Marianna sent a displeased Savannah to her room to do some schoolwork and asked Will to join her in the study, where they sat side by side on the sofa. Esme was reading in her sitting room. At first, Will was mortified that Esme had spoken to his mother about matters so intimate but also relieved that he could unburden himself. He had always had a close relationship with his mother, whom he adored and found easy to talk to.

"It is not Esme's fault, Mama. Not at all. I am so sorry that she feels she is the problem. I have done something I am ashamed of, and it haunts me." He saw the aggrieved look on his mother's face as she seemed to grasp what he was inferring. "Before I married her."

"You were intimate with someone else? When you were engaged?"

"Not formally engaged but—"

"A prostitute? Is that why you are ashamed?"

As usual, his mother did not mince her words.

"No. But as good as." Will adjusted his shirt cuffs and exhaled heavily. "She seduced me. I let her seduce me. It is difficult to explain the power she had over me and I could not resist her. She was so beautiful, so alluring, so different. Knowing. Confident. Free-spirited. So mocking of convention. Skilled, Mama, if you understand me? And afterwards, I was so ashamed. I thought she was a lady, but she was a siren, a vampire, who used me. Esme is so pure and innocent in comparison and, when I try to love her, I see the face of the other woman mocking me and I am consumed with guilt and disgust. I do not feel worthy of my wife."

Will's head slumped to his chest. Telling his mother something so personal, which showed him in such a poor light, shamed him. Just thinking of Leonora Brown made him feel sick. Who she was would go with him to the grave.

Marianna took his hand and said quietly, "You have always been an honest person, Will. I am glad you feel you can confide in me. I cannot bear the thought of you being unhappy. It was a mistake. God knows, we are all guilty of making mistakes. I must ask you, Will, if you think you have rushed into this marriage? You were engaged and married within months."

"I am thirty years old, Mama. Esme is twenty-eight and wants children. What is the point of delaying? I think we are suited, and the marriage will be a happy one if…" He looked up at the ceiling. "If we can be as a husband and wife should be."

Marianna released his hand and patted his knee. "I am relieved you are not having second thoughts at least. You know you love Esme. You must look at your wife and see her for what she is and how superior she is to this other woman, in her beauty, her nature, her character, and possibly as the mother of your children. Court her again, Will. Talk to her. Spoil her with your attention. Remember what it was that attracted you to her." She leant across to hug him and kissed his cheek. "She loves you, Will. Very much. I hope by talking to me you feel a little better and less guilty."

Her role as confidante and counsellor did not end with the advice that she gave them. She arranged for them to have dinner in their room, hoping Esme would have the courage to do as she suggested. When they both came down to breakfast together the next morning, their faces betraying their shared intimacy, she was relieved.

THIRTEEN

Over the next few months, Cuthbert Robson made two further visits to Longridge. The first was in the company of Mr Billington, a wealthy corn merchant from Melchester who wanted to buy Marquis. Marianna entertained them both to luncheon before they went off to inspect the stallion. The dining room was the only room in the house to give a hint of the Hamiltons' wealth, as the glass-fronted cabinets displayed the precious silver and priceless porcelain acquired by successive generations and a pair of ornate, silver candelabra graced the long, highly polished mahogany table. And as the artefacts impressed, so Marianna sparkled and charmed her guests.

They came to take their leave of her and as Mr Billington, more than satisfied with his purchase, climbed into the carriage to return to the railway station, Robson took her hand and touched her cheek. She did not rebuff him.

"The horse was sold before he even saw him. You bewitched him. Andrew will make the arrangements to transport the horse and I shall come for my mare next week."

She smiled and said, "I look forward to it."

Her words sang in his ears all the way home.

The second visit was to look over the mare and to confirm his initial desire to purchase her, and, if he was honest, it was an excuse to see Marianna again.

The horses were gone as Robson had promised, apart from the mare he wanted. The Kerrs were gone too, not to Thorneythwaite, but back to Scotland, where Andrew had found a position at the racing stables where he had started as a stable boy. Marianna was sorry to see them go, as was Savannah, who had grown up with their children. Thomas had married. Had to marry, Ada informed her, and the wife not much older than sixteen. He had moved into one of the cottages next door to Sarah and Ezra, who had married not long after the Kerrs had left. Marianna did not think he deserved the stable master's cottage. He was yet to prove himself.

Robson arrived for a third visit, in the mid-afternoon, at Newbridge Station, where Marianna, now out of mourning, waited to meet him as she had been shopping before collecting Savannah from school. She had invited him to stay the night. He was interrupting his journey to Castleton to visit his daughter to discuss the transport arrangements for his mare with Thomas. Badger, who had not encountered Robson before, eyed him and his bag warily as he climbed in and gave a low growl.

"I am sorry," said Marianna. "He is usually a friendly dog."

"He can probably smell my dog on my clothes."

"You still have a dog?"

"Not Sam, obviously," he said, referring to the dog he had owned at Loop Hall, and gave her a look, and she laughed.

"Obviously."

The tension between them had eased since his first visit. There was no stiffness or forced politeness; they were more comfortable with one another. They waited on the road by the school, away from the prying eyes and idle tongues itching to know the identity of the stranger with the widow. The school bell rang and, before long, Savannah was grinning at the carriage window and climbing in, before kissing Badger on the head and putting him on her lap.

"Good afternoon, Mr Robson," she said, offering him her hand. She had been told he was coming. "How nice to see you again. Do you like my Badger?"

Such a confident child, he thought, *and so very like her mother.*

"Indeed, I do." He smiled at her, and she beamed at his obvious good taste.

When they arrived back at Longridge, they took tea together and, afterwards, Marianna asked Savannah to accompany Mr Robson to the stables so he could make sure they were looking after his mare, and he could talk to Thomas. When they returned, he helped her with her arithmetic homework, played with Badger and let her beat him at chess. Then, dinner over, Savannah tucked up in bed, the servants dismissed, Marianna and Robson were alone in her sitting room. She poured him his preferred drink of whisky with a splash of water, sat opposite him on one of the armchairs by the fireside and asked, "How long have you lived at Moss End Farm?"

He described how, a few years after she had left Loop Hall, he had used a bequest from his parents to buy the farm, as it had long been his wish to own his own property, and he wanted to safeguard Eleanor's future.

"Is she married or dedicated to her pupils?"

"That is why I am going to Castleton. I am to meet the man who apparently wants to marry her."

"Will she give up her position? Will she have to give up her position? Personally, I do not see why she should."

"No. Not a chance. She has worked hard for all she has achieved. I am so proud of her."

"Are you pleased with your decision to have your own farm? Do you enjoy being your own master?"

"I do. I have to say there is a lot less to think about than my job at Loop Hall entailed. My mistakes now affect me alone, not the hundreds of people who depended on the estate for their livelihood."

"I never asked if you married again?"

"No." Robson got up abruptly, saying he would retire after a long day. He put down his unfinished drink on a side table and thanked her for her hospitality. He brushed his lips over her hand and paused as if on the brink of saying something, then simply bade her goodnight.

Marianna undressed and stood looking at her reflection in the mirror. At the end of their first meeting at Longridge, when

Robson had taken his leave and she sensed he wanted to kiss her and take the first step in rekindling their relationship, he had angered her because he had forgotten her circumstances as a widow in mourning. He had also annoyed her because she wanted to be in control. If anything was to happen, just as it happened at Loop Hall, it would be because she wanted it. Tonight, she wanted it. She was a little frustrated he had not kissed her goodnight on the cheek... or the lips, as she would have responded to let him know she was willing. She unpinned her hair and brushed it out. She put on her silk robe and touched some perfume behind her ears and on her throat and then, after a moment's consideration, between her breasts. She opened the door carefully and padded silently, barefoot, along the corridor to one of the guest rooms in the opposite wing of the house. She turned the door handle and breathed a sigh of relief that he had not locked it. She stepped into his room. She was surprised to see he was still dressed and sitting, silhouetted by the lamplight, in a chair by the window, staring into the darkness. He seemed preoccupied and did not hear her. She crossed the floor and stood before him and let the robe slide from her shoulders. He looked up in surprise. His eyes never left hers, but his hands gripped the arms of the chair.

"So, you come to me again, Mrs Read?"

He turned his head away from her to stare into the blackness of the night beyond the window. She was confused. Had she misread the signals he had sent out these past weeks; the way he looked at her, the hand touching her cheek, the light kiss? Tears of humiliation pricked her eyes, as she stooped to gather her robe round her trembling body and made for the door. He heard the handle click.

"Marianna," he whispered. "Stay." He had instantly regretted his sarcastic, wounding words. They echoed the pain she had caused him by rejecting him all those years before and not coming back to him as he had hoped. And more than that: he had been sitting worrying, agonising, whether he dare go to her, where her room was. He had wanted to go to her, but his masculine pride would not have borne another blow if she had spurned him. If he let her go now, he might lose her forever.

He rose from the chair and went to her, wrapped her in his arms and kissed her and she returned his kisses. He slipped the robe from her and began to undress, dropping his clothes to the floor, and then lifted her in his arms, carried her to the bed and lay her down. She glowed in the lamplight. He paused above her, in wonder at her, her beautiful face, her thick, richly coloured hair, her beautiful body, her breasts, her rounded belly, the curves of her, the lusciousness of her. There was a hint of a knowing smile on her lips. She pulled him down on her. He whispered, "I have never stopped loving you."

He returned two nights later at her invitation, happy to interrupt his journey home from Castleton to be with her again. When they were alone after Savannah had gone to bed, they took their unfinished drinks from dinner, went to her sitting room and sat beside each other on the sofa. Marianna asked him about his meeting with Eleanor's suitor.

"It seems to me to be more of a business arrangement than a love match. He is much older than her, a bachelor still at fifty-odd years of age – nothing wrong with that I suppose – and comes into the school to teach the classics. I feel he is looking for a comfortable home and a guaranteed position for as long as she is headmistress. As for Eleanor, I think she is lonely. And desperate."

"You sound cynical, Bertie."

"To be honest, Marianna, I don't care. She is old enough now to make her own decisions. I do not want to interfere. She is my only child, a dutiful daughter, and I love her dearly, but she has her own life. I do not want to lose her by expressing my reservations too freely."

"How are you able to spend time away from your farm?"

"I have a man who helps me. He was a stockman originally but knows horses, and I have labourers."

"And tomorrow you take your mare. Then what?"

"I'll settle her in and then find a stallion to cover her."

Marianna glared at him. "You know what I mean."

"That depends on you," he said. "As it always did."

Again, the words he thought but did not mean to say slipped out. Marianna rose abruptly and put down her glass a little too forcefully, so it rapped on the table and the contents splashed out. She went out through the door into the rose garden. She walked along the path to the furthest arbour and sat down on the bench. It was still light, the evening sky suffused with the pale yellow of the setting sun. The air was filled with the lingering, gentle scent of the early roses. She sighed. She had given herself to him willingly two nights ago and he had pleased her; it had been a long time – two years – since she had loved a man. But even though she had lain with him, there was still a bitterness in Robson that niggled him because of what had happened all those years ago. She had told him she had to return to the family who had lost her but if it did not work out, she had promised to come back to him. She did not go back to him. *What does it matter?* she thought. He lived a train journey away; he had a life. Why should she countenance a more permanent relationship? "Oh, William," she said, sighing, twisting her fingers together. "Why did you leave me again?"

She heard Bertie's footsteps on the path and hastily brushed the tears from her eyes. He sat down beside her, took her in his arms and rested his chin on her head.

"I'm sorry," he said. "Your leaving of me all those years ago hurt so much. I hoped and hoped you would come back to me. I loved you so much."

"You knew I had to come back here for the sake of my parents."

"Then you found him, didn't you? That is why you did not come back."

"No." She began to weep silently. "He saw us together. He came back to Loop Hall and saw us and thought we were married and Will was your son. By some fluke, he ended up here – a long story – and it was he who told my mother where I was. She knew when she came to Loop Hall to take me home that he was alive and never said a word. I suspected it was he who told her because no one else knew where I was. That is also why I came back to Longridge. To find answers. But I was too late. By the time I got here, he was gone. To America." Marianna was sobbing more loudly, and he hugged her close to comfort her. "I married a lawyer from Manchester. Then Will met his father by chance many years later as he had returned to live near Liverpool. My husband died so we were able to remarry. These last years with him have been the happiest of my life."

Not once did she call him by his name. He was too precious. He meant everything to her. He was her William. For Robson, it was difficult to name the man who had never left her thoughts, their love for each other beyond words, and he was jealous. Jealous that he had never known such shared, deep love or had the chance to find it with her; jealous of the man who, although dead, had such power over her. Marianna sobbed and sobbed, and Robson hugged her tighter and stroked her face. She had not wept so deeply for a long time. Her shoulders convulsed with the pain of her racking sobs, and she covered her face with her hands. He sat silently, waiting for her to calm herself. There was nothing he could say to ease her sorrow.

"He did not drown," she said at last, gulping in breaths of air and drying her tears on the handkerchief he offered her. "He was not on the coach. Do you remember the riot in Melchester? You went to look for him for me. I always remember how kind you were to me at that time. He had an accident. He lost his memory." She lied. It was simpler.

"You knew, didn't you?" he said gently. "You always knew he was alive because you loved him so much. There was a special bond between you, and I am glad you found each other again."

Robson could not compete with what they had; he had to accept it. He had told her, years ago, when he first asked her to marry him that he would be second best; he could not be jealous of a dead man. How could he be jealous now? William Read was dead. He loved her. He had always loved her. Now he had the chance to make her love him again. Marianna looked up at him through her puffy, red eyes. His words were noble and kind. But then he was always kind. He was watching her, his eyes full of compassion, hurt and love for her. She kissed his hand and they sat quietly as she recovered and her breathing steadied. He broke the silence.

"This is a lovely garden."

"My late mother's pride and joy. I know nothing about horses and nothing about roses. Mr Dummigan looks after it." She shivered.

"Come," he said, standing up and offering her his hand. "The sun is gone and there's a chill in the air. Let us go back inside."

Later, when the house was quiet, the maids asleep in the attic, Savannah snoring gently, Badger curled up beside her, Marianna crept along to Robson's room. All those years ago at Netherton when William disappeared, she had craved physical contact, which Robson satisfied. In the early years of her marriage to the homosexual Bennet Foster, she sought comfort, but never found it, in the arms of other men. Now William was gone, she needed fulfilment, the fulfilment she found in the pleasure of sexual contact. The first time Robson had loved her, two nights ago, he had made her want more. Cuthbert Robson, at sixty-two years of age, was still a handsome man. He carried himself well, was smartly dressed, his body still firm and, when he smiled at her, his eyes crinkling and sparkling, she felt the tug of attraction that had first drawn her to him years ago, and he had lost none of his skill in lovemaking. She knew she was a beautiful woman: men turned to look at her, even now at the age of forty-nine, and she still had her figure and the body those men in her past lusted after.

The other night, she saw in Cuthbert Robson's eyes, as she had seen in all men's eyes, the desire and then the gratitude as they spent themselves inside her. But Bertie, like William, was a kind, thoughtful, unselfish lover and, like William, there was a giving and sharing. But William was the love of her life and her best friend. Robson could never match the love she felt, even now, for William. Yet she needed to be held, caressed, touched, roused, satisfied. That night she stayed longer; they made love, they talked, and, as the first grey light appeared through a chink in the curtains, she kissed him, laughed and said, "I must fly before everyone wakes up." She had not felt as contented since William died.

So, just as at Loop Hall, they came to an arrangement. He would come to her once a fortnight if possible. He would leave the mare for the time being on the pretext the stabling at his farm was undergoing refurbishment and then, in future, if they really needed a pretext for his visits, that he was advising her. They would not make or seek any other commitments from each other, and she told him quite firmly that she would not marry again, for the sake of Will and Savannah, and the need to safeguard the Longridge estate for their future. This arrangement suited them both.

On his next visit, as they dined with Savannah, Robson asked her how she liked school and where she was going to go the following year. Marianna wished he had not asked as it was a touchy subject between them.

"I hate school. I hate Mr Ollerton. If Mama sends me away to boarding school, I shall run away. How can I be separated from Badger, who will pine for me most dreadfully as I will pine for him?"

He looked across the table at Marianna who was rolling her eyes.

"My daughter has a school near Castleton, Savannah. The girls are taught all the usual subjects: sewing, piano—"

Savannah groaned.

"French, mathematics—"

Savannah groaned again.

"Science. When I was visiting not long ago, some of the older girls were dissecting a frog."

Savannah's eyes lit up. "Really?"

"Indeed. They also play tennis and do archery—"

"Archery? You mean bows and arrows?"

"Yes."

Savannah looked impressed.

"We could make a trip to Castleton, and you could have a look round and see what you think."

Marianna was annoyed that Bertie had taken it upon himself to interfere in this aspect of Savannah's life and organise something without consulting her. She forced a smile as Savannah turned on her pleading look.

"May we, Mama?"

Within days, Savannah had been excused from school and they were in a cab approaching Westhaven Academy for Young Ladies. It was a large, country house, square, solid and imposing, in its own spacious grounds with a view of the estuary and the Scottish hills in the background. Girls dressed in the uniform of navy blue dresses, white pinafores and navy blue cloaks were strolling across the lawns in front of the house or sitting on benches, chatting and laughing, in the winter sunshine. Curious eyes followed their progress. Savannah, overwhelmed by the daunting building and the stares of so many pairs of eyes, clutched her mother's hand nervously as they ascended a flight of stone steps to the front door, where Miss Eleanor Robson was waiting to greet them. She shook their hands and kissed her father's cheek. Marianna realised immediately that Eleanor had not recognised her: Bertie had not told his daughter who they were.

Eleanor Robson was tall, dressed in a pale blue, sprigged cotton print dress, a woollen shawl fastened round her shoulders, her hair piled up in curls on the top of her head. A bunch of keys hung from a belt round her waist and a gold fob watch was pinned to her chest. She had been a plain-looking child, as Marianna recalled, but the passing years had been kind to her: she had grown into her features and could be described as handsome. Like her father, she carried herself well, which, with her height, gave her an imposing presence. Her manner was calm and authoritative, her movements controlled, her speech measured. She gave the impression of a self-contained, cold woman. A small, diamond ring glinted on her finger.

She led the way across the highly polished, wooden floor in the hallway to her study, a large, light-filled room with two windows overlooking the front lawns and the entrance to the house, and a fire glowing in the fireplace. The visitors removed their hats, coats and gloves.

"Father, sit there please," said Eleanor, pointing to an armchair in a corner by the door. "Mrs Hamilton-Read, Miss Hamilton-Read, please take a seat here," she said, indicating two chairs positioned in front of the wide, oak desk set at right angles to one of the windows. When they had settled themselves, Miss Robson wasted no time in directing her first question at Savannah.

"*Comment t'appelles-tu?*"

Savannah looked startled.

"You do not know any French?"

"No, ma'am. It is not taught at my school."

"What do you consider to be the most useful discovery beneficial to humankind?"

"Potatoes," Savannah answered, without giving the question much thought.

Marianna stifled a smile. Bertie coughed to hide his laugh. Miss Robson raised her eyebrows.

"Is that the best you can come up with?"

Panic-stricken, Savannah looked to Marianna for inspiration, but her mother was studiously examining her fingers.

"What was the title of the last book you read?" Miss Robson asked brusquely.

Without hesitation, Savannah replied, "*Robinson Crusoe*. Although I did not like it very much. His days seemed so tedious, and he had no one to talk to for a long time."

"Is that so? Describe to me very succinctly your favourite thing and why it is your favourite thing."

Savannah, again without need for much thought, launched into a very detailed description of Badger, ignoring Miss Robson's instruction for brevity, and had barely begun to elaborate on all his fine qualities and amusing behaviour and why she loved him when Miss Robson interrupted her.

"If five apples cost two pennies each and four pears cost three pennies each, how much change will I receive from a florin? Answer as quickly as you can."

Mental arithmetic! Savannah looked in despair at her mother whose facial expression did not alter and then stared at the ceiling for a moment and then back at Miss Robson.

"Why are the pears more expensive than the apples?"

Marianna groaned inwardly. She had been warned not to be precocious. She knew that her daughter was stalling to give herself time to do the calculation. She saw Eleanor's eyes narrow as she looked from Savannah to her and back again.

"Answer your own question, Miss Hamilton-Read."

Savannah's brow furrowed and she put her finger to her mouth.

Her darling papa had told her something. She said, inwardly pleased with herself, "There is a glut of apples at harvest, so they are cheaper."

Miss Robson was impressed. She suppressed a smile. "So how much change will I receive?" she asked as she reached to the side drawer in her desk to retrieve a brochure which she handed to Marianna. Again, Marianna detected the narrowing of the eyes. She sensed Eleanor was trying to draw out from her memory who it was this woman, seated opposite, reminded her of.

"Tuppence," answered Savannah triumphantly.

Miss Robson nodded and turned her attention to Marianna.

"The brochure explains our fees, dates of terms, uniform, what the girls need to bring with them, rules, the subjects we teach and so on. Our ethos is that girls should be educated to go out and do good in the world, their minds opened to opportunities, not be churned out as the perfect little wife, an appendage to her husband, but as an equal to any man."

"Very impressive," said Marianna. "And not before time." *Most parents*, she thought, *would consider it more desirable for their daughter to make a decent marriage.*

"Good," said Eleanor, rising from her seat. "I have some free time to show you round personally." She smiled at her father. A favour to him. A bell rang and the babble of chatter coming from outside began to subside.

"The start of afternoon lessons," explained Eleanor. "We shall go upstairs to the dormitories first and avoid the crush in the corridors as the girls make their way to class."

They had viewed the dormitories, each room containing a huge chest of drawers and six or eight neatly made beds with a chair at the foot. There were trunks on the chairs as the end of term approached and the girls were beginning to pack away their belongings. Miss Robson informed them that the older girls enjoyed the privilege of single rooms. They were introduced to the matron who attended to the girls' welfare. They saw the communal bathrooms, prep rooms, music rooms, art room and library, and were descending the main staircase to see the classrooms and dining room on the ground floor when Eleanor placed her hand on Marianna's arm. Her father and Savannah were already walking along the corridor, talking animatedly. She hissed venomously in her ear, "I know who you are. It took me a while to recall where I had seen you before and put your face to the name. If you break his heart again…"

Marianna turned to confront her and saw the determined set of her jaw, the glint in her eye, the jealous resentment she had seen in the young girl's eyes who saw her as a threat to her own claim on her father's love. In that same instant, she knew she would not entrust her daughter to this woman's influence. She did not trust her to be kind to Savannah. She pulled her arm away angrily and continued down the stairs. As far as she was concerned, there was no point in prolonging the visit. Eleanor Robson's parting words stopped her in her tracks.

"Did he tell you about his wife?"

FOURTEEN

Marianna could not wait to get home. Savannah chattered away to Robson on the journey about what they had seen, and she tried to join in. She had been relieved when Eleanor had sent for one of the senior girls to accompany them on the rest of the tour, excusing herself by saying she was busy and they shook hands, briskly and frostily. She watched Robson as he looked out of the train window at the snow-capped fells and bare trees in the wintry landscape or turned to Savannah to answer a question or point something out to her. Savannah seemed to like him; they were relaxed in each other's company. But Savannah liked anybody who paid any attention to her or admired Badger. Robson glanced at her occasionally and smiled; she smiled back at him, but her eyes did not. He had lied to her.

When they got home, she wished she could send him packing. She wanted nothing to do with him. Not even a confrontation. She would write to him that she had no wish to see him again. Savannah yawned all the way through dinner, so it was not a battle to send her off to bed. And then, as soon as she could, she said she was tired too.

"I thought we might spend some time together and you could tell me your opinion of the school."

"Savannah will not be going to that school."

"Oh! And your reasons?"

"I do not need to discuss my daughter's education with you," she said crossly.

"Is something wrong, Marianna?"

"I am tired. Please excuse me."

Marianna lay in bed and could not sleep. Eleanor Robson's words taunted her: *Did he tell you about his wife? If you break his heart again…* Was she condoning her father's adultery? Why had he lied to her? Was he repeating his past behaviour when he had cheated on Eleanor's mother before she had known him? Did she care he was married if it meant she could lie with him? Would it trouble her conscience? But he had lied to her, and he had not told Eleanor who she was. Why not? She heard the gentle knock on her door and the handle turn. She was glad she had locked it. The thought of that liar imagining she would sleep with him and allow him to love her in William's bed, the bed her beloved William had died in, revolted her.

Robson came down to breakfast in the morning room. Savannah was feeding crusts of toast to Badger. There was no sign of Marianna.

"Mama has gone for a walk," said Savannah, pre-empting his question. "And I am off to school."

Robson helped himself to a plate of scrambled eggs from the covered dish on the sideboard, poured himself a cup of coffee and picked up a newspaper.

"Do you wish me to take you?"

"No, I can go on my own, thank you. Well, not really on my own as Thomas will drive me. But I will let you look after Badger for me. He will be company for you."

"It will be my pleasure." He smiled at her. She was an enchanting child. "I shall be gone when you get back from school."

"Oh, well, I'm sure I shall see you soon. I'd better go." Savannah scraped back her chair and got up. "Be good for Mr Robson, Badger." She patted the dog on the head and then came round the table and planted a kiss on Robson's cheek. "Thank you for yesterday. It will not be so bad at that school and if I have any complaints, I know who to complain to." She grinned at him and skipped out of the room.

Marianna, her face pinched and pale, arrived ten minutes later as he drained the last of his coffee.

"Savannah has gone to school. Have you had breakfast?" He got up to pour her a cup of coffee.

"I met her on the drive. I'm not hungry."

"Do you often go for a walk so early? Did you enjoy it?" he asked, placing the cup on the table in front of her.

"Yes, thank you." She pushed the cup away. "I'd prefer tea."

"What is wrong, my love?"

She glared at him for not caring if the servants overheard his intimacy.

"You seem out of sorts. Have I said something, done something wrong?"

"You know you have."

He raised his eyebrows.

"Not here," she said, rising from her chair, and walked purposefully from the room.

He followed her to her sitting room and closed the door behind them. She refused to sit and stood in front of the fireplace; her face and her eyes had darkened.

"Why have you lied to me?"

Cuthbert Robson looked away from her cold, angry stare and muttered, "Eleanor."

"I cannot understand your deception," said Marianna. "Where do I begin?" She spread her hands in incomprehension. "You do not tell your daughter who I am. You hoped she would not recognise me and your secret was safe? You do not tell me you are married. Worse. You lied. Blatantly. In this very room." Marianna began to pace the floor, her voice rising in anger. Her face was thunderous, her cheeks tinged with red flecks. "To what end, pray? To use me? Revenge? Revenge for what I did all those years ago? To toy with me, my emotions, my feelings, and then disappear? To give me a taste of my own medicine?"

He was watching her, his face impassive.

"Well," she said, stopping suddenly in front of him, "you have nothing to say, Mr Robson?"

"Nothing," he said quietly. "There is no excuse."

"Then please leave. Take your damned horse and leave." Her

words were calm but uttered through gritted teeth. He did not move, but continued to look at her, a look she thought provocative. "Did you hear me? I ask you to leave my house immediately."

He said softly, "I will leave when you have heard what I have to say. Please sit down."

She gasped at his insolence. "Who are you to tell me what to do? I most certainly will not."

"Remain standing, as you wish, but I shall not go until you hear me out."

Marianna believed him. There would be an impasse until someone conceded. It was her house: he should do as she asked, if he was a gentleman. But she could see her innate stubbornness was to be outmatched and the quicker he said what he wanted to say, the quicker he would be gone. Marianna sat down stiffly in a chair as far away from him as possible.

"I did not tell Eleanor who you were as I thought she would have forgotten you; she was only a child when you knew her. She saw when you left how much you had hurt me, and she resented you anyway if you recall. Westhaven is a good school. She is a fine teacher. Modern in her ideas. You were impressed with what they are trying to do there. I wanted to do something for you. I did not want to poison the atmosphere by dragging up the past. You would just be the mother of a prospective pupil. If you did not like the school, then nothing was lost. That is the truth of it."

Marianna was painstakingly examining the pattern of the silk rug under her feet; she wanted him to leave, say his piece and go. He could say what he liked, true or not. She would not delay him by responding. For him, his next task was to explain the existence of his wife.

"She is an invalid."

"She!" Marianna exploded. "You betray her, and you cannot give her a name?"

"Emma."

"Well, there we have it." Marianna rose suddenly to her feet and swished her skirts into position, marched to the door and held it open for him. Robson got up more slowly and shook his head sadly.

As he passed her, he said, "Good day, Marianna. Perhaps when you are calmer, you will compare my circumstances with your own… All those years ago."

She slammed the door behind him. When she knew he had left the house, she ran upstairs to her room and threw herself on the bed. Rage and frustration consumed her, and she punched the pillows as the tears flowed. She rolled onto her back and stared at the ceiling, angrily rubbing her wet cheeks. *Perhaps when you are calmer you will compare my circumstances with yours.* His words echoed. He was calling her a hypocrite. She had gone to him at Loop Hall, seeking a physical relationship, despite protesting her belief that William was not dead. She had been an adulterer too.

She had forgotten Ellen Greenwood was coming to have luncheon with her and Robson. She had decided to introduce him to her dearest friend. Her heart sank. She could not face her, and she would have to come up with an excuse to explain his absence. Perhaps she could send a note to say she was unwell. There was a knock on the door. It was Sarah.

"Mrs Greenwood is here, ma'am."

"What? What time is it?"

"After twelve, ma'am."

She had fallen asleep.

"I'll be down presently. Offer Mrs Greenwood some refreshment."

Sarah saw her distressed state, her hair askew, her puffy eyes.

"Shall I do your hair, ma'am?" she asked kindly.

"No, thank you, Sarah. Tell Mrs Greenwood I am on my way."

Marianna went into the bathroom, splashed her face and examined herself in the mirror as she tidied her hair. She decided honesty was the best policy. Ellen was her confidante and closest friend, and she was in need of a friend. She hastened down to the drawing room and stood for a moment to compose herself before opening the door. Ellen rose to take her hands and kiss her cheek.

"Good day, my dear. How was your trip to Castleton? How did you find the school? Tell me all." She pulled Marianna down beside her on the sofa. "Will Mr Robson be joining us shortly?"

"He is gone, Ellen," she said bluntly. "We have had a disagreement. A very unpleasant disagreement as I have found out something. Oh, I shall come straight out with it, Ellen. He is married."

"Oh, my dear! Is that why you have been crying?" asked Ellen tenderly. "How did you find out? Did he confess all?"

"It's a long story." Marianna explained what had happened.

"So, you will give him up?"

"How can I not?"

"What did he mean she was an invalid?"

"I have no idea. I did not allow him to explain. It was enough he had lied to me. I asked him to leave."

"But you were happy, Marianna. Or happier, at least. What a shame." They looked at each other for a moment. Ellen patted her arm and said, "Did you hope to marry him, Marianna? Is that why you are upset?"

"No. Never. He knew I would not consider it. Now I realise that his willingness to always come here was convenient for his own, now obvious, reasons."

Ellen cleared her throat nervously. "But if she is an invalid, Marianna, he seeks his comfort elsewhere. You are a widow. What is the harm? You are both discreet. He is good for you. You have confided in me how he pleases you."

"I have known you long enough, Ellen Greenwood, not to be shocked by the things you say. But he lied to me, Ellen. Why did he not tell me from the start? Is it just me he seeks comfort from or are there others?"

The subject of Robson was dropped as they took luncheon in the dining room. Instead, they discussed the founding of The Rational Dress Society, which railed against the physical restraints imposed by women's dress. Neither Marianna nor Ellen, on the advice of her husband, wore corsets or the fashionable bustle.

"Richard," said Ellen, "is relieved that common sense may prevail, and women will desist from contorting their bodies into these ridiculous shapes. It is not healthy, and he says the damage they are doing will become apparent as they age."

"I prefer to be comfortable. Even more so as I get older. Do women succumb to fashion for themselves or to please men?" Marianna asked.

"I think some women like to follow the crowd. How they must suffer for it."

"Well, I will not allow Savannah to torture herself for the sake of vanity and someone else's idea of femininity."

After luncheon, they went for a stroll, arm in arm, well wrapped up in the crisp winter sunshine. Away from the chance of being overheard, Ellen asked, "Have you given any more thought to selling Longridge?"

"I cannot do it, Ellen. I have tossed and turned in my bed at night, fretting about it. This house is too big for me and Savannah. When William was alive, I did not notice it as much, but now… I would like to live at Hapenny How, but I cannot do that either, as William and I planned to live there together. I do not want to live there without him…" A sob rose in her throat and Ellen squeezed her arm. "I must stay here. Look after the house and estate for Will and his family. It is what my father wanted. Generations of our family have lived here. I must accept my responsibilities and fulfil my duty. So, you see, Ellen, I have no choice."

They had rounded the corner of the house and Marianna opened the door into the walled garden.

"It is a little patch of paradise, Marianna. The smell is overwhelming and the colours are dazzling in summer. But now, in winter, you can see clearly the structure, the geometry, and the thought that has gone into the planning of it."

"Yes," agreed Marianna. "My mother had many faults, but I have to concede she had taste and an eye for things. This is most definitely her pièce de résistance. Will was frightened of that statue when he was a boy," she said, nodding in the direction of Pan, who stood in the middle of the central bed of rigid, skeletal roses. "The horns."

"He does have a rather leering, off-putting glare," said Ellen. "So, Savannah, I assume, will not go to Westhaven?"

"No. How can I have anything to do with that family? Truthfully, I did not care for his daughter. Formidable. Determined.

Impressive. Admirable qualities, I grant you. She may have a flock of young girls in her care, but they seem to be a means to an end, a project, a business. I think she is a disciplinarian and, knowing who Savannah is, she would make her miserable. The school would not suit Savannah's nature at all."

"Richard and I have been discussing the college in Penistone for Izzy and Maddy. Of course, they will not go away until a year after Savannah, but we have been thinking about it a lot and this school has much to recommend it. It is closer to home for one thing, so the girls can come home at the end of the week. I am not ready for all my children to desert me for months on end. I do so miss Jack. The house will be like a tomb when they are away. I have the details if you are interested."

"Thank you, Ellen. I think that is a good idea and the school has a good reputation," said Marianna, taking her friend's arm. "Savannah will miss Badger and if I can hold out the carrot that she will see him every week she may be persuaded. Then, the following year, Izzy and Maddy will be there, and they can travel together on the train."

A few days later, Marianna was in the study looking over the household accounts when Sarah came in with the post. There was a letter from Robson, an envelope containing a banker's draft. He had sent her the money for the mare and the cost of transporting her to his farm. The coded message was that he accepted that he would not see her again. She ripped the draft into tiny pieces and tossed the shreds into the fire.

FIFTEEN

Savannah had been relieved when it was announced that Penistone Ladies' College was closing three weeks early for the summer holidays due to an outbreak of sickness among the junior girls. One more year and she could leave. School bored her. No, that was not accurate. The long days confined to the school buildings and grounds and the never-ending list of rules bored her, stifled her. If she had not the opportunity to go home at the end of the week or did not have her friends, Amy, Connie and Sophia, she would have gone mad. Apart from mathematics, which she loathed because she could not seem to grasp the principles and there was no Jack with his infinite patience to guide her and explain, she liked most subjects and excelled in them, especially English and history, both taught by Miss Harper, who was fearsomely clever and encouraged her pupils to think and express themselves, constantly challenging them to justify their opinions. She had also discovered a talent for French and seemed to pick it up more quickly than her classmates and was able to converse reasonably well with Mademoiselle Gobillon. But always at the back of her mind was what was the point of it all? What could she expect to do with this expensive education? Yes, she was glad to be home.

Jack was home too from university at the end of his second year of medical studies and, one afternoon after luncheon, he cycled up the hill from Dene House to call on Savannah. He was shown into the drawing room, where she and her mother were examining the contents of a large box filled with tissue paper.

"Good afternoon, ladies," he said. "What have you got there?"

"It's my dress for the Mayor's Ball. It has just been delivered and we were inspecting it," said Savannah. "I'll try it on later, Mama."

"Are you looking forward to the ball?" asked Jack.

This would be the first time Savannah, now seventeen years old, was allowed to attend the annual charitable ball held in the Newbridge music rooms, known as the 'Holroyd' after the benefactor who had paid to have them built.

"I am," said Savannah. "Only you must promise not to monopolise me and let me dance with other young men who might catch my eye."

Jack laughed. "Izzy and Maddy are furious because Mother says they are not old enough to go."

"There is always next year," said Marianna.

"Are you looking forward to it, Mrs Hamilton-Read?"

"I shall be exhausted by the end of it, as will your mother." Marianna and Ellen were on the organising committee. "But all the tickets are sold, which is a relief, and it always raises a lot of money for our charities which makes the effort worthwhile."

Savannah asked Jack if he would like to go for a walk up Longridge Fell and he said yes.

"Don't forget, Savannah," her mother reminded her, "we are helping to sort clothes and food parcels at St. Thomas's at three o'clock."

"I hadn't forgotten, Mama. We won't be long."

She and Jack walked, one behind the other, up the narrow sheep track, with Badger bringing up the rear, and paused, panting from the exertion of the climb, to admire the view.

"We are so lucky to live in such a beautiful place," said Savannah.

Below them, the roof and chimneys of Longridge poking through the trees, in the far distance, under the pale sun, the glinting silver of the sea in the bay; all around them, the rolling hills and soaring fells, the fertile, green valleys and dark, hidden cloughs. The cotton grass in the boggy ground below them semaphored in the breeze and bees hovered above the wild thyme. From the fields below floated the bleats of the sheep and a curlew called above their heads. Badger wandered off to sniff in the heather at the scatterings of rabbit droppings. Savannah glanced at Jack who was smiling at her.

"Penny for them. You were miles away."

"Oh, just thinking about Papa and how he loved coming up here. The view, you know."

"You still miss him, don't you?"

"I'll miss him until the day I die." She turned away abruptly. "Let's put the stones on the cairn."

They tossed the stones they had gathered on the way up on top of the mound.

"Do you think Badger was a little out of breath coming up?" Savannah asked.

"He is getting on a bit. Perhaps he should lead a quieter life."

"He's not so old. Perhaps he is ill. I don't think he will manage the walk to Devil's Seat. We can stay here for a while."

Savannah whistled to the dog, and he came and lay down on the grass nearby. Jack took her hand and pulled her down beside him as he sat down.

"We had some good times there, didn't we?" Savannah waved her hand towards the bay. She remembered the last time she had been there with her father, snuggled on his lap as they shared the binoculars, and he patiently told her again the names of the birds strutting across the sands or wheeling in the sky. "What was your house like over there?" she had asked him.

"Very small, but very cosy. A friend of mine lives in it now."

"Can we go and see it?"

"One day, perhaps."

That day never came. Jack was speaking.

"Pardon?"

"My! You are away with the fairies today! I was saying we did have some very good times. You were very competitive, I seem to recall, with collecting shells – mussel shells mostly – and making sure you had the most by pinching mine when I wasn't looking."

"You should not have let me get away with it. You were too obliging, Jack Greenwood."

She smiled at him. She had not seen him since Christmas, as he had holidayed in France with university friends at Easter, and she thought he had grown up a lot since he had gone away to university. He had always been a handsome boy, but now his voice had deepened further, and the stubble was visible on his chin and lip as he had stopped shaving since he came home. He seemed more masculine, more mature. He was well liked, always courteous and attentive, and her mother was very fond of him. Savannah was struck for the first time that she was attracted to him, not as a friend, but as a possible suitor. She reached for his hand and held it.

"You have another year of school. Will you make it?" He knew how frustrated she was by the rules and regime of her school.

"I will have to. Mama will not let me leave. What she thinks I will do with all this education, I have no idea." She dropped Jack's hand and waved her arm in a sweeping gesture. "Education is a gift, a privilege not to be spurned," she said pompously, mimicking the headmaster. "Your parents pay well to send you here. Do not let them down." Savannah plucked a blade of grass and began to pick it to pieces. "I have an idea I might want to travel. To Europe. Or America. Will has been."

"Izzy and Maddy are in awe of you as always. They tell me you and your friends have a certain reputation for speaking out about the injustices you see and asking to change petty rules."

"We need to do something to amuse ourselves and keep our sanity. Ask yourself, Jack, what is the point of it all when women struggle to be accepted for their brains and intelligence? What chance have I of going to university and becoming a doctor?"

"Would you try? Women are accepted at universities. Do you have the stomach for it? Don't moan about it, Savannah. Do something. I wouldn't expect anything less from you."

"I won't even have the opportunity to take on Longridge. It is Will's. And to be married off and expected to do nothing but sit around and be decorative... Ugh! I'd die of boredom."

"You'd be busy if you had children."

"Is that all a married woman has to look forward to? Is that how you see your future wife? A breeder of perfect little copies of you?"

"That's a bit harsh. Have you forgotten your promise?"

"What promise?"

"Down in the wood. Before I left for boarding school you gave me first refusal on an offer of marriage."

"Oh, Jack. Surely you don't think—"

She saw immediately she had hurt his feelings. He often took the opportunity to remind her of that childish promise, but she thought he did it to tease her.

"I meant it then and I mean it now. I absolutely and totally love you."

The image of her parents years ago here on the fell came back to her. The opportunity was too good to let go.

"Very well, if you love me, prove it." She pushed herself to her feet and walked over the brow of the hill to the less exposed, more private hollow, kicked off her boots and lay back on the grass, arms by her side, straight as an arrow, but Jack did not move. "Well," she called to him. "I'm waiting. Come and show me. Come and kiss me."

Jack demurred. "But that is an order," he called back, "and, if I may say so, somewhat forced and unnatural."

Savannah sat up and shouted to him, "You are the one at university. You are the one learning things that might actually be useful in this world. So, I presume you know how to kiss a girl? So prove it. Come and love me."

He came down to her, pushed her back gently on the grass and lay beside her and told her to close her eyes. He had thought about this moment for a long time. To love Savannah. Not the quick, embarrassed pecks they exchanged as children but the long, lingering, wet kisses, tongues exploring mouths, hearts pounding, hands wandering in search of the mysterious places, entering those mysterious places. He was learning more than medicine at university. He wet his lips. Her eyelashes fluttered and her lips parted as she felt his warm breath on her cheek. She pictured the movements of her mother and father kissing all those years ago in this very spot and her fingers went to his hair, then she moved her hand to place his on her breast and she felt his tongue push into her mouth, and she could hear his pantings as he sought out her mouth again and again. She did not want to open her eyes and spoil the magic of all the sensations and tinglings she could feel charging her body. She felt his fingers unbutton her bodice and then the warmth of his hand against her skin moulding her breast and his fingers stroking her nipple. Then he was on top of her, and his hand was pushing up her skirt, her petticoat, sliding into her drawers, between her legs, and she was trembling. She pushed herself against him as she responded to the strange but not unpleasant sensation in her private parts. Then nothing. She opened her eyes. He was staring down at her, a look of desperate panic on his face. He pushed himself off her, sat up and turned away from her.

"Sorry. Sorry. Sorry." He was shaking his head. Badger had wandered up to him and was looking at him, head cocked to one side.

"What on earth are you doing?" asked Savannah, more in frustration than anger. "Why did you stop?" She raised herself on to her elbows. Badger lay down abruptly at the sharpness of his mistress's voice.

"You are not that kind of girl, Savannah," muttered Jack.

"What kind of girl might that be? My mother has a lover. You can be my lover. I know all about it. I know what happens. I am here. You are here. You say you love me. Show me. Come back and do it again."

Jack turned his head to look at her over his shoulder and said, his voice trembling with emotion, "No. I cannot. You are so special to me. I want to wait until we are married."

"Married? Some chance! I intend to marry a man who knows what he is doing! You say you love me. Then show me. Prove to me you are a man. Love me. I want you to love me. All the way," she demanded. "Here. I shall lie down, and you must come to me," she said, raising her skirts.

"Stop it, Savannah. This is not the way."

She scowled at him, pulled on her boots, heaved herself to her feet, dropped her skirts, and then swiped him round the head in frustration. "Damn you, Jack Greenwood! I wanted you. I wanted you to love me. What pathetic excuse of a boy are you?" She stalked off down the hill, fastening her bodice and whistling to Badger, who bounded after her. If Jack came anywhere near her, said another word, she would slap his face.

Savannah was stretched out on the chaise longue in her bedroom, her eyes closed, listening to the sound of a fly buzzing near the window, banging against the glass in its futile attempt to escape. Badger snoozed on the floor next to the book that had dropped from her grip as her eyes had slowly closed in resignation at her inability to concentrate. She was feeling on edge and there were butterflies in her stomach. There was a knock on the door and her mother came in. Badger jumped up and trotted across the room to greet her.

"Are you ready, darling?" asked Marianna, bending down to scratch Badger's ears.

She sat up slowly. "I don't want to go."

"But the Greenwoods are expecting us. Jack is expecting you."

Savannah slumped back and groaned. It was the afternoon of the Greenwood's garden party. She placed her hand on her forehead. "I have a headache. Really, Mama, I do not feel well," she lied.

"Can you not make the effort? They will be so disappointed. Jack will be disappointed."

Jack. Jack. Same old Jack. Same old faces. Same old conversations. How are you, Savannah? How is school? What will you do when you leave? On and on. And Jack, who had humiliated her, who had let her down. Puppy-eyed, doting, fetching a lemonade, attentive, come and make up a four for tennis, walk with me, Savannah. Drone, drone. Buzz, buzz.

"Send my regrets, Mama. I have the rest of the summer to visit them."

"Well, if you insist."

Savannah watched from behind the curtain until the gig driven by Cuthbert Robson disappeared down the drive. She checked herself in the mirror, patted her hair and dabbed scent behind her ears. Badger had settled himself in the warm spot on the chaise where she had been lying.

"Stay, Badger," she said. "I'll be back soon."

She crept downstairs to the study, let herself out of the French doors and hurried down the road to the stables. She skirted round the back of the building and waited on the corner to ensure the coast was clear. One of the yard cats was sitting by the barn door, licking its paw. She hissed at him, and he ran off. She scuttled into the barn and up the ladder to the hayloft. She undressed, unfastened her hair, and arranged her naked body carefully and, she hoped, seductively, on the loose hay. The clock on the pele tower struck two and it was not long before she heard his steps on the ladder and his face appeared.

Since returning from school, Savannah was on a mission – a mission hatched among her gang of friends, a gang of four who called themselves the Musketeers, as Dumas's book was a favourite. They were the cleverest in their class, frustrated by the rules that constrained them and often questioned authority. They were never insubordinate or rude and were tolerated with bemused affection by their teachers.

On a wet afternoon, before they left for the early holiday, the bored Musketeers had gathered to discuss their plans for the summer and a scheme was dreamt up, with much giggling, and a challenge issued with a financial reward for the winner. The moment she arrived home, Savannah was determined to win. She wanted to be the first to write to her friends to claim victory. She had sensed an opportunity on the fell and Jack had let her down.

The day after the doomed walk with Jack, she asked Thomas Longmire, the stableman, to accompany her on a ride. Since the death of her father and because of her own riding accident, her mother insisted she did not ride out alone. When they returned to the stables, she said, "I seem to have pulled a muscle in my shoulder, Thomas. Will you help me down?"

"Of course, Miss."

She swung her leg over the pommel of the saddle and placed her hands on his shoulders and, as he put his hands round her waist to take her weight, she fell forwards into his arms, her topper falling to the ground.

"Oh, I am sorry," she lied as she clung to him, her arms round his neck, and gazed, with what she hoped was a meaningful look, into his eyes.

The day after, she went riding again and they walked the horses through the wood at her suggestion.

"Stop," she said and slid from the saddle.

Thomas dismounted. "Is summat amiss? Is the pony lame?"

"No," she said, dropping Ladybird's reins, "but you can come here."

Savannah had known Thomas all her life. He was thirty-two years old, tall and gangly and pleasant looking, with a gap between his front teeth which she saw often as he was always smiling. Nothing seemed to bother him, nothing was too much trouble. He knew his station, but they were always easy in each other's company, and she looked on him more as a friend than a servant. He came and stood before her, eyebrows raised in question. Without too much thought, in case she lost her nerve, she put her arms round his neck and reached up on tiptoe to kiss him. What surprised her and, at the same time, slightly alarmed her was the fact he kissed her back immediately. He did not hesitate to consider if it was the right way to behave. Before she knew it, he had pushed her back against a tree trunk, one hand round her waist, the other fondling her breast as he smothered her in kisses. It was as enjoyable as it had been with Jack. She was excited again as she had been with Jack. Then his hands were pulling up her skirts, his fingers groping their way up her britches. She pushed him away.

"Not here, Thomas," she panted. "Someone might see."

The next day, her mother left after breakfast to go to Melchester for a meeting with the accountant who audited the estate books and luncheon with Bertie Robson at the King's Head hotel. Savannah waited until the hour Thomas told her his wife was going to take the children to visit her mother in Newbridge and crept down to the stables and her mission was accomplished. They had their first assignation in the hayloft. He had kissed her once on the mouth, lifted her skirts and petticoats quickly, unbuttoned his flies impatiently, pulled down her drawers and touched her briefly before entering her. She waited, eyes wide open, staring at the cobwebs hanging from the rafters, as he did his business and wondered whether that was it? The Musketeers had talked about it and wondered how it would feel. One had an older, married sister who had described it as a form of ecstasy but, as far as Savannah was concerned, it was slightly painful; there was a smear of blood on her petticoat; it was uncomfortable and thoroughly disappointing; and he had covered her leg with his sticky seed. He rolled off, buttoned his flies and pulled her skirts down. He looked a little too self-satisfied for her liking.

"Do you wish to do it again?"

"What? Now?" he asked in astonishment. "I won't be able to reet off."

"No, I mean tomorrow?"

"Why not? She's out again in th' afternoon."

Savannah thought his use of the pronoun was coldly dismissive of his wife, or perhaps he could not say her name because of what he had just done.

"Next time, do you think you could take me into account and make it more pleasurable for me?" She could not tell the Musketeers that it had not been worth the effort and subterfuge, the risk of discovery or that she was just useless at it.

"It's not always good for a lass th' first time," he said.

"How do you know that?"

"She weren't th' first nor th' last. I only married her cos she were pregnant. I'll tek me time next time an' any time thou likes after that." He grinned at her, his tongue poking through the gap in his teeth.

Despite his admission that he was a serial adulterer, she went back to him, having convinced herself he must be well-practised and would provoke the elusive ecstasy she craved. And again she wondered why poets wrote such gushing twaddle about love. She needed to keep trying until he succeeded in bringing her to fulfilment. The Musketeers needed to know what lay ahead of them. Perhaps it was not her but him that was useless. He did not seem to take any time to consider her at all. She desperately wanted to experience the ecstasy she had been told about. Although the mission was accomplished, she had taken an unsatisfactory bite of the forbidden fruit.

Thomas moaned as he withdrew. She had arched her back and pushed hard against him in a desperate attempt to feel something, anything. She uncurled her legs from round his thighs and untangled her fingers from his hair. Another disappointment. She wiped away his juice from her stomach with some hay and wondered if it would be more pleasurable if he stayed inside her.

"Savannah!"

It was her mother. In the stable yard. Badger barked.

"Fuckin' shit!" muttered Thomas, pulling up his trousers and scrabbling in the hay for his shirt.

"Ssh!" hissed Savannah, fumbling with her undergarments.

Badger was in the barn just feet below them and whining.

"Savannah!" Her mother called again, and she could hear her steps on the cobbles. Then she sneezed. Badger yelped. Her mother started to climb the ladder. There was nowhere to hide. Marianna saw the terrified look on the stableman's face and the panicked look on her half-dressed daughter's. Marianna said nothing and descended the ladder. She waited in the yard. Thomas did not appear, but Savannah did, a few minutes later, her face crimson with embarrassment, and picked up the excited dog.

"Jack is here," said Marianna.

Savannah groaned.

Marianna turned to walk back to the house. "He was disappointed you had decided not to visit, and I told him you could probably be persuaded to attend. I knew there was nothing wrong with you. He insisted on coming to fetch you."

Savannah struggled to keep pace with her mother and put Badger down.

"Of course, you were not in your room. Only Badger. Your little friend there has betrayed you."

"You do not expect me to speak to him? To Jack?"

"I most certainly do. You will go and clean yourself up and you will attend the Greenwood's party."

"Mama. Please, no."

She was surprised by her mother's quiet calmness. She had not uttered a word about what she had just witnessed. Marianna turned to face her daughter. Her eyes blazed.

"You will do as you are told."

SIXTEEN

The guard had closed the carriage door and Savannah leant through the window to kiss her mother's cheek. She settled back into the seat opposite Bertie, who was to make sure she caught the connecting train to Liverpool. She had told her mother she wished to travel alone and was annoyed Bertie had offered to accompany her as she did not know what they would talk about on the journey. She was embarrassed, as he knew everything. She was glad when the train began to pull out of Newbridge Station, and she would find something to stare at out of the window. It had been a difficult few days. The grey weather matched her mood.

As they rattled through the countryside, she stole glances at Bertie. He was a lovely man and she liked him very much. *Quite handsome*, she thought, *for a man of his age, although a little grizzled.* But, since he had reappeared in their lives, her mother was happy, which was good enough for her. He was kind to her and good company. Over breakfast they would often discuss and argue about the events reported in the newspaper and he would patiently answer her questions, especially why, following the Reform Act, women still could not vote, for which, they both agreed, there was no answer. They went out riding together and, like her father, he knew a lot about horses. She recalled the afternoon during the Easter holidays several years before when she had been allowed to sit in on a meeting in the study – provided she remain silent and work on her sampler – with her mother, Will and Bertie. It was something that had stuck in her mind: that this man was involved and included in something so important to her family. The desk was covered with maps of the estate and pieces of paper with columns of figures. They were discussing ways to keep the estate financially viable. Her mother had already spent money on the farms in line with plans discussed with her father. Now Marianna was asking the men's opinion on another of William's ideas – opening a shoot; something Bertie, the former steward of a large estate, was familiar with. At the end of each opinion expressed, the same question was asked: Will it work? Her mother wanted to sell Lowside Farm to release capital to purchase the Newbridge Hotel which had recently been put up for sale. She had grand ideas for refurbishing it as a place to stay for the shooting parties, and it could also be used for wedding receptions, events, and a holiday destination for all the visitors flocking to the area, thanks to Mr Wordsworth. Will's suggestion that Hapenny How, a farm that was doing well with a hard-working tenant, might fetch a better price was dismissed. Marianna had too much emotion invested in it to ever sell it. Her mother stood, arms folded, brow furrowed. Bertie stroked his chin. Will, fingers splayed on the desk, hunched forward over the plans. Then a little voice – hers – piped up. "A grand idea!" And they laughed with surprise.

"What is it?" Bertie was regarding her with a bemused look. She did not realise she had been staring at him.

"You know we all love you, Bertie. You are very much part of our family."

"That is very kind of you to say so." He smiled fondly at her, wondering where this affectionate compliment had come from.

"Was your daughter as troublesome to you?"

"Not in this way," said Bertie, thinking of his solemn, humourless daughter, devoted to her school and destined to be a spinster since she had, within two months, broken off her engagement to the classics master for reasons she did not divulge. "This will all soon blow over."

"I hope so, Bertie. I hope so."

Her thoughts returned to the afternoon of the Greenwood's party where she had endured hours of excruciating embarrassment, as she felt everyone was looking at her and knew what she had done, and guilt as Jack fussed over her and she wished the ground would swallow her up. Afterwards, she had been summoned to her mother's bedroom. They had settled side by side on the bed, something they often did to have a chat, and now a tactic Marianna decided to use to put her at ease in the hope her daughter would confess all and not feel it was to be an interrogation. At first, Savannah had grovelled and asked for forgiveness, then promised she would go back to school and study hard.

Her mother interrupted her, "Why have you behaved like this?"

She had to explain the 'mission'.

"So, for the sake of a guinea, you chose to throw yourself at a servant? That is all you are worth?"

"Thomas is a friend. He is not a stranger. I have known him all my life and Jack wouldn't do it."

"Jack? You asked Jack?"

"Not exactly. We were kissing but that is all. He wouldn't do it."

"Of course he wouldn't. Jack is a gentleman and has too much respect for you."

Marianna's fingers twisted in her lap. She did not know what to say to her daughter but knew that she had to try and make Savannah realise, not for the first time, that her recklessness had consequences. How would William have handled the situation? What would he have said to his beloved daughter? Bertie knew better than to interfere. She was on her own. She had already decided there was no point in being angry; she did not want to damage their close relationship.

"Was this the first time?"

Savannah squirmed. They were so close she knew her mother, just by looking into her eyes, knew everything concealed within and it would be pointless to lie. What would her mother think of her when she told her no?

"Thomas is married, Savannah. Did you have no consideration for his wife and children?"

"He does not love her. He told me."

"Of course he did. Did he tell you other sweet things to entice you? Have you no judgement, Savannah? When a man wants something, wants to seduce a woman, he charms her, tells her things she wants to hear."

"He does not love her. He had to marry her. Anyway, even if it makes you hate me more, Mama, I went to him."

"I do not hate you, darling. But you have been foolish and reckless. But then that has always been the way with you." Marianna sighed. "I feel I am partly to blame for your behaviour. I have always been honest with you and answered your questions and prepared you for womanhood. A few years ago, I told you Bertie would be coming to visit sometimes because we were lovers. I explained to you what that meant and what happens between a man and a woman. My failing has been in not explaining to you the emotional aspects of a relationship, which are as important as the physical. My failing has been in not emphasising how precious the sexual act is, and your love must not be given away cheaply. You do not love Thomas any more than he loves you. You wanted to know what it was all about, and he is a man who will take it when offered. I did not anticipate having this conversation with you so soon. I suppose I still regard you as my little girl and want to protect you…" She sighed again. She *had* failed to protect her child. "It would seem you have taken matters out of my hands. I hope it was worth it. Thomas will be dismissed."

"Oh, no, Mama. Please don't. It is all my fault."

"How can he stay here after what has happened? He has overstepped the mark. Did you think of the consequences should you be discovered? How can I trust a man who has done this? How can I look him in the eye knowing what he has done? I will ask Bertie to help me to find him another position, and I will give him a reference only for the sake of his family and because I recognise the fault lies as much with you as him and, until that is arranged, you will go to stay with Will. I have already written to him. And you will not be returning to school, Savannah. I will have to think of something else for you. Let us hope that you are not pregnant."

She had been able to reassure her mother on that score. Thomas had known what to do in that regard. Her mother informed her that what Thomas did was not enough. She had to learn to take responsibility for herself and had told her what was required. Savannah had also asked, "Why is it so disappointing and is it always the same for a woman? Will I have to endure the act forever and not feel anything? Is there something wrong with me? What do I need to do?"

"Well, you are no longer my little girl, so there is no harm in telling you all that I know. It is more pleasurable certainly when you love and care for someone."

As the train rattled on towards Melchester, Savannah recalled the details of this long, intimate conversation with her mother, and it was disappointment she sensed, not in the fact she had lost her virginity, but with whom she had lost it. Her mother had not lectured her on her lack of morals, her wantonness, how she would never find a husband as she was tarnished goods. She had the feeling that her mother was sad for her that she had not waited to find a man she loved and who loved her, rather than throw herself at the first man willing to take advantage of her. If it had been Jack, who everyone knew doted on her, her mother would have been less sad. Savannah was sad too, and sad that she had risked her reputation on this lovemaking business that had not lived up to its promise.

But what she was to do in Liverpool to occupy herself she did not know. Her mother had said she would be company for Esme, who was heavily pregnant and would appreciate someone helping with her sons, William Bennet and Theo, even though they had a nursemaid. She wondered too how long her banishment would last. She supposed it would depend on how long it took for Thomas to find another position. How would Badger cope without her? She was worried about him.

At Liverpool, Will met her off the train and turned away when she tried to kiss him. His frostiness was not a good omen. In silence, they followed the porter who trundled her luggage on a trolley to the station forecourt, where a cab was summoned to take them to Will's home in the suburbs. Will had done well and now had his own law firm, which had expanded and thrived alongside his growing reputation and list of clients. He had aged well and was a strikingly handsome man who reminded her of her father, apart from the Hamilton eyes they had both been blessed with. She loved her much older brother as he was always kind and protective of her. His house, which reflected his prosperity, was a detached villa set behind a red-brick wall and iron gates, overlooking a large, tree-filled park with wide avenues, ornamental gardens, fountains and a boating lake.

After she had freshened up, Savannah went to face Esme who was, surprisingly, sweet and kind to her, and she wondered if she knew of her disgrace. Her nephews were pleased to see her. On the other hand, when summoned to Will's study after dinner, she had to endure an hour-long lecture on how disappointed he was, how she had wasted her education and the money her mother had spent on it, how selfish and immature she was, lacking any morals or standards of behaviour expected in a young lady, pausing only to take a sip of the drink he had poured for himself without offering her one. He had never spoken to her before in such a hostile manner and it upset her. She listened to him, hands clasped in her lap, eyes cast down demurely, not saying a word until he had exhausted his extensive vocabulary of scathing adjectives to denounce her behaviour and leaving her with nothing but the offer of a simple apology.

"I am sorry, Will." She tried to keep the tears she wanted to shed under control because she knew they would only rouse him more. "I have let everyone down. I can understand your anger. At least Esme has been kind and civil to me."

Will glowered at her. "Esme has not been told the reason for your visit. She thinks you are here out of the kindness of your heart. She is eight months pregnant, Savannah. My duty is to see to the well-being of my wife and not give her cause to worry."

"I am grateful you have let me stay with you."

"Mama asked me. I care only for Mama, and I would do anything for her."

His choice of words about duty and only seeming to care for their mother struck her as odd – a slip of the tongue? But she did not dwell on it as he was shaking his head sadly to reinforce his disappointment in her. He reached for his pipe and waved his hand to dismiss her so she could escape at last from the interview in which she had played only a small part.

The first few days passed uneventfully. A letter from her mother did not mention when she might go home. Savannah rose when she wished and then, whilst the elderly nursemaid, Miss Atkinson, who had once looked after Esme, rested, she would play counting games, sing songs and read to her nephews. In the afternoon, she would take them to the park to feed the ducks on the boating lake; play with a ball; chase each other with sticks, pretending to be knights on horseback; play hide and seek; or stop and talk to the many people walking their dogs, who knew who the boys were.

Walking back home one afternoon after feeding the ducks, both boys holding her hands, William Bennet said to her, "I am so glad you are here, Aunt Savannah. You are so much fun."

"I am glad to be here as you are two of the nicest little boys I know."

Savannah had noticed that of the two, William Bennet, who resembled his father with his dark hair and the Hamilton eyes, was the most reserved and often seemed troubled. At five years old. Theo, fair-haired and grey-eyed like his mother, was a bundle of energy, noise and mischief. His brother, a year older, was not.

"Mama gets tired and cross, and Papa is always working," said William Bennet.

"I'm sure your mama does not mean to be cross. It is hard work having a baby but, after the baby comes, she will be her old self again. And your father works hard so you can live in a nice house next to a nice, big park for you to play in." She knew, despite the pregnancy and Will's long hours at work, that both parents were loving and attentive.

William Bennet looked up at her and seemed on the verge of tears.

"What is it?" asked Savannah, bending down to hug him. Theo stood watching them, his thumb in his mouth. William Bennet cupped his hand round his mouth and whispered in her ear, "Papa is angry with Mama and Mama is angry with Papa and cries. I hear them sometimes, shouting, when I am in bed."

"Oh, my dear," Savannah whispered back. "I'm sure it is nothing. Grown-ups often shout. They have big, loud voices, don't they?" She was at a loss as to what to say to such a young child that would not upset him further. "Shall we have a race to the gate?"

At the end of the week, a note arrived from Aunt Lizzie inviting Savannah to stay at Meadowside for a few days. She wondered who had told her she was at Will's. However, she was glad to go as there was an atmosphere in the house which she did not understand, and Esme did not mind. Aunt Lizzie was waiting for her on the front steps as she got out of the cab after the short journey from Liverpool and hugged her warmly. After she had deposited her small case in her bedroom, she went downstairs to take tea with Aunt Lizzie in the sitting room.

"How's your mother?"

"She is well."

"You're helpin' Esme, I believe, who's also in good health?"

Savannah breathed a sigh of relief. It would seem Aunt Lizzie had not been told of her misdemeanour.

"Yes, but she tires easily and complains of her size and how awkward she is. She is convinced she is having twins."

"I think you get bigger with each successive child. I certainly found it so. And your brother's well and lookin' forward to bein' a father again?"

"I believe so, but it's hard to tell. He has not said much about it."

She did not want to tell Aunt Lizzie that she thought Will was unhappy. She knew he was disappointed with her, but there was something else. When they sat down together for dinner, he seemed withdrawn, as if his mind was elsewhere, and had to be prompted several times to answer a question. Afterwards, he would go up to the nursery to read to the boys and then shut himself in his study to smoke his pipe and drink his whisky. She wondered if he had problems at his law firm and had to bring his work home.

"He looks so much like his father," said Aunt Lizzie, who used Will's law firm to look after her affairs. "Each time I see him, he reminds me of William. I do miss him, Savannah. He was so good to us. Never forget him, Savannah. He was a good man, a good man." Aunt Lizzie brushed away a tear. As did Savannah.

Through the sitting room window, they saw a cab coming up the drive and, shortly after, Lizzie's daughter Beth, and son-in-law Robert, came into the sitting room with their daughter, Millicent. They had been shopping in Liverpool. Savannah had not seen Milly, who was a year younger than her, for a couple of years. Cousin Beth, who was plump and friendly, and her husband, who was as thin as a rake and very reserved, doted on their only child. She was a sweet-looking, kind, young woman who attracted people to her with her wit and good humour. She kept them all entertained at dinner with the conversation revolving mainly around her cousin's nuptials due to take place in late August when Milly was to be one of the bridesmaids. Aunt Lizzie rolled her eyes good-naturedly at Savannah.

"You'll have guessed, my dear, from all this talk of preparations, that it'll be the weddin' of the year in Liverpool, if not the North of England."

"Dorothy has found the most perfect dress for me, Savannah," said Milly, "from the best dress shop in Liverpool, 'La Parisienne'. It still needs a few alterations."

Milly launched into a pitch-perfect rendition of the conversation with the proprietress of the shop, who spoke English with a French accent but failed to disguise the local one she had been born with.

"You may mock her, Milly," scolded her mother, "but she is a very fine seamstress trained in one of the best fashion houses in Paris."

"She is, Mama, but why pretend to be French? It's ludicrous!"

Milly turned to Savannah and said, "Why don't you come with me and Mama next week for my fitting and you can hear her for yourself?"

SEVENTEEN

Savannah did not have to wait long, as a note from Milly arrived within days of her return to Will's house, inviting her to meet her and Beth on Friday at the Adelphi Hotel for lunch first, and they would go to the dress shop afterwards. Will was going in late to his office and said she could ride into the city with him. During the night, Esme had thought she was going into labour and her doctor had been summoned. It was a false alarm and Savannah had slept through it all. The cab was late arriving, and Will said he would prefer to go straight to the office as he had a noon appointment with an important client. The cab could take her on to the hotel afterwards.

"If you do not mind, Will, I should like to go to the Walker Gallery. I have some time before meeting Beth and Milly so I could walk from your office."

"I will ask one of the clerks to walk with you."

"No need, Will." She knew he did not trust her. "It is not far."

"I insist."

"I insist I can walk by myself. I know my way around."

"As you wish. You are so aggravating, Savannah, but I do not have the energy to argue with you."

He sighed, sank back against the seat and fumbled in his pocket for his pipe, thought better of it and put it away. Again, Savannah thought he looked careworn and troubled. Perhaps the result of his disturbed night? Will looked across at her.

"Have you taken time whilst you have been here to consider your behaviour, Savannah, and how to mend your ways?"

"I have, Will, and I shall endeavour to behave more appropriately," she replied in a measured tone in order to appease him and win her way back into his good books.

"I am pleased to hear it. I do not like Mama to be upset."

They rode along in silence for a few minutes. Will stared at Savannah so she looked out of the window at the people walking in the street as he was making her feel uncomfortable; no doubt going over in his mind what she had done and what a nuisance she was.

"I recommend the turtle soup for your lunch."

Savannah turned back from the window, a look of surprise on her face. "I thought turtle soup was fiction. *Alice in Wonderland?*"

"They keep them in tanks of water in the basement, so it is freshly made. Very expensive, though."

"Ugh! It sounds remarkably cruel to me. I do not think I can bear the thought of an animal being killed beneath my feet."

"You eat beef, do you not? And lamb? How do you think they end up on the table?"

"But the cows are not slaughtered within earshot."

Will smiled wearily at her and shook his head.

"I thought I might buy a present for Esme's birthday next week. What do you think of a book? *The Mayor of Casterbridge* by Mr Hardy? It is recently published, and I know she likes to read his books."

"Yes, she does. She will appreciate your kind thought."

"What have you bought for her?"

"I have an account with a jeweller. That is what she always wants. She chooses her own piece. She knows what she likes."

Savannah thought it strange that Will would not buy something for his wife as a surprise. He saw her puzzled look and said, "I never get it right. I do not know what appeals to my wife's tastes."

"Will?"

"Hmm?"

"No matter."

She wanted to say something to him, ask him if all was well with him but, somehow, she knew he would not confide in her. He thought her immature and irresponsible, not the kind of person to ask for advice.

They parted outside his office and Savannah headed for the gallery that she knew well, as she had been several times with her mother when they came to stay with Will. She wandered round the rooms on the ground floor and then decided to make her way to the hotel. The streets were thronged with people, carts, trams and taxi cabs. Many heads turned to admire the beautiful girl: a policeman touched his helmet in salute and a barrow boy whistled. Savannah was wearing a dark blue fitted dress with three-quarter-length sleeves and a large bow at the back which showed off her figure and which she hoped would impress the owner of 'La Parisienne', despite the fact she eschewed the fashionable bustle. A small, velvet hat was perched at a jaunty angle on her head. She wore her hair loosely plaited and coiled at the nape of her neck, as she hated the fuss of the latest fashion for pinned curls piled high on the head. She carried a lace parasol, borrowed from Esme, and her purse hung from her wrist. She passed St. George's Hall, where a huddle of pigeons flew up at her approach and attracted the attention of two young men sitting on the steps.

"My," said one, puffing out his cheeks as she passed by. "She's beautiful. Perfect."

"Perfect in every way," said the other, tossing away his cigarette and rising to follow Savannah. "Come on," he said to his companion.

They paused on the pavement outside the hotel as Savannah disappeared through the door.

"What about our meeting?"

"We have a half hour yet. I'm sure you are dying to wet your whistle with a cup of English tea."

His companion hesitated.

"You look fairly presentable. Come on."

Savannah had settled on a sofa in the corner of the hotel foyer to wait for Beth and Milly. It was busy and noisy: businessmen, lawyers, ladies meeting friends congregated before moving into the dining room. As a young woman on her own she attracted some disapproving looks and kept her eyes cast down. She looked up in surprise as a young man addressed her.

"May we join you?"

She was taken aback by him. He was beautiful. She looked at him quizzically. There were plenty of free chairs.

"I am waiting for someone," she said, lowering her gaze. Her heart was beating fast.

"We are visitors here in this fine city," he persisted, "and wondered if you would suggest some landmarks that we may be interested in."

She looked up at him again. He was tall and slim, soberly dressed in a dark brown suit. His eyes twinkled at her, and a grin curled the corners of his mouth. He was dark eyed, his long, wavy, dark hair and the neat line of his trimmed beard framed a handsome face crowned by high cheekbones. He was exceedingly handsome; she had never seen such a handsome man and his accent, soft and lilting, intrigued her. She could not stop herself returning his grin.

"Oh, sit down." She laughed. "As if I believe all that nonsense."

The handsome one sat down next to her. His friend, who was not as tall but heavily built, smiled shyly and sat down opposite them. He was not as well-turned out and looked uncomfortable. He was mousy haired and blue eyed with a pleasant, open face, but was nowhere near as attractive as the man sitting beside her.

"Conor Clare," the handsome one said, offering his hand. "This is my good friend, Hugh Furlong." She shook their hands. "And who might you be?"

"Savannah Marianna Hamilton-Read."

"My, that is a mouthful. But your first name… Enchanting."

"You cannot stay long," she said, ignoring his attempt to charm her. Her mother had warned her. "I am expecting my cousin and her daughter. We are having luncheon before going shopping."

"We shan't stay long then, sadly. Do you live here in this fine city, Savannah?" asked Conor Clare, leaning close to her.

"I am staying with my brother and his family for a while. His wife is expecting a baby soon. I am helping out."

"So where is home?" asked Conor.

"Near Newbridge."

"Never heard of it!" Conor laughed.

"Where do you come from?" she asked, charmed by the brogue.

"Ireland."

"And your business in Liverpool?"

Conor tapped his nose. "Wouldn't you like to know?"

It is he, she thought, *who does most of the talking.* His friend was silent, fiddling with his cap, embarrassed to be there, although she was aware he could not take his eyes off her. A member of the hotel staff approached, and Savannah waved him away as Milly and Beth had still not arrived. In a way, she hoped they would be delayed a bit longer as she was enjoying herself and Mr Clare's attention.

"So, what does this brother of yours do?"

"He is a lawyer."

"Aha! Has a nice big house, does he?"

"Near Sefton Park. Do you know it? It is worth a visit."

"Do you know, Miss Savannah Big-Mouthful-of-a-Name, I might just do that. What do you think, Hugh?" Hugh nodded. "My friend has been struck dumb by your beauty. Forgive him! Well, Savannah, if you are expecting company, we'd best be going. It was a pleasure to meet you."

Mr Furlong was already on his way out of the main door as Mr Clare took her hand, brushed his lips across her knuckles and stared into her eyes. She felt a flutter in her stomach, a stirring, and began to blush. And then he was off with a backward wave.

Savannah was walking briskly back to Will's house along one of the many wide paths that dissected the park when she saw him. He was leaning against the trunk of a tree smoking a cigarette. She had an hour or so to herself after luncheon and decided to get some fresh air now the rain showers had passed over. She stopped in surprise: that she would see him again and why he would be loitering in the park. There was no sign of the silent Hugh. It had been three days since they had met, and she had not stopped thinking about him – and here he was. He tossed away the cigarette, waved to her and walked languidly towards her, hands in trouser pockets, and her heart skipped a beat. Why? She hardly knew him. Yet there was something alluring, animalistic about him; he walked like a prowling lion approaching his prey and she knew he had only to ask, and she would be a willing victim.

He was dressed, more flamboyantly this time, in a grey linen suit, a gold watch and chain attached to the pocket of his pale blue, striped waistcoat and a neckcloth tied in a floppy bow under his stiff collar. Unlike the gentlemen strolling in the park, he was hatless.

"Are you following me?" she asked.

"I have been in this park for two days, waiting to see you and trying to work out which house is your brother's. I saw you yesterday walking with two small boys, so I kept my distance."

"Why did you want to see me?"

"Why? What a stupid question! I am smitten."

"Don't be ridiculous. You do not know me."

"I fell for you the other day when I saw you walking through town. Do you think it was mere chance we turned up at the hotel?"

"Don't be so ridiculous," she said again, flattered by his words and unable to keep the giggle from her throat.

"I was watching you as you came along the path. Do you always walk at speed?"

"I like to walk. At home I walk a lot. Up hills too. Here, people saunter because they are encumbered so by their dress. I should like to lift my skirts and run."

Conor laughed. "Saunter with me," he said, looping her arm through his.

"I have not got long. I have to look after the children as their nurse is going to the dentist."

He tightened his grip on her arm. "You are not going anywhere until you agree to meet me tomorrow and the day after and the day after that." He led her to a small copse of trees and bushes that shielded them from anyone walking along the path. He positioned her against a tree and placed his hands on the trunk either side of her head and stared at her: the heart-shaped face, the full lips, the eyes fringed with thick lashes.

"You have the most stunning eyes. I struggle to decide on the colour. Dark blue. Purple almost."

She stared back, the warmth of a blush rising to her cheeks, and then he leant slowly into her, his eyes never leaving hers, and began to kiss her. She tasted the stale bitterness of his cigarette. At first, her mother's words rang in her ears, but she could not help herself and soon she was responding to him, eyes closed, heart pounding, until he stepped back, gasping a little, and laughed.

"My word, you know how to kiss. Have you done it before, Miss Unbelievably-Long-Name?"

"Stop making fun of my name," she said huffily.

"Don't pout," he said, although he was thinking how invitingly kissable her lips were and pulled her into his arms and began to kiss her again.

"Now," he said, holding her at arm's length, "I'd better tell you all about myself so you know you can trust me and will agree to see me again."

They walked, him leading the way, from the cover of the trees to a bench in one of the shelters further along the avenue, which Savannah checked could not be seen from the house. She hoped, too, none of the neighbours would pass on their daily dog walks. She sat down and folded her hands in her lap, asking him to sit away from her for the sake of propriety. He sat back, casually crossed his legs and stretched his arm along the back of the bench. His fingers climbed up her back to stroke her neck. She knew she should object to this improper behaviour in public, but she did not as she liked the intimacy of it.

"So," he said, "I am Conor Clare as you know. Twenty-six years old. And I hasten to add, a gentleman, although you may not think so. A gentleman does not drag young ladies into the shrubbery."

She laughed.

"However, in my defence, I am an Irish gentleman, not a stuffed-shirt, English gentleman, and we do things differently in Ireland."

Thank goodness, she thought, casting her mind back to the disastrous episode with Jack.

"And you are?"

She smiled at him. "Savannah Marianna Hamilton-Read, as you already know. Seventeen years old. And you must decide whether I am a lady or not. After all, I went willingly into the shrubbery."

He laughed. His fingers crawled up her neck and twined a loose curl. She edged closer to him. "Now," he said, running his thumb and forefinger down the line of his moustache, "to win your heart and make you fall hopelessly in love with me, I'll tell you I am an orphan."

"Oh! I am so sorry," gasped Savannah.

"Do not shed tears for me, my sweet, little English rose, for I am a grown man," he said, waving his free arm theatrically. "My pain has ebbed after so many years and the tragic tale has a happy ending. I was taken in by a wealthy relative. Like all good fairy tales."

Savannah was horrified by his glibness. "Mr Clare, I feel you do not take things such as the loss of your family very seriously and I wonder if you have any feelings at all. My papa died when I was young, and I miss him every day."

Conor's hand dropped to her shoulder and gave it a squeeze.

"I'm sorry to hear that. I have not experienced pain such as yours, as I do not remember my parents at all. They died of sickness when I was three. My sister remembers them. She is four years older than me. She's called Orla, by the way. Tell me about your father."

They spoke for almost an hour. She told him about William and the day he died, her face clouding over as she spoke fondly of him. She told him about Marianna, how beautiful and kind she was and how much she had loved William. She told him about Longridge, the house and the countryside, which was as beautiful as any she had seen. She told him she was worried about Badger. She told him about Moth and Ladybird. She told him about her school and how she wondered what to do with her life. The minutes flew by. She talked to him as if she had known him for years and felt no awkwardness in his company. He listened, asked questions and seemed genuinely interested in what she had to say. He listened, watching her face; her beautiful eyes shining with tears at one moment, with joy at another.

"We are becoming good friends, you and I," he said warmly, and he went on to tell her how he and his sister had been taken to Boston in America to live with a great-aunt, who had married a rich Irish American. When he died two years later, his aunt, Norah Archbold, returned to Ireland to fulfil a desire to live for a few years in her homeland. She bought a large house not far from Dublin and a few miles away from the town where she had lived as a child. For him and his sister, it had been an idyllic childhood. As he spoke affectionately of his aunt, his sister, and his life, she edged her hand along the seat to seek out his and they entwined their fingers. The lion had ensnared his prey. Savannah had fallen in love with Conor Clare.

EIGHTEEN

A book clutched in her hand, Savannah left the house in a rush for her third meeting with Conor, telling Esme, who liked to take a nap after luncheon, she was going to read in the park as she had done the previous afternoon. The children were with Nurse Atkinson in the nursery. Conor Clare was waiting for Savannah by the bench, but they decided it would be more prudent to walk further into the park and found another seat under some elm trees on a less frequented path. They kissed before sitting down.

Conor picked up the book she had brought and raised his eyebrows.

"Hmm! *Treatise on Crimes and Misdemeanours*. I should imagine that's a fascinating read for some people," he said, handing the book back to her.

"I just grabbed it from the hall table on my way out in my haste to see you. It's obviously Will's. Do you have a favourite book?"

"No." He laughed. "That sounds like I don't read at all. Let me change my answer. My favourite book is the last one I read." He laughed again. "That's not true either. I read *Daniel Deronda* and hated it. Far too long. I didn't finish it. What about you?"

"We do not have much time to list my favourites."

"All right. Quick-fire questions. What's your favourite colour?"

"I do not have one."

Conor laughed. "This is not going to work either."

"Well, what is your favourite colour?"

"I couldn't tell you because I do not know the name of the colour that matches your eyes. I thought lapis lazuli, but… not quite. Something darker."

"What did you do after our meeting yesterday?"

"I was extremely miserable and moped for the rest of the day. The hours dragged and I could not sleep last night. And then you were late, and I was in agonies as I thought you had come to your senses and decided not to see me again."

Savannah smiled. She did not tell him that she had not slept well either, her mind racing with thoughts and feelings that made her skin tingle and her heart race. "The cook burnt the rice pudding for luncheon," she explained. "We had to wait whilst she made some more, as it is my nephews' favourite dessert."

They lapsed into silence. He took her hand, kissed it and held on to it, rubbing his thumb gently across the skin.

"What are you thinking about?" he asked at last.

"I wish I could sit here all afternoon."

"Will you meet me tomorrow?"

"I cannot see you tomorrow." The tears bubbled to the surface. "It is Esme's birthday and her parents, sister and my cousin's wife and children are coming to tea."

"Don't fret," he said, wiping away the tears. "There is always the day after. Can you meet me then?"

"Oh, yes. Please, yes."

Conor cupped her face in his hands and stared into her eyes.

"Savannah? You feel it, don't you? There is something happening between us."

"Yes." Her voice wavered. "I feel it."

Connor Clare, wearing his plain, brown suit, was waiting for Savannah in front of the Municipal Buildings as they had arranged at the end of their meeting on the previous Friday. Two long, frustrating days to fill with entertaining her nephews and enduring the visits of Esme's and Will's friends before she would see him again. They walked briskly along the road. She was wearing her plainest dress and jacket as he had advised to avoid drawing attention to herself. She felt as though she was floating above the pavement beside him as she was so happy and cast furtive glances to feast her eyes on his beautiful face. They turned into a narrow street of identical, small, tired-looking, back-to-back houses not far from the docks. They walked past a gaggle of dirty-faced children absorbed in a game of ollies and through a short tunnel under a railway line to a wider street with wider terraced houses and back yards and entered the first in the row. Savannah had lied to Esme, saying she was going shopping for a gift for her mother. She knew what she was doing. She knew what was going to happen. She knew she had never wanted something so much in her life.

Within minutes of going upstairs, they were naked in the narrow bed in the narrow, sparsely furnished bedroom. His soft, brown eyes stared deep into her soul, his dark hair fell over her face, and he was caressing her and touching her and whispering to her. How beautiful she was, how much he desired her. He was kissing, touching, caressing every part of her that she did not know could give such pleasure. Clumsy, diffident Jack. Crude, selfish Thomas. Who were they compared to this beautiful man who gave her at last the ecstasy she longed for? No thoughts either for a schoolgirl wager. This was her moment. Hers alone. And then he entered her. Again, her body trembled to its core. This was more than pleasure. She was dreaming. In heaven. Drifting to a place of dreams on clouds of pleasure. She did not want it to end. Everything else was forgotten.

They barely spoke afterwards. He lay behind her, his arms and legs wrapped round her, and nuzzled her neck. She felt cherished and warm and… happy. Her eyes flitted round the room. She had the impression that it was not his as there were, apart from his clothes in a heap on the floor and his smoking equipment, no personal effects to be seen. The curtains were drawn partly across the window and one of the hems was down. It was not perhaps the most salubrious place to have enjoyed such pleasure. The walls were covered in a drab, faded wallpaper, the pattern lost to the passing years; there was a brown stain on the ceiling, but at least there were clean sheets on the bed. Then, without warning, he turned her over, climbed on top of her, balanced on his arms stretched either side of her and watched her intently, and she could not take her eyes off him; she was hypnotised. His eyes were warm and gentle and suffused with the knowing of a man who loved women and knew what women wanted.

He stares at her; he knows all, he is older, he is a man. His eyes are black, the pupils dilated with all the things he has seen and knows, and she cannot stare him out because she is young, a woman, and women do not know, are not allowed to know, all a man knows because that is the way of the world, and her eyelids flutter once, then more quickly because she needs to hide her ignorance, She does not want to fail; she does not want to disappoint him. Yet there is a questioning in his eyes, a hesitancy, which she does not understand. He blinks, and whatever it is has gone. Is this why he is now asking her again if it is safe? She had forgotten to think about it; she cannot remember; she does not care. She nods. He enters her again and loves her and still his eyes never leave hers as he gives himself to her, gives her everything he knows, and she drifts away again on wave after wave of pleasure as her eyes fill with tears of utter happiness.

He helped her dress and ran his fingers through her hair as he tidied it for her, and she lifted her face to seek out his mouth and she wanted him again. How was it possible to feel like this? To be desired and wanted and to desire and want so intensely in return. But he shook his head.

"You need to go home. You must not be late. We need to be careful. Can you come again tomorrow?"

She started to weep.

"What is it?"

"I don't know. I feel so emotional. I cannot explain it. I don't want to be parted from you for even a minute."

"It is only until tomorrow. Come downstairs and I shall make you a cup of tea. There is time for that. Isn't that the English answer to all your worries, my sweet, English rose?"

They went down the narrow staircase. The door to the front room was ajar and she could see it was being used as a bedroom.

In the gloom, as the curtains were undrawn, Savannah could see that it was very untidy with an unmade bed, and clothes scattered on the floor. The kitchen was at the back of the house, and she was surprised to see Hugh was there. He smiled shyly at her as he got up to pull out a chair for her. There was another man standing by the open door, smoking a cigarette, who barely turned to acknowledge her. She thought, as a pink flush bloomed on her cheeks, that they had been alone in the house.

"That rude ruffian is our friend, Finn O'Driscoll," said Conor by way of introduction. "This is his house. He's an old friend from home which is why we stay here."

O'Driscoll turned his head, nodded and went back to staring out of the door.

"Don't mind him. He was never one for polite conversation."

In response, O'Driscoll hacked up a wad of phlegm and spat it out into the yard. Hugh grimaced and shook his head in apology to Savannah.

"Hugh, make us a cup of tea, will you?" said Conor.

The kitchen, like everything else in this house, was small and cramped. Dirty dishes were piled up in the sink and a rag, an apology for a curtain, hung to one side of the grime-smeared window. They sat round the small table stained with cup rings, crusted food remnants and cigarette burns. Savannah shuddered inwardly at the squalor and thought of Ada's pristine kitchen at home. O'Driscoll stubbed his cigarette out on the step with his boot, kicked the butt into the yard and shut the door. He took up a position, arms folded, and leant back against the sink. Savannah was in his direct eyeline, his cold, blue eyes boring into her as though he was appraising her, and she was undergoing some kind of test. She felt uneasy and did not have the nerve to stare him out. He seemed older than Conor and Hugh, rough-looking, shabbily dressed, and unshaven. When she dared to glance up at him, he was staring at her, tobacco-stained fingers stroking his stubbled chin.

"How's your tea?" asked Hugh. "Would you be wanting some more milk or sugar in it? I sometimes brew it too long."

"No, thank you. It's fine."

There was an uncomfortable silence. Savannah wondered if Conor's friends had heard anything – the springs on his bed had made a lot of noise – and what must they think of her?

"Do you have family in England, Hugh?" she asked brightly to stimulate a conversation.

"No. I came to work so I can send money home." Walk? Savannah was puzzled by his pronunciation until he said, "Jobs are easier to come by in England. I work in the docks with Finn."

For a moment she wondered why they were at home rather than at work, but the cold, disdainful stare of Finn O'Driscoll's scrutiny convinced her not to ask that question.

"Do you miss your home and family?"

O'Driscoll snorted and rolled his eyes. She could see Hugh was embarrassed by him. Conor was tracing his finger round one of the stains on the table. He looked ill at ease, troubled. She wanted to take his hand to reassure him and, more so, herself, but Finn O'Driscoll's sneering look unnerved her.

"Not really. I try and get home once a year if I can," replied Hugh.

"Well, Savannah, drink up," said Conor, rapping his knuckles on the table. "Hugh will walk you to the cab as I have business to see to."

He accompanied her to the front door and whispered in her ear, "Same tomorrow. Same time."

Savannah and Hugh walked in silence until they reached Dale Street.

"Why aren't you at work today, Hugh?" asked Savannah to quench her curiosity as they waited to cross the road.

"The work's casual, so it is."

"I don't understand."

"Some days we don't get taken on. It depends if there's enough work."

"Oh! I see. Does that make things difficult for you?"

"Sometimes. But when we do get taken on the pay's good. Some days we do overtime, so it seems to balance out, so it does."

"What is it Conor does? What is the business he has to see to?" asked Savannah. "I've asked him, but he doesn't give me a straight answer."

"He doesn't need to do anythin'. He works for his aunt who sees him right," replied Hugh.

"He has spoken of her. So why is he here in Liverpool?"

A look of panic flitted briefly across Hugh's face. "Visitin' his friends. Me and Finn. He has the time to do as he likes."

"But if you don't mind me saying, I find it difficult to see what you have in common?"

Hugh chose not to answer and took her arm as they crossed the road, dodging between the wagons, trams, cabs and piles of steaming horse manure, towards the Municipal Buildings.

"Do you have anyone special, Hugh?" Savannah asked when they reached the safety of the pavement.

He blushed and said, "No, I don't have the time but…" He stopped.

She had walked on a few paces before realising he was not beside her. She turned back. "What is it?"

Hugh had stuffed his hands into his pockets and was looking at her sadly.

"I'd give my right arm to find someone like you, so I would. Conor's a lucky man."

"I'm the lucky one, Hugh. I have never met anyone like him before. He quite takes my breath away. I have never seen such a beautiful man."

Hugh wondered how many men, beautiful or otherwise, Savannah had met in her short life. She seemed so innocent.

"Watch your step with him, Savannah. Don't get too involved. Don't get in too deep."

"What do you mean?"

Hugh glanced at the people passing round them and lowered his voice.

"He likes women, Savannah. He's broken many hearts."

"I don't think he will break my heart."

"You're young and sweet and too trustin'. He's my friend. I've known him a long time, so I have. I'm not betrayin' him by tellin' you to take what he says with a pinch of salt."

"Why are you trying to turn me from him? Are you jealous, Hugh? I think you are. I've seen the way you look at me."

"You'd never give someone like me a second glance. I like you, Savannah. Have your fun as he will have his, but don't expect it to last."

"Well, I suppose I must thank you for your brutally honest words," she said sarcastically. "I shall make my own way now, Hugh. I don't need a chaperone."

She turned abruptly and stalked off, leaving him to stare after her retreating figure until she was swallowed up in the crowd of pedestrians.

The wind blowing in from the river carried the threat of rain and Savannah quickened her step as she approached the square in front of the station, where there would be a line of waiting cabs. Then she stopped. It was Will who had caught her eye, standing beside a cab on the pavement outside a hotel in a side street. A well-dressed young woman was flicking something from his lapel and then she reached up to touch his cheek. Savannah shrunk back into the doorway of a shop and peered round the corner and watched as her brother lowered his head to kiss the woman on the lips, in broad daylight, in a public place, and then helped her into the cab.

Will! Will! No! No! No!

Hugh could hear the muffled voices of Conor and Finn in the kitchen, which ceased abruptly as he opened the door.

"She sent me packin'," said Hugh. "A mind of her own that one, to be sure."

Finn glanced at Conor. "Not too much of one, I hope."

"What do you mean?" asked Hugh.

"Nothing," said Conor.

"Right," said Finn, scraping back his chair, "I'm off to the pub. Would you be comin', Hugh?"

"No, you be on your way. I'll not be long after you. I want to have a word with Conor."

Finn grabbed his jacket hanging from the peg on the back of the door and went out, slamming the door behind him.

"I should be off too," said Conor. "There's a load of quality furniture come in from a big house in Cheshire and I've been promised first helping."

"Wait, Conor," said Hugh, resting his hands on the back of a chair.

"What is it?"

"What were you and Finn discussin' just now. You shut up when I came in."

"You know the rules, Hugh. You only need to know what you need to know. Safety first."

"Why did you bring Savannah here when you have no need? It's not a suitable place for a girl like her and Finn is so rough. It's embarrassin'." A troubled look flitted across his face as something dawned on him. "You're not plannin' something involvin' her, for the love of God?"

"As I said, none of your business, Hugh."

"But it is my business if I live here." Hugh straightened up. "I'm as much at risk as either of you, so I am. You had me meetin' the Belgian fella the other day."

"That's because you'll be dealing with him next month and he needs to know who you are."

"So, this between you and Finn is somethin' else?"

Conor took out his watch, flipped the lid and looked at it pointedly before saying in exasperation, "Look, Hugh. I'm new to this." He snapped shut the lid and replaced the watch in his pocket. "Finn's in charge. I'm only doing it because my aunt asked me because of the nature of our business. Finn had an idea and he asked me to do something about it. That's all you need to know."

"Involvin' Savannah? This isn't right, Conor. She's too young. She's too innocent."

"Enough, Hugh, or I would think you were soft on her." Conor got up. "I need to go, or I'll miss out. If you've no work tomorrow, make yourself scarce when she comes. I'd appreciate the privacy." He retrieved his cigarette case from another pocket and lit a cigarette, tossing the spent match into the sink.

"You're a rogue, Conor. She's a child." Hugh glared at Conor.

"Believe me, she is not." Conor inhaled deeply and blew out the smoke. "She knows what she is doing. She's—" He stopped himself.

"I'll be tellin' you somethin' else, Conor," said Hugh, coming round the table to face him. "You've no respect for women. Since the hair started growin' on that lip of yours, you've treated women cheaply. You don't know the damage you do when you have had your fill."

"Shut your mouth, Hugh, before you say something we both regret and fall out."

"I will speak my mind and you'll listen to me whether you like it or not, so you will." Hugh clenched and unclenched his fists. *Conor can be so arrogant*, he thought. "It's a game to you, isn't it? What your aunt does, what we do here, it's a game to you because you're bored and don't have to earn a livin' same way as the rest of us. You don't care what we believe in. The same with women. You chase them – old, young – have your way, move on to the next. You're shallow, Conor, And you hurt people. You're somethin' else, Conor. You're a bastard."

Conor stared long and hard at Hugh, who had never in his life spoken to his friend like this.

"Talkin' of which," said Hugh, the side of his mouth lifting in a sneer. "I wonder how many little bastards—"

"Shut your mouth, Hugh," Conor said again, thrusting his face forward and glaring. "Or I'll shut it for you." He waited for his friend to rise to the bait, but Hugh stared him out. They were both breathing heavily. Then Conor said, "You have no idea what I think or what I feel. You have no right to judge me."

He dropped the unfinished cigarette on the floor and ground it under his shoe. He pushed Hugh aside on his way out of the kitchen and slammed the front door behind him.

NINETEEN

Savannah returned the next afternoon to meet Conor in front of the Municipal Buildings and was relieved when he told her they would have the house to themselves. She had used the excuse of not yet finding a suitable gift for her mother to leave Will's house again without arousing too much suspicion in Esme. They made love. Afterwards, they lay naked on top of the bed, their arms and legs wrapped round each other, so close, so warm, so safe, staring at each other.

After a while, Conor's eyes drooped, and he dozed. Savannah watched him as his breath fell on her face. She pulled away from him and began to examine him: the first man she had seen completely naked. She wanted to look at every part of him as he had looked at her, without embarrassment, without him knowing. His body was slim, not muscular like Thomas's, and there was a patch of dark hair on his chest. His legs were long and, like his arms, covered in dark hair. His face. She caught her breath at the beautiful, sleeping face. The dark brows and thick lashes; the thick hair, unkempt as always; the high forehead; the long, straight nose; his mouth, thin-lipped; his moustache and beard that framed his face. She touched his cheekbones. She studied him intently, trying to understand why he was so beautiful. She recalled the drawing lessons at school when they had been taught proportion and symmetry. His face was almost symmetrically perfect, everything was in proportion: it was a model of perfect proportion. He had been blessed. She wanted him again. She began to kiss him and moved her hand between his legs. His eyelids fluttered and opened, and he smiled at her.

Afterwards, Conor went to make her a cup of tea. Hugh was right. The house was grubby and made him ashamed, and no one took care to keep it particularly clean. He spied the crushed cigarette on the floor, picked it up and tossed it in the bucket under the sink. He carried the tea up to the bedroom and sat on the bed next to Savannah.

"Can you meet me tomorrow?"

"Yes," she said. She sipped the hot tea and put it down on the dresser. Too strong for her taste!

"Would you prefer to meet somewhere else? You could come to my lodg—" He checked himself. "A hotel, perhaps, where it's more comfortable, with a bigger bed?" He laughed.

She looked at him in horror as she recalled the image of Will and his woman on the street outside the hotel. Who knew where else he might entertain his lady friends?

"Oh no! Someone might see me. My brother is well known. Here is more anonymous."

She was right and he was relieved. Anonymous for her and for him.

"As long as you don't mind. I know this house lacks certain comforts and you deserve much better."

"I don't mind as long as I am with you."

"Tell me more about your family. I've heard about your parents. What about this well-known brother of yours?"

"I love him very much. He has his own law practice. He is very clever and kind and generous. He is married with two sons and his wife is expecting another baby soon. He is much older than me and has taken on the role of paterfamilias. He is very cross with me at the moment. I am in disgrace."

Savannah wished she could take back her last words, but it was too late.

"Why? What have you done?"

She blushed and looked at Conor, who was trying not to laugh at her discomfort.

"I cannot imagine you guilty of misdemeanours, apart from me."

"Oh, I am guilty. Even more so now with you."

"I'm intrigued. Explain yourself."

Savannah decided to tell him about the Musketeers and the unsatisfying encounters with Thomas.

"You have upset me, Savannah."

"Why? It upsets you to hear I was not a virgin when it is apparent from the way you behave and what Hugh told me that you were not either. It is acceptable for you as a man to behave in such a way, but not me because I am a woman?"

"Hugh should learn to keep his nose out of my business," muttered Conor. "No, I'm upset that I may be the subject of a dissection of my success or failure as a lover by your schoolfriends and that you have been using me."

Savannah laughed at his mock offence. "Would you like me to tell you how I would score your efforts? Would you like me to tell you how you could improve?" She got up, hitched up her dress and sat astride him. "Do you know," she said, stroking his face, "you are very dashing and as I imagined D'Artagnan to be?"

"I'm flattered. Are you my Madame Bonacieux?"

"Mmm. Would you like to show me now what improvements you could make? *Tu veux refaire l'amour, monsieur?*"

"I'd like nothing more." He kissed her. "You are very young. There are almost ten years between us and yet…"

"And yet?"

"You are not how I imagined a schoolgirl to be—"

"I'm no longer a schoolgirl," she interrupted. "So, you would expect me to be silly, frivolous, tiresome, giggling and ignorant?"

"You are none of those things, which is my point. And your confidence, your lack of shyness with me in bed."

"My mother," explained Savannah.

"Ah! I see. You must be very close to your mother."

"I am. More so after Papa died. We comforted each other. Now I am older, no longer a schoolgirl" – she grinned at him – "we can talk about anything."

"It would seem so."

The front door slammed.

"Damn!" he said and sighed. "Where does the time go?" He lifted her off his lap, pulled her to him and kissed her slowly, and she put her arms round his neck and did not want him to stop.

"You will come again tomorrow for certain?" he whispered in her ear.

"Of course. Why would I not? I love you, Conor."

"Come then," he said, taking her by the hand. "I'll walk with you. To the Municipal Buildings at least if you are afraid of someone spotting us together."

On the Friday, Esme stopped her in the hallway to ask, "Where are you going this time, Savannah? It is taking you a long time to find something to please your mother. And I am not sure Will would be pleased to know that you are going out unchaperoned."

"Oh, do not concern yourself, Esme. I can look after myself. And traipsing round shops can be so boring with someone who cannot make up her mind. I should not like to inflict that on anyone." She was desperate to see Conor as it would be difficult to think of an excuse to leave the house the next day and Sunday with Will at home, far more suspicious of her, watching her like a hawk. "I enjoy wandering round the city. It is so different to Longridge and the shops in Newbridge do not compare."

"You are bored? The boys are too much for you?" asked Esme.

"No, I love them dearly. But I do enjoy the time on my own."

Esme patted her arm. "I understand. Will you have some thought for me when there are three of them?" She laughed.

* * *

They lay in each other's arms, him on his side to make room for her on the narrow bed. She explained she would not see him for two days, as she would not be able to pull the wool over Will's eyes as she did with Esme. He asked her why there was such an age gap between her and Will. It was comforting to share her family's complicated history with someone, and he listened patiently to her edited account, stroking her cheek or twirling a strand of her hair round his finger. He was struck by her eloquence and the maturity of her empathy and understanding.

He told her his aunt had sent him to a boarding school not far from Dublin, run by Jesuits when he was eleven, and he had hated it. He had run away twice and was thrashed on his return. His aunt had bribed him to finish his education by saying she would take him to Europe if he stuck it out. He described the places they had visited in Germany, France and Italy, the museums and palaces and castles his aunt had insisted on showing him and his sister, how knowledgeable she was, all self-taught. She had opened his eyes to enjoying art and culture for its own sake, not as a badge to impress and display one's education. He went to Trinity College in Dublin to study law, as his school encouraged its pupils to acquire an education befitting a gentleman to be employed in some capacity to benefit the British Empire. He left after a year, as it did not interest him. His aunt encouraged him to go to London, where he lived with Orla and her family, and he found a job as a porter at Sotheby's, where he worked under a man called Jocelyn Digby, who taught him everything he knew about paintings and furniture. Conor had never had such a long, intimate conversation, expressed his feelings so freely, with any of his many conquests, or even his sister or female friends and, inspired by Savannah's honesty, he surprised himself by his own willingness to open up to her.

Conor helped Savannah to dress as he liked to do it, and then he sat down on the edge of the bed, pulled her onto his knee and hugged her. "Will you come to Ireland with me?"

"What? Are you going back soon?" Her eyes welled with tears. "Please say you are not going back?"

"I am. My business in Liverpool is done and I am needed at home. I told you about Enniscourt. There are things needing to be done there and I have already stayed longer than I intended."

He had told her about his home, and she often wondered why he chose to stay in this poky, shabby house in a run-down, backstreet in Liverpool. He seemed to have money, as he was well dressed, his watch and chain were gold, he wore a gold ring on the little finger of his right hand and his cigarette and vesta cases were silver. Did his aunt keep him on a tight rein?

"When are you going?"

"Monday."

"No," she cried, flinging her arms round his neck. "Stay! Stay! This will be our last meeting."

"Come with me. For a holiday. For a few days."

"They won't allow it."

"Who?"

"My brother, for one."

"Don't tell."

He reached over for his cigarettes on the chest of drawers and lit one, his cheeks hollowing as he inhaled, highlighting the fine sculpture of his face, and tilted his head as he blew the smoke slowly through pursed lips into the air above her.

"Are you serious? And put that out. I don't want to go back smelling of that."

He squeezed the end of the cigarette between his finger and thumb, placed it back in his cigarette case and said coldly, "Well, we had better say our farewells now. I doubt we shall see each other again." He pushed her unceremoniously off his lap, got up and held out his hand to shake hers. "It was fun whilst it lasted."

He was repeating the words Hugh had used. Savannah dropped to the floor and her hands flew to cover her face. So, it was all a game to him after all, as her mother had warned her, despite the last few days when she thought they had become so close, friends as well as lovers.

"But I love you," she sobbed.

"Prove it. Come with me. I have a ticket for you already and have sent a telegram to my aunt, who is expecting you because I thought you would come as I know you love me as much as I love you."

Surprised, not by his presumptuous behaviour in thinking she would agree to accompany him to Ireland, but by his declaration of love – he had never said that he loved her before – she peered up at him through her tears. He was smiling at her, his eyes creased with laughter and twinkling at her.

"You think I was using you? A diversion to amuse me whilst I was here?"

TWENTY

Hugh was waiting for Savannah in a cab round the corner from the house. Thankfully, Will had gone to his office. Esme had stayed in bed to rest. Miss Atkinson was watching the children in the nursery on the top floor. She left a note for Will on her dressing table. When they noticed she was missing and found it, she would be well on her way. She clutched her smallest suitcase into which she had crammed as much as she thought she might need, grabbed her purse and crept down the stairs, opening and closing the front door as quietly as she could, then walking as quickly as her heavy, bulging suitcase allowed.

As they made their way through the suburbs and bustling streets of the city to the docks, Savannah said to Hugh, "Do you know Conor's aunt?"

"Yes."

"What is she like? I'm a little nervous about meeting her."

"She's a wonderful woman, to be sure. No child goes to school in Ballymore lackin' a pair of boots. No family goes hungry in times of hardship. Not one person in Ballymore has a word to say against her."

Savannah nodded. Hugh's glowing words made her more nervous. She had another question for him. "I still do not understand how you and Conor are friends. How long have you known each other?"

"Since we were boys. I took pity on him, so I did, when he first came to the school in Ballymore. With his nice clothes and funny, American accent, he was a target. A gang of boys waylaid him on his way home after his first day. I'd to pull him out from under a pile of bodies punchin' and kickin' him. His nice new clothes were torn and dirty. They didn't like him cos he was different… and rich."

"It was a brave thing for you to do."

"I was bigger than most of them, so I was, although you wouldn't think it to see me now. Anyway, they liked him well enough when they got to know him better and he became one of the gang and got into scrapes with them. He had a way with him, even then, that made friends easily."

Savannah smiled. She was aware of that trait. "What kind of scrapes?"

"Oh, now then…" His face creased as he laughed, remembering. "Things naughty boys get up to. Stealin' apples from Old Ma Boyle's garden. Takin' the milkman Billy Flynn's pony from the yard out into the country to learn to ride whilst Billy was catchin' up on his sleep, him havin' to be up early in the mornin' and all… I could write a book, so I could, of all the things we did."

Savannah grinned. "Did you get caught?"

"Oh, surely. A clip round the ear usually. Conor's aunt made him get up every mornin' at the crack of dawn for a week to help Billy with the deliveries."

"And Mr O'Driscoll? How does Conor know him?"

"He doesn't know him well at all," said Hugh. "People from home know him and told me there was a spare room at the house he rents so I'd somewhere to stay when I came to work here." Hugh thought for a moment and then added, "Have a care, Savannah. You've only known Conor a short time. He's swept you off your feet, so he has, with those looks of his and that charm. There's so much you don't know about him. About us."

"What do you mean?"

The cab had come to a halt, and Hugh got out to help Savannah down. He carried her suitcase and guided her through the crowds of passengers, dockers and porters to the ship's berth, where he handed over the suitcase and ticket.

"You didn't answer my question," said Savannah.

He hesitated before diffidently planting a kiss on her cheek. He had said too much already. "No matter. I'll see you when you come back."

Conor was already in the cabin and hugged her. "I thought you might get cold feet, or someone might try to stop you."

The crossing was unpleasant, and Savannah lay on the bunk feeling ill and trying not to lose her dignity by vomiting all over the cabin floor as the boat pitched and rolled in the Irish Sea. Conor fussed over her, teasing her about how green she looked, until she snapped at him to leave her be. She was irritated that he was so unaffected by the ship's motion. The bad weather had delayed their arrival; they had to ride out the storm as it was unsafe to enter the harbour. The carriage sent from Enniscourt had been waiting for them for hours. Savannah heard Conor mutter angrily at the driver, a stout, smartly dressed man with a florid complexion, who smelt of drink.

As they trotted through the city streets, she could not keep her eyes open and fell asleep, her head cradled in Conor's lap. She was jolted awake when the carriage came to a sudden halt, and she sat up in alarm.

"It's all right," said Conor. "There's an accident on the road." He settled her in the seat before opening the door and jumping down. A wagon had overturned, shedding its load of potatoes, and was blocking the road. The wheel had sheared from the axle and a thin, grey-haired old man and a young, pale, pinch-faced boy, both dressed shabbily in patched clothes, had been tossed into the road.

"Walsh," said Conor to their driver, "give me a hand."

Wanting to be useful, Savannah climbed down from the carriage to hold the reins of their horses, and watched as Conor and Mr Walsh helped the victims to their feet. Neither was injured, just bruised and shaken. Together they heaved the wagon out of the way.

"Now, you're sure you are both unhurt?" asked Conor.

"We're fine, sir," replied the old man.

The boy had begun gathering the undamaged potatoes and was piling them up by the side of the road. Savannah expected Conor to return to her and they would soon be on their way, but he said to the old man, "Were you headed for Dublin?"

"That's right, sir."

"There's a wheelwright at the forge in Ballymore. I can send him out to you."

"That's good of you, sir. I know Mr O'Flaherty."

"And let me take care of the expense."

"There's no need, Mr...?"

"Clare. Conor Clare of Enniscourt. I insist. Good day to you both," he said, shaking the old man's hand.

Savannah watched and listened, her heart swelling with love and pride at Conor's kindness and consideration. What she witnessed reassured her that the kindness and consideration he showed her was genuine, a true part of his nature, not a show to continue to deceive her and win her over falsely as her mother had cautioned and Hugh had hinted at.

In the mid-afternoon, they arrived at Enniscourt. They trotted up the short drive to the front of the house. There was no garden to speak of, at least not what Savannah understood to be a garden – manicured lawns and flower beds – rather, an overgrown field that may once have been a lawn, but the grass now grew untamed and was choked with weeds; the white, fluffy seeds of rosebay willowherb floated across the drive. A short, thin, white-haired man, sleeves rolled up, a pipe clenched between his teeth, was flailing with a machete at the overgrown bushes and shrubs that grew to one side of the house, tossing the branches and cuttings behind him into a haphazard heap next to a smouldering fire.

And the house! Savannah could not believe her eyes. It was enormous: at least twice the size of Longridge or would have been if half of it had not fallen into ruin. Conor had warned her of the state of it, but still, she was not prepared for the sight of it. The south-east-facing house was built in the Palladian style in grey stone, and an extra wing added at a later date, which had doubled the size of the original house. But the extension was a wreck. The roof was missing, and a spindly tree grew from one of the chimney stacks still standing. Mounds of bricks and stones stood where walls had already been demolished. The windows were either paneless or the glass was smashed, the floors of the upper storeys had collapsed to the ground floor and timbers hung precariously from the few remaining joists. Tarpaulin sheets had been attached with ropes to the chimney stack to one side of the inhabited part of the house and huge, timber joists placed against them to hold them in place. The facade of the habitable part was covered in a blanket of ivy that grew untamed up parts of the wall, partially covering some of the attic windows, and seemed to be holding the house up in its smothering embrace. Rusty marks where the gutters had overflowed stained the stonework where the ivy did not grow.

A young girl, dressed in a brown frock and white pinafore, her hair untidily tucked under a white cap, was perched unsteadily on a step ladder, throwing soapy water onto a window of one of the ground floor rooms and using a mop to wipe away the suds. She scurried down as the carriage approached the door, dropped the mop into the bucket, wiped her wet hands on her apron, curtsied and ran to open the front door for them.

Conor helped Savannah down from the carriage and said, "Well, here we are. Welcome to Enniscourt."

The girl stared hard at Savannah. Rudely, she thought, as her eyes travelled from her face to her feet and then back again as Conor led her into the hallway.

"Fetch the cases please, Niamh, and then show Miss Hamilton-Read to her room."

The girl scuttled off.

"You'll want to freshen up first. Ring the bell and Niamh will bring you down to the sitting room. I'll introduce you then." He squeezed her hand to reassure her.

The hallway was gloomy. There was a console table pushed up against one wall under a large, gilt mirror with two chairs either side, and little else. A plump, black cat was stretched out on the floor tiles and lifted its head for a moment to inspect the arrivals before returning to its snooze. Conor took Savannah's hat and coat and tossed them onto one of the chairs as Niamh came into the hall with the suitcases.

"This way, Miss Hamilton-Read," she said.

Conor kissed Savannah's cheek. "See you in a minute or two," he said, and disappeared through one of the doors off the hallway.

The wooden stairs, scuffed with the tread of many feet, creaked under their weight as Niamh led the way. There was a slight smell of damp and mildew on the landing that made Savannah wrinkle her nose.

"The outside wall in the rooms on that side of the house is damp," explained Niamh, seeing her discomfort. "Because of next door. But only upstairs on that side. It's the chimney, I've been told. The rest of the house, this bit, is sound, so it is."

She went to the end of the corridor, put down Conor's case and opened the door to her bedroom, and it was a relief for Savannah to see how bright and welcoming the room was. There was a four-poster bed with rose-coloured brocade drapes, a dressing table and chair, a toilet table, and two armchairs near the fireplace. Thick oriental rugs covered the wooden floor and two windows, framed by blue velvet curtains, had wonderful views of the Wicklow mountains in the distance. Niamh put the suitcase on the bed and said, "I'm to take you down for tea, so ring the bell by the door when you're ready, Miss. I'll unpack for you, Miss, but first I'll fetch you some hot water."

"Oh!" said Savannah in surprise. It would seem Enniscourt did not enjoy the same comforts of plumbing she was used to. "There is a bathroom?"

"Opposite, Miss."

"Where is Mr Clare's room?"

"Two doors along. Why would you be wantin' to know that?"

Savannah was surprised by the boldness of the question and the sharpness of the girl's tone. "Oh, I hoped I was not too far from other people in a strange house."

Savannah, who had changed out of her travelling clothes, stood nervously on the threshold of Mrs Archbold's spacious sitting room, wondering how she would be received. Like her bedroom, it was filled with natural light from the tall windows, but which, Savannah noticed, were smeared with streaks. The girl had not done a good job. The drapes were faded with the sunlight and the rugs on the floor, although expensive looking, were worn. The furniture was old but seemed to her to be of a high quality. There was a scattering of silver boxes, porcelain figures, photographs in silver frames, bonbonnières and glass domes housing tableaux of stuffed birds on various side tables, and the walls were covered in pictures: landscapes, hunting scenes, portraits, still lifes, religious scenes. She had never seen so many paintings in one place other than a museum. If Mrs Archbold did not care much for the décor, she certainly cared for fine things. Conor rose quickly from his chair and came to take her arm.

"Aunt Norah, this is Savannah Hamilton-Read."

Conor's great-aunt was a large, obese woman in her sixties, squashed into an armchair that Savannah thought she might have to be chiselled out of. Her bulk flowed over and hid the arms of her chair. Propped up against a pile of books on one side of the chair were two silver-topped canes. She was dressed in black. Her thin, pure white hair was piled up on the top of her head and covered with a handkerchief-sized piece of black lace which barely hid the bald, pink patches on her scalp. Her small, button eyes disappeared behind the hillocks of her bloated cheeks. A large brooch of diamonds and pearls was pinned at her neck, under the folds of her many chins, and rings of gold, diamonds, emeralds and topaz adorned every pudgy finger. As Savannah approached to shake her outstretched hand, Mrs Archbold reached for the pince-nez which dangled on a gold chain over the shelf of her enormous bosom and perched it on her nose to look her over.

"A little pale," she said in a drawl, a mix of Irish and American accents.

"Savannah's not a good sailor, Aunt," explained Conor.

"Very pretty," she said, clamping Savannah's hand in her vast paws. "Just as you described, Conor. No wonder he could not wait to show you off. And soft, long-fingered hands," she said admiringly as she released her grip, "which means, I am sure, you have a gift for the piano."

Savannah laughed and replied, "I am afraid not, Mrs Archbold. I have been told I thump the keys. And I have no gift for painting or sewing, much to my mother's chagrin, as she is very talented. Although I am not too modest and will say I ride very well, play a mean game of tennis and my French is good. Will I do, Mrs Archbold?"

Mrs Archbold collapsed back in her chair, emitting an exhalation like a pierced puffball and laughed. "You will do very nicely. Oh, yes! Very nicely indeed," she said, looking past Savannah to Conor and nodding.

Savannah breathed a sigh of relief, saw Conor smiling at her, and began to relax.

"Come and sit next to me, child, and tell me all about yourself, your family and where you live. And your name, child! You can explain to me why you are named after a town in Georgia. Conor, will you ring for tea, darling?"

As they sat chatting, Savannah noticed Mrs Archbold's eyes began to droop after half an hour and, before long, her head dropped to her chest and she was fast asleep. Conor held his finger to his lips and beckoned to her to come with him. They crept out of the room.

"Let's go for a walk," he said.

They left the house by the front door. The girl was back on the step ladder, swiping another window with the mop. She stopped to watch them with what Savannah interpreted as a scowl. The man with the machete had disappeared and left the fire to smoulder, the freshly cut branches and leaves hissing in clouds of smoke.

"I need a cigarette. Aunt doesn't like me smoking in the house." He took out his cigarette case.

"I agree with her. You should stop."

Conor grinned at her, suitably chastened, and put the case back in his pocket. Savannah, troubled by pangs of guilt at her behaviour in sneaking away from Liverpool, asked Conor if he would send a telegram to Will on her behalf to say she was well and would return soon, which he said he would do the following day.

"I was extremely nervous about meeting your aunt, but she's very kind. Is your aunt unwell?" asked Savannah as he threaded her arm through his and they made their way along the weed-ridden gravel path. "It is unusual to fall asleep in the middle of a conversation. I must have bored her."

"She is. You are too polite to mention her size. She has arthritis. It is very painful for her, and her joints are stiff, which makes it difficult for her to move about, and she sleeps badly. She takes laudanum to ease the condition." Savannah had seen the small, blue bottle amidst the clutter on the side table. "The doctor has put her on a diet to help to make her more mobile and ease the weight she carries. Now she eats like a sparrow which makes her light-headed and tired."

"How sad for her."

"Yes, it is. It is only in the last few years she has been like this. She was in pain, ate for comfort, and this is how she is. She used to be gregarious, always out visiting, travelling, having people to stay." Conor sighed. "I do my best to entertain her but… Mrs Walsh will be glad you are here. She's a fine cook, and it will make a change for her to provide something other than the boiled and steamed offerings she makes for my aunt."

"She seems to have a passion for art. So many pictures and paintings."

They had walked away from the house through a gate into a field where sheep grazed. A rutted track bordered by nettles led to a large, stone barn nestled in a copse of trees.

"Come down here," said Conor. "I want to show you something."

He heaved back one of the big wooden doors of the barn and wedged it open with a stone. Inside was an Aladdin's cave of furniture: wing chairs resided on sofas; dressing tables jostled for space with wardrobes; bed frames imprisoned side tables; glass-fronted cabinets hosted lamps; hat stands leant drunkenly; mirrors hung on walls reflected the contents – mahogany, yew, velvet brocade, leather and brass – into infinity.

"What is this?" gasped Savannah.

"Aunt Norah loves her pictures. They are kept in the house. She would travel round Ireland to country houses, where she had heard on the grapevine that the owners were in financial difficulties and buy their art from them at a very good price. Some of them are valuable. The lady in the black dress near the fireplace—"

"I saw it. It's beautiful."

"A Tissot. The painting of the Magi is a Poussin. Many more. Bargains. You should ask her about the pictures. It gives her pleasure to talk about them. Then, of course, people heard about her, and they would come to her and offer her pictures or furniture, or anything they were desperate to sell, or she would go to house sales."

"She is a magpie and collects it all? To store it in a barn?"

"No, not at all. It is sold. To Americans who want to fill their homes with authentic, antique furniture. I crate it up and send it to dealers."

"I see."

"And now she is somewhat hindered, I have been travelling since I left London to go to England, Scotland and Wales in search of pieces."

"Why did you not tell me this in Liverpool? Did you think I would not care for a tradesman?"

"Do you care for a tradesman?" he asked, taking her into his arms.

"Only this tradesman here whom I want to kiss me. Now. This instant."

Conor and Savannah took an arm each and hoisted Mrs Archbold to her feet. Conor passed her her sticks, and they made a painful progress to the dining room; another room filled with antique furniture and more pictures. A many-branched silver candelabra in the middle of the long, polished, mahogany dining table glittered with candles; a matching sideboard groaned under the weight of claret jugs and silver trays, crystal decanters and glasses; and a glass-fronted cabinet was filled with porcelain dishes and plates.

Once seated and comfortable, the pain left Mrs Archbold's face and she was entertaining company, talking about her late husband and their busy social life in Boston, where her two sons and three daughters still lived. They were married with their own families and had settled lives and did not mind in the least when she told them she was returning to Ireland with Conor and his sister.

"I wanted to travel in Europe," she explained. "Oh! The places we have seen, eh, Conor?" She sighed. She had only intended to stay for a few years. "I don't know what happened, Savannah." She chuckled. "I'm still here! Nearly twenty years!"

"Do you visit your family often or do they come here?" asked Savannah.

"Yes, they visit but not often. I was in Boston two years ago, but I must confess the journey tired me and, like you, Savannah, I am not a good sailor."

"I have inherited that from my late father. It was one of the reasons he gave up travelling to America."

Niamh came in to clear away the soup dishes and returned with a wide, heavy tray holding the dishes for the main course. She was dismissed by Conor, who got up to carve the roast beef and serve the vegetables.

"A small portion for me, Conor dear," said Mrs Archbold. "But if you would be so kind to refill my glass."

"Do you mind if I ask why part of the house seems to be falling down?" asked Savannah, once Conor had taken his seat after serving them.

"Of course I do not mind," replied Mrs Archbold. "I would think you a very stupid girl not to have noticed half the house is in a ruinous state and I am relieved you had the nerve to ask the question. Conor is to be congratulated he has a young friend with some gumption."

Mrs Archbold wiped her mouth on her napkin and placed it beside her plate. She took a sip of wine. Savannah noted that, although she picked at her food, this was her third glass.

"The house was owned years ago by an Englishman, Oliver Roberts, a harsh and cruel man who had enriched himself at the expense of his tenants and workers. Ah! The English," she said meanly, her eyes narrowing and disappearing into the folds of flesh on her face. "Masters of all they survey and coveters of what remains of the globe they have yet to conquer."

"Aunt, I'll remind you that Savannah is English," scolded Conor.

"I am sure Savannah is educated enough" – she smiled condescendingly at her – "to know full well the history of her country and the avaricious tentacles of the British Empire spreading throughout the world. Or perhaps, as is so often the case, the truth is varnished or history rewritten to flatter the perpetrators of injustice, and the grubbiness of the master's deeds are hidden or ignored, wiped from the pages of English children's history books."

Savannah detected a tone of bitter aggression in Mrs Archbold's voice behind the forced smile and wondered if she was affected by the drink and forgot her manners.

"The English who were responsible for forcing my family to leave Ireland after they were reduced to starvation and obliged to eat nettles and weeds. People then were dying of hunger and typhus. There were bodies in ditches where they had died in their sleep. Bodies on the roads. Dogs scavenging on corpses—"

"For which Savannah is not personally responsible," interrupted Conor, glaring at his aunt as Savannah looked at him in alarmed embarrassment.

"No, indeed," said Mrs Archbold, "and you are quite young, my dear, and have probably lived a sheltered life where the nastiness and cruelty inflicted on our people has not troubled you at all or their struggles made you lose a wink of sleep."

Savannah bristled and put down her knife and fork. "I may be young as you point out, Mrs Archbold, but I am aware of recent events and Mr Gladstone's attempts to bring about Home Rule. Crimes have been committed by Irishmen on innocent people, murders which—"

"You were telling us about the house," Conor broke in as he was becoming increasingly perturbed by the drift of the conversation. "I'm sure you have made it all up, Aunt."

He got up to fill her glass as an excuse to place a warning hand on her shoulder.

"You know very well that I have not made it up," Mrs Archbold said testily. "It was a well-known story in these parts. I was told it as a child."

Savannah sensed from her peevish tone and the strong look Conor gave her over his aunt's shoulder that she might launch into another belligerent tirade, so she said, "I'd like to hear it, Mrs Archbold, if you wouldn't mind."

Conor nodded at her, relieved she had correctly interpreted his look, and sat down.

"Very well, my dear. I forget myself and I apologise if I was a little rude. I do not like the English, but I will make an exception in your case. The Irish have always been a dignified and hospitable people who would give any guest in their home their last crumb. Yet, they were denied the same rights as other citizens because of their religion—"

"Aunt Norah!" Conor cut in. It seemed Mrs Archbold, her tongue possibly loosened by drink, could not resist dropping into the conversation yet another poisonous jibe at the English. She went on as if nothing was amiss and this was another suitable topic of conversation at the dinner table.

"Where was I?" Mrs Archbold peered into her wine glass. "Yes. To advertise his wealth and importance, as so many did, Oliver Roberts decided to extend his house. However, his plans and grandiose ideas went beyond his means. He sacked the architect and builders and decided to employ his own men to complete his vain folly. But they had no skill and hated him, so they took the wages he offered and took no care in the building of it. One night, a year later, there was a terrible storm, mighty trees that had stood for centuries snapped like twigs and the winds howled like hurricanes and lifted the roof off and blew out the windows. Slates and glass and pieces of shattered furniture were found miles away carried by the tempest which some said had been sent by God to punish Oliver Roberts for his evil ways. Of course, he had no money left to repair it. He had to sell up and the next family to live here could not afford to repair all of it and tired of the constant expense. I bought it from them for a reasonable sum. I have spent a lot of money to restore the part we live in now and Conor is helping me to find the money to either rebuild the wing next door, or part of it, or knock it down. We have many heated discussions, don't we, Conor dear, on the best course of action?"

"Indeed, we do."

"What would you do, Conor?" asked Savannah.

"Knock it down. It would be far too expensive to rebuild, and the house is big enough as it is."

Mrs Archbold finished the last of her wine and, scowling at Conor, growled pettishly, "You win. Knock it down. Let us hope neither of us come to rue that decision."

TWENTY-ONE

Savannah had undressed and was sitting at the dressing table in her nightgown and robe, mulling over the conversation at dinner and what she should make of Mrs Archbold's outburst. She was a witty, amusing woman and knew a lot about art, but her mood completely changed in an instant, and her clearly expressed distaste for the English had made Savannah uncomfortable, so she resolved to avoid mentioning politics in Mrs Archbold's presence, not that she was competent to discuss politics. When Niamh had brought the dessert, the atmosphere had changed again, and it was back to stories about her life in America and Conor and Orla.

She was about to unpin her hair when Niamh came to return her travelling clothes, sponged and pressed, and to take away the water Savannah had washed in. As Niamh wiped out the basin, Savannah said, "Will you stay a moment and brush out my hair?"

"As you wish, Miss."

Niamh took the proffered brush and grasped the thick, glossy hair that glowed in tints of black and auburn and chestnut in the lamplight. So unlike her own mousy hair and Mrs Archbold's thin, coarse hair that often came out in clumps as she brushed it.

"Ouch!"

"Sorry, Miss." Her first stroke, she had tugged too hard.

Savannah studied Niamh's reflection in the mirror. She was

short and plump with a wide, round face, sallow complexion, large, grey eyes, an upturned nose and a small, sulky mouth.

"You are not a lady's maid?"

"I am, Miss, to be sure. And a housemaid, laundrymaid, cook's assistant and general all-round dogsbody. All on me own since Mary left. That's Mr Doyle's daughter. She's just after havin' a baby. She'll be back in two weeks. Not a day too soon as far as I'm concerned. Up at four to clean out the fires and we've fires nearly all year round on account of the damp. Off to bed once the mistress is tucked up safe and sound. Seven days a week. One afternoon off a month."

"You have a lot to say."

"It bothers you?"

"No, I like your accent."

"It's a joy to speak to someone, so it is. I'm on me own most of the time except when I help Mrs Walsh in the kitchen. We chat at mealtimes, the two of us, but she goes home at seven to Mr Walsh, who drives the carriage and looks after the horses and does odd jobs. It's just me and the cats. There's three of them on account of the wreck next door that brings the mice. The time sits heavy, especially in winter when the mistress is in bed by eight. It's better when Mr Clare is here. He talks to me sometimes."

That's kind of him, thought Savannah.

"Then I'm off to me room up there" – she jerked her head towards the ceiling – "once I've checked the lights are out, the doors locked, the fires covered. You've lovely hair, Miss, so you do. Not like me. Why she named me Niamh... I think it's her little joke."

"I do not follow."

"Niamh, the beautiful goddess with the golden hair. Well, she got that wrong, didn't she?"

"Who? You talk in riddles."

"Mrs Archbold. Calls me Niamh, so she does."

"That's not your birth name?"

"No idea, Miss. The nuns called me Bridget. The missus came to the laundry at the convent in Dublin, picked me out and brought me here."

"You are an orphan?"

"No idea. Left on the doorstep probably. I saw that often enough when I was there. But at least I'd some friends back then to talk to."

"How old are you?"

"Nineteen, Miss. So I've been told, anyway. I've been here for years. Well, it seems like years, so it does."

"But you like it here?"

"Like it?" She pulled a face in the mirror. "Do you leave it down, Miss, or shall I put a ribbon in?"

"Leave it down. Thank you, Niamh."

"That's pretty," said Niamh, spying the necklace on the dressing table as she put down the brush.

Savannah turned in the chair and smiled at her. "They are kind to you here?"

"I suppose so. It's better when Mr Clare comes, but they hardly notice me. Although," said Niamh, lowering her voice, "they forget I have eyes and ears, so they do. If you're understandin' me?"

Savannah took heed. "Conor, Mr Clare has a sister. Do you know her?"

"Orla. She got away, so she did, as soon as she could." She saw Savannah's raised eyebrows. "She told me when she came to stay once. I do her hair too. She went off to London to work as a governess. She's married to a very rich Englishman, Mr Broughton, and has three wee boys. He owns a bank or somethin'. They come sometimes, but not the Englishman. Mrs Walsh says he's scared of the old woman. They fight like cats and dogs, the three of them. Lord knows what about. We can hear them shoutin' at each other down in the kitchen."

Niamh went to turn back the bedcovers.

"And there is no other family? No other visitors?" Savannah thought she would take advantage of Niamh's willingness to speak freely.

"Sometimes," said Niamh, smoothing the bottom sheet. "Mr Doyle comes to tackle the garden. The delivery boy comes with the order. The neighbours call sometimes. Then there are the Americans."

"Mrs Archbold's relations?"

"I don't think so. Mrs Walsh is told to order in more food as the investors are comin', so she goes to get the better meat from Delaney's in town rather than from Furlong's store in the village."

"Furlong? Do they have a relative called Hugh?"

"No idea, Miss. I don't know them." Niamh stood beside the bed with her hands clasped. "Mrs Walsh says the missus is tryin' to get the money to repair the house, probably to sell it and make a profit and move somewhere smaller. Why she wouldn't go back to America, I've no idea. I'd go at the drop of a hat." Niamh plumped the pillows. "You've seen the size of her," she said. "What a weight she is to lift out of her chair and into bed! I sometimes worry about me back, so I do. She struggles to get about, although Mr Clare makes her go for a walk to help her lose weight. She sleeps downstairs now, as she can't manage the stairs no more. Sometimes Mrs Walsh says the house is for Mr Clare for when he gets married. I don't think she rightly knows the truth of it. The speculatin' passes the time for us, so it does. And Mrs Walsh remembers the old days when there were parties, and the house was full of people from Dublin and all over and servants to do all the work. Not like now." She sighed. "Well, I'd better go," said Niamh, collecting the bucket of slops and jug from the toilet table. "Is there anythin' else you might be wantin'?"

Niamh looked forward to when Conor was at home. It gave her something to think about during the day, during the long silences as she went about her tedious tasks. She hoped she would bump into him as they passed on the stairs, or he would lift his head from the newspaper when she put out his breakfast or be awake when she took in his hot water for washing. Best of all, when he took her to one side and asked when she had had her monthly, then she knew, depending on her answer, that he would come to her, and she would lie naked and trembling under the sheet, waiting, waiting for the creak of the floorboard outside her bedroom door.

Niamh tapped gently on the door to Savannah's room and, with the jug of hot water perched on her hip, turned the handle and entered the dimly lit room. She placed the jug next to the basin on the toilet table and went to open the curtains.

"Leave them."

She jumped out of her skin. Conor Clare's head appeared above the blankets. That is why he had not asked her the question yesterday. He was grinning at her, like the proverbial cat that had got the cream. Her hand flew to her mouth, as her cheeks and the tips of her ears turned scarlet. She scuttled across the room to the door, away from his mocking stare; his face telling her what she had worked out for herself. *Why would I come to you, you plain, little dumpling, when I have this beauty?*

She closed the bedroom door but did not move away. She pressed her ear to the crack between the door and the frame.

"Come here, you little vixen."

It was *her* cheek his soft hair would brush.

A giggle.

It was *her* mouth that would taste his lips and tongue.

A creak of the bed.

It was *her* fingers that would slide down his back as she opened her legs to him.

She stifled a squeal of jealous rage.

The bell had rung in the kitchen. She was summoned. Miss Hamilton-Read was dressed and sitting in front of the mirror. She held out the hairbrush to Niamh.

"You did such a good job. Will you brush it for me again, please?"

Did he run his fingers through that hair? Of course he did. She took the brush and pressed the bristles into Savannah's tresses.

"Careful, Niamh. That was my scalp."

"Sorry, Miss."

Savannah saw the scowl on her face in the mirror.

"You seem cross this morning, Niamh."

Cross? she thought as she banged the brush on Savannah's head causing her to wince. *Cross does not quite cover it.*

"How pretty you are," he had said to her. "I like plump flesh," he had said as he pulled away her hands modestly covering her sagging, floppy breasts, hoping he did not notice the rolls of fat round her stomach. He lay on top of her and pumped her, rolled away, and was gone. It was a treat for her if he stayed long enough to hold her for a minute and she could breathe in the warm, musky smell of him. He was *her* secret. He was *her* treat. He was *hers*. He alleviated the boredom. What was *she* saying?

"Miss?"

"That will be all, Niamh. Thank you."

For the rest of the day, she watched them as often as she could. She spied on them. Him with his arm round that neat, little waist as they walked outside. Him sat up close to her on the sofa in the sitting room, stroking her smooth, soft cheek, twirling a lock of that shiny hair round his finger. Him leaning forward to whisper something in her ear and making her laugh. How she was mad with jealousy. And he would not come to her whilst that English bitch was here to see to him.

The days passed in a fug of smouldering resentment and frustration for Niamh. It seemed Conor Clare was utterly charmed by Miss Hamilton-Read, constantly touching her, her face, her hands, his eyes lighting up when she came into the room. He read to her, they cuddled, they kissed, they went for walks in the grounds and coaxed Mrs Archbold to join them. Miss Hamilton-Read went out of her way to endear herself to the mistress of the house by asking her about the paintings, volunteering to fetch things for her, asking if she was comfortable, pouring her tea, chatting to her as if they were old friends. All this Niamh saw. She hated Miss Hamilton-Read with all her heart. Miss Hamilton-Read was everything she was not: beautiful, clever, charming, alluring, a lady. A lady? Miss Hamilton-Hoity-Toity-Read was no lady. On that they were equal.

Thursday morning and the English bitch was still in bed, exhausted from his attentions the night before, no doubt. She was clearing the plates away in the morning room. He was talking to Mrs Archbold and, as usual, they paid no attention to her.

"She is completely besotted with you," said Mrs Archbold. "You seem to be attending to her very well, if you catch my drift?"

Conor smiled at his aunt. "It is not a hardship. She was no virgin when I first had her."

Niamh nearly dropped the tray she was carrying and eased herself out of the room. But she did not return to the scullery. She put the tray down gently on the floor and waited behind the door that she had left ajar.

"Although I must confess I…" Conor thought better of what he was about to say. "She is quite beautiful, don't you think? You will agree, Aunt, she is very natural and not in the least conceited."

"Then it is certainly no hardship for you to keep her satisfied," said Mrs Archbold.

Niamh swallowed a shriek.

"We can use her weakness for you to our advantage. If it works this first time, we can use her again. She told me she stays with that brother of hers two or three times a year. Then when you tire of her you can find another."

Conor winced. His aunt smirked.

"You're a young man, Conor. I know all about young men and their appetites. I am grateful you have the decency to conduct your affairs elsewhere so I do not hear any gossip. Enjoy yourself, until I find you a respectable woman to marry and you have to come to heel." She winked at him.

Conor smiled weakly, sipped his tea and watched his aunt enjoy his discomfort before he tried to score a point of his own. "You nearly scuppered the plan with your excoriation of the English the other evening. I was worried she might go off in a pet. I'm glad you've toned it down."

"Have you prepared the package?"

"Not yet, but it's all in hand. I need to go into town this morning to send a telegram to her brother to expect her tomorrow afternoon."

"How will the money get to our friend?"

"I've arranged for Furlong to meet her off the boat and see her home. She will give the parcel to him."

"When will the guns arrive?"

"Next month. Off Ardlare."

The front doorbell rang. Niamh picked up the tray, taking care not to rattle the crockery, and hurried down the stairs to the scullery to deposit the dishes, before rushing back to answer the door as the bell rang for the second time and Mrs Walsh opened her mouth to scold her.

"Good morning, Niamh. I heard Mr Clare was back."

"In the mornin' room, Miss."

Taking the coat held out to her, she watched as Philomena Byrne admired her reflection in the hall mirror, patted her hair and strode off. She heard her cry out as she flung wide the door, "Good morning to you both."

"Phil!" said Conor, taken by surprise. He grimaced at his aunt.

"Pour me some tea, Conor. I'm parched. I've walked all the way. Are you not going to give me a welcome-home kiss?"

The bell rang in the kitchen and Niamh plodded up the back stairs with a jug of hot water to Savannah's room.

"I thought I heard the doorbell. It is early for visitors," said Savannah, who was propped up against the pillows, her tousled hair tumbling round her shoulders, the sheet pulled up to conceal her nakedness, as she had not long since made love with Conor.

"Miss Philomena Byrne."

Savannah raised her eyebrows for an explanation.

"Mr Clare's fiancée, so she is."

Niamh turned away to hide the spiteful smirk that crossed her face as she saw Savannah's look of baffled dismay and confusion.

"They are in the mornin' room." *This'll be interestin', sure enough,* she thought.

Half an hour later, Niamh heard the front door bang and watched from Savannah's bedroom as Philomena Byrne walked briskly down the drive, angrily shoving her arms into the sleeves of her coat. *Someone's upset,* she thought, and went back to making Savannah's bed. She removed the under sheet and saw where he had left his mark. She held the sheet to her face and breathed in. *How long before he comes back to me? The bitch is leavin' tomorrow.* As she shook out the clean sheet and tucked in the corners, Niamh was already forming a plan. What had the mistress said? *We can use her weakness to our advantage.* In the name of Jesus! She may come back to Enniscourt. *Not if I have anythin' to do with it.* The package. What were the names they had mentioned? Money. Guns. In the name of

Jesus – she crossed herself – the Virgin Mary, Holy Saint Joseph *and* all Holy Saints! What was that all about?

"She is not my fiancée," said Conor, sucking on a blade of grass. It was a beautiful, warm, early afternoon and he had driven Savannah in the trap to a local beauty spot, the Fairy Pool. He tied the pony to a tree and led her along a narrow path through long grasses and reeds to the lochan. The waters rippled, dark under the deep blue sky, dragonflies hovered – the fairies of the legend he told her – grasshoppers whirred, a startled moorhen paddled away angrily, and the reeds and bullrushes hissed and rustled in the welcome breeze. Although there was no one about, he took her to a secluded patch of fresh grass in a hollow and shook out the blanket he carried, and she lay with her head in his lap, looking up at his face.

"We have known each other since we were children, went to school together, played together, and it has long been assumed, especially by her, that we would marry."

"I know someone like that," said Savannah. She noticed Conor's quizzical look and regretted her words as she did not want to bring Jack into the conversation. He was in the past, a pale shadow compared to this man. "Just because you have been friends does not mean you will be a compatible match. It is irritating when other people think you should make such a commitment." She frowned, then said, "Miss Byrne is very beautiful."

Philomena Byrne had looked up in surprise when Savannah entered the morning room, and it was obvious from the look on her face she knew nothing of her or her visit. She was of medium height and slim with long, russet hair tied back with a green, velvet bow to match her green eyes, set in an oval-shaped face with a smattering of freckles across her nose. There had been some conversation, which continued unabated after Savannah sat down to eat her breakfast, about shared acquaintances and local gossip, and Savannah, upset and unsettled by the information imparted by Niamh, listened politely until Miss Byrne decided to take an interest in her.

After learning who Savannah was and that Connor had invited her to stay, Philomena quickly understood the situation and she had snarled, "Up to your tricks again, Conor? She is no more than a child," and had stormed out of the room, slamming the door behind her.

Mrs Archbold had said, "Take no heed, Savannah. All the Byrnes have a quick temper."

"Yes, she is beautiful," Conor was saying. "But the difference between you is that she knows it and uses her beauty to get her own way. You are the most beautiful, unaffected woman I have met."

"Have you taken her to your bed too?" asked Savannah, watching him carefully.

"What? A good Catholic girl like her. Her father would horsewhip me."

Savannah sat up abruptly. The angry, hurt expression on her face could not hide the offence his words had caused. "And I am not good? I am too free and easy?"

"Come here," he said, pulling her towards him. "I like Phil but I do not love her. She has no chance now that I have met you. If I am going to marry anyone, it will be you, Miss Hamilton-Read, if only to rid you of that mouthful of a name." He laughed. His eyes twinkled mischievously as he leant towards her, his arm went round her waist and his lips sought hers.

"Damn!" he exclaimed as he fell off her, breathless and flushed, and buttoned his flies. "Look what you do to me." He jumped up, took both her hands, pulled her to her feet and helped her straighten her clothes. He held her face in his hands and said fondly, "Is it possible there is just one person in the world meant for me and I have found you?" He frowned, bit his lip, and then laughed. "Come on, you little temptress, I'll get some food sent up to your room and we'll spend the rest of the afternoon in bed. How does that sound to you? You go home tomorrow. Let's make the most of the time we have left. I cannot stop thinking about you and, when I think about you, I want you."

They drove back to Enniscourt. At the end of the drive, Conor halted the pony and turned to Savannah, took her hand and said, "I want you to do something for me."

"Of course."

"I have a present for Hugh and want you to give it to him when he meets you off the boat."

"Is it his birthday?"

"No. We had a disagreement and I want to make it up to him."

"A disagreement?"

"Nothing really. A few words. I want to give him some books as I know he likes them. He loved reading them when he was younger."

"What are they?"

"Have you read Edgar Allan Poe?"

"No."

"An American author. Aunt Norah brought his books with her from Boston. Macabre and mysterious stories. They appealed to the young, impressionable Hugh."

Conor stood naked before the mirror on the dressing table. Savannah, her hair scattered around her face, her mouth slightly open, was dozing, as the wine had made her sleepy. He stared at his reflection and saw the handsome face, the chiselled features, the soft, brown eyes staring back at him which women told him they loved the most about him. Women, young and older, whom he had flattered and charmed – the words so rehearsed, repeated so often – in order to seduce them as he had Savannah. Married women who had sneaked him into their houses when their husbands were away. Young women who met him in hotel bedrooms away from the clutches of their parents. Then he was bored and moved on to the next conquest. His aunt knew of his behaviour and accepted it, provided it did not come to her ears from another source. Did others know? Philomena Byrne did. Did he have a reputation? Did he care? He didn't ever think about it. Hugh was right. He was aimless, selfish, and did not care for the women he used. The grass was greener elsewhere. He enjoyed the chase. He was a rogue, not a bastard. He hoped he had not created any bastards despite the precautions he took. He did not hurt women physically, but he did play with their emotions. What was to become of him? How much longer could he carry on in this way?

He examined his face and frowned. He was unsettled and hung his head, trying to sort out his jumbled thoughts. He turned and watched Savannah, who had not stirred and was breathing softly. He was transfixed by her. Was she the woman for him? The one person in the world meant for him? He had used that line before. Many times. But this afternoon, it had slipped out without any premeditation on his part. And he had meant it. He shivered. In that instant, he knew his life was about to change. He wondered what mysterious spirit had entered his body, what mischievous sprite had invaded his mind to make him think so. There were no voices in his head telling him to act one way or the other; it was not his conscience that troubled him. Whatever it was, supernatural or not, he knew. He looked back at his reflection to see if anything had changed, if the sprite was still hiding behind his eyes, but he could see no difference. The frown creasing his brow was still there, the eyes soft, the nose long and straight, the cheeks hollow, the lips fine, the beard carefully trimmed, the hair long and wild after their lovemaking. All unchanged, except there was the beginning of a smile, a twitch at the corner of his mouth, and he knew for certain his life was about to change.

He straightened up and went to sit on the edge of the bed beside her. He picked up her hand and held it gently. The difference in years between them worried him. Mature for her age, yet her inexperience of life and her sweet innocence worried him. The thought he might one day lose interest in her, as he had done with all the women he had known before, worried him. He dropped his head and closed his eyes. His own behaviour worried him. Could he change? For her? Could he resist the temptations of other women? He raised his head to look at her. She was beautiful. Every part of her was beautiful: her face, her body, her nature. She was sweet, charming, intelligent, more than satisfied his urges, a match for him in every way despite the age difference. She was confident and could look him in the eye and hold his gaze; young as she was, she could hold her own, there was a spark in her, and she made him laugh. He had only known her for days. Yet he knew.

He dressed quietly so as not to wake her. He had matters to attend to: the books, the money, and he had forgotten to go into town to send a telegram to her brother.

Savannah smiled at Niamh, who stood behind her brushing her hair, but she seemed distant and did not return her gaze or smile.

"Is something wrong, Niamh? You were very chatty the first night but have got progressively less so."

How did she expect her to be? It was her who had brought the tray of food and wine up to them. Him, half naked, with his arms round her waist nuzzling her neck. Her, in her robe, half-open to show off her fine, firm breasts. They had not even had the decency to wait for the servant to leave before mauling each other. She had set down the tray without a word and then listened at the door to their lovemaking, her fist stuffed into her mouth to stifle the rage welling in her throat as she heard the moans and whimpers and sounds of pleasure that never sounded in her bed.

"It's been a long day, Miss, so it has."

"I won't keep you then."

Niamh replaced the brush on the dressing table and turned to go.

"One minute, Niamh." Savannah picked up the necklace that Niamh had admired that first evening, took Niamh's hand and folded it into her palm. "I want you to have this. A thank you for looking after me."

Niamh's bottom lip quivered. "I cannot be takin' this." *Why did she have to be so kind?*

"I want you to have it. Please take it."

"No one ever gave me a present before." She stared at the small stone glinting in the lamplight. A moonstone, she had told her, on a silver chain. "It's very pretty, so it is. Thank you, Miss."

She bent down to kiss Savannah's cheek and ran from the room. Up in the attic, Niamh knelt by the side of her bed to say her prayers, the necklace nestled in her clasped hands. Tomorrow, after they had left for Dublin, she would go to Miss Byrne and tell her what she had done that very afternoon when she had sneaked out of the house, certain that Miss Byrne would be pleased with her for removing a rival for Conor Clare's affection. Philomena Byrne's reaction, however, would surprise her as she slapped her face, hard, twice, raged at her, denounced her as the most stupid 'eejit' she had ever met. In her jealousy and desire for revenge on the girl who had usurped her, Niamh had failed to foresee the knock-on effect of her actions and had not considered the consequences for Conor Clare, Mrs Archbold and, ultimately, herself.

TWENTY-TWO

The countryside flashed past the window of the carriage; the wooded slopes, the fields vibrant green in the early morning sunlight, and smoke rising from the chimneys of the white-washed cottages by the side of the road, but the brightness of the day did not find its way into Savannah's heart, and she looked through a mist of tears as she clung to Conor. At the port, he cupped her face in his hands and kissed her, a lingering kiss as if they knew it would be some time before they kissed again. She could not stop weeping and she clung to him more fiercely. She thought her heart would break.

"You will come soon?" she sobbed. "As you promised?"

"I will."

"You will ask her, as you promised last night?"

"Yes, I will come and ask her. Now dry your eyes and let me see that smile again so I can remember your beautiful face and the spells you weave."

"I love you so much," she whispered.

"I know you do." He looked away from her for a moment as she waited for him to say the same. "I wish I had someone to travel with you."

"I'll be fine." She was uneasy. A sickening quickened in her stomach.

"Remember to lock the cabin door. And you will remember to give Hugh his present?"

"Yes, of course." *Why is he like this?* she thought. *Talking of nothing?*

"Then I'll see you soon."

He had not told her he loved her. Despite his promise, she was filled with doubts about him. The sickening rose and she swallowed hard. Hugh had warned her to take his words with a pinch of salt.

"You will come?" she asked again. "You will come and ask my mother?" Savannah saw what she thought was a trace of uncertainty in his eyes. She was right to doubt him. She began to cry again. "You will not come. I will not see you again. Despite everything…" She could not speak.

"Hush," he said as he hugged her. "I will try…" He kissed her quickly, turned and hurried away before she saw his tears. Sprite or no sprite, he was bewitched. Conor Clare had fallen hopelessly in love with Savannah.

Relieved to be off the boat, as she had spent most of the crossing mulling over Conor's ambiguous words and flippant attitude, Savannah trotted down the gangplank, her suitcase in one hand, the parcel of books for Hugh, wrapped in brown paper, in the other, searching for him in the bustle of people on the quayside. He was waiting by a pillar near some luggage trolleys. He waved and came towards her. Then, as if from nowhere, two men were by her side and, for a moment, she thought Will had sent them to collect her to make sure she went home.

"Miss Hamilton-Read?" asked the short, fat one.

"Yes."

"Come with us, please."

"Who are you? Has my brother sent you?"

She looked round anxiously for Hugh and saw his startled face, his hands spread wide in questioning confusion, and then he was escorted away by two uniformed policemen.

"Just come with us," said the taller, thin one, taking her suitcase in one hand and her arm in the other. His companion relieved her of the parcel. "We don't want to make a fuss, do we?"

"Thank you, Sergeant," said the fat one to a man standing immediately behind Savannah.

She turned round to see the gentleman who had offered to carry her suitcase to the cabin before the boat left Dublin.

"But I don't know you," said Savannah, trying to shrug off the tall one's hand. But he only tightened his grip.

"Police, Miss Hamilton-Read."

After giving her name, which irritated her as they already knew it, and Will's home and office addresses, Savannah had been taken downstairs to a small, windowless room in the basement of the police station. They asked her, politely enough, to sit on one of the four chairs positioned round the wooden table and disappeared. She did not know how long she sat. In silence, worried, upset and completely baffled. Then the door opened, and Mr Fat came into the room. He had a glass of water which he placed in front of her and sat down with a grunt in a chair on the other side of the table. He took a notebook and pencil from the inside pocket of his jacket, placed them carefully on the table and reached again into his jacket pocket for a handkerchief and mopped his brow. She could feel her legs trembling. They seemed to be waiting for someone. The door opened and Mr Tall and Will came in. She rose unsteadily to greet her brother, relieved to see him and that he would sort out this preposterous mistake but was ordered quite forcefully by Mr Fat to sit down. Will sat beside her. Mr Tall – she had been told their names but, in her bewildered state, had not registered them – went to stand in the corner and leant back against the wall, crossed one leg in front of the other and folded his arms.

"Why am I here, Will?" Savannah asked, her voice barely more than a croak.

"The police have had a tip-off. The parcel you were carrying. What is in it?"

"Books," she said. "Only books."

She glanced at both of the policemen. Mr Tall, his expression unreadable, was watching her closely. Mr Fat, beads of sweat on his brow, was writing in his notebook.

"Books," repeated Mr Fat, looking up from his writing. "Books for whom?"

"Hugh. My friend, Hugh Furlong. A present. The man you took away."

"Where have you been for the last few days?"

"In Ireland. You know that. You saw me disembark from the boat."

Savannah thought it another stupid question and Will, sensing her annoyance, placed his hand on her arm as a warning not to antagonise her interrogator.

"Where in Ireland?" asked Mr Fat, reaching into his pocket for the handkerchief to mop his brow.

"Enniscourt. Not far from Dublin, near a village called Ballymore."

"Why?" asked Mr Fat, scribbling furiously.

"Why?"

"Why did you go to Ireland?" he asked, all his questions put to her without looking up. All Savannah saw was the top of his head and the flecks of dandruff in his oily hair.

"I was invited by a friend."

"What kind of friend?"

Savannah squirmed in her seat.

"Male? Female? Name?"

"Conor Clare. Enniscourt belongs to his aunt, Mrs Archbold. She's Irish and American."

She saw Mr Tall's mouth twitch. She recalled the conversation that first evening at Enniscourt and, for some reason, she felt instinctively it would be wise not to reveal Mrs Archbold's anti-British sentiments.

"What business does Mr Clare pursue?" asked Mr Fat.

Savannah thought for a moment and replied, "He is an antiques dealer." She hoped it would give Conor respectability. "He is very knowledgeable about furniture and art."

"Did you see any other people at the house?"

"What do you mean? Servants?"

"Visitors. Were there other guests?"

"No."

"Mr Clare was with you all the time you were there?"

"Yes, except when he went to send telegrams to my brother."

"Do you know where Mr Furlong lives? You should if you bring him presents."

This time he looked at her with a barely concealed sneer. Savannah gave him the address. Then Mr Fat placed his hands on the table and, scraping back his chair, heaved himself to his feet and said, "We will be back. Do you want anything to eat, Miss Hamilton-Read?"

Savannah shook her head. She had no appetite as she was frightened and could not understand why they were asking her such questions. When they had gone, leaving the door ajar, she turned to Will and asked, "What is the meaning of all this?"

"They think you may have brought money across from Ireland."

"Money?"

"Money, Savannah. They think you are mixed up with people, Fenians, who want to buy guns and dynamite to kill British people."

Her face went white. "No. No. No. I swear to you, Will, on Mama's life, I know nothing of this. Fenians? Good heavens! Why have they brought me here?"

"A tip-off from the police in Ireland. You have been watched since you left this place, Enniscourt. Tell the police everything, Savannah. It will be better for you in the long run to cooperate if it goes to trial."

"Trial? What are you talking about? I have done nothing wrong."

"If they find something, Savannah, you will be charged as an accomplice. If found guilty you will go to prison. You know they hang those guilty of treasonable crimes?"

She began to cry.

"Stop it, Savannah," said Will, mercilessly. He had lost patience with her behaviour these last few weeks, and he was determined to make her suffer; even exaggerating the consequences for her as he was not privy to all the information the police had and what the outcome would be. She was no longer the sweet, little girl he took riding. She was no longer a sweet, little girl. He had made a promise to his father when she was born, and he had asked himself more than once recently whether he should have acceded to his mother's request to return to Longridge after his father's death where, perhaps, he would have taken a more prominent role in her upbringing. His mother had not failed in that regard, but Savannah obviously needed a father figure. But at the time, he was a young man, he did not want the responsibility, and he still had fish to fry. He shook his head. "Once more you do something reckless with all its consequences. Have you learnt nothing? Are you so stupid and selfish? Mama has been beside herself with worry. How can you behave like this? A note? A telegram? So weak and stupid you fall for any man who sweet-talks you? And look where it's brought you."

He had hissed the words at her and was interrupted when Mr Tall came back in.

"A word, Mr Hamilton-Read."

They disappeared into the corridor, and she could hear them whispering together. It seemed to take a long time. Then Will came back into the room and said, "You are to spend the night here, as you are to be questioned further. I shall arrange for you to have some of your personal things."

"Will, please," she pleaded. "Don't leave me here."

He ignored her and left.

The cot was hard, the mattress lumpy, the blanket thin and smelly, and she had hardly slept. Despite what Will had said, she was not questioned again. A policeman in uniform had brought her a tray of food that she was unable to determine what it was meant to be, never mind stomach it. She had gone over and over in her mind the image of Conor handing her the parcel and asking her to make sure Hugh received it. What did it all mean? She was cold, stiff, hungry and felt dirty, and wondered how much longer she would be detained when the door opened.

"Good morning," said Mr Fat gruffly. "We are letting you go. Choose your friends more wisely in future, Miss Hamilton-Read. If we have any more questions for you, we know where to find you."

Will appeared in the doorway beside him and they shook hands and, after collecting her suitcase, he took her out to a waiting cab.

It was very early in the morning, the sun pale and the air chilly, and there were few people about, a milk cart, a shopkeeper rolling out his awning. The horse's hooves echoed, and the wheels rumbled on the cobbles.

"What happened to Hugh?" asked Savannah.

"They let him go."

"So they should. We did nothing wrong. I have been treated abominably," she said severely.

"Mama is here," Will said after a few minutes. "You had better think of something to say to her to make up for your appalling behaviour. If she sends you to a nunnery, it will be too good for you."

He did not tell her that he was, because of his line of work, well acquainted with one of the detectives. The other, the tall, thin one, he did not know why he was there and assumed he had been sent by the Metropolitan Police in London. They had informed him the evening before that they had nothing to charge her with, nothing had been found, the parcel was in fact a couple of books, and they had gone to Furlong's address and found nothing suspicious. He had asked them, as a favour to him, to keep her in the cell overnight to teach her a lesson.

"And Esme about to give birth and you cause her to worry. She feels let down by you, as you have deceived her with all your mysterious disappearances. She is horrified she has facilitated your disgraceful behaviour."

"You do not need to adopt that tone with me, Will," Savannah snapped at him. "You can climb down from your high horse."

"Do not dare to speak to me like that." He turned to her, red-faced with anger and indignation.

"I shall speak to you how I wish. You are my brother, not my father. Do not lecture me on my morals and conduct. You need to examine your own conscience."

"What on earth are you talking about?"

"I saw you. With that woman outside the hotel."

"I beg your pardon?"

"I saw you. Do not insult me by denying it."

He took her chin, twisted her face towards him and glared at her. "I have nothing to deny. You do not understand what you saw. She was a client."

Savannah pushed his hand away and snorted derisively. "Is that so, Will? You know to what I refer then? Another appointment. Is that so? Is that your word for it? As you wish."

Her mother was waiting in the hall of Will's house, grim-faced, and declined to kiss her, which she had never done before. "You look dreadful."

"So would you if you had spent a night in a cell."

"Don't be clever with me, young lady. Go and bathe and then join me for breakfast."

Marianna watched her daughter eat and said nothing. Although she was extremely hungry, Savannah found it difficult to swallow her food under her mother's unrelenting gaze and kept her eyes firmly on her plate, for if she looked at her just once she did not know whether she would explode in anger or tears. Her mother's coldness upset her.

"Have you finished?" asked Marianna curtly. "Will is waiting for us in his study."

Savannah sat down in an armchair. After knocking out his pipe in the grate, Will sat down next to his mother on the sofa opposite. Savannah thought they were like a pair of stern-faced Spanish Inquisitors. This was the second time in as many weeks she had been in this room, and she was to be reprimanded again. She could not look at either of them because she knew how upset they were. For this she was sorry, but she was not ashamed of Conor. She could hear William Bennet and Theo in the hallway waiting to go for a walk with Miss Atkinson and she wished she could go with them and so avoid the grilling that awaited her.

The front door closed. Marianna spoke.

"Have you learnt nothing? I sent you here whilst I cleaned up the mess you left behind at home. Will was kind enough to let you stay and how did you repay his kindness?" She waved the note Savannah had left on the dressing table and began to read aloud. "'Dear Will, I am going away for a few days with a friend. I will let you know when I intend to return. Please do not tell Mama.' No word of explanation. No idea with whom or to where."

"I sent telegrams, Mama."

"Pshaw! What did they tell us? How did that make us feel better? Have you any inkling at all of the worry and vexation you have caused Will and Esme? Will especially, as I had entrusted you to his care. Have you any inkling of how this has affected me? Are you such a selfish, self-centred, spoilt, self-indulgent... brat?" Marianna turned to Will and, without stopping to take a breath, said to him, "Is my role as a parent done? Should I cast her out and leave her to her own devices? Would her father forgive me? Is it my duty to keep her close or let her loose?"

Will clasped his mother's hand. Savannah did not fully comprehend what her mother was saying and before she could begin to unravel the meaning of her words, Will set to.

"Can you see how upset Mama is?" he asked. "How upset we all are, Savannah? Can you begin to imagine the thoughts swirling in our minds as we wondered if you were safe? We were on the point of notifying the police when your first telegram arrived. Can you imagine the consequences? The gossip? The damage to your reputation? What on earth were you thinking? You thought it was a jaunt? A jolly jape? A lark?"

He waited for an answer. She twisted her fingers together, sighed and shuddered as she struggled to put into words – genteel, acceptable words – the effect Conor Clare had had on her, the bliss of their lovemaking, but she could not.

"You see?" said Marianna in exasperation at her silence. "You see? She has no shame. No consideration. She feels no responsibility for her actions."

"I do, Mama," Savannah said quietly. There was no point in trying to justify her behaviour. "And I beg your forgiveness. And I beg your forgiveness too, Will, and I will apologise to Esme. I am, as you say, Mama, selfish, spoilt and reckless. And I await your punishment and will accept it without complaint." She looked pleadingly at her mother. "But please do not cast me out. Where would I go? I love you so much, Mama. And you too, Will. I could

not bear it if I was never to see you again. You don't mean it, surely?"
She laughed nervously.

"Those doleful eyes may have worked on your father, Savannah,"
said Marianna scornfully. "But they will not work on me. Of course
I would not cast you out. Those words were said in desperation at
your indifference to our feelings. However," she said, lowering her
voice, and speaking emphatically, "things *will* change. Your behaviour
must change. You must consider more carefully the consequences of
your actions and learn that all men are not the same. Some men
are not honourable, Savannah." Savannah glanced quickly at Will as
her mother mentioned honourable men, but his expression had not
changed from the severe and disapproving one he had adopted from
the beginning. "You are too gullible," her mother was saying. "You
are too easily distracted by their attentions to see them for what
they are. And when they have taken what they want, Savannah, they
will drop you without a thought for you or your feelings."

Her mother looked bereft, and Savannah shot up from the
chair and went to give her a kiss and Will a hug. She may be all
of the things her mother described, but she was a generous, kind-
hearted, sensitive young woman, despite her bravado.

"I am so very sorry. I cannot say it any other way than that."

Will said, "I will accept your apology, for I believe you are sincere.
I promised Papa when you were born that I would look after you.
It saddens me that I have let him down. But look how much you
have upset Mama, and I will not stand for it, Savannah. I cannot
bear to see Mama so distraught." His words struck home. The night
she was born, Savannah now realised, he had been more concerned
about his mother than the unborn child. "My goodness, you have
tried my patience to the limit these past few weeks. You must listen
to Mama, and you *will* change your ways. Still only seventeen years
old and already two lovers."

"Will!" cried Savannah. "Please." She sat down heavily in her
chair. He was determined to make her suffer.

"What? I state the truth, do I not? This man. What is his name?
Conor Clare. The man you have been with is also a lover, for why else
would you run off with him? You do not like the sound of it? You do

not like what I am saying when it is the truth? Your reputation will be ruined if this gets out."

She glared at him, a look warning him to hold his tongue. How could he be so hypocritical? Did he not have a reputation to uphold?

"Enough, Will," said Marianna. "Savannah is not stupid." Will snorted. "She understands."

Marianna rose and said to Savannah, "We are going home. Go and say what you need to say to Esme. Then pack your things."

"Mama—"

"Now!"

TWENTY-THREE

On the journey home, Savannah told Marianna she thought Will was unhappy. Marianna raised her hand to silence her.

"I know all about it. It is Will's business, not ours."

Savannah did not disclose what she had seen in the street outside the hotel. It was obvious her brother was unfaithful to his wife and, thinking about all the other comments he had made and what William Bennet had told her, she doubted they still loved each other. She wondered if her mother knew that. The rest of the journey passed with few words exchanged. Her mother read a book. She stared out of the window.

The new stableman, Edmund Sill, collected them from the station. He was in his forties, married with grown-up children and, Marianna hoped, a more trustworthy employee than the disgraced Thomas. Ada was waiting in the hall. She welcomed them home and then asked to have a word with Marianna. They moved to one side, where Ada whispered something, and Marianna's head dropped.

"Oh, no. Not this too."

Ada patted her arm affectionately and, casting a sympathetic look in Savannah's direction, went downstairs to the kitchen.

"Do you wish to rest?" Marianna asked Savannah.

"I do, Mama, but first I'll go and see Badger."

"No, Savannah."

The sharpness of her mother's voice told her that something bad had happened to Badger. Marianna took her arm and guided her into the drawing room.

"Sit down, darling," she said, sitting beside her.

"He's dead, isn't he?"

Her mother nodded, her eyes brimming with tears. Savannah's face crumpled and she began to sob.

"When?"

"Yesterday afternoon. Arthur has been looking after him whilst I was away. He stopped eating, and yesterday Arthur was worried enough to send for the vet as he wouldn't get out of his bed. The vet thought he had a cancer."

"I knew something was wrong with him and I was not here for him."

"He did not suffer, Savannah." He had been put to sleep. "We must take comfort from that." She tried desperately to find the words to ease her daughter's bruised heart. "He had a wonderful life here and we all loved him very much."

An hour later, Marianna found Savannah curled up on her bed, eyes wide open, staring vacantly into space.

"Savannah, I have had an idea."

Savannah jumped at the sound of her mother's voice; she had not heard her enter the room. She sat up and swung her legs over the edge of the bed. "What is it, Mama?" she asked, smoothing out the creases in her dress.

"We should bury Badger beside Papa."

"Is that allowed?"

"It is the Hamilton plot, beside the Hamilton chapel, on Hamilton land. I am a Hamilton. I shall do as I please."

Arthur Dummigan had collected a spade from his tool store and had already dug a small grave at the foot of William's by the time they arrived. Savannah had not been to the burial ground since her father died. She carried her beloved dog wrapped in one of her lace shawls. She kissed the bundle and placed it gently in the ground and they watched as Arthur filled in the hole, patted the soil flat with the back of the spade and replaced the turves of grass.

He shouldered the spade, touched his cap and left them. Marianna had picked two roses from the garden and placed one on Badger's grave and replaced the faded rose on William's. Savannah read the inscription on her father's headstone. *William Read. Aged fifty years. Beloved husband and father. Till all the Seas.*

"Will Badger have a stone, Mama?"

"Why not?"

"Why William Read?"

"Because that was his name. When he was taken as a child to Coldbarrow, he vowed to return to his family. Every night before he went to sleep, he repeated his name so he did not forget who he was. That is a powerful thing for a young child to do. He was never a Hamilton. I had his stone inscribed thus out of respect for him and everything he stood for."

"What does 'Till all the Seas' mean?"

"They are words by the Scottish poet, Robert Burns, and we heard it sung by an old friend of ours when we lived at Netherton. We promised to love each other until all the seas dried up."

"Which means forever."

"Yes."

"Do you believe Papa is in heaven?"

"If you mean will we see him and Badger again, I would hope so. We are not a religious family, but I pray to God, Savannah, in my own way. Whether that is a sign of faith or superstition, as your father teased me, just in case there is a heaven, I do not know. But if there is a heaven, your father is surely there."

They stood, arms round each other's waist, lost in their own thoughts.

Savannah lay in bed, the curtains drawn, not sleeping, eating little of the food that was sent up on trays. Why was life like this? Her father gone. Badger gone. Conor gone. Her mother came to talk to her to try and shake her out of her misery; she listened but did not speak. Richard Greenwood came to talk to her; it was obvious he had not been told everything, and she listened but did not speak. She longed for Conor. Her body writhed in pain in the long, dark hours of the night with the yearning for him, the lust for him. She tossed and turned. She wept. She got up and paced the floor. She stared out of the window at the shadows on the lawn, the black silhouette of the wood. She heard the lonely, frantic peep of an oystercatcher flying overhead. She lay on the bed, eyes wide open, staring into the nothingness where she could not escape her thoughts. She was haunted. Words. Deeds. Names. Hugh: *There's so much you don't know about us.* Mr Fat: *Choose your friends more wisely.* Mrs Archbold's acerbic comments about the English. What was Philomena Byrne to Conor? Why did Hugh need to work in Liverpool when there was the family shop in the village? Was he telling the truth about why he and O'Driscoll were at the house instead of at work? Conor needing to disappear to attend to business. What kind of business? The American visitors the police had been interested in, but she knew nothing of them other than what Niamh had told her. The parcel. Where was the money the police were looking for? Conor had used her. Conor had duped her. She wept. Words, words, words. *Is it possible there is just one person in the world meant for me and I have found you? He likes women, Savannah.* Conor's beautiful eyes. Conor loving her. Again and again. Conor. Conor's beautiful, beautiful eyes. His beautiful face. His kiss. His breath on the nape of her neck. His tongue exploring. His touch. Her body writhed with longing for him.

The third morning, she woke from a troubling dream and struggled to understand it and why she had woken from it. Masked men – although she could not see their faces, she knew they were Will and Jack – chased her along a never-ending road and she knew they were dangerous, she was in peril, and she had to reach the door of Enniscourt to be safe. But she woke up before she got there. The dream had unsettled her, and she felt anxious. And alone. She lay in bed, staring at the ceiling, and began to realise that she could not keep pent up all her thoughts, fears and desires. She could not continue to hide herself away. She needed to talk to someone, as she recognised that she was harming herself and would make herself ill. She was close to her mother, trusted her, trusted her advice, though she did not want to upset her by asking if she would have made wiser choices if her father was still alive, implying that her mother was somehow to blame for the way she had turned out. Would she have a better understanding of men if he was still alive to advise her? If he would have protected her by sniffing out the unsuitable ones? If she could have spoken as freely to him about love and what men wanted? If she had not participated in the wager? If Jack had loved her, would she be in this predicament? If. If. If. Her whole life so far, for all her seventeen, nearly eighteen years of it, was one big *if*.

She got up slowly, sluggishly, from the bed, took a sip of water from the glass on the bedside table and tottered across the room to open the curtains. It was a beautiful day; the sky was cloudless. The clock in the pele tower was striking the hour. She counted. It was nine o'clock. Crows wheeled above the trees in the wood and a pair of blackbirds hopped across the lawn. She dressed, wearily, as she was weak and light-headed with hunger, and went down to breakfast. She would tell her mother about Conor. About everything. Everything.

Later that afternoon, Savannah lay on the sofa in her mother's sitting room. She had just read a letter from Amy, one of the Musketeers, that had arrived in the morning post. It was very brief.

There is a dearth of even barely attractive members of the opposite sex in this town and most I would not allow within six feet of me! I have never seen so many pimple-faced, buck-toothed ninnies in my life! Have you had better luck?

The heavy cloak of sadness and lethargy was swallowing her again. Luck? Was it luck to have fallen in love with the most beautiful man in the world and lost him? No letter from him. What did that mean? He did not love her. That was the truth of it. Already forgotten about her. Moved on to the next stupid, gullible woman to fall for him. The door to the rose garden was open and she could hear the bees busy foraging among the flowers. She felt numb. She missed Badger who, had he been alive, would now be sitting on her lap, nudging her with his damp nose, appealing to her with his sweet, brown eyes to snap out of her sadness. She felt guilty too as she knew he was not well when she had left for Liverpool. But in that she had no choice, she reasoned. Still, she could have asked to come home sooner to be with him. She must remember to thank Arthur for his kindness. Conor. There he was again, back in her thoughts. How was she ever to forget him?

She heard the door open, and her mother appeared at her side.

"Jack is here."

"Send him away."

"This is rude, Savannah. He has called twice now to tell you how sad he is about Badger. He is your friend. He will cheer you up. He missed you at the Mayor's Ball."

"I have no interest in Jack Greenwood. If you let him in to see me, I shall leave the room."

"I am not pleased with you, Savannah. I am running out of things to say to him. He is upset that you will not see him. You should take care of your friendships."

The following day she still moped, languishing on the sofa in her mother's sitting room.

"Come for a walk with me, Savannah. You need to bring the colour back to your cheeks."

"I do not care to, Mama."

"Then go for a ride. I am sure Ladybird could do with the exercise."

"No, Mama. Please. Let me be." Savannah rolled onto her side and turned her back on her mother.

"How long is this behaviour to continue?" said Marianna, sitting down at the end of the sofa so she could see Savannah's stern, pale face, her eyes constantly brimming with tears.

"Until I pine away to nothing."

"You are beginning to tire me, Savannah, with this mood of yours. You are seventeen, for goodness' sake! There are years ahead of you to amuse yourself with flirtations—"

"Oh, Mother!" Savannah interrupted her angrily and glared at her. "How can you insult me by saying it was a flirtation? I told you what he meant to me and how much I love him and now you have forgotten and do not begin to understand at all what I am going through."

"I understand perfectly. But how you can allow yourself to throw away your life and the opportunities that await you because of a duplicitous, lying rogue is beyond me. Your obtuse, stubborn refusal to see him for what he is begins to aggravate me, Savannah."

Marianna got up, skirts rustling, and left the room, returning some minutes later with a leather-bound book with gilt-edged pages and a letter.

"I want you to read this," she said, handing the letter to Savannah.

Savannah wiped her eyes on her sleeves and shuffled into a sitting position.

"Who is it from?"

"Your father. To me."

Marianna sat by her feet and waited for her to finish reading it. Savannah began to cry again as she recognised her father's handwriting, the long, swooping downstrokes with the little curl at the end.

My darling Marianna. My darling love. My darling wife. My darling friend,

For you are all these things to me. When I sleep, I dream about you and in my dreams you are perfect, the most perfect woman a man could ever conjure in his wildest imaginings. Imagine then how I fear to wake and that perfect woman dissolves with the fading darkness. Yet what do I have to fear? For when I open my eyes and see you lying beside me, knowing that until my eyes close in sleep once more and my perfect woman returns to my dreams, I have a woman more perfect, more beautiful, more loving and loved than any dream can conjure up.

Know this, my darling Marianna, I have loved you all my life and will love you beyond my life till all the seas gang dry and if there is a heaven and life eternal that is where I shall wait for you to come to me.

Your devoted William.

Savannah was sobbing uncontrollably, and Marianna moved to take her in her arms. Many minutes passed before she regained her composure.

"It is beautiful, Mama. Did he write it when he was wooing you?"

"No. I did not know of it until the day his will was read out. I do not know why he gave it to Mr Birch to look after." She shrugged her shoulders. "I can guess it was to be read only after he died. I wanted you to read it to help you understand what love is. Love means different things to each of us, I know, but for me, the purest, deepest love is love given freely by both, without conditions, without expecting one should give more than the other, and knowing the other reciprocates, totally, your feelings. Giving and sharing, Savannah. You must learn the true meaning of love and not give it away too cheaply. You have made some poor choices and you have been ill-used."

Savannah kissed the bottom of the letter where her father had signed his name, folded it and gave it back to her mother. "I hope someone will write to me like that someday. You have been so lucky, Mama."

Marianna reached across to the side table where she had left her book.

"Now I want you to read this. Not all at once, as it is rather long. It is an account of my life and my thoughts on what has happened to me. A memoir, if you like."

"Did Papa ever read it?"

"Of course. Your papa and I had no secrets. You will read of my mistakes, things I have done that I am ashamed of, my life with your father, my deep, deep love for him in all its forms. It is personal, truthful. Very, very honest in fact, and it may embarrass you. But you will see me as I am, as I have been, good and bad."

Savannah spent hours reading her mother's memoir, even late into that same night, snuggled up in bed, the lamplight glowing on the pages. She knew of Coldbarrow and her parents' early lives but not how each of them had suffered.

William was often overcome by waves of sadness at Coldbarrow because he remembered his family, knew who he was, and could not understand why he had been taken from them. 'But then I had you,' he told me. 'And things got better.' This sadness gave way to disappointment when we arrived in Mossbrook and his dream of his family was shattered: his father dead, his two brothers gone, Lizzie married and pregnant. I did not suffer these bouts of sadness because I could not remember my family at all. Although, the scent of a rose climbing up a wall reminded me of something. My sombre moods came later when we lived at Netherton. Our dear friend, Walter Fleming, had been talking about his time as a soldier in Spain and began to count in Spanish. The words and the chiming of a clock lit a spark, a spark flitting in the shadows of my mind that, try as I might, I could not blow on to increase the flame of memory. I came to believe that my parents had abandoned me. I did not know who I was.

Savannah did not know the truth of how they had been separated at Netherton and could not believe how much her father had endured, falsely arrested and transported to Australia. She learnt the reason for his fear of the sea after he had almost drowned following the wrecking of the convict ship in the Atlantic Ocean. They had never told her that part of their history. She wept when she read of her mother's pain at his loss and anguish at the thought of bringing up his child alone. She gasped when she read Bertie Robson had been her mother's lover all those years ago at Loop Hall when she thought William was gone, and the passionate love they had enjoyed, the physical need her mother had for a relationship, and she wondered if he ever knew about the lost baby. She shuddered at the coldness and demanding nature of her grandmother, the spitefulness of her Aunt Verity, and wished she had known her grandfather. This was the family she had never known. She wept again when she read how William and Marianna had been so close to being reunited and how her grandmother had been responsible for denying them that opportunity, not even telling Marianna that William was alive until she questioned her directly. She was astonished by the revelations concerning Bennet Foster and understood why Will had named his eldest son William Bennet, recognising the close friendship he had had with his stepfather. She was more astonished that her mother had taken lovers and was saddened by the shame and guilt she felt at these casual, loveless affairs. There were pages describing her parents' eventual reunion, the indescribable joy, the lovemaking, the passion, the holiday in Scotland when they had stayed in bed for days, loving each other but seeing little of the sights, their plans for the future, the news they would have a second child. Her mother had written after one night of passionate lovemaking, *I love beyond words. I am loved beyond words. His name is William Read, and I whisper his name and feel him all around me.*

Marianna wrote about how often she and William talked about the past, the strangeness of their childhood and how it affected them, their love for each other, and their happy life at Netherton until cruel fate had intervened.

I asked William if he ever suffered black moods after he was taken from me. He told me that he did because what happened to him was beyond his control, but he learnt to smother them as he realised he could do nothing to change anything. I asked him why I continue to have them. I always fear to enjoy any happiness or good things that come my way. He thought it was because I was lonely. I had no one to confide in. My father was dead, my mother and sister were hostile, Bennet Foster was distant. And Agatha Mislet had a lot to answer for, filling children's heads with all that fire and brimstone nonsense from the Bible, making us feel guilty. I love this man, my husband. He is so kind and understanding. He does not belittle my feelings or dismiss my worries. He listens and offers words of comfort. 'Be kind to yourself, Marianna.'

Savannah understood why there had been no more children after her.

Savannah's birth terrified William and upset him in equal measure. He does not lie with me at my fertile times, as he fears for my life, which he says is more precious to him than his own. Each day, each night my heart fills with love for him. Each hour, each minute, each second we are apart is bitter, sweetened only when he comes back to me. I cannot wait to lie with him. I cannot wait to feel his touch, his kiss. I cannot wait to feel him inside me when we are one. My beautiful, beautiful man.

When her father died, she had written simply, *He is gone.* There was nothing written after her father's death until more than three months later she wrote, *Today I read my darling William's letter for the first time. I did not have the courage to do so before now as I feared for my state of mind. I have been plunged into the depths of misery and despair. Dark, dark days when I have contemplated the worst act a human being could wish upon themselves to be with him again. It is only my darling Savannah and the thought of her, so young, losing both of us that stills my hand. How I wish I had read his words sooner, so beautiful, as they have brought me comfort and I will treasure them always. I have had to be brave for Savannah's sake – she is a lost soul without her beloved papa – and I will treasure always the comfort Will has brought me. I can only pray that the pain, the emptiness we all feel will ease. I long for my darling William so much my body is in pain, my heart completely broken. I wake in the morning and reach for him but…*

The words stopped. She imagined her mother could not continue as her grief was still too much. Sometime later, she had written, *I bless the day Badger came into this house. The little fellow is a joy and has done more to help Savannah come to terms with the loss of William than I could ever do.*

Savannah shed tears again for them both. Bertie Robson had disappeared from the scene at some stage, and she had not paid much attention at the time. She was too young, did not know they were briefly lovers again, but she read the reason why and, as she turned the pages, how he had come back into her mother's life after his wife died two years later and he had written to her, regretting his dishonesty and begging to see her again. Marianna had told her at the time why he was there and what he meant to her. She wrote, *Savannah is home for the holiday, and I have explained to her why Bertie Robson comes to Longridge. She understands what sexual love is and knows he is my lover. But I have told her I will never stop loving her father. William is the first and only true love of my life.*

She skipped over the pages where her mother revealed the pleasure that she got from Bertie, as it was too much; she wondered how she could look at them and not imagine them together, which would be embarrassing. She also felt it would be dishonourable to the memory of her father to read it, although she did not disapprove of her mother finding that kind of love again. Her mother inspired such love, had inspired two men to love her. She understood too, as her mother wrote so vividly, how much she craved physical love, and it began to dawn on her why she had been allowed to read this memoir; why her mother had shared the most intimate, most revealing details of her life. Her mother had lain with her father when she was very young and before they were married. She had lain with Cuthbert Robson even though she was convinced William was not dead. She had lain with other men because her second husband could not satisfy her. Her mother understood her, wanted her to learn the meaning of an honest love, to understand the difference between carnal, selfish urges and true, unselfish, lasting love. She had to understand this if she was ever to be happy.

As the pale light of dawn filtered through the gap in her bedroom curtains, she extinguished the lamp and got up to go to her writing desk. She took up a pen and wrote under her mother's last entry, *I hope one day I will love and be loved forever. Be it a fraction of the love between my darling papa and mama, I shall be happy. Savannah H-R.*

TWENTY-FOUR

They were in the walled garden, aprons covering their dresses, their faces shaded from the morning sun with wide-brimmed straw hats. The air was heavy with scent and hummed with insects. Savannah was helping her mother to deadhead the roses and other spent blooms. She had been home for ten days.

"I am not surprised you remembered the scent," said Savannah, watching a bumble bee, heavy with pollen, totter drunkenly on an open rose flower.

"What do you mean?"

"When you were taken as a child to that place. In your memoir, you described a rose growing there and the scent; you could remember the smell of the roses but not from where. I am not surprised. It is quite overwhelming."

"Yes, that is true." Marianna stood upright to ease the stiffness in her back and wiped her hand across her brow. "And I remembered the sound of the clock on the tower."

"I cannot imagine," said Savannah, tossing a handful of swollen seed pods into the basket that lay on the path between them, "what it must be like to lose a child in that way." She looked at her mother. "You would not have sent me away, Mama?"

Marianna smiled at her fondly. "No, of course not. You are too precious to me and what would your father have thought of me?"

"Am I the daughter you hoped for, Mama?"

"What a strange thing to ask. You are you, Savannah, and I wouldn't change a thing."

Savannah dropped the scissors into the basket and went to hug her.

"I am so sorry I have vexed you as much."

Marianna kissed her cheek. "It is passed now."

"But I loved him, Mama. I could not help myself. I will never find love like that again."

"You will." Marianna saw the dejection in her eyes. Savannah did not believe her. She was going to mention Bertie Robson but decided against it. Savannah loved her father too much and it was not appropriate. Anyway, she felt differently about Bertie. Compared to William, it was not the same intense love. She took her daughter's hands in hers.

"Promise me, Savannah, that you will come to me when you are troubled or want to know something, which I will answer to the best of my ability. It does not matter what it is, you know you can confide in me, don't you?"

"Yes, Mama, I know," said Savannah. "You are my best friend in the world."

They went back to their pruning. After a few minutes, Marianna said, "You know, darling, I wonder if you should go back to school after all. It would give you time to think about what you would like to do. Miss Harper has written to me. She says you have such abilities—"

"I think not, Mama!" Savannah looked at her mother in horrified astonishment. "To live with all those silly girls and endure all those petty rules—"

"So, you think you are all grown up now when I beg to differ? It is your immaturity which has landed you in so much trouble."

"Mama, I have read your book. Tell me how you were different to me at the age I am now."

There was a silence. *Touché*, thought Marianna. It was she who had made her feelings known to William and kissed him first and lay with him when she was... How old was she? Savannah was right.

"What would you like to do instead?" asked Marianna, bending to her task.

Without hesitation, Savannah replied, "If Papa was here, I would help him with the horses and learn all I could from him. But, Mama… Will the pain of losing him ever go away?"

Marianna straightened up again. "No, darling. But each time you think of him, remember how much he loved you."

"It upsets me to think I have let him down. Would Papa have been disappointed in me?"

"Yes, Savannah, I think he would, as like me, he would have hoped you were more responsible by now. He would have been very worried about what you had got yourself involved in, and if he got his hands on that man… But, like me, he would forgive you." She wanted to change the subject. Savannah seemed so much brighter and was beginning to think more positively about the future. Conor Clare was out of the picture and Savannah would forget him and move forwards. "We are your parents. You never stop loving a child, Savannah, however much they vex you. Well, I do not know about you, but I am quite warm. Shall we stop and have some of Ada's lemonade?"

She picked up the basket and left it on a bench in one of the arbours and they removed their aprons and hats. Savannah linked arms with her, and they walked back along the path to her sitting room.

"You know, Mama, I think I would quite like to have a farm."

"Is that so?" Marianna laughed. "You told your papa you wanted a zoo, one time. Do you remember?"

"There's someone at the door, ma'am."

Sarah stood on the threshold of the sitting room.

"Who is it?" asked Marianna, looking up from her embroidery. "I did not hear the bell."

"He wouldn't say. But…"

"But?"

"He's very handsome, ma'am," said Sarah, lowering her eyes and blushing crimson.

Savannah jumped to her feet, a beaming smile on her face, and threw her book on the chair.

"Show him in, Sarah."

"Savannah!" exclaimed her mother as Sarah shut the door. "Is this wise?" Her intuition told her who it was.

Savannah smoothed her hair and patted her skirts, swallowed hard, patted her hair and smoothed her skirts and then stood, heart beating frantically, waiting.

Conor Clare was shown into the room and Savannah, unable to contain her emotions, flew to him, flung her arms round his neck and kissed him on the mouth and he kissed her back. They seemed to have forgotten they were not alone.

"Really, Savannah!" hissed Marianna.

Sarah could not believe her eyes and sidled out of the room. Conor unwound Savannah's arms from his neck and held out his hand to Marianna. He was struck immediately by her beauty and elegance and the determined, hostile set of her face.

"Conor Clare," he said.

"I know who you are," she replied coldly, refusing his hand, but taking in the handsomeness of him, the casual smartness of his dress, his self-assurance.

He saw where Savannah had inherited her stunning eyes, but the iciness he saw in them did not surprise him and, in truth, alarmed him.

"You have half an hour, Mr Clare, and then I shall ask you to leave." Marianna glared at Savannah. "I shall ask Sarah to bring you some refreshment." And then she left them alone.

"I've walked from the station. I've left my bag there," Conor said, holding Savannah at arm's length and looking at her from top to toe. "I was not sure of my welcome."

"You look tired," said Savannah.

"I've been travelling for two days. My God, I have missed you."

They walked into each other's arms and kissed each other hungrily: eyes, mouth, hands.

Then, as if something had just occurred to her, Savannah pulled abruptly away from him and said, "Why are you here, Conor?"

"You said to come and ask your mother for your hand."

She stepped back further in bewildered amazement at his earnest face. "Are you quite mad? You saw how she was with you just now. She thinks you are the devil incarnate for what you have done."

"When she knows me, she will change her mind."

She was surprised by his confidence, his arrogance. "And me? You do not ask me if I have not changed my mind and still wish to marry you after what you have done."

There was a tap at the door, and they moved further into the room to allow Sarah to deliver a tray of tea and sandwiches. She tried not to stare as the gentleman thanked her but needed to imprint his every feature in her mind as she had been instructed to do by the intrigued staff waiting below in the kitchen. When she had gone, Conor and Savannah sat down, and she offered him a plate of sandwiches. He took two and ate them immediately, as he was very hungry, he told her. She poured him some tea and he took a swig and put the cup back down on the tray. He glanced round the room and admired the understated elegance of it, so unlike other women's sitting rooms he had visited that were cluttered with furniture and the tasteless knick-knacks he despised. He saw the collection of family photographs and the discarded embroidery hoop on the side table, the rosewood sewing box on the floor. He knew Savannah's mother was an accomplished needlewoman.

"Why did you not write to me and let me know you were coming?" asked Savannah, interrupting the silence.

"I was afraid you would refuse to see me."

"You were right to think so, but you thought if I saw you in the flesh, I would be unable to resist you?"

"Because you love me."

"Why did you not write to me when I came home? You must have heard your plan failed. You never thought to write and enquire about me and explain yourself? Do I count for nothing?"

"There is no excuse for that. In my defence, let me tell you what happened."

Savannah looked away from him. The scent from the rose

garden was overwhelming and, despite the breeze it allowed into the room, she went to close the door as she thought she might faint. It gave her a moment too to consider his words and how she should respond. She loved him with all her heart but… She sat down again. Her mouth was dry with nerves. She took a sip of the now lukewarm lemonade. She breathed in deeply.

"Tell me why I was dragged into your plot."

"Yes," he said. "I need to explain. But know this, Savannah, it may have started out one way, but it did not end as it was intended."

He took her hand and kissed her fingers. She jerked her hand away. He sensed her anger and made no comment on her reaction. He went on to tell her he had been arrested at the port not long after he left her and spent three days in a police cell. He had been questioned repeatedly about his supposed involvement with the Republican Brotherhood, Fenians, Americans, his aunt, his business, Savannah, Liverpool.

"I have even given up smoking as they took away my cigarettes and I found I did not miss them. Are you pleased with me?"

She ignored him. "So, three days in a cell and" – she counted on her fingers – "seven days have passed since then and no word from you."

"I had some things to do. I have had to help my aunt leave for Boston. She has instructed me to get on with the work on the house without delay, so I have had to find workmen. I stopped in Liverpool briefly to see Hugh and asked him to help me."

"You know then that the police took me away as Hugh witnessed it."

"Yes, he told me, and I am so sorry, Savannah. It was not meant to happen."

"But it did, Conor, and I have never been so scared in all my life."

"Sorry," he said again. "I regret that happened and frightened you."

They were silent for a moment. Savannah still could not understand his motivation. His aunt, yes; she had made her anti-British, Republican sympathies plain, but Conor had never, in her hearing, expressed such sentiments.

"You wish Ireland to be an independent state?"

Conor paused before replying, "Yes. Yes, I do."

"But these people you mention kill innocent people. They plant bombs. You are connected to them?"

"The police said they had been given information to connect me to them. They went to Enniscourt and turned the place upside down, emptied the barn, and found nothing. There was nothing to find, Savannah. The whole episode was upsetting for my aunt." His explanation was brief. He omitted to say that his aunt had always been careful and burnt incriminating correspondence; that it was Philomena Byrne who had immediately gone to Enniscourt to tell his aunt what Niamh had done so they were prepared for the arrival of the police, and that the day before he had accompanied her to Dublin, when he had gone to send a telegram to her brother, he had dug a hole in a field and buried the money she was expected to deliver.

"In that case, why were you arrested? Why was I questioned? I spent a night in a police cell, Conor. It was humiliating and unbearable."

"I am sorry. I didn't know about that. I don't think Hugh did either. He never mentioned it. Someone passed on information to the police."

"Who?"

"Niamh. She told Philomena Byrne that she had gone to the police."

"Is Miss Byrne mixed up in this?"

"No! Phil thought she was making it all up to be spiteful."

"But why? What could Niamh know? She seemed rather simple to me."

"She was jealous of you."

"Me? Why? I was kind to her."

"Apparently she has feelings for me and resented you being at Enniscourt."

Savannah's suspicions were aroused. She edged away from him. Niamh's angry silences after that first morning. Hugh's words: *He likes women. Take what he says with a pinch of salt.*

"Have you lain with Niamh, Conor?"

278

There was a split second, a twitch of the mouth, before he answered, "No."

She knew he lied. He took her hands, but she balled her fists and edged further from him. "Have you used me, Conor? Did you think to use me to bring the parcel of money to Hugh?"

He leant towards her and touched her cheek. She swiped his hand away.

"I was going to," he said. "That is the truth. I saw you in Liverpool and I saw an opportunity to use a pretty girl, an innocent, English girl to act as a courier, a go-between."

"A go-between. Between whom exactly?"

She was determined not to let him touch her. He had picked her out, wheedled his way into her affections as part of a plan. She felt sick. He knew she did not believe him about Niamh and he needed time to think of how he was to win her round, so he helped himself to another sandwich, settled himself on the sofa and nonchalantly crossed his legs. He would play his game – seeking a truce, as she played hers – putting up barriers. She watched his every move, her face impassive, trying hard not to give in to the feelings stirring inside her. He took another sip of tea before replacing the cup on the tray. They sat in strained silence. He could feel the heat of her anger until he could stand it no longer. He had come a long way to see her and did not want to fail. She needed to understand certain things. He sat up straight and turned to face her.

"You may have gathered from a certain conversation with my aunt that she harbours anti-British sentiments. This is a result of what happened to her family and many Irish families during the famines. Her mother, a brother and two sisters died of hunger and disease. Her father emigrated with her and another brother to America. She married well, as you know. She was a great beauty in her younger years – if you can believe it. Her husband, an Irishman whose family had settled in America years before, was rich and, after he died, she came back with Orla and me. She was already using his money to fund a charity she set up to help stricken Irish families settle in America and find employment, and she continued this work when she returned to Ireland. I believe she was approached about six months ago. Some people from Boston she knew from her charity work came to see her to persuade her to help them. It was a natural progression for her to help the Irish cause."

"I'm sorry, Conor, but this is nothing to do with me. I cannot be involved in this. I cannot know someone who is involved in this."

"Let me finish, please. She was to use the sale of furniture and paintings as a front to enable sums of money to pass between America and Ireland without arousing suspicion."

"The investors."

"Pardon?"

"Niamh called them the investors. The Americans who came to the house and had to have the better meat. She thought they were giving your aunt the money to repair the house."

"Indirectly they were." *The better meat?* he thought. *What is she talking about?* "I didn't realise you and Niamh were such friends."

"Why are you telling me this anyway? You said the police found nothing. How can you tell me this and not expect me to go to the police myself with your revelations? You knew about it and you sympathise with her beliefs."

"Yes, I do. But I believe there are better ways to achieve our ends. I have always known this. Violence begets violence. But I swear to you that I did not know until two months ago what she was doing. Until then, I thought it was a legitimate business. Then she decided to involve me. I wish she had not. She was very persuasive. She has done so much for me, and I depend on her financially."

"So where did I fit in?"

"The parcel was for Finn. Hugh knew nothing. Yes, one of the books was for him, but I was to hollow out the pages of the other and fill it with the money intended for a contact who was going to buy guns and dynamite."

Savannah could not believe what she was hearing. "Will was right. My God! I could have hanged! You would have me hanged?"

"Of course not. I didn't think anyone would pay any attention to you. They would see a young English girl and who would suspect she could be involved in our business? You were travelling to visit friends. And if they did stop you, they would see you were innocent, from a good family, and had been used. That is what happened. I did not travel back with you in order not to arouse suspicion. We were never sure we were not being watched. They would never have suspected if it had not been for Niamh. She overheard us discussing the plan."

Savannah looked at him in horror, at the seeming lack of concern for the consequences of his actions on an innocent person. Her.

"You did not travel back with me to save your own skin." She looked at him in disgust. "You loved me. You made love to me. Every day. Every day we were together. Loving. Passionate. How could you love me like that and not mean it? Had you no care for my feelings?" She cried out, "Liar! Liar! Liar!"

"But I did mean it. I fell in love with you. How many days did we know each other? Such a short time and I fell in love with you. I did not realise how much until the day before you left. Up until then, I convinced myself I was playing a part, denying my own true feelings. I am no saint, Savannah. You were not the first. I have made love to many women. But I have not loved them as I love you. That is why I did not go through with it. I buried the money in a field the day before you left. Before the police were involved. I had already made up my mind that you would not be part of this. You know nothing was found in the parcel I gave you. You mean too much to me. Because I love you. I love you, Savannah."

She ignored his impassioned declaration. "But you have bought weapons before?"

"No." He was frustrated that she did not seem to heed his declaration of love; it had fallen on deaf ears. Nor did it seem she wanted to forgive him. If only she would turn those beautiful eyes on him. If only she would let him kiss her. If only she would melt just a little. He wanted her to kiss him. He did not know this side of her, the coldness, the determination to resist him. He was worried. "No, I have not bought guns before. This was the first time my aunt was involved in something like this. I was only the intermediary passing on the money. I told my aunt I would not do anything more than that." He did not tell her that he had facilitated the meeting with the contact and the task of buying and collecting the guns was down to Finn O'Driscoll and Hugh.

"Pah!" She looked at him in disgust, not believing she could have fallen for such a man. "What is the difference between someone who enables the guns to be purchased and the man who pulls the trigger?" She thought for a moment. "How did you think this plan of yours was going to work? You surely did not think I would be allowed to travel to and from Ireland without my family knowing? That I would be allowed to do this?"

"I would arrange to meet you in Liverpool when you visited your brother and ask you to deliver packages for me, telling you they were for business contacts."

"Really? You would pretend you cared for me, sweet-talk me, tempt me back into your bed and all the while…" She shuddered as a thought came to her. "And another woman, a girl, stupid and gullible like me, would be invited to Ireland in my place."

Savannah could not hold in the tears. She began to weep, the tears flowing unchecked. She could not keep up the facade of indifference and deny her feelings for him any longer. She fumbled in her sleeve for her handkerchief and wiped her eyes.

"But I loved you. I loved you so much. I love you so much." She broke off and heaved a sigh which caught in her throat. "You lied to me. You tricked me. You have made me out to be a fool. The day in the park. Those words you spoke to me. You asked about my family and seemed genuinely interested in me, but it was all part of your act, wasn't it? To fool me. Stupid, little girl! Why should I be of interest to an older, handsome man? I know that you were flattering me, twisting me round your finger, manipulating me. I know that now. Do you know how stupid and embarrassed I feel by letting myself be flattered by you, the idea that you had come to the park looking for me, waiting for days to see me so I would fall for you and let myself be used by you?" She stopped to take a deep breath and wiped her eyes again.

"Savannah," he said softly to quench her rising agitation, but she did not hear him.

"Every step you took, one step closer to your bed and the ultimate conquest. You lied to me. The first day I lay with you. You lied to me. That horrid, common O'Driscoll man. He was staring at me. Was I on show so he could see if your plan would work? Hugh. Was he part of it?"

"Savannah." He tried again to interject.

"They knew. They knew you were sleeping with me as part of the plan. They were laughing at me. The silly, little, English girl, her head turned by the handsome, charming Irishman. You tricked me into going to Ireland with you knowing how much I loved you. What a dupe!" she cried, punching the seat with her fists. "What a stupid, stupid fool I am." She covered her face with her hands. The shame of it all. Her mother was right. She was reckless and unthinking.

Distressed by her anguish, he shuffled along the sofa to be close to her. "Listen to me," he demanded. "The first time we made love I fell in love with you. The second time we made love that afternoon, do you remember? I do. I stared into your eyes to test myself, quite dispassionately, to make sure you were just another woman giving me pleasure and that you meant nothing to me, and I could carry out the plan. But I knew as I stared into your beautiful, beautiful eyes that you had stolen my heart. I felt something I had not felt before; something that I was unaware of that began in the park in Liverpool. A feeling that I knew you even though I had just met you. I had to keep denying it because of the plan hatched by O'Driscoll. I was struggling, Savannah."

She did remember. She raised her head and wiped the sodden handkerchief across her face, but she could not look at him. There was something she had seen in his eyes, some hesitancy, something she did not understand as he looked down at her that day, and then he had loved her. She had never known anything like it. Never felt anything like it. Never known it was possible. But she knew it often later; with him it was possible, as though they were one being, as the waves of pleasure rolled through her. He was giving himself to her. Giving and sharing, as her mother described. He wanted to please her, watching her as his love thrilled every nerve in her body and she had struggled not to weep with sheer joy. *Take his words with a pinch of salt, Savannah.*

He took her silence as an indication she was prepared to hear him out and explained to her that, by the time he was to present her to Finn O'Driscoll that afternoon for approval, he knew he could not go through with the plan, but he still wanted her to come to Ireland, otherwise he thought that he might not see her again. "I told you I loved you. I told you you were not a diversion," he reminded her. "It was the truth, Savannah. And the days we spent at Enniscourt… my love was deepening, and I was torn between what my aunt wanted, my loyalty to her, and what I felt for you."

He told her that he had strung his aunt along knowing that, after he left Savannah in Dublin, he would have to go back and face her wrath when she learnt he had not used her after all. He told her again that Hugh knew nothing of the plan. He moved towards her and tilted her chin. "Look at me, darling Savannah."

Reluctantly, she raised her puffy, red-rimmed eyes to him.

"I have done things I am not proud of. I have lied to you. I have slept with many women for my own pleasure." He took a deep breath. "I will confess to you now, I slept with Niamh to satisfy myself. It is unforgiveable. I am ashamed of myself for taking advantage of her. But you must believe in me now. Why do you think I have come all this way? I had to see you. I think about you all the time. When we are together, I cannot explain it, you fill me with happiness. Words cannot do justice to how I feel about you."

Conor cast his mind back to her bedroom at Enniscourt when he felt the change come over him, when he struggled to understand what it was that had taken possession of him. Next to his overwhelming love and need for her sat the realisation that not only did he love her, but he also cared about her, more than he had cared for anyone in his life before. She had taught him to care. She had taught him to be less self-centred, less selfish.

"I want you to allow me to love you, to show how much I love you."

His eyes, so soft and warm, were an open book; his thoughts and feelings were not hidden from her, they were there in plain sight, honest, and appealing to her to forgive him and give him another chance. She could feel her resistance dissolving and she wanted to throw herself into his arms, for him to hold her and everything would be as it was at Enniscourt when the world was a happy place. The cold steel wrapped round her heart. *Take his words with a pinch of salt, Savannah.* She was calmer, more composed, more resolved.

"You used me, Conor. How can I be with someone who is prepared to let innocent people be killed? You lied to me, Conor. How can I ever trust you?"

"Because I am here. Come all this way. Confessed all. Bared my soul."

"You are the most beautiful man I have ever seen. I have been with another man. I told you. But it was nothing compared to what I found with you…" The tears spilled over again. "Each time you loved me, I did not know it was possible to feel these things. You were kind and sweet to me. And I loved you. I loved you. But I am a silly, seventeen-year-old girl. What do I know about love? And you are a beautiful man, Conor. Women throw themselves at you. How can you resist? I want to love and be loved by someone as my parents loved each other. I do not trust you, Connor. I cannot trust you. And without trust, there is no love."

TWENTY-FIVE

Conor was banished. Savannah had wanted to summon Edmund Sill to take him to the station, but he refused the offer. Another minute waiting and he would have broken down. Savannah had not even given him the chance to take his leave of her mother, whom he saw watching him from an upstairs window as he made his way down the drive, no doubt glad to see the back of him. His heart was heavy, he was weeping, and he did not know what he would do. He had seen a future with Savannah, but she had cast him out. She knew about his past and, even though he knew she loved him as much as he loved her, she did not trust him. His past had caught up with him and taught him another lesson. He was in despair. Savannah watched him too from the sitting room window, tears falling silently, as he disappeared from view.

Marianna came downstairs to comfort her daughter and, as she opened the door, Savannah almost knocked her over. She had let her head rule her heart and her heart was breaking. Marianna grabbed her arm.

"What are you doing?"

"I am going after him." She pulled her arm away. "I love him, Mama. If you will not meet him properly and talk with him to understand why I love him, then I will go with him."

"Savannah, please, darling," Marianna called after her as she opened the front door. "Remember how he behaved. What he was prepared to do."

Savannah stopped on the threshold. Her red-rimmed eyes shone, and her face was wreathed in happiness. "But he didn't do it, Mama. He didn't go through with it because he loves me."

Edmund Sill was sent to collect Conor's bag from the luggage office at the station. In the meantime, there was an awkward interview between the three of them as Marianna failed, despite their attempts, to be convinced of Conor's suitability as a suitor, never mind husband to Savannah. She was horrified to hear he came to ask permission to marry her daughter. But Marianna was a wise and astute woman. If she let them be together, without opposing their relationship, then the affair might wither naturally when one or the other came to their senses.

So, Conor had been invited to stay and, at luncheon, Marianna was, despite her misgivings, impressed by his intelligence and charm, and she hoped he was behaving naturally and not putting on a show for her benefit. Savannah had obviously told him a lot about her family and Longridge, and he asked all the right questions. But Marianna also saw that he was nervous and kept glancing across the table at her, as if he was half-expecting her to throw him out of the house at any moment should he betray anything that offended her or fell short of her expectations.

She went for a walk by herself after luncheon to mull over what she should do. When she returned she asked them both to join her in her sitting room.

"I have decided," Marianna said, standing before them as they sat meekly on the sofa holding hands, "that I will allow you, Mr Clare, to court my daughter. But know this. I will not agree to a marriage. You will not be engaged. Savannah is too young." She saw Savannah's eyebrows shoot up. "Although I married young, at the age Savannah is now, I had known her father for years. Savannah may know you as a lover, Mr Clare, but she does not know fully your character, and nor do I. It is too soon to make a decision about marriage, despite your request. You accept this?"

Conor said he did.

"Savannah?"

"Yes, Mama. And I thank you from the bottom of my heart for allowing us to be together." She beamed at Conor – who seemed bemused by Marianna's frankness – and began to rise from her seat.

"I haven't finished," said her mother, causing her to sit down abruptly.

"You are lovers. I will allow this…" Marianna could not think of the right word. "I will allow this situation to continue. You may share a bed."

Conor looked up at her in disbelief. Had she just said what he thought she had said?

"I will not have you creeping through the house in the middle of the night, Mr Clare, and we all pretend we do not know what is going on. My servants are loyal and discreet. In public, you will both be discreet and behave in the proper manner. For your sake, Savannah."

Savannah was blushing. Conor had not taken his eyes of Marianna, confused by this turn of events and this extraordinary, liberal-minded woman.

"I do not know what to say," he said.

He remembered Savannah had told him how close they were, how frank the discussions about sex had been, but still her mother was prepared to breach the usual conventions for her daughter.

Marianna saw the waves of confusion and incredulity cross his face as her words sank in. "Do not be fooled by me, Mr Clare. I have my reasons. I do not see myself as a hypocrite. You may know I have a companion." She saw from his face that Savannah had told him and did not feel the need to explain. She said, "And I will also add one more thing. I have instructed Savannah previously on how to take care of herself, so she does not fall pregnant." Savannah's blush intensified as she recalled the conversation they had had after the Thomas affair. "Therefore, in light of my generosity of spirit, I ask you, Mr Clare, to do what is required of you to ensure the same. Do I make myself understood?"

Conor had never in his life been part of such a frank conversation and was astonished by her bluntness and found it difficult to not look away from her unrelenting gaze. He felt he was being tested. He must behave like a gentleman, convince Savannah's mother of his integrity. He rose to shake Marianna's hand.

"You have my word. I can assure you we already…" He could not bring himself to say the words they all knew he meant. "I love and care for your daughter, Mrs Hamilton-Read."

"Then you must show me. Now, Savannah, if you don't mind, I should like a few words in private with Mr Clare."

Savannah left them and closed the door behind her. Unsure what to do with herself, she began to pace the floor in the hallway, overwhelmed by her mother's sympathetic attitude and wondering what on earth they could be talking about. One thing she did know was how much her mother loved and understood her.

"Sit down please, Mr Clare," said Marianna, preferring to remain standing as she felt it gave her some authority over him. "I believe you owe me an explanation. You will tell me all about yourself, your background, politics, how you support yourself, why you thought to endanger my child and why I should not ask my servant to escort you immediately to the railway station. I want to know what kind of man I have allowed under my roof. I advise you too, Mr Clare, you will never tell my daughter what to do. She is young but she is her own woman, so do not misjudge her abilities. You will respect her. I have brought her up to know her own mind and her own worth. No man who truly loved me ever told me what to do and I have always been the equal of any man. As is my daughter. And I warn you now, Mr Clare, if you so much as look at her in the wrong way, you will suffer the consequences."

Ada knocked on the study door and came in with a tray bearing a pot of tea and the household accounts ledger tucked under one arm. She placed the tray on the desk and handed the ledger to Marianna before pouring out the tea and sitting in the chair on the opposite side of the desk. Despite the greying hair and stiffening gait, she was still the same kind-hearted, loyal Ada.

"Thank you, Ada. Is there anything in particular you wish to draw my attention to?"

"No, ma'am. The figures are correct. The bills needin' paid are there. Everythin's in order."

Ada looked forward to these weekly meetings when she discussed the menus and informed Marianna of the business of the household, financial and personal, that enabled Marianna, who trusted her implicitly, to run a smooth and contented household. The servants and tenants were treated well and with respect. Marianna was well aware how much loyalty was to be gained by behaving in a certain way; she had been a servant herself once. There was a special bond between these two women, formed on the night of Savannah's birth when Ada had been such a calming influence and reassured a concerned and helpless William as much as her, and which was strengthened after William's death when Ada had gone about her work, taking charge of household matters and giving Marianna time to grieve. Marianna found Ada's common sense and down-to-earth, good-naturedness comforting.

"I'll deal with this shortly, Ada. You may have to order some more provisions as our unexpected guest at luncheon will be staying with us. For how long, I am not certain. He is a friend of Miss Savannah's." Savannah had taken Conor to the stables to meet Moth and to go out riding.

"Ah!" Ada nodded. "The 'andsome gentleman. Sarah's all of a dither and she a married woman with littl'uns an' all!"

Ada sipped her tea and looked across the rim of the cup at Marianna, who pursed her lips and looked back.

"Ada, I have known you for nearly twenty years. You are one of the kindest people I know and I trust you. You know I consider you to be more of a friend than a servant."

"That's kind of you to say, ma'am. You know I'd do anythin' for you if I could."

"Ada, I always speak plainly with you."

"And you wish to tell me about Miss Savannah and this gentleman?"

"You are as sharp as a tack, Ada Dummigan." Marianna laughed with relief, as it seemed she was taking too long to get to the point of what she wanted to discuss with Ada.

"Well, ma'am, it was not 'ard to guess when Sarah comes back down to the kitchen and tells us they were kissin.'"

Marianna shook her head. "It is Savannah we are talking about, Ada. Impetuous as always. It will soon be obvious to the servants that they are lovers."

Ada replaced her teacup and saucer on the tray and, without so much as a blink of an eye, said, "And it will be none of the servants' business, ma'am. I will see to it there's no gossip downstairs, at least not in my 'earin'. In fact, I'll read the Riot Act and if there's so much as a peep out of them…"

Ada left the words unsaid as Marianna understood what she meant. This had already been the case not long after Bertie Robson came regularly to stay. Not only that, but Ada was very fond of Savannah and protective of her. She had loved her as if she was her own since the day she was born and had watched her grow up. She would not have a word said against her.

"It's your private business, ma'am, and Miss Savannah's. And the young gentleman's name?"

Marianna did not care what others thought of her own behaviour. As long as her friendship with Ellen and Richard Greenwood endured – and they had always been supportive – she could not care a fig what the others in their social circle thought of her association with Cuthbert Robson, and she knew they did not think much of it. Some shunned her completely. Others, those who gratefully accepted the donations she made to their pet charities, were more inclined to turn a blind eye. But Savannah needed protecting and she did not want her daughter to be the subject of local gossip, especially if Mr Conor Clare disappeared from the scene sometime soon. The fewer people who knew, the better. To achieve this end, it might be prudent to avoid familiar company as much as possible for as long as this liaison continued.

Marianna closed her eyes and sighed. "Am I doing the right thing, William?" She did not want the tongues wagging in Newbridge but, more importantly, she did not want the Greenwoods to know, not yet at least. She was pondering what she should do when an idea came to her. She opened a side drawer in the desk and pulled out a sheaf of letters, including the recent ones from Geoffrey, now happily married and settled in New York, and rifled through them until she found the one she was looking for: the last letter from Alessandro Paluzzi, the lover of her second husband, Bennet Foster, who always wrote just after the anniversary of his death in Italy. Each time he asked her to visit him at his villa near Florence. Now seemed as good a time as any to accept his offer.

TWENTY-SIX

The three of them went to Melchester for luncheon the following day to meet Bertie, who was not expecting the extra guest. As they dined at the King's Head Hotel, which overlooked the busy square in the town centre, Marianna put forward her proposal of a holiday in Italy and would Bertie be able to drag himself away from Moss End for a couple of weeks? Savannah pointed out they would miss the start of the shoot, but Marianna waved her hand dismissively and said she would ask Will to take charge and act as host, and Mr Brotherton, the gamekeeper, knew his business. By the end of luncheon it was agreed, boosted by the knowledge that Conor had been to Italy with his aunt, and plans made – the dates, the passports, the acquisition of tickets. Marianna was pleased to see Conor settled the bill.

Conor and Savannah went shopping, as Conor was in need of more clothes and would require a cooler selection for summer in Italy. Bertie and Marianna waited for them on one of the many benches in the shade of the trees that surrounded the square: the square where Bertie Robson had first set eyes on her and William more than thirty years ago as they stood on the steps of the town hall at the hiring fair when he had taken William on as a groom for the Loop Hall estate. Marianna itched to know what Bertie thought of Savannah's young man, but he said it was too soon to form an opinion, although his first impressions were that he was charming.

Bertie then escorted them back up the hill to the station, and Marianna stopped on the way at the Post Office to send a telegram to Signore Paluzzi.

The following afternoon, Savannah and Conor took a picnic down to the river. They deposited the rug and picnic basket under the ancient oak tree that stood in the middle of the field and then walked up to the chapel, as Savannah wanted to show Conor the graves of her father and Badger. He asked her what the quotation on William's headstone meant. They stood, their arms wrapped round each other, Savannah's head resting on Conor's chest. Neither spoke as there was no need for words. After a few minutes of contemplation, Savannah broke the silence.

"We had better go before the ants carry away our picnic."

They walked hand in hand across the mown field, where fresh grass was already regrowing, and were glad to reach the shady coolness of the oak tree. The Home Farm cows had congregated in the copse of trees at the far end of the field to sit out the muggy, afternoon heat, munching lazily on snatches of grass, their ears twitching irritably against the flies. The air was still and there was hardly a sound except grasshoppers whirring and the river babbling gently over the stones. They tucked into Ada's offerings and then settled back against the tree trunk.

"Have you recovered from this morning?" asked Savannah, barely able to conceal her amusement.

They had walked up Longridge Fell in the cooler morning air after an early breakfast. They had set off on equal terms, but Conor had struggled up the last incline and collapsed at Savannah's feet at the summit, where she waited for him, laughing at his discomfort.

"You were cruel not to warn me of the effort required," Conor replied. "But it was well worth it. The views are magnificent."

She laughed. "You would have suffered more in this heat." She mopped her face with a napkin. "Are you close to your sister?" Conor had written to Orla that morning to inform her of his situation and the forthcoming trip to Italy. "I sometimes wish I had a sibling closer in age than Will."

"Yes, very close. Orla looked after me. She mothered me when I was young. Even now, she takes a motherly interest in what I am up to. She knows everything there is to know about me."

Conor reached into the basket to retrieve an apple.

"Is she as beautiful as you are?"

Conor laughed. "You think me beautiful, Savannah?" He took a bite of his apple. His eyes twinkled mischievously.

"You know I do." She laughed, digging him in the ribs.

"Well, I think she is beautiful. She is a beautiful person and very kind. A doting mother of three boys, and a loving wife."

"Her husband is rich and owns a bank, I have been told."

"Owns a bank! Who told you that? No, let me guess!" He took a last bite of his apple and tossed the core into the grass. "What an imagination that girl has! David works for a bank, a good position. They are not rich but comfortable."

Savannah took his hand and rested it in hers on her lap. "Do you feel different because you did not know your parents? I mean, do you think how your life might have been if they had not died?"

"I was too young when they died to remember them. I cannot recall how hard our life was. I know only what Orla has told me, and she saw everything through the eyes of a child who experienced it without understanding why it was happening. It seemed to be the way life was: to feel cold and to be hungry."

"I see a similarity between what happened to you and to my father. Will told me, when I was old enough to understand, what my father had told him and the effect events he endured had on him. Papa thought he would have ended up, like his father, working in a cotton mill with no hope of a better life. Then his life changed. I have already told you he was taken from his family and later, he lost my mother, and this put him on a different path which, ironically, led him to a better life, materially that is. The same with you when your parents died, and your aunt gave you opportunities."

"That is why I shall always be grateful to her, Savannah. I know she has caused some… upset, for want of a better word, and I take my share of responsibility for that, but I cannot deny my affection for her, and I will not give up my connection with her."

"Nor did I mean to suggest you do. She is your family. I know how precious family is."

"She took Orla and me in. We were not abandoned. She told us that, even if she had not been married to a rich man, she would have taken care of us. It was her Christian duty to do so. Aunt Norah never made us feel guilty for enjoying the more privileged life she gave us and treated us the same as her own children. Nor were we made to feel beholden to her. So, to answer your question – do I ever think how my life might have been? I do not. I appreciate what I have, although some would say..." He remembered the bitter exchange with Hugh. "Some would say I have abused my privileges but... well... you know all about that." He looked bashfully at her. "I am sad my parents died but, truthfully, I have no memory to mourn, unlike you with your father. I have no memory of them, what they looked like, how they were."

Savannah sighed. "I don't know which is worse. The pain of not knowing them or the pain I feel because I remember Papa so well and miss him so much."

"Is that not the price we pay for loving someone?"

"Then please, I beg you, Conor, please do not die for I could not bear it."

He put his arm round her shoulder and hugged her. "I have no intention of doing so."

A squadron of ducks glided low over the river and landed noisily on the water.

"Come," said Conor, "let's change the tenor of this conversation. We have been far too serious on such a glorious day. We'll feed the bread crusts to the ducks." He began to remove his footwear. "What about a paddle to cool us down? Those stepping stones look very inviting."

"Can you skim stones, Conor?" asked Savannah as she removed her shoes and stockings. "We used to skim stones. My friends and I. When I was younger."

"You are looking at the champion stone-skimmer of Ballymore." He laughed as he helped her to her feet.

The shadow passing the sitting room window, which landed on the page she was reading, alerted Marianna, who was dismayed to see Ellen Greenwood alight from her carriage. She was relieved that Conor and Savannah had taken a picnic down to the river and hoped, if they returned and Savannah recognised the Greenwood carriage, she would have the wit to enter the house by a different door and keep out of sight. She placed her book on the side table and breathed in deeply.

"Good afternoon, my dear," said Ellen as Sarah showed her into the sitting room. She offered her cheek for a kiss. "I was just passing and thought I would drop in."

"Just passing to where, Ellen? The road is a dead end, as you know. Please sit down, and don't fib. Tell me the real reason for your visit. Would you care for some tea? Or I have lemonade here."

"Lemonade, thank you. It is so warm. Too warm, really. Lemonade may be more refreshing."

Marianna poured her a glass from the jug on a tray on a side table and handed it to her. She took a welcome sip.

"Mrs Dummigan should give the recipe to Mrs Dixon as hers is just a little too sharp."

"The reason for your visit, Ellen?" asked Marianna, who already had an inkling.

"Indeed, Marianna. Who is the young gentleman you have staying with you? Someone saw you all leaving the station yesterday."

Dora Cavendish, thought Marianna. She was walking her dog near the station as they came out to the waiting carriage, arched her eyebrows and gave Marianna the cold shoulder when she wished her good afternoon.

"My! News does travel fast," said Marianna, trying to laugh it off.

"You did not mention to me the last time we met, just three days since, that you were expecting visitors, so my curiosity was piqued." Ellen peered expectantly at Marianna over the top of her glass as she took another sip.

"Mr Conor Clare. A friend of Savannah's."

"Oh!" said Ellen, somewhat taken aback. She put down her glass. "I have not heard her mention him before. A new acquaintance? Did she meet him in Liverpool? Are they at home? Are we to meet him? Would you all care to come for tea on Saturday?"

"So many questions! And I shall regretfully refuse your invitation, as Bertie comes on Friday and we have already made plans."

Ellen turned to face her friend and look her in the eye. "I know you so well, Marianna. You have never really explained Savannah's sudden departure for Liverpool, so she missed the Mayor's Ball. Then Richard attended her when she was in bad humour. And now this visitor. You are being evasive and giving little away. I can only surmise it is to spare me embarrassment because Mr Clare has intentions towards Savannah, and you are thinking of Jack. He has called three times and she has refused to see him. I wonder if it is coincidental." She rose to leave, seeming more than a little peeved. "I am upset on Jack's behalf that Savannah has not had the courage or the decency to speak to him directly."

Marianna bit her tongue. Speak to him directly? About what? Ellen seemed to think there was an understanding between Jack and Savannah, or she hoped there was, which was certainly not the case. Savannah had never said as much to her. Marianna stood up to see her out, knowing that Ellen was upset with her too, as they always confided in each other, but she was not ready to explain this situation.

"You read too much into it, Ellen. Savannah did not see Jack as she was upset about Badger," she explained, knowing her feeble excuse was only half the story. "Mr Clare arrived the day before yesterday. He is a friend she met in Liverpool," she lied, knowing that if this 'friendship' went wrong, Jack, as Savannah's oldest and closest friend, might be needed to pick up the pieces. She would have encouraged her friend to stay a little longer, take tea, but feared the return to the house of Savannah and Connor. She would leave the news of the trip to Italy for another day. The suddenness of it would arouse more suspicions and would upset Ellen further.

The next day, Savannah rode Ladybird to Dene House to speak to Jack. She accepted her mother's argument that he was owed an explanation, as a long-standing friend, for her neglect of him, and to thank him for his concern for her but, please, not to divulge the true nature of the relationship between her and Conor or the forthcoming trip to Italy.

The meeting did not go well. They went to sit in the summerhouse overlooking the tennis court at the end of the garden. She told Jack that she valued his friendship and hoped it would continue and apologised for not seeing him when he visited. But she could not stop herself from restricting the conversation to generalities and went on to say that she did not have the feelings for him that he had for her. Jack was crestfallen and wanted to know who this new friend was, and took her reticence as a sign that Mr Clare meant more to her than she was revealing. He began to jabber at her that he had known her longer than this new friend, they had memories, they had secrets, he loved her, had always loved her, and how could she break her promise to him, especially in light of her behaviour on the fell when she was ready to give herself to him?

He grabbed her hands, lurched towards her and tried to kiss her. Savannah was appalled at his clumsiness, boorishness and pig-headedness in not accepting what she had just told him.

"How dare you?" she cried, shoving him away. "How can you continue to believe the words of a nine-year-old child have any substance when I have never repeated them since? How can you behave so presumptuously when I have simply been honest with you? If you had behaved like a man when you had the chance, instead of behaving like a pathetic *boy*, I may have seen you in a different light."

Instantly, she regretted her harsh, demeaning words. He was her dearest friend and she had wounded him – badly. Jack was devastated. The colour drained from his face and he got up slowly, his body slumped as if all the air had been sucked out of him, and his eyes filled with tears in pain at her treatment of him.

"Jack. I'm sorry. Please…"

Without a word, he left her. He knew he had lost her. They did not speak to each other again for years.

Whilst Savannah was out, Conor wandered round the house and stopped on the landing to look at the portraits of William and Marianna. Having met Marianna, he knew the artist, a woman whose name he did not recognise, did not need to flatter them. The style was loose and soft, impressionistic and accomplished. The artist had used large, sweeping strokes that captured the relaxed, natural pose they had adopted. In her portrait, Marianna was sitting at the end of a chaise longue, a white rose in her hands resting on her lap, her embroidery on the seat beside her. She was beautiful and exuded warmth. In his portrait, William was leaning back, seemingly at the other end of the chaise, his legs crossed, one arm draped along the top, an open book beside him.

Conor stared at William for a long time. He was handsome, his dark hair flecked with grey and his brown eyes warm and kind. Savannah had her mother's beauty and determination, but he reckoned she had her father's nature. He looked to be an intelligent man, compassionate, caring, a friendly man. Conor wished he had known Savannah's father and wondered what he would have made of him. Both subjects were smiling, their faces turned slightly towards each other as though they were having a conversation and sharing a private joke. Conor half-expected them to burst out laughing, step out of their frames and go to each other. It was obvious from the light in their eyes how deep was their love for each other.

Marianna watched Conor from behind her bedroom door; she had been there for a few minutes, unseen, watching him. Her coldness towards him was gradually dissipating as she saw the tender way he behaved towards Savannah, but she was stubborn, and it was too soon to let him realise that her attitude towards him was changing. Conor approached William's portrait and touched it gently, his hand resting there for a few seconds. Then he noticed her, and both were embarrassed: she for seeming to spy on him, he for his display of emotion. Marianna composed herself and came out on to the landing.

"He was the best of men."

"I know it. I see it." Conor smiled at her shyly. "Would he have liked me?"

"I doubt it."

Conor was stung by her words.

"You are the man who has stolen his beloved daughter's heart. He would have had to share her with you," said Marianna, brushing past him to go downstairs.

Bertie came to Longridge at the end of the week to stay for a couple of days. It had been agreed between him and Marianna when they met in Melchester that he would come for moral support and to give her his considered opinion of Mr Clare. It was soon obvious the two men got on, as Savannah discovered when the three of them went out riding. Conor was happy for some male company. After dinner, he and Bertie adjourned to the games room to play billiards and enjoy a brandy and cigar before retiring for the night.

Bertie Robson knew the rules. Marianna would come to him. Her non-negotiable rule was not allowing him to love her in William's bed but, at least now, after all these years, she did not creep back to her own room. He had made love to her but knew her mind was elsewhere. As she snuggled up to him, she asked, "What do you think of him, Bertie?"

"I like him, Marianna. You might not wish to hear me say so, but I do. He is intelligent, educated, extremely well read and absolutely charming. They seem besotted with each other."

"The first flush of romance," scoffed Marianna. "They have known each other for days not years. He is so handsome I fear in time he will wander, as he will be unable to resist the attentions of other women. Did you see the way the women in Melchester looked at him? You could almost smell the lust in their eyes."

Bertie chuckled. "You were turned against him from the start because of what he did or, rather, what he intended to do. You will have to learn to forgive him as Savannah has done."

"But do I trust him, Bertie? What if he harbours these violent beliefs and this is all a ruse?"

"Your imagination is running away with you, dearest. I do not think he has any such beliefs at all; he does not strike me as a violent man. Sympathy for the cause, yes, but not the methods. He told me he got sucked in somewhat by his aunt's persuasiveness."

"A weakness of character then?"

"No, I don't think so. My gut feeling is he is a fine young man. More misguided loyalty perhaps. He is in awe of you, Marianna. For your dignity and the way that you have behaved. The way that you have welcomed him. And a little frightened, I think. What have you said to him?"

"What any mother would. I tell you, Bertie, if he hurts her, I will cut out his heart with a blunt knife."

Bertie chuckled again and hugged her. "I believe you."

"Was I right to allow him to stay here and share her bed?"

"Unconventional, I'll admit. Not many mothers would have done the same." He kissed the top of her head. "No, I think it was wise and pragmatic. You do not want to lose her. She must learn from her own mistakes, much as you might want to protect her."

"You are right about losing her. I feared if I had not taken this option, she might have run away with him and I would never see her again."

"She would not do that. She loves you too much. And I think she cares for me too."

"And if she falls pregnant?"

"Let us cross that bridge when we come to it. You are her mother. What do you think you will do? Love her and care for her."

They lay quietly for a minute or two until Bertie asked, "Are you content, Marianna?"

"Content! I have not been content since Savannah left school. One thing after another. Have you seen how many more grey hairs I have?"

"I meant content with me?"

He came to her as often as he could and sometimes she came to him at Moss End. He knew she would never marry him or even agree to live with him. She was too independent. She would not give up Longridge and, in truth, he did not want to give up his farm, although he wondered often about its viability. Yet he harboured a lingering fear it would endanger their relationship if either one conceded to give up something. When he was away from her, he missed her but was never certain she missed him. It had been the same years before at Loop Hall.

Marianna sat up and peered at him in the gloomy light. He looked sad.

"Why do you ask? I have not given you reason to think otherwise?"

"No. No, you have not…" His words trailed away.

"You mean do I love you?" She nestled back down next to him and kissed him. "I do."

The next morning, after breakfast, taking the first step to establishing a better relationship with Conor, Marianna took him to the study to show him her father's private book collection and invited him to read whatever he wanted. He was touched by the gesture. That afternoon, she went to look for Savannah and Conor to ask if they wished to go for a walk with her and Bertie to find them snuggled up on the sofa in the study. He was curling a lock of her hair round his fingers, and she was telling him about the birds in Audubon's *Birds of America*. It was one of Henry Hamilton's most precious books and one of William's favourites. He had often cuddled Savannah on his knee when they had looked at it together. Marianna felt a lump come to her throat. She was so envious of them. So young, so in love. She thought of her and William when they were first married. How those precious moments were sometimes blighted by her sense of dread that their happiness would be snatched away from them. She hoped her daughter would not be so troubled. She crept away. She would go for a walk by herself. Lost in her own thoughts and memories.

TWENTY-SEVEN

Alessandro Paluzzi's letter in response to Marianna's telegram and subsequent letter was effusive and enthusiastic and, of course, her fellow travellers would be very welcome. Signore Paluzzi lived with his companion, Sebastian Nardini, in a villa surrounded by vine-clad hills and sun-baked fields bordered by cypress trees and dusty roads, on the outskirts of a village in the hills near Florence. The visitors were relieved to be there after days of travelling by rail and staying in hotels en route.

The three-bedroomed house was small, clad in sandstone bricks, with a terracotta-tiled roof, shuttered windows and marble-tiled floors. The rooms were simply furnished, adequate for the two gentlemen living there, and the rooms on the ground floor opened on to the terraces around the house, lending it a spacious and airy ambience. The largest room was the sitting room, which had an open fireplace topped by a thick, stone mantel, around which was grouped an over-plump sofa, three equally plump armchairs and two marble-topped, gilt-legged side tables. A large, carved walnut cabinet filled the wall opposite. At an angle in one corner stood a baby grand piano. An archway led into a smaller room which was lined from floor to ceiling with book-laden shelves. There was a small garden where a path – bordered by lavender, rosemary and salvia, and terracotta urns filled with citrus trees and roses – led to a seat under an ancient, gnarled olive tree. Beside it, a small patch of earth where they grew herbs.

The Italians, both in their forties, who were also enjoying their summer holiday, were charming and attentive hosts. Alessandro, a teacher of English, was of medium height and plump with a head of luxuriant, silver hair above dark, merry eyes; a jolly, witty man, a bon vivant. Sebastian, who worked in a bookshop, was plump too, shorter, completely bald, quieter in nature, and waved his hands enthusiastically when he spoke in his broken English, his gestures translating the words he could not find. He amused them enormously.

The two men lived discreetly and quietly and looked after themselves – apart from the woman who came once a week to see to their laundry and would have nothing to report to the inhabitants of the village, as they had separate bedrooms. Sebastian gave up his for the use of their guests and slept on a cot on the terrace which, he reassured them, he did often in summer. Alessandro had offered to engage a maid for his guests, but they were perfectly happy to see to their own needs. It was hot and the visitors lived as their hosts did: sleeping or resting at midday, not venturing out without a hat or parasol, as the sun was merciless, and eating late in the evening on the terrace under the vine which draped luxuriantly across the beams as the sun sank behind the twinkling lights of Florence in the distance, and the crickets in the grass and the nightjars chirred.

There was no timetable. The guests slowed down and relaxed. They ate well, as Sebastian was an enthusiastic cook and tempted their taste buds with *crostini toscani*, *pappa al pomodoro*, *pasta*, plates of *prosciutto*, *mortadella* and *salame*; fresh vegetables drizzled with olive oil; cherries, figs and peaches; and packages of cakes and pastries from the *pasticceria* in the village. They sampled the local wine. They visited the church with its beautiful Renaissance frescoes, the ruins of a Roman amphitheatre and the castle on a hilltop. They woke to the sound of church bells summoning the faithful to Mass. They played chess and backgammon, helped themselves to books from their hosts' impressive collection or listened to Sebastian sing pieces from the opera in his warm, tenor voice as Alessandro accompanied him on the piano. Sebastian was particularly captivated by Savannah and would whisk her away to sit with him under the olive tree as he gave her lessons in Italian and sometimes in the local dialect. They went several times to Florence, setting out in the early morning to embark on the coach which stopped outside the inn in the village, returning in the late afternoon, exhausted but replete with knowledge, experiences and memories, as there was so much to see: the Duomo, the Ponte Vecchio, San Lorenzo, the burial place of the Medicis, churches and galleries. At the Uffizi, Conor, who had visited Florence with his aunt and sister, impressed them all, not only with his knowledge, but also his ability to explain the beauty and emotion in the paintings they viewed. He had long discussions with Alessandro about them. The others left them to it: Bertie, who whispered to Marianna that he had had a surfeit of culture, preferred to find a shady spot to sit and have a quiet drink with Sebastian; Marianna and Savannah escaped to explore the shops, particularly the leather shops, and buy gifts to take home.

One evening, after a trip to Florence, they dined as usual on the terrace in the glow of the lanterns on the table and scattered along the low terrace walls. As the night sky darkened and the scent of lavender, thyme and rosemary hung heavily in the air, plates were pushed aside, appetites sated, and the conversation lulled. Conor noticed the tears on Savannah's cheeks. He leant towards her and whispered, "What's amiss?"

Savannah shook her head to deny anything was wrong and quickly brushed away the tears. But her mother had seen.

"What is wrong, darling?"

Savannah blushed as all eyes turned to her. She gazed at each anxious face in turn: Alessandro at one end of the table, Sebastian at the other, watching her with concern – dear, sweet Sebby – her mother next to Bertie, Conor at her side.

"Isn't this the best way to spend one's time?" she said simply.

"Then why the tears?" asked Marianna.

"Because…" Savannah began to sob. "Because…"

Conor put a comforting arm round her shoulder as she dabbed her face with her napkin. "Come," he said softly. "Do you wish to walk a while in the garden and tell me what troubles you?"

She shook her head and tried to smile as they all waited for her to compose herself. Marianna wondered if her emotion was a consequence of drinking a little too much wine; she had acquired a taste for it on this holiday. Savannah swallowed hard as she collected her thoughts, thinking quickly about what she was to say, what she could say, to distract them.

"Today we saw many beautiful paintings of women and I am a little confused. Some of the women were nudes and clearly the objects of men's lust—"

Alessandro interrupted her. "Many of the nudes were painted for the patron's private viewing and were probably not meant for public display. That is my explanation if you were offended by them."

"Offended yes, but not in that way. In contrast, there were paintings of the Madonna, a symbol of purity and the personification of motherhood, an object of veneration. Two extreme views of women that I find difficult to accept, as if women are either one or the other."

"And this has upset you?" asked Conor. "Because you are angry that women are not portrayed to show all their qualities?"

"In a way, yes." Inwardly, she thanked him for the suggestion. "But I was annoyed because I was thinking of you, Conor, and how much I love you because you treasure me for who I am, my qualities as well as my shortcomings. I am sorry…"

Savannah grasped Conor's hand and looked round the table again at the perplexed faces, all wondering why she was so upset, and she could not tell them the truth. She knew she had begun to dig a hole for herself as she had no idea where this theory that she was conjuring out of thin air was heading and she should have brushed off their concerns earlier. Now she needed to find a way out. She was also aware she may have drunk a little too much Chianti and saw Conor discreetly move her glass out of reach. The wine had certainly loosened her tongue and, she felt, made her a little reckless, and so she ploughed on regardless as it seemed she had a captive audience who still waited for her to tell them what she meant.

"Earlier, Conor and I were looking at one of your books, Alessandro, and there was a picture of the Arnolfinis. It is a picture that represents, if I am correct, married love, and it is very moving.

Conor explained the symbolism to me and, if I am correct… sorry, I seem to be repeating myself. The wife may or may not be carrying their child." She paused and swallowed hard. "She may have died in childbirth and the picture painted in her memory or in memory of the love between husband and wife. I think I am remembering… but anyway, to me, it is a truer picture of what love is; not putting women on a pedestal for their purity or their… you know… what men want from them but showing the deep bond of love and friendship and respect between a man and a woman. Their shared life. Well…" Savannah paused again and glanced round at her silent, slightly baffled audience. "I saw something in that picture that spoke to me. At least… I am sorry, I am not expressing myself very well. I am still so young, so I probably do not know what I am talking about." She was running out of steam. "Sorry, I apologise. Am I a little tipsy?" She laughed self-consciously. "I am a little embarrassed. I'm rambling so I'll stop talking."

"Do not be embarrassed," said Alessandro kindly. "*In vino veritas*. And do not apologise for being young, my dear girl. The young have feelings and thoughts as worthy as their elders. I see it with my students. You are saying, if I understand you, that your love for Conor has… Ah, what is the word? Deep? Deepened over the time you have known him, and it is a beautiful thing to say, Savannah."

Conor put his lips to her ear and whispered, "Indeed it is. *Ti amo*."

She inclined her head and looked at him as her eyes filled with tears again. She rubbed them away and then, as if filled with a second wind, thinking her jumbled words must have made some sense and, against her better judgment, she set off again on this strange voyage.

"It is not just that, Alessandro. There is sadness in the picture too, sadness for a lost love. Both you and Mama have lost someone you loved very much and now you are with someone else. Did Mr Arnolfini find someone else? Am I silly to think there is just one person in the world meant for me, as Conor once said of me? Is it a chance in a million that I have found the love of my life?" Savannah reached up to touch Conor's face. "Someone I love beyond words. If I lost him…" Savannah's hand dropped to her lap. "If he did not love me any more for whatever reason…" Her voice cracked and she looked to her mother. "Would I find someone to match Conor? Would the second love be as wonderful?"

"You will not be rid of me so easily," said Conor, laughing.

But despite his levity, the relaxed atmosphere of the evening meal had long dissipated as Savannah monopolised the conversation and no one could think how to divert it to a happier topic. Marianna wondered if, by directing the questions at her, Savannah expected her to answer. She wondered if Savannah was basing her questions on what she had read in her memoir. She wondered, too, how she was going to answer such leading questions with Bertie sitting next to her. She wondered what troubled her daughter, as it was something more than the subject matter of some artworks they had viewed earlier in the day. She wondered if she should suggest Savannah should go to bed. Bertie was fiddling with a knife. Alessandro was watching her closely. Conor had removed his arm from Savannah's shoulder and looked bemused. Sebastian was staring at the moths batting the glass of the lantern above his head.

"Savannah, please," implored her mother. "Must you speak like this and spoil what has been a very pleasant evening?"

Savannah was not to be deterred. Ignoring her mother and without thinking of the effect on those around her, she said, "I am trying to… understand, Mama. Forgive me, I did not wish to upset anyone. I just wonder, as both you and Alessandro have experienced this, whether there is a… compromise the second time; a weighing-up to be made because… you do not want to be alone?"

There was a sharp intake of breath from Marianna, and she regretted she had not taken the opportunity, minutes before, to tell Savannah to go to bed. Bertie cleared his throat. They both understood perfectly the balance of their relationship that had certainly been weighed up, mostly by her. But Savannah's careless words demeaned Bertie and how much he meant to her, how much he had helped her. He was second best but not second rate. She reached for his hand and gave it a meaningful squeeze.

Sebastian looked blankly from one face to the other, not quite sure he had understood, with his limited English, what was being said. It seemed from the tension he sensed, despite his lack of comprehension, that Savannah had managed to upset her mother, discomfort Bertie, unsettle Conor and baffle Alessandro who was, at that moment, pondering the complexities of the relationships between his guests and the curious change in the atmosphere. It was Bertie who came to the rescue.

"I think, Savannah, that if you lived in Italy, you would find a handsome, charming *signore*. If you lived in France, a dashing, debonair *monsieur*. So, in my opinion, there is not one person specifically created for each of us. Some people are fortunate and find the love of their life; others do not or wait a long time."

"That is true," agreed Alessandro. "I loved Bennet Foster and I love Sebastian. Two quite different people. And I can reassure you, Savannah, that it is possible to find love again."

Alessandro noticed this comment disconcerted Conor, who shifted in his seat. *What on earth was Conor making of this?* he thought. It was time to put an end to it all. He picked up his glass.

"Let us drink to love and friendship and a long, happy life for each of us. And then we should move inside away from the insects and have some music, I think."

Marianna raised her glass to her lips but did not drink. She would apologise to Bertie later if he had been offended by what Savannah had said. She was, however, more perturbed by the sombre tone of Savannah's words and the idea she might lose Conor and wondered if she was succumbing to the dark thoughts that often plagued her. It was something she had never noticed before in her daughter until the time she shut herself away for days after returning from Liverpool, which she had put down to a grand sulk more than anything else. But maybe it was something more akin to her own breakdown years ago. She resolved to speak to Savannah about it, to find out where the darkness came from. She watched as Conor helped Savannah to her feet and whispered something. Savannah nodded and smiled at him. But Marianna could see there was something troubling her.

Two days later, Bertie went home as planned as there was work to do on the farm, confessing to Marianna that, although the long journey home on his own did not appeal to him, he was glad to go as the heat exhausted him. Alessandro gave him his copy of Dickens's *Pictures from Italy* to help pass the time in the days ahead. And now Bertie was gone, Marianna became melancholy, thinking of William, how they had had such a short time together, and wondering whether he would have enjoyed this holiday as much as she had. They were to go to Venice for a few days, and Alessandro took her under his wing and did his best to comfort and amuse her. They visited all the famous landmarks and Conor bought Marianna a beautiful millefiori paperweight from the glassworks in Murano as a thank you for treating him to the holiday. They went back to the villa for two more days before returning home.

On their last evening, Conor insisted on inviting them to dinner at a small restaurant in the village. Afterwards, as they walked back in the ghostly light of a full moon, Marianna took Alessandro's arm and they fell in behind Savannah and Conor, who had taken charge of Sebastian and were guiding him up the road, as he was a little intoxicated. They could hear Savannah coaxing him. "*Attento!* Not far now, Sebby. *Attento!*" to the slurred sounds of an aria from *The Marriage of Figaro*. Marianna and Alessandro laughed together at the comical sight in front of them. The air was warm and scented, the dusty road like a silver ribbon up the gentle slope of the hill.

Alessandro said, "A good evening, I think, with excellent company. Conor is a charming and clever young man."

"He is. He has a prodigious memory. I can barely remember what happened last week." Marianna laughed. "I want to thank you, Alessandro, for a wonderful holiday and for inviting us to your beautiful home and country. You must come and visit us at Longridge soon. You are more than welcome."

"I am so pleased you accepted my invitation at last. I have always wanted to meet you. It is a shame I never got to meet your husband." He patted her arm. "Your letters to me after Bennet died were so kind. He spoke of you often, you and Will. He was very fond of you both."

"As we were of him. You have found love again, Alessandro. Are you happy? You seem very contented."

"I am. I was a very young, innocent man when I knew Bennet. He was my first love, my teacher. We were master and pupil and my English improved immeasurably. I was a little in awe of him, I think. He was so intelligent and cultured. I will never forget him. This is different with Sebastian. We are the best of friends. I feel it is a more balanced relationship – if you understand me? We are so similar in temperament and interests and equal in age. And you, *cara mia*? Mr Robson is a fine gentleman."

"Yes, he is a very dear friend."

"I sense a little reticence there. I sensed something during the meal that evening before Bertie left."

"Savannah embarrassed me, Alessandro. She knows I loved her father more than I can ever love another man. Please do not misunderstand me. I care for Bertie, and I do love him, but I do not love him in the same way I did William."

Alessandro stopped and turned to face her and saw the pain in her eyes.

"We have both experienced the same thing, have we not? *Cuore spezzato*. Broken hearts. What did Tennyson write? ''Tis better to have loved and lost than never to have loved at all.' Yes, we were both broken. There was a crack in our hearts but now here we are, years later… *Riparato*. Hmm. What is the word? Repaired? Mended? Yes, mended. Do you think so?"

"Sit down here, Sebby. *Qui! Qui!*" Savannah's anxious voice floated down from the terrace.

"Have you hold of him, Conor? *Questa sedia*, Sebby."

"*Che… rag… rag… azza deli… deliziosa…*"

"*Non capisco*, Sebby. *Cosa hai detto? Caffè penso.* He needs coffee, Conor."

"Savannah has learnt a little Italian, Marianna," said Alessandro admiringly. "You didn't answer my question. You are mended?"

"No, Alessandro. I don't think I am. It was agony when he died, and I lost so much. Even now, I feel a searing pain, like burning coal, in my heart. Yes, I have memories, but I cannot take comfort from them as they emphasise the regret of so many unfinished conversations, unfulfilled hopes and dreams. What we had no longer exists. In truth, the loss is beyond pain. Our future together was extinguished. It was so cruel. I loved him so much. The problem is, Alessandro, I do not know where he is. I do so hope and pray there is a heaven, for where else am I to find him? I so want to be with him again."

Alessandro cupped her face in his hands and kissed each cheek.

"What a special man he must have been. How fortunate you were to know him and love him. You will see him again, *cara mia*. Have faith. And his daughter. Your daughter. *Bellissima. Deliziosa.* Indeed, what a delight she is."

TWENTY-EIGHT

On their return to England, Conor took his leave in London as he wished to visit his sister, and then he would go on to Enniscourt. He promised to return to Longridge as soon as he could. He had already explained to Savannah and repeated to Marianna that his aunt had been overwhelmed by the shock of the police raid and how close they had come to being arrested, imprisoned or worse. Having reconsidered her direct involvement in Republicanism, she had gone back to Boston – relieved Conor had failed in his task by falling in love – to live with her eldest son, taking her favourite artworks with her. Conor had been instructed to arrange for the demolition of the derelict part of the house, make the rest sound, and sell it along with what was left of the contents with the intention of splitting the proceeds between him, his aunt and sister. He had begun the process of employing the workers before he went to Longridge and they had been on site for a month, overseen by Hugh Furlong, who had returned to live permanently in Ireland after Conor had asked for his help. For Hugh, it was not a difficult decision to leave Liverpool, as he was as unnerved as Mrs Archbold by their experience.

It was a week later that Savannah knew that she was pregnant. She had an inkling in Italy. She had left her little diary in which she recorded her dates at home, but she was convinced her monthly was late. The thought she might be carrying Conor's child had caused her to panic. The thought he might reject her had caused her emotional outburst at dinner when she had tried to contain how frightened she was of losing him. When her mother had taken her aside the day after to ask what troubled her, she did not dare say, as she was certain Marianna would be disappointed, and it would spoil the holiday. Now she was sure of her condition, she had no idea how to break the news or what her mother would say at their failure to heed her instructions. It was not a planned event, and it must have happened when she was in Liverpool on the first day that he had loved her. She had been so consumed by her passion for him, wanted him so much, was so lost in the thrilling pleasure of it all, the ecstasy, she had forgotten everything her mother had told her. It was only in the days after Conor had taken steps to protect her. She was not sure how Conor would react to the news either.

She told her mother as they walked round the rose garden one afternoon. To her surprise, her mother, whom she expected to be, if not angry, at least disappointed, hugged her close.

"Oh, Savannah, my darling girl. You never do things by halves. Come. Let us sit."

They settled themselves on the nearest bench.

"Is this what troubled you in Italy?"

"I had an idea."

"Then why did you not confide in me?" her mother asked, taking her hand.

"Mama, I have let you down so much these last few weeks, I felt you would despair of me for failing to heed your advice, and it did not seem right, in the circumstances, to spoil the holiday. After all, I was not one hundred per cent certain."

"You were upset because you thought Conor might not stand by you? That is what the discussion about the Arnolfinis and all the questions about finding love a second time were in aid of?"

"Yes, Mama. I did not intend to ramble on so, a little incoherently, I think, as I was a little drunk. You were all looking at me, waiting for me to explain my tears, and I could not tell the truth. Conor and I had looked at the picture of Mrs Arnolfini carrying a child in one of Alessandro's books… when I was blathering about the pictures that we had seen earlier that day… it came back to me and overwhelmed me and made me cry. Conor and I have known each other for such a short time, and although I think I know and understand him, this is such a big thing. It is not planned. I really do not know what he will say. And if he—"

"If he abandons you, he will not be worth an atom of our breath. He will show himself to be unworthy of you. I have to say, Savannah, and I agree with you, we have not known him long, but we know him well enough, don't you think?"

Marianna was not pleased with the news, but, seeing her daughter's determined acceptance of the situation and the happiness she had found with Conor, and having got to know him better, she softened her position and said Savannah should go to Ireland to tell Conor he was to be a father. Privately, she hoped he would do the right thing and marry her daughter. Or, at least, stand by her.

"We shall go to stay with Will as planned next week," said Marianna, taking control of the situation, "and we shall see Esme's new daughter. You can go to Ireland after. Write to Conor and tell him of the change in your plans. I must speak to Will too and try and smooth out any bumps in your relationship with him before he meets Conor. Eventually." *And*, she thought, *I must face Ellen.*

Lizzie came one afternoon to see the new baby, Charlotte. Marianna was shocked by her appearance; she looked worn out, her skin pale, and seemed to have lost a little weight. After taking tea with the family, Marianna suggested they took a turn round Will's garden by themselves, and then they settled on a bench under an old apple tree.

"What is amiss, Lizzie," Marianna asked. "You do not look well."

"I had a fall the week before last. I took a dizzy turn. George says I am a little anaemic, which he said explained my light-headedness and my itchy skin, and my blood pressure is low, but nothin' serious. I am gettin' on, you know, Marianna. These little things are sent to try us at my age."

"Why don't you come back to Longridge with me?" Marianna suggested. "You can have a holiday, and I can look after you, spoil you."

"Thank you, Marianna, that's kind of you. A change of scenery will do me good. Will your gentleman be there?"

"Would you like to meet him?"

"I think I would, Marianna."

It was generous of Lizzie to say this, as she had loved her brother, and it had been difficult telling her about Bertie, but Lizzie knew William was the love of her life and irreplaceable.

"Are you well, my dear?" Lizzie asked. "You seem preoccupied. I know… it is probably none of my business and I will not take offence if you tell me so, but I sense that all is not well between Will and Esme."

"You are family, Lizzie. You may ask. And it is clearly becoming more obvious. I know you will be discreet, Lizzie—"

Lizzie interrupted. "Say no more at present. I am sorry to hear it. This is not the time or place to discuss it. On the other hand, I was intendin' to ask if there is somethin' amiss with Savannah? She seems a little pale, distracted, dreamy almost. Is she pinin' for the Greenwood boy?"

"No," said Marianna. Lizzie had not been informed of recent events. "Another reason why I would like you to come to Longridge. I need to talk to you about family matters."

"Are there money worries, Marianna?" asked Lizzie in alarm, grabbing Marianna's arm. The income William had provided for her depended on his investments which were now managed by Marianna and Will. "Have I been too extravagant with the household expenses?"

"Calm yourself, Lizzie Hindle. Of course not. Family matters." She waved her hand towards the house.

Will had been told when they first arrived in Liverpool. The three of them convened in his study again. He was horrified, glared at Savannah and stalked out of the room. Marianna had to pursue him to calm him down.

"It has happened. There is nothing we can do about it except give Savannah our love and support. You must meet Mr Clare. You will like him, Will."

Savannah had refused her mother's offer to allow Sarah to accompany her to Ireland, as she wanted to be alone with Conor, and Sarah had her own family with Ezra to look after. However, Will had heard of a widowed gentlewoman who was sailing with her maid to visit her son, an army officer stationed at Dublin Castle, and arranged for Savannah to travel in their company. Her mother and Will accompanied her to the port. Will even kissed her cheek in parting when he had seen her settled in her cabin. She was anxious on the voyage. Conor would wonder why she was coming to Ireland when it had been agreed he would come to Longridge. In her letter, she had not mentioned she was pregnant, only that she missed him. Although she was sure of his love for her, she did not know if Conor wanted a child. It was not something they were expecting to discuss so soon. They had never discussed marriage either, since Marianna's veto. There were many things they had not discussed in this whirlwind of a romance, as they were so wrapped up in each other and neither thought further than the day ahead of them. But now they must. Where were they to live? Would he live in England? How would she feel if he asked her to live in Ireland, so far from her mother? What would Conor do? He had said he would like to continue selling pictures and furniture to America and travel to France to find more treasures. The idea of having a farm had been blossoming in her mind, but where? And of course, the most pressing question of all: would he ask her to marry him? More to the point, would he want anything to do with her, rendering all these other questions irrelevant? Conor met her off the boat and she waited until they were at Enniscourt before she told him her news. She was taken aback by his reaction and relieved. He was overjoyed. He did not mention marriage.

They were happy, happy days. Wonderful days. End-of-summer days. She helped him clear the rooms in the house, starting in the attics. Broken items of furniture, boxes of musty papers and chests of moth-eaten clothes were taken away to be burnt on a bonfire. Anything that was of value or interest, which would be of use to him in his new business, was stored in one of the bedrooms. She found him, one afternoon, standing by an attic window, lost in thought. He jumped when she crept up behind him and put her arms round his waist.

"What are you thinking about?"

He had found an old, wooden trunk which contained notebooks filled with his scribblings and drawings, his and Orla's toys, treasures and books from their childhood.

"I'm a little bit sad, I suppose. Thinking back to when I was a boy and how happy I was in this house. The fun we had. Orla. Our friends. Aunt Norah shouting at us to keep the noise down or chasing us outside to play. Now it's so quiet and it's sad, you know, thinking that those times are gone…" He sighed. "But I'm not sad anymore, as I have you. For our child," he told Savannah, picking up the trunk to take it downstairs.

A man came from a Dublin auction house to catalogue the art and furniture Conor did not want and they were taken away to be sold. Conor had already written to Jocelyn Digby at Sotheby's, who sent a man to view some of the more valuable pictures his aunt had left behind, as they would fetch a better price in London. He had been impressed and left with several of them.

As the rooms emptied, they moved into Mrs Archbold's quarters on the ground floor and lived there. Savannah had found an old roll of muslin in the attic and fixed it across the windows to give them privacy from the workmen outside. They needed that privacy. Mrs Walsh, her long, thin face a picture of outraged indignation, came in the mornings to cook their breakfast and luncheon and do their laundry. They told her they would see to their own supper to be rid of her as she scowled and tutted at them so much. Mr Walsh came to see to the horses and helped Mr Doyle to bring some order to the grounds. In the afternoons, with Mrs Walsh out of the way, Savannah would busy herself in the kitchen, preparing simple meals for supper and making scones and cakes as Ada had shown her, which she would carry out on a tray with a pot of tea for the workers. They were always cheerful, laughing and chatting – the *craic*, Hugh called it. She did not always understand what they were talking about, but they made her laugh and told her what grand cakes she made.

Niamh had been dismissed by Mrs Archbold and returned to the convent laundry in Dublin. It was assumed she had taken one of the cats with her, as no one saw it again and they knew how fond she was of them. Conor gave another away to one of the workmen's children as he disliked them but allowed a small black cat with green eyes to stay, as Mrs Walsh complained about the mice. Philomena Byrne never showed her face, but everyone in Ballymore, and possibly further afield, knew what was going on at Enniscourt. Mrs Walsh kept them well informed of the 'disgraceful goings-on' at Enniscourt.

"We are bohemians," declared Conor, scoffing at her small-mindedness.

Some days they did not dress because of the heat, and wandered round the house, her in a nightgown, him bare chested, as they went about their work. They laughed constantly. When, at last, they were alone, they made love whenever and wherever the fancy took them. They ate in bed. They bathed together. One evening, Savannah bathed alone. She stood up just as Conor walked into the room and instinctively covered her modesty with her hands.

He gasped. "Don't move." He stood transfixed. "More beautiful than Botticelli's Venus," he whispered as he came to her, lifted her out of the bath and carried her, dripping wet, to the bed. He undressed and lay down beside her and pulled her on top of him. Beads of water glistened on her swelling breasts and rounded stomach. Their child was growing inside her. He was filled with love and tenderness for her. He gazed, his soft, dark, liquid eyes gazed deep into her soul, and she melted with love for him.

They went for walks, barefoot, in their nightclothes in the grounds, their way lit by lamps, and loved each other. They went in the carriage to the Fairy Pool several times and he loved her each time. Mr Walsh drove them to Dublin and was warned not to get drunk in any of Dublin's many pubs as Conor took her for luncheon at the Shelbourne and, afterwards, they walked in St Stephen's Green. They went back to Dublin to have dinner and see a play at the Gaiety Theatre, and Mr Walsh did get drunk and Conor had to drive them home. They played cards and chess; she often won, he never let her win out of sympathy. At night, they curled up on the bed, his face lit by the glow of the lamp, her head resting on his chest listening to the beat of his heart as he read to her; she did not mind what he read as long as she heard the sound of his gentle, lilting voice. Sometimes, when she read to him, having deliberately chosen something in French, knowing he liked to hear her speak it, he would sit at her feet and then he would kiss her toes and make her giggle, his fingers would climb up her legs and the book would be cast aside.

Savannah and her mother exchanged weekly letters. Marianna waited for the news that they would be coming back to Longridge to marry. Savannah wrote only of the progress being made on the house, her happiness, and her love for Conor.

TWENTY-NINE

The leaves that lingered on the trees glowed gold, russet and bronze. The air was chill. Summer was over. The days were drawing in. The fire was lit in the evening. The ruin was demolished; the ground cleared; the ivy on the main house trimmed; the rusty stains on the exterior walls cleaned; the external window frames painted; and the gardens tidied. The house was back to its original state, and everyone agreed looked so much better. Scaffolding had been erected to begin the repairs to the side wall of the house the following week before the workmen moved inside to carry out further repairs and redecoration in the bedrooms affected by damp.

On the Sunday, Conor decided to tackle what remained of the furniture piled up in the barn. Hugh came to help. Conor went to fetch the horse and wagon to take away the damaged pieces which were to be burnt on yet another bonfire. What remained, Conor had arranged to be shipped to America.

"You look well, Savannah. Carryin' a child suits you, so it does." Hugh was the only one at Enniscourt who knew.

"Thank you, Hugh. I am very well and so very happy. He loves me, Hugh, despite your warnings." There was a tacit understanding not to mention what had happened in Liverpool.

"I know he does. He's a changed man, so he is. I've seen him happy before, as it's his nature to be happy, but this time it's different.

He's content, at peace, as if after all this time, he's found somethin' worth cherishin' and holdin' on to."

"I am cherished, and I cherish him."

"He loves you somethin' fierce. He's told me how fierce he loves you."

"And when next you talk about me, Hugh," said Savannah, laughing, "you can tell him how much I love him for I am sure it's been at least an hour since I told him."

The next day, the sky blackened, and it rained heavily.

"Will you look at that! 'Tis wettin' rain," said Hugh dolefully.

"Is not all rain wet?" Savannah chuckled.

"Ah! Now that is not the question of someone well used to Irish rain," explained Hugh. "We have different grades of rain, so we do. Stay with us long enough, Savannah, and you'll learn the difference."

She did not know if Hugh was teasing her.

It rained for the rest of the week, and so the work on the outside of the house was halted and the workmen moved indoors. Conor had engaged an agent to seek out buyers for Enniscourt and, at first, there was little interest and he began to fret. Money left by his aunt was disappearing quickly in wages for the workmen and the materials needed to do the repairs. The weather and the shorter daylight hours did not help his mood. It took all Savannah's charms to wheedle his concerns from him.

He was sitting back in an armchair one evening, and she sat astride him with a pair of scissors in one hand and a comb in the other to trim his beard and moustache. She liked to do it for him. He opened one eye to watch her: her face a picture of concentration, her tongue peeping from the corner of her mouth, as she snipped delicately and blew away the hairs.

"I can see you watching," she said. She stopped and looked at him. "Have you ever thought of shaving it all off?"

"Would you like me to?"

"I dare you."

Conor accepted the challenge and, half an hour later, presented himself to her. Savannah stared at him.

"D'Artagnan has gone. You look younger."

"But you still think me beautiful, or I shall grow it back."

He sat back down on the chair, and she sat astride him again and kissed him.

"Either way, you are exceedingly beautiful. Now, please tell me what is wrong. You have been distracted lately."

"I do not want to worry you."

"But I am worried because you are keeping something from me."

"Money, Savannah."

"I can ask my mother to send me extra next month."

"No, it is not money for our day-to-day needs. It's the money to complete the work on the house and pay the wages."

"I have money," she told him. "From when my father died. I can write to Mama and ask how I can release it."

"I won't hear of it," he replied. "It is my aunt's house. She has underestimated the expense, or I have overspent. I shall have to telegraph her to transfer some more funds."

"I do not mind, Conor. If you need it, I shall ask for it. You can pay me back when the house is sold."

He hugged her. "You are so sweet and kind. Thank you for the offer, but no. I will see to it."

They were cuddled up on the sofa in the sitting room, deciding what to have for supper. It was already dark, and the only light came from the glow of the fire. It was so comfortable, and he could smell her and feel her breath on his cheek as she stroked the stubble on his unshaved face. He sat up suddenly.

"What is it? You made me jump."

He wriggled round on the sofa so he could see her face and placed a hand on her stomach.

"I love you."

"And I love you." She smiled at him tenderly, but he was not smiling. "What is it, Conor?"

"I love you," he said again. He seemed to be struggling to say something. "I love you. *Ti amo. Je t'aime. Ich liebe dich.* Simple words in whatever language you speak. Just three simple words in English that do not do justice to how much I love you."

Savannah sat up too and took his hand but did not say anything as he was frowning.

"I have done things I am ashamed of, Savannah. You know what they are, so I do not need to ask again for your forgiveness. I will only add that my behaviour towards women has been crass and dishonourable. Women are to be respected and treated well. I have learnt that from my time with you. You are young, Savannah. Young in age, but not in character and wisdom and kindness and intelligence and love. I have never in my life cared as much for another human being as I care for you. I care for you and the unborn child. I could weep with happiness when I think about you and the child, and the love we have for each other that made the child. I have to pinch myself sometimes to reassure myself that this is happening. That you are with me. That I have found you and that you want to be with me. I have never in my life loved another human being as much as I love you. I want you to know that. We tell each other every day, many times every day, that we love each other. Three simple, little words. I want you to know what those three little words mean for me."

Savannah hugged him close as he buried his face in her hair and began to sob.

"That day I left Longridge when you told me I was to go was the worst day of my life. I thought I had lost you. You will never leave me, Savannah? Promise you will never leave me."

She was startled by his emotion, as she had never seen him like this. He had never broken down before, not like this. She had only seen him cry once: when she ran after him down the drive at Longridge, and his tears of despair turned to joy when he heard her call his name and she threw herself into his arms. He always seemed so sure of himself, so certain about everything, which she found comforting. She wondered why he had shown this side of himself now. She wondered if it was the near darkness of the room that had given him the courage to expose his deepest fears. She kissed him to console him. She stroked his face to soothe him. It upset her to see him so distressed. She wrapped him in her arms and whispered softly, "Why would I leave you? I love you too much. You mean everything to me."

Conor was very attentive and caring, but often it seemed his mind wandered, consumed by worries about the work on the house, until a letter arrived a few days later from the Dublin auction house with news of the sale which had gone better than he hoped and, the following morning, he told her he needed to go to Dublin. Savannah wanted to go with him to buy some new clothes to accommodate her expanding figure, but Conor was adamant he would go alone. She was not pleased. When he returned in the dark of the late afternoon, the workmen had already gone home, and he told Savannah to stay in the sitting room and not to leave. She was intrigued and a little annoyed he would not tell her why, but he was intransigent, and disappeared into the dining room and locked the door. She was beginning to worry and wonder what he was up to when he came into the sitting room and said, "Miss Hamilton-Read. Would you do me the honour?" and held out his arm.

"Conor?" She giggled. "Why all the secrecy? What have you been up to all this time?"

"Please, Miss Hamilton-Read. No questions! Come with me."

He took her arm, led her across the hall to the dining room and opened the door. She gasped. In the centre of the empty room was a small table and two chairs. The fire was lit and candles, so many she could not count them, flickered on the mantelpiece and on the windowsills. The table was covered in a white cloth and a red rose lay in her place. He held her chair for her and poured her a glass of wine.

"Thank you," she whispered and reached up to touch his face. "What a lovely surprise."

"I shall be back in two minutes," he said, kissing her cheek, and disappeared through the door to the kitchen downstairs. He returned, carrying a tray with two plates of salmon in a dill sauce with green beans and boiled potatoes, that he placed with a flourish on the table before bowing to her.

"Have you cooked this?" said Savannah, leaning forward to breathe in the aroma. "Still I do not know everything about you."

Conor sat down opposite her and raised his glass.

"To us," he said. "To you. The most beautiful woman I know."

"This is so romantic, Conor." she said, biting into the salmon.

"Goodness! It's delicious. Sorry! My surprise did not sound complimentary. It is truly delicious, Conor." She smiled at him. "You seem much happier today."

"I am. Let us toast the money from the auction and hope there is a letter soon from Sotheby's. And," he added, "a prospective buyer is coming next week."

They clinked glasses.

"To good news! I have been thinking, Conor, that the house is so bare perhaps we should find some furniture in the pieces you have left to make it more homely and attractive to a buyer."

"That sounds like a good idea." He clinked her glass again.

When they had finished their meal, Conor tipped back in his chair and looked across the table at her. She was radiant and so beautiful, simply dressed in a light frock, a paisley shawl draped round her shoulders, her hair loose, her eyes dark and sparkling in the candlelight. A smile played on his lips.

"What are you thinking?" asked Savannah, intrigued.

Conor rocked forward, rose from the chair and went round the table, feeling in his waistcoat pocket as he got down on one knee. He took her hand and she gazed at him, understanding, but not quite understanding, what was happening and, as the words came from his lips, "Savannah, I love you so much. Please will you marry me?" her arms were round his neck before he had finished speaking and she was smothering him with kisses. "Yes. Yes. Yes."

He toppled backwards and she fell on top of him. They were laughing, hugging and kissing.

"Here," he said, sitting up and pulling her onto his lap. "Let me at least put the ring on your finger."

She offered him her hand and he slipped on the platinum band with a diamond solitaire.

"It is beautiful," she said. "And it fits. How did you know my size?"

"Aha!" he said, tapping the side of his nose. He had knotted some thread round her finger when she was sleeping and taken it with him to Dublin.

"Thank you from the bottom of my heart." She sighed, extending her hand in front of her to admire the diamond glinting in the candlelight. "I was not expecting this at all."

"I'm sorry that I did not take you with me to Dublin but now you know the reason why. We shall go soon to buy the clothes you need."

From the day Savannah had returned to Enniscourt and told Conor about the baby, they had not discussed marriage. Savannah knew her mother wanted her to be married before the baby came, but Conor never asked her and she did not press him, although she thought once she might ask him, but feared the answer. As the days passed, days filled with love, days of freedom, carefree days, it did not seem to matter. They lived on the fringes of society, answering only to each other, worrying not a jot what people thought of them. Marriage was for conformists. They were bohemians. Until now…

"Thank you, Conor, for everything," she whispered. "I love you. I love you. I love you."

"And I love you. Come," he said, getting to his feet and scooping her into his arms. "Let us go to bed."

A letter came a few days later from her mother, in response to a telegram, who congratulated them both. Marianna wanted to know if they would return to Longridge to be married. They were lying next to each other on the bed having just eaten breakfast, and still not dressed, and had exchanged amused looks when Mrs Walsh had knocked on the door to hand over the letter to Conor with a thunderous scowl on her face to convey her disgust at them.

"We cannot marry here," said Savannah. She pointed to her stomach. "It would scandalise your neighbours and the good people of Ballymore and beyond. Mrs Walsh would have a heart attack."

"And you are not Catholic, and I have not been to confession or Mass for years," said Conor, who was twirling in his fingers the ammonite he had found in the toy box.

"My mother suggests our chapel. She will arrange something if we wish."

"I will marry you there if that is what you want, but it may be difficult as I was baptised a Catholic."

"I am not baptised at all. My mother will look into it. I shall write to her."

"I wouldn't raise your hopes about it, Savannah. Church people are very uncompromising about the rules."

"If it is not possible it does not matter so long as we are married somehow, and you can rid me of my mouthful of a name."

He smiled and pinched her cheek. "Not a grand affair, Savannah."

"No, not at all. You have seen it. It is a small chapel. Family only." She bit her lip. "My papa would be there, in spirit at least. You must invite Orla and her family. I'd love to meet them. Perhaps a few friends. Hugh for example."

"You won't invite your old schoolfriends to come and inspect me?"

"I should think not, for they will giggle and make eyes at you and show themselves up to be silly girls. It will reflect badly on me." She thought for a moment. "I will not promise to obey you, you know."

"I don't expect you to. I have been told by your mother—"

"My mother?"

"Yes, when I came to Longridge, she made it quite plain that you will be my equal in all things. But rest assured, darling, I did not need to be told. I've been brought up under the influence of two wonderful women, remember?"

"Well, we are both in agreement. Equals. Partners in life." She sighed. "It would be lovely to be married at night, with candles, and if it snowed, that would be magical. Although…"

"Although?"

"Where does a newly married couple go on honeymoon in winter?"

"What does it matter as long as there is a fire to keep us warm and a fine bed?"

She picked up a pillow and hit him. "Although…" she said, lifting her nightdress and climbing on top of him.

There was a knock on the door and Savannah rolled her eyes and got up to answer it. It was Mrs Walsh, whose eyes widened as she took in the now obvious swelling under Savannah's nightgown.

"The postboy's brought this. He's just found it in the bottom of his bag."

"Thank you, Mrs Walsh."

The cook turned away in disgust. "Morals of alley cats," she muttered.

Savannah closed the door, knowing the news would be circulating in Ballymore by the end of the day. The letter was from Will. She tore it open as she made her way back to the bed.

"It is from my brother. He sends his congratulations and wishes us well, but—"

"But?"

"He says he hopes I intend to marry promptly considering my condition. Really! How tactless! What has it to do with him? He would disapprove of me marrying in a church as he has no religious convictions."

"Neither do I, Savannah. How can anyone have a literal belief in the Bible when objects such as this have been discovered?" He opened his hand to show her the ammonite. "How can anyone believe Noah saved two of each species of animal when the bones of creatures, strange, unidentified beasts, have been found scattered across the world, beasts that never entered the ark. The Bible is myth. The Flood is fantasy. If the Old Testament is such, who is to say the New Testament is not the same?"

"Will has read books about the discoveries of these creatures called dinosaurs," said Savannah, making herself comfortable beside Conor. "He liked to frighten me when I was younger about the size of these monsters. He has read Mr Darwin's book too and talked to me about it."

"Well, there is something we would have in common if I should ever have the opportunity of meeting him."

"You were quite vehement just now. Are you uncomfortable about marrying in a chapel? Honestly, I'm not too bothered where we marry."

"If you wish to do it and it can be arranged – which I'm sceptical about, Savannah – I will do it for you."

"Is that what you and Orla argued about? Religion?"

"How do you know about my arguments with Orla?" He nodded. "Niamh! Is there nothing she did not tell you? I am not religious at all. I keep my beliefs private, Savannah, especially round here where people will be offended by them, such is the strength of their faith. Orla has faith. As does my aunt. Yes, we argued. Or rather, I would say, they were heated discussions. About religion and many other things. We like to argue. I like to provoke them." He laughed.

It was late November. The trees were bare. It was a fine, sunny day and Hugh and Conor had borne Savannah, wrapped in blankets, on a chaise like the Queen of Sheba, and placed her on the grass. Enniscourt was sold. The work inside the house was finished and Conor had promised the new owner that the pointing on the exterior walls would be completed before they moved out. He was impatient to finish the work whilst the weather held. Savannah settled back in her cocoon of warmth and rested her hands on her belly, waiting for their baby to move. She had never been so happy. And soon she would be Mrs Clare.

THIRTY

Marianna Hamilton-Read died peacefully in her sleep. She was seventy-nine years old. She had lived long enough to ride in an automobile, speak to someone who lived miles away by means of the telephone, and know that a Frenchman had crossed the Channel in a flying machine. Yet there were rumblings in the world beyond the fells and valleys and bay she had loved so much. Europe was trembling and on the brink of an unimaginable horror. The Hamilton-Reads, the Hindles, the families on the estate, families across the world would send their men to the bloody swamps of Flanders and the rocky shores of Gallipoli, and elsewhere, and many would not return. But they did not know this as they gathered in the house at Longridge to mourn the matriarch of the family. She had been dead for a week and today the house was full of her children, grandchildren, nieces, nephew and friends, come to mourn the woman they had loved and who had loved them.

Will had helped to dig the grave of his beloved mother the day before and had come back covered in dirt and weeping. William's grave had been opened up to receive her. Savannah sat with her the night she died, with William's photograph clutched to her chest. She was frail, her body exhausted. She had said she was tired; she had lost her appetite and took to her bed. It seemed as if she had decided it was time to go. She opened her eyes just once that night and a faint smile hovered on her lips.

"He's waiting for me, darling," she whispered. "I have seen him. I'm ready to go to him. I have waited so long to be with him again."

Savannah looked around her mother's room; everything just as she had left it. She went to her desk and pressed the secret button, which opened the top drawer, to retrieve the leather-bound book. Next to it was a small, black, velvet box, an inch square. She removed the lid and caught her breath. Inside, tied with black ribbon, was a lock of her father's hair; the one that flopped over his brow. She touched it gently before replacing the lid and putting the box in the purse hanging from her wrist. She took the book and went to sit in the chair by the window where her mother spent hours sewing, reading or just staring at the view, lost in her memories; the chair her parents had bought for their cottage when they lived at Netherton, which Marianna refused to leave behind when she returned to Longridge; the chair she said helped her feel closer to William.

Savannah flicked through the pages to where she had written in the book all those years ago.

I hope one day I will love and be loved forever. Be it a fraction of the love between my darling papa and mama, I shall be happy. Savannah H-R.

She did not know, as this was the first time she had seen the book since then, what else her mother had written. Under her own words, Marianna had written, *Conor Clare has come into our lives. What will it mean? It is an infatuation. I do not know which of them will be the first to hurt the other and bring it to an end.*

She smiled to herself. How wonderful her mother had been, despite her concerns about Conor. To confound public opinion. To scorn the gossip and let them be together.

"There you are, Mama."

She looked up. Framed in the doorway was their daughter, married now, happy, and heavily pregnant with her second child. *How beautiful she is*, thought Savannah. She did not have the Hamilton eyes. She had her father's eyes.

"Uncle Will says we are leaving in half an hour."

"He sent you in your condition to find me?"

"I am not ill, Mama," she scolded, "and perfectly capable of managing a flight of stairs. Are you all right?"

"Yes, very sad but I'm fine. Just thinking about her. How much I loved her and how much she loved me despite all the worry I caused her when I was younger. I shall miss her terribly. She was a marvellous mother and my best friend. I hope one day the same will be said about me." She smiled optimistically at her daughter.

"That would be telling, Mama," Her daughter laughed then said seriously, "Uncle Will is on his third whisky and quite maudlin."

"Go and take the glass from his hand. He will not argue with a pregnant woman. I'll be down shortly."

Savannah flicked through a few more pages and saw the entry for the trip to Italy. Such a wonderful holiday, tainted only by her fears that she was pregnant. She turned more pages and Conor's name jumped out. What did her mother write about him when she knew him better?

Conor Clare is wickedly handsome, not at all vain – although he knows he is admired – charming and intelligent. He loves her so much and she him. I doubted his sincerity and his intentions but, so far, he has given me no cause to doubt him. He is a man who knows who he is, very assured, very personable.

Savannah leant back in the chair. She closed her eyes as her mind drifted back to those wonderful days at Enniscourt.

It was a fine, sunny November day. The trees were bare of leaves. Despite her concerns, Conor had gone up onto the scaffolding to lend a hand with the repair work. Hugh was up there too with one of the other workmen, whose legs dangled over the plank and was busy repointing the stonework. She heard them laugh and shaded her eyes to watch. Conor waved to her, and she waved back.

Savannah shuddered. Birdsong floated across the lawns from the wood to join the thrum of the conversations of the mourners gathering in front of the house. Savannah screwed her eyes tight to blot out the sight she had never forgotten.

Conor leans over the rail to haul up a bucket filled with cement mixed by the workman on the ground. The railing gives way. Conor falls. It is still vivid. Falling so quickly. The sound, a dull thump, as he hits the ground. The scream. The awful, shrieking scream. She hears it still. The howl like a banshee. Until she realises it is her. Running. Almost tripping over the blankets he had wrapped round her. Screaming. Running to cradle his bloody head, the eyes wide, blank, in his beautiful face, and his beautiful, broken body in her arms. She holds him as he dies...

Savannah gulped to stifle the sob that rose in her throat.

Her mother came with Bertie, not to celebrate her daughter's forthcoming marriage but to bury her lover. She could not remember them coming or how they knew to come, but she was aware they were there. She vaguely remembered they stayed in a hotel but could not remember where. Her mother did not, could not say anything. She knew her words were useless. She knew exactly how her daughter was feeling. Bertie cradled her in his arms, singing softly to her, lullabies, nonsense, rocking her until she fell asleep.

Orla came from London with her husband, David Broughton. His sister was beautiful and kind to her. She sat with her in her room, and they comforted each other.

"Does Mrs Archbold know?"

"Yes, I telegraphed her as soon as I heard the news. She is heartbroken. Conor was another son to her."

Later that day, Orla told her, "I have arranged the funeral and Mass, Savannah."

"Conor was not religious."

"He despised all religions and saw them as a means of oppression. We used to argue about it all the time, amongst other things. But do it for me, Savannah. He did not receive absolution before he died. I want his soul to rest in peace. For all his faults, Savannah, he had a beautiful soul."

"I ask one thing, Orla. We shall not wear black. When I think of him, I do not see black but all the colours of the rainbow."

"I have a photograph of him, taken when he visited me in London in April. I want you to have it. He wrote to me about you. He never wrote to me about his women, but he wrote about you. He loved you with all his heart. You and the child. He told me all about you when he visited me on his return from Italy. He never stopped talking about you. You are as beautiful as he described. We shall stay friends, shall we not? You will write to me about his child?" Orla kissed her on the cheek and hugged her tight.

"I promise," said Savannah.

Conor's funeral was a blur. The day was a blur. It was drizzling. The countryside was a blur of mist. The church in the village packed with villagers come to see the wanton, pregnant English girl, the subject of so much local gossip. They did not understand the service, when to sit, stand or kneel. It seemed to go on and on. There were bells. There was incense. The air was thick and smothering and she fainted into Bertie's arms.

She could not remember coming home to Longridge, nor the days that followed. Then their child was born. If it is a boy, she had told him, he will be Conor William Clare. If it is a girl, he had countered, she will be Erin Savannah Clare.

She realised she was crying and sought her handkerchief to dry her tears before she smudged the ink in her mother's book. Marianna's words jumped out of the page at her.

That is all I had too. A photograph. His child growing in me. The memory of his love.

And she had his ring, which she still wore, a little tight now, on her right hand. Savannah realised then how much her own life had mirrored her mother's. But not what happened after Conor died.

The dark, dark days before their child was born. All the time she carried the growing child, she had been seized with panic and wished she could die. She had sunk into an all-consuming melancholy, filled with feelings of dread that grew heavier and heavier and enveloped her in their crushing embrace, and her thoughts grew darker. She walked up Longridge Fell, alone in the early morning light, and wanted to walk away into the empty distance because she did not know what lay there and she would walk until she was no more and that was what drew her: the not-knowing, the nothingness, which would surely be more bearable than the pain she endured now.

It was Edmund Sill who found her. Fortunately, she had not been gone long. He had seen her footprints in the light covering of snow leading up the fell. He had saddled Ladybird and followed her tracks and saw her, silhouetted against the grey skyline, as she climbed slowly and ponderously up Devil's Seat. She was in her nightgown, a shawl round her shoulders, barefooted, shivering violently, her feet red with cold, her lips almost blue, staring over the edge at the jagged rocks below by the time he reached her.

"Come away, Miss," he had said, quietly, gently. "You must be very cold now. Think of the child. Think of Mr Clare and take care of his child." He had lifted her, oblivious, a dead weight, onto Ladybird's back and put his overcoat round her and brought her home. She sat, swathed in blankets, in front of the fire in her mother's sitting room.

Ada came with a drink of hot chocolate and gathered her in her arms, murmuring softly, "It will be all right, my little pumpkin. It will be all right."

She told her mother she did not want the child who would remind her daily of what she had lost. Marianna tried to reason with her. She told her something her father used to say: 'When all is hopeless, have hope.' She told her she would care for them both and not to act rashly, do something she might later regret. When she saw the child, she would change her mind. But Savannah was adamant, and a couple had been found, a childless clergyman and his wife, to take the baby.

When Savannah's time drew near, Marianna rented a house in Manchester for a month, as the clergyman lived in the city and they needed to be away from Longridge. Lizzie came to stay, and she was grateful for her calming presence and the sympathetic way in which she dealt with Savannah as she herself was at her wits' end. If Lizzie, a devout Christian, disapproved of Savannah's behaviour, she never showed it. She was a kind, compassionate woman and saw the parallels with Marianna's own life and knew how much Savannah suffered. Marianna hired a nurse, and a doctor came frequently to examine Savannah and was engaged to deliver her. The day she was born, Marianna wrapped the unnamed girl in a shawl and, unable to contain her grief, desperate for Savannah, pale, wild-eyed, silent, to change her mind, left the bedroom to hand over the baby to the wet nurse engaged by the new parents. As the nurse disappeared down the stairs to the sitting room where they were waiting with Lizzie, Marianna heard a howl and the door was flung open and Savannah was running after the nurse, screaming, "No! No! No!" She grabbed the baby from the startled nurse's arms and clutched her to her breast. "She is all I have of him," she wailed to her mother. "He would not forgive me. When I see him in heaven, he will turn away from me if I let her go."

Would she and Conor have been happy, lived happily ever after? Would their love, the passion, have survived? Would he have loved her and only her? Would he have pursued his political beliefs and brought her grief? Impossible to know. Did it matter now? The months she had known him had been the happiest of her life; each day lived at the peak of loving and being loved. And she had his daughter to remind her of the times she shared with him. Marianna, in her last hours, had seen William in heaven. If there was such a place, it would be Conor she looked for. "I love you, Conor," she whispered as she fingered his ring and the tears fell. "I love you still. *Ti amo. Je t'aime. Ich liebe dich*. I love you. I love you. I love you." He was her beautiful man.

A letter came from Orla with another letter enclosed from Mrs Archbold as well as a banker's draft for the sum of two thousand pounds.

"I cannot accept this," Savannah said to her mother. "Look how much she has sent! It's blood money. The woman is a criminal and may be responsible for the deaths of innocent people."

"Accept it," said Marianna. "It is Conor's money, as she explains in the letter. This is his share from the sale of Enniscourt. Conor did not leave a will. She wants you to have the money, you and Conor's child. She is doing what she thinks Conor would want, for you and his daughter to be looked after."

"Then I shall put it away for her. I will not touch it."

She needed something to do, and she asked her mother to find her a farm. Bertie suggested she live with him for a few weeks before he moved out to see if it was what she wanted, and she had gone to Moss End, taking a nursemaid with her to help look after Erin. Erin Savannah Conor Clare, now ten months old. Bertie's farm was sold. Her mother had asked him to give it up and live with her at Longridge. It had not been a difficult decision, as his heart was no longer in it and he had begun to feel his age as the physical tasks tired him. Apparently, she had asked him on the boat coming back from Ireland. The suddenness and shocking nature of Conor's death, the snuffing out of such a young life, and Savannah's grief and heartache, had devastated her. "Life is too short, Bertie, and we don't have much time left." He wanted more than anything to be with her and spend the rest of his life with her.

Savannah had asked him if he knew her father when he lived on the Loop Hall estate.

"Not well, Savannah. It was me who hired him, and the times I worked with him, I liked him. He was well respected and had a wonderful way with the horses."

It was bitterly cold that February night. The moon glinted on the water frozen in the troughs and cast a silver sheen across the yard. Colin, the stockman, had woken them with a loud banging on the door at two in the morning. One of the cows was struggling to give birth and he needed help. Bertie told her to go back to bed, but she insisted on going with him, throwing one of his old coats over her nightgown. When they got to the barn, the unborn calf's legs were protruding from the birth canal. Colin had already tied a rope round them.

Together, he and Bertie, now in his shirtsleeves, began to pull, stopping now and then to catch their breath and reposition their feet to brace themselves to pull again. After ten minutes, it was all over and, two minutes later, the calf had struggled to his feet.

"Come on," said Bertie. "Still time for a few more hours in a warm bed."

His face was grey in the moonlight, and he was sweating.

"Are you unwell, Bertie?" she asked as she closed the barn door behind them.

He was staring hard at her and then he clutched his chest and, without warning, fell heavily to the ground at her feet.

What had her mother written about him? She turned the pages.

He always knew he was second best, but he loved me with all his heart. He had never stopped loving me despite the pain I had caused him. He was a gentleman, a dear friend, kind, gentle and wise. I shall miss him. And I loved him too.

Savannah was crying again. She went to sit at her mother's writing desk and glimpsed the paperweight Conor had bought in Venice. She picked it up to admire the wonderful colours and wondered if Erin would like it. The women who came after Marianna. Would any of them match her? Esme would not. She liked Esme. But she was not to be mistress of Longridge. Too sweet and docile for Will and more preoccupied with her children to give him what he needed. He sought the attention and excitement he craved elsewhere. She tired of his infidelities and divorced him. He sold his law practice and came back, a wealthy man, to help their mother run the estate with his second wife. What was the name of the silly thing, half his age, he had brought home to Longridge once for the shoot? Louise? Savannah could not remember her name. What was he thinking? At least he did not marry her. She had announced at dinner that the three most important things in her life were sex, horses and dogs. She had embarrassed William Bennet, Theo and Charlotte. Will had thrown back his head and guffawed to hide his own embarrassment.

Marianna had said in riposte, quick as a flash, as cool as a cucumber, "In that particular order, my dear? Because as far as I can see, you have more dogs than babies at home."

Savannah chuckled at the memory. Will soon came to his senses and married Margaret, a childless widow who remained childless, and neither seemed bothered by it. They were well suited and adored each other.

Will liked the finer things in life and lived as a country gentleman, pursuing the interests of a country gentleman: hunting, shooting, fishing. There were more staff at Longridge too, with a butler-cum-valet, a housekeeper and a cook, kitchen maids, personal maids for his wife and Marianna, housemaids who lived in. He had put on weight in his later years but was still handsome, and she had never seen him so contented. William Bennet lived nearby too, so the Hamilton-Read line would continue, she hoped, for some time yet.

The sound of wheels and horses' hooves on the drive brought Savannah out of her reverie, and she glanced out of the window. The hearse had arrived, with her mother's coffin hidden under a mountain of flowers, and drawn by four black horses, the plumes of feathers dancing on their heads. Will had spared no expense. They would follow the coffin in the early spring sunshine to the family chapel for a simple service in accordance with Marianna's wishes before she was laid to rest with her beloved William.

And she had her farm. Thomas Crossley retired from the tenancy of Fell Foot and his family did not wish to take it on, so she moved in with Erin as her mother's tenant, retained the shepherd and stockman and, after three years, Marianna, impressed and somewhat surprised by her dedication and hard work, gave it to her. She lived there still.

Someone coughed. It was Theo. "Father is getting impatient, Aunt. I have been sent to tell you we are leaving now."

"I'm sorry, Theo. I got distracted." She replaced the cap on her mother's pen and blew on the ink to dry the words she had written.

She picked up her purse and got up to put her mother's book back in the drawer. Before closing it, she blew again and reread her words.

I loved. I was loved. He is and always will be the greatest love of my life. Forever. His name was Conor Clare.

It is possible to love again. Differently. Contentedly. Happily. He loves me and has always loved me. His name is Richard John Greenwood. My beloved Jack.

Savannah M. Greenwood.

READER'S NOTE

In 1974, following the Local Government Act of 1972, the administrative county of Lancashire was reformed, and the counties of Cumberland and Westmorland became Cumbria, absorbing areas like the Furness peninsula and the town of Barrow, which had once been Lancastrian. The fictitious town of Kirkby by Sands in Lancashire would nowadays be part of Cumbria.